THE
UNEXPECTED
Everything

THE UNEXPECTED

Everything

Morgan
MATSON

Waterford City and County
Libraries

SIMON & SCHUSTER

First published in Great Britain in 2016 by Simon & Schuster UK Ltd
A CBS COMPANY

Originally published in the USA in 2016 by Simon & Schuster BFYR
an imprint of Simon & Schuster Children's Publishing Division,
1230 Avenue of Americas, New York, NY 10020

Copyright © 2016 Morgan Matson
Jacket photography copyright © 2016 by Meredith Jenks

1 3 5 7 9 10 8 6 4 2

Simon & Schuster UK Ltd
1ˢᵗ Floor, 222 Gray's Inn Road
London
WC1X 8HB

www.simonandschuster.co.uk

Simon & Schuster Australia, Sydney
Simon & Schuster India, New Delhi

A CIP catalogue record for this book
is available from the British Library.

PB ISBN 978-1-4711-4614-5
eBook ISBN 978-1-4711-4615-2

Printed and bound by CPI Group (UK) Ltd, Croydon, CR0 4YY

MIX
Paper from
responsible sources
FSC® C020471

Simon & Schuster UK Ltd are committed to sourcing paper
that is made from wood grown in sustainable forests and supports the Forest
Stewardship Council, the leading international forest certification organisation.
Our books displaying the FSC logo are printed on FSC certified paper.

For Justin Chanda,
editor and friend

ACKNOWLEDGMENTS

Justin!! In order to thank you properly for the hundreds of things you did for this book, these acknowledgments would go *very* long. So I'm going to try to limit myself to two. You know what? Make it three. I'm not driving. Thank you for your patience and enthusiasm—for believing in this story right from the beginning, and your unshakable confidence that we'd have a book by the end of it, even when it was months late and hundreds of pages too long. Thank you for your beyond-amazing notes. As ever, you knew what this story was before I did, and helped me find it draft by draft. And thank you for being so wonderful to work with—between the LOTR notes calls and emoji-filled emails, it's always such a joy. I couldn't have done this without you, and I'm so lucky to get to work with you.

Thanks to Emily Van Beek, my wonderful agent and fierce supporter. Thanks also to Molly Jaffa, Amy Rosenbaum, and everyone at Folio.

Lucy Ruth Cummins, I didn't think a cover could be more beautiful than SYBG's. But then you added PUPPIES. You're a genius. Thank you for making my emoticon dreams come true. And a huge thank-you to Meredith Jenks for the gorgeous photos!

The people I'm fortunate enough to work with at Simon & Schuster are the absolute best. Thank you to Chrissy Noh, Katy Hershberger, Jon Anderson, Anne Zafian, Michelle Leo, Katrina Groover, Dorothy Gribbin, and Lucille Rettino. And a special shout-out to Alexa Pastor for reading every draft!

I share a writing office with three of the finest people in Los

Angeles. Rachel Cohn, Leslie Margolis, and Jordan Roter, thank you for everything. I promise I'll start refilling the water cooler.

Thanks to Anna Carey, Jennifer E. Smith, and Jenny Han. Jenny, here's to that night in Italy!

I'm so fortunate to know Jessi Kirby and Siobhan Vivian, brilliant writers and wonderful friends. Thanks, you guys, for the encouragement and support.

Thank you to Jane Finn and Katie Matson. And thanks especially to my brother, Jason Matson, the bravest person I know.

And, of course, thanks to Murphy, without whom this book would have been written much, much faster.

The Elder looked across to Tamsin in the firelight. "Pay close attention when people tell you stories," he said. "At their core, every story you've ever heard comes down to two things. *Someone goes on a long journey* or *a stranger comes to town*."

Tamsin considered this as the fire crackled. "But can't it sometimes be both?"

The Elder looked at her for a long moment, like he was seeing something she was not. "Yes," he finally said, his voice grave. "Very occasionally, it can."

—C. B. McCallister, *A Murder of Crows*. Hightower & Jax, New York.

Chapter ONE

I flexed my feet in my too-tight shoes and made myself stand up straight, trying to ignore the rapid-fire clicking of the cameras going off all around me. It was still really hot out—despite the fact it was getting close to five—but I was wearing a knee-length tweed skirt and a white button-down shirt. My hair had been blown out and curled, and I was wearing pearl earrings and a light application of makeup. It was not the way I would normally have looked on a Wednesday afternoon in early June, but this was anything but an ordinary Wednesday.

"Thank you all so much for coming today," my father said from behind the podium that was currently in the middle of our front porch. He shuffled his papers for a second before taking a deep breath and going into his prepared speech, the one I now knew by heart, since Peter Wright, his chief of staff and main strategist, had made me listen to it over and over until I could do so with absolutely no change in my expression, like all of this was old news to me by now, and nothing my dad was saying would catch me by surprise.

For a moment, as the now-familiar words started to wash over me, I just blinked at the podium. Where exactly had it come from?

Did Peter travel around with spare ones in the back of his SUV?

". . . regret that the people of Connecticut might have lost any of their trust in me," my dad said, snapping me back to the present moment. I fixed my eyes on him again, hoping that my face hadn't betrayed anything other than a supportive daughter standing by her father. If it had, this story, which was already dominating the twenty-four-hour news channels and had spilled onto the networks, would just keep getting bigger.

It wasn't like I didn't understand why. A prominent congressman, one of the stars of the party, is suddenly caught up in a scandal that threatens to upend not only his career but the next national election—the headlines practically wrote themselves. If it had been someone else, I would have looked at the round-the-clock coverage and shrugged, figuring it was to be expected. But now that it was happening here—my front yard, my porch, my father—that certainty was totally gone.

My eyes drifted to the wall of reporters and photographers in front of me, the news cameras pointed toward us, the relentless sound of shutters clicking, all of it letting me know every moment was being captured. The press knew when there was blood in the water. It was evident enough by the fact that our front lawn was now packed and news trucks lined the block. They'd been here ever since the story broke, but until a few hours ago, they'd been kept from getting near our house by the guard at the entrance to Stanwich Woods, the planned community we lived in in Stanwich, Connecticut. Since normally this job consisted of waving in residents while reading magazines, I had a feeling whoever was working was not thrilled that they now had to fend off national media teams.

The headlines and news reports had been inescapable, all of them leading with the fact that my father had once been tapped as the vice presidential candidate before withdrawing five years earlier. Everyone brought up that he'd been widely considered to be a strong candidate for the VP spot again in the next national election, or even higher. Reporters commented on the story with barely concealed glee, and the segments and headlines were each worse than the last one. *Rising Congressman Falls to Earth. Congressional Corruption Brings Party's Star Low. Walker Trips Himself Up.* I'd been around the press practically my whole life—but it had never felt like this.

My father, Representative Alexander Walker, had been a member of Congress since I was three. He'd been a public defender before that, but I had no recollection of it—of a time when there weren't voters to court and messages to craft and districts to analyze. Some of my friends' fathers had jobs that they did and then left the office and forgot about, but that had never been my dad. His work was his life, which meant it was mine, too.

It hadn't been so bad when I was a kid, but in the last few years things had changed. I'd always been part of the Alex Walker brand—the daughter of a diligent single father who worked hard for the people of Connecticut—but now I was also a potential liability. Countless examples of politicians' kids who'd tanked, or at least threatened to damage, their parents' careers were laid out for me as cautionary tales and clear examples of what I was *not* supposed to do. I would not say anything offensive, or anything that could be interpreted as such, in a public forum or in earshot of the media. I would not be photographed doing or wearing anything even mildly controversial. I had the same social media accounts as everyone else, but mine were regulated by a series of interns and I wasn't allowed to post to them without permission. I'd had a week of media training when I was thirteen, and after that I'd never strayed too far from the message, from the words that were vetted and scripted and written for me. I didn't cause my dad, or his team, any trouble if I could help it.

It wasn't like I never did anything that made waves—I'd once, without thinking, ordered my regular latte on a campaign stop, and his staff had had a two-hour meeting about it. Then they'd had a one-hour meeting with me, complete with an agenda labeled ALEXANDRA, despite the fact that nobody who actually knew me ever called me by my real name. I was Andie, and had been since I was little and couldn't quite manage the four-syllable name my parents had landed me with. "Andra" was the best I could manage at two, which turned into Andie, and fifteen years later, here I still was. In the end it was decided that when there was press around, I could no longer order five-dollar iced sugar-free vanilla soy lattes—they didn't want me to seem like a rich kid, throwing her money around while the people of Connecticut struggled to put food on the table. They also didn't want to offend the dairy lobby.

It didn't seem possible that after years of being beyond careful, watching all the tiniest details, and trying never to make a mistake, we'd ended up here anyway. But not because of anything I'd done—or even anything my dad had done, according to the version of events Peter had been giving the media ever since this broke. But this was happening because someone in his office had (allegedly) taken charitable contributions that were intended for my dad's foundation and funneled them into his

Morgan Matson

reelection campaign fund. Apparently, when it was discovered during an audit that my dad's foundation was nearly bankrupt, people began asking questions. Which had led to this, to today, much more quickly than I could get my head around.

Two weeks ago my life had been normal. My dad had been in D.C., working as usual, I'd been finishing up the school year, hanging out with my friends, and planning how to break up with my boyfriend, Zach (by the lockers, right after his graduation, quick and fast, like ripping off a Band-Aid). Two weeks ago my life had been going to plan. And now there was a podium on the porch.

I let my eyes fall for just a second to a spot on the lawn where a thick cable was laid out, flattening the grass. A month ago my dad and I had shot promo photos and ads there for his fall campaign, my dad in a jacket but no tie, me in a skirt and cashmere sweater. There had been fake fall leaves scattered over the grass, turning May into October. I hadn't asked if these had been purchased, or if some intern had had to make them, because I really hadn't wanted to know the answer.

We'd been shooting all day, first stills, then video, my dad and I walking across the lawn together, like this was totally normal. As if we ever got dressed up to walk across the lawn and have a chat, just for fun. As we were nearing the end of the day, the director had looked at the two of us and sighed. "Don't you guys have a dog or something?"

My dad had been on his BlackBerry as usual, not even hearing this, and it had fallen to me to give him a smile and say, "No dog. Just the two of us." And he'd nodded and said something to the guy holding the silver disk that bounced light onto us, and we'd moved on, into the next setup, projecting the image of a small, happy family once again.

Now, though, I didn't know if those mailers or ads, complete with my dad's campaign slogan—"Toward the Future"—would ever be used. From where I was standing on the porch, it wasn't looking so good.

"I will say again that I had no knowledge whatsoever of this misuse of funds," my dad said, snapping me back to the present moment. His voice was getting low and serious, and I could practically sense the press grow still, like they knew they were getting what they'd come for. "But the fact is, this violation of campaign finance regulations originated in my office. And since it was an office under my control and my leadership, I must take responsibility. As you know, I've asked for an independent investigation, one that can get to the bottom of how this occurred. I've directed my staff to cooperate to the fullest extent. And while the investigation is ongoing—"

Here my dad drew in a breath and rubbed his wedding ring with his thumb, his nervous tic. Apparently, he'd lost four the first year he and my mother were married, and so she'd bought him a crazy-expensive one in the hope that he might hold on to it. He had, but ever since, he'd been absently checking for its existence. The press sometimes commented on the fact that he was still wearing it, five years later, but I had a feeling today that would not be one of the questions shouted at him from our lawn. There were much bigger headline-generating fish to fry.

"While the investigation is ongoing, I will be taking a leave of absence. I feel that I cannot serve my district or my state effectively while this is being investigated. I will be donating my salary to the Ovarian Cancer Research Fund."

I hadn't heard about the charity—it wasn't in the last draft of the speech Peter read to me, and I tried not to let any surprise pass over my face. But I couldn't help wondering if it had been a last-minute addition, or if this was just something they hadn't thought I needed to know.

"I will be taking this time away from Congress to reflect on any actions that might have brought me here and to spend time with my family." My father glanced over at me, and I gave him the smile that Peter had made me rehearse that morning. It was supposed to be supportive, encouraging, and kind, but couldn't be too happy. I had no idea if it came off or not, but all I could think as my dad turned back to the press was how strange this all was—this bizarre theater we were performing for the national press on our front porch. "I will not be taking any questions at this time. Thank you very much for your attention."

He turned away from the podium as the reporters on our lawn started yelling questions. As we'd practiced, I walked toward my dad, and he put his arm around my shoulders as someone pulled the front door open from the inside. I glanced back to see Peter stepping smoothly up to the podium, answering the shouted questions my dad had walked away from.

The second we were inside, my dad dropped his arm and I took a step away. The door was firmly shut behind us by one of the interns who'd arrived with Peter last week. The intern nodded at my dad, then hustled out of the foyer, fast. Most of the interns—I never bothered to learn their names unless they were particularly cute—had been avoiding him since the story broke, not meeting his eye, clearly not sure how to behave. Usually, they were unshakable, following his every move, trying to prove themselves invaluable, the better to get a job later. But now, it was like my dad was radioactive, and just being around him might damage their future job prospects.

"Thanks," my dad said after clearing his throat. "I know that can't have been easy for you."

It was only years of practice and ingrained media training that kept me from rolling my eyes. As though my dad had ever cared about what was easy for me. "It was fine."

My dad nodded, and silence fell between us. I realized with a start that we were alone—no Peter, no constantly buzzing BlackBerry. I tried for a moment to remember the last time it had been just me and my dad, together in a way that hadn't been staged for the cameras, engineered to appear casual. After a moment I realized it had probably been December, my dad and I driving together to a post-holiday charity event. He'd tried to ask me about my classes, until it became painfully clear to both of us that he had no idea what they were. We'd given up after a few minutes and listened to the news on the radio for the rest of the drive.

I glanced up and saw our reflection in the hall mirror, a little startled to see us standing next to each other. I always wanted to think I looked like my mother, and I had when I was little. But I was looking more and more like my dad every year—the proof was being reflected right in front of me. We had the same freckly skin, same thick auburn hair (more brown than red, except in the light), same thick dark brows that I was constantly having to tweeze into submission, same blue eyes and dark eyelashes. I was even tall like him, and lanky, whereas my mother had been

Morgan Matson

petite and curvy, with curly blond hair and green eyes. I looked away from the mirror and took a step back, and when I looked up again, it was just my dad reflected back, which felt better—not like the two of us were being forced into a frame together.

"So," my dad said, reaching into his suit jacket pocket—undoubtedly for his BlackBerry. He stopped after a second, though, and dropped his hand, when he must have remembered it wasn't there. Peter had confiscated it so that it wouldn't go off during the press conference. He'd taken my cell phone too, which even I had to admit was a good idea—my three best friends had a tendency to start epic text threads, and even if my phone had been on silent, its buzzing would have been distracting and probably would have spawned a story of its own—*This press conference is like sooooo boring! Texting daughter can't even pay attention as Walker's career hits the skids.* My dad stuck his hands in his pockets and cleared his throat again. "So. Andie. About this summer. I—uh . . ."

"I won't be here," I reminded him, and even saying the words, I could feel relief flooding through me. "My program starts the day after tomorrow." My dad nodded, his brow furrowed, which meant he had no idea what I was talking about but didn't want to tell me that, just wanted to look concerned and engaged. I'd been watching him do it with opponents and voters for years, and tried not to let myself be surprised that he hadn't remembered. "The Young Scholars Program," I clarified, knowing telling him was the simplest path out of this. "It's at Johns Hopkins."

"Ah," my dad said, his brow clearing, and I saw he actually was remembering, not just pretending to remember while waiting for Peter to whisper something in his ear. "Of course. That's right."

The program at Johns Hopkins was one of the best in the country, designed for high school students who were planning to be pre-med in college. My friend Toby insisted on calling it pre-pre-med-med, and the fact that I kept telling her not to only seemed to be making the name stick. You stayed on campus in the dorms, took advanced math and science classes, and got to shadow interns and residents on their hospital rotations. I'd known I wanted to be a doctor since I could remember. I had a story I told to reporters about my dad giving me a toy stethoscope for Christmas when I was five that actually wasn't true, but I'd said it enough now that it *felt* true. When I was applying to the program, I was confident I'd get in based on my grades—I did well in all my subjects, but I did great in math and science; I always had. And it didn't hurt that one of my dad's biggest supporters was Dr. Daniel Rizzoli, who was the former provost of Johns Hopkins. When he'd handed me my letter of recommendation, handwritten on heavy, cream-colored paper, I'd known I was in.

I'd been looking forward to it all year, but with everything that had been happening, I was practically counting down the minutes. My dad could stay here and sort things out on his own, and hopefully by the time I came back in August, things would be settled. But either way, in two days this would no longer be my problem. In forty-eight hours I would be gone. I would be in a dorm room in Baltimore, meeting my new roommate, Gina Flores, in person for the first time, and hoping that her tendency to never use exclamation points in any of her texts or e-mails was a weird quirk and not actually indicative of her personality. I would be reading over my syllabus for the millionth time and getting my books from the campus bookstore. I would hopefully have met someone cute at orientation already, halfway to my summer crush. But I would not be *here*, which was the most important thing.

"Are you all set with everything?" my dad asked, and I wondered if this sounded as strange to him as it did to me, like he was reading badly written lines he hadn't fully memorized. "I mean . . . do you need a ride?"

"I'm fine," I said quickly. The last thing I needed was to have my dad drive me onto campus trailed by a CNN news truck. "Palmer's driving me. It's all arranged." Palmer Alden—one of my three best friends—loved any opportunity for a road trip, and when she'd seen me looking into buses and car services, she'd jumped into action and started planning our route, complete with mixes and snack stops. Her boyfriend, Tom, was coming as well, mostly because he insisted, since there was a rumor that *Hairspray* was going to be our school musical next year, and he wanted to do some "method research."

"Oh, good," my dad said. Peter must have finished answering a question, because suddenly the shouts of the press outside got louder. I winced slightly and took a step away from the door.

"Well," I said, tipping my head toward the kitchen. My phone was in there, I was pretty sure. Not that I even really needed to check it, but I wanted this to be over. The whole day had been strange enough, and we didn't need to keep adding to it by trying to have the world's most awkward conversation. "I'm going to . . ."

"Right," my dad said, his hand reaching toward his suit jacket again, out of habit, before he caught himself halfway and dropped it. "And I should . . ." The sentence trailed off, and my dad glanced around the entryway, looking lost. I felt a sudden flash of sympathy for him. After all, my dad always had something to do. He was beyond busy, his day scheduled to the minute sometimes, always in the center of a group of staff and handlers and interns and assistants. He ran his team; he was respected and powerful and in control. And now he was standing in our foyer without his BlackBerry, while the press tore him apart just a few feet away.

But even as I felt bad for him, I knew there wasn't anything I could do or say. My dad and I fixed our own problems—we took care of them ourselves, didn't share them with each other, and that was just the way it went. I gave him a quick smile, then started toward the kitchen.

"Andie," my dad said when I was nearly to the kitchen door. "I . . ." He looked at me for a moment before putting his hands in his pockets and dropping his gaze to the wooden floors, which seemed impervious to scratching, looking as brand-new as the day I'd first seen this house, like nobody actually lived here at all. "Thank you for standing up there with me. I know it was hard. And I promise I won't ask you to do that again."

A memory flashed before me, fast, just a collection of images and feelings. Another press conference five years earlier, my mother, her hands on my shoulders, squeezing them tight as I tried not to flinch while the flashes went off in my eyes. The way she'd leaned down to whisper to me right before, when we were standing behind the doors of my dad's congressional offices, the synthetic hair of her wig tickling my cheek, so unlike the soft curls I used to wind around my finger whenever she would let me. "Remember," she'd said, her voice low and meant only for me, "if things get too dramatic, what are you going to do?"

"Mom," I'd said, trying not to smile, but fighting it with every millimeter. "I'm *not*."

"You are," she said, straightening my dress, then my head-band. She tugged on the end of her hair and arched an eyebrow at me. "If things are going badly and we need a distraction, just reach up and yank it off. They'll forget all about what they were asking your dad."

"Stop," I said, but I was smiling then; I couldn't help it. She leaned down closer to me, and I felt my smile falter as I could see just how thin she was, her skin yellowing underneath the makeup she'd carefully applied. How I could see the veins in her face, the ones that we must all have—but on the rest of us they were hidden, not exposed where they shouldn't be.

How the press conference had gone on longer than they'd expected, how my mother had left me to go stand with my dad when he started talking about her. It had all been about her, after all—the reason he was pulling his name from consideration for vice president, despite the fact that it was going to be him, everyone knew that. It was *supposed* to be him. How hard I'd fought not to cry, standing alone, knowing even then that if I did, that would be the story, the picture on the front page. And when it was over, how my dad had given me a hug and promised me that was that, and I'd never have to go through another one of those again.

"Really," I said now, my voice coming out sharper than I'd expected. My dad blinked at me, and I held his gaze for a moment, wondering if he even remembered the last time we'd done this, or if they all blended together, just another promise he'd made that he couldn't actually keep. "Because I've heard that before."

I didn't want to see if he understood what I meant. I wasn't sure I could take another fake furrowed brow, not about something like this. So I just gave him a nod and headed into the kitchen, walking twice as fast as usual, ready to put all of this far behind me, and suddenly feeling, for the very first time, that nobody gave rats the credit they deserved for abandoning the sinking ships. They were the smart ones, getting out while they still could. After all, they saw the way things were going, and they were just looking out for themselves. And so was I.

PALMER

> Andie!! How are you doing?

BRI

> You looked great on CNN.

TOBY

> Totally great. Did you do that thing with the curling iron? Remember, the thing you promised months ago to teach me?

BRI

> Toby.

TOBY

> What? I'm trying to say she looked good. And that I would like to as well.

Morgan Matson

How are you holding up?

In the safety of my own room, I looked down at my phone and felt myself really smile for what I was certain was the first time that day. I could see Peter had been right to keep my phone away from me—it looked like these texts had started right around the time my dad's speech was wrapping up.

I crossed over to my bed, phone in hand. We'd been in this house five years, but my room hadn't changed a whole lot since the day we'd moved in. It had been professionally decorated, but by someone who clearly didn't know they were designing for a middle schooler. It was all taupes and beiges and subtle patterns, everything matching, like a bedroom suite had just been picked whole out of a catalog. After all this time, it still sometimes felt like I was sleeping in a hotel. I had my makeup and jewelry organized on my dresser, framed pictures of my friends, and clothes folded on the chair in the corner, but aside from that, there was very little that marked this room as mine. I flopped down onto the bed, kicking my shoes off and settling back against the throw pillows, getting comfortable, since these text chains could go on for hours.

I glanced down at the last text, Palmer's, and hesitated, my hand over the keypad. I leaned closer to the window that was above my bed—it was open slightly, and I could hear voices drifting up to me. I looked out and saw the press conference had wrapped up. People were wandering around the lawn, and there was no sign of either Peter or the podium.

I turned my back on everything that was happening outside, hoping that maybe the next time I looked, everyone would be gone, the flattened grass the last reminder of what had taken place there only a few hours before.

ME

I'm fine.

PALMER

Really?

BRI

REALLY?

TOBY

?

ME

Totally fine. The press conference was a pain,
but it's my dad's issue, not mine.

BRI

Hm.

ME

What?

TOBY

She's saying she doesn't believe you.

PALMER

How can you tell?

BRI

No, Toby's right. I don't. But we can discuss it later.

ME

There's nothing to discuss

BRI

Yes there is

TOBY

And when we discuss it, why don't you also show me
the curling iron thing?

PALMER

Toby, I thought we were going to be supportive.

TOBY

I AM being supportive! I even tried to drive over
and be there for Andie, but the guard at the
gate wouldn't let me in.

ME

He wouldn't let you in?

TOBY

No! Something about needing to be on a list,
national security, I don't know.

ME

      Sorry, T. This should be back to normal as

            soon as all the press is gone

TOBY

    Well, I was offended. He knows me, after all.

    We go way back, me and Ronnie.

PALMER

    His name's Earl.

TOBY

    Oh.

PALMER

    But anyway!

    We're going out tonight.

ME

          We are?

BRI

    We are. We voted, and it's a necessity.

TOBY

    Absolutely. That's what I tried to tell Ronnie.

PALMER

    Earl.

Morgan Matson

BRI

> There's a party. We're all going.
>
> We think you need it after everything that's happened.

I turned and looked out the window again, at the press corps that weren't leaving nearly as quickly as I wanted them to. There were now reporters lined up in front of the house, cameras pointed at them, no doubt recapping what had just occurred. It didn't seem like I was going to be leaving unnoticed any time soon.

ME

> I'm not so sure that's going to happen, guys.

TOBY

PALMER

> No, it totally will!

BRI

> Don't worry

PALMER

> We figured it out.

ME

> But the press are still all over this place.
> We'd need a way to get me out of here unseen. . . .
> Don't know how that's possible.

Andie, RELAX. We have a plan.

I looked down at that sentence, feeling a tiny stab of nervousness. The fact that nobody would tell me what exactly this plan *was* had me concerned. Especially if Toby was the brains behind it. I moved a little closer to my window, still trying to keep myself out of sight, and pushed it open more. There must have been a reporter doing her recap practically right beneath me, because suddenly I could hear it crystal clear, her miked voice traveling straight up to me.

"The last time the congressman was the focus of this much attention was five years ago, when, due to his wife's failing health, he withdrew his name abruptly from Governor Matthew Laughlin's unsuccessful presidential campaign, despite the fact he was seen as the front-runner for the VP slot. His wife, Molly Walker, died from ovarian cancer six weeks later. It's unclear what this latest upset means for the congressman's future—"

I slammed the window, shutting out the reporter on the lawn, and picked up my phone again.

ME

A party actually sounds great.
Let's do it.

Chapter TWO

"Okay," I heard Palmer say as the car slowed down and then turned left. "We're almost there. Andie, how you doing?"

"Um," I said from where I was lying between the seats on Palmer's minivan's floor, under a blanket that seemed to be covered in equal parts dust and cat hair, "I've been better."

"Just a little bit longer," Bri said from above me as what felt suspiciously like a foot patted my shoulder.

"Better safe than sorry," I heard Toby say, with the blithe assurance of someone who wasn't currently trying not to breathe through her nose.

"Toby, do I make a right?" I heard Palmer ask, as the car slowed and then stopped.

"To get to Ardmore?" I piped up from beneath the blanket, then sneezed twice. "It's a left, then another right."

"How can you know that?" A corner of my blanket lifted up, and there was Bri—a piece of her, at least, just wide brown eyes and side-swept bangs. "You can't see anything."

"She's making it up," Toby said confidently as the blanket dropped again.

"Check your map," I yelled up through the blanket, then started to cough on the dust I'd inhaled.

"It's . . . ," Toby said, and there was a long pause in which she must have checked the directions on her phone. "Seriously?" she asked, not sounding impressed, but annoyed.

"Told you," I said. I hadn't been trying to track where we were going ever since we'd left my house, but there were some things you couldn't turn off, and I liked always knowing where I was and how to get where I was going. It was the reason, whenever we needed to go somewhere in separate cars, everyone always followed me.

"Quick, drive around in circles to confuse her," Toby said, and I heard Bri laugh.

"I don't think the party's going to be worth all this," I said, as the car made, sure enough, a left and then another right. It slowed even more and started to feel like it had pulled off the pavement and onto the side of the road. It was amazing how much more you could tell about these things when you were lying on the floor.

It turned out that the plan to get me to this party had been Palmer's, and I had to admire her thoroughness. Palmer lived three houses down from me in Stanwich Woods. She'd taken a walk after the press conference to scout things out and had seen—even though the media was supposed to have cleared out—that there were several news vans parked in front of the Stanwich Woods gate, no doubt hoping for another scoop.

So she'd picked me up at my house, and then she'd smuggled me—hiding under the blanket—past the vans. Even though I was pretty sure we were in the clear and that nobody was tailing us, I

Morgan Matson

stayed hidden as we drove to pick up Toby and Bri. Luckily, it was only one stop—it almost always was. All four of us were best friends, but Toby and Bri were *best* best friends and basically inseparable.

We headed to the party right after picking them up, which was good, since I was nearing the limit of my endurance for being stuck under a blanket. But even though I couldn't breathe very easily, I was glad we were taking these precautions. I knew that if I were caught going to a party hours after I'd stood next to my dad, the responsible daughter in pearls, it wouldn't be good for anyone.

"Of course it'll be worth it," I heard Bri say, and a moment later, someone whisked the blanket off of me, and I blinked, trying not to sneeze from all the dust motes that were now floating through the van.

"Air," I said gratefully, as I took a big gulp of it and sat up, looking around, trying to see where we were parked and if there were any other cars near ours. "Are we far enough from the house?"

"Yes," Palmer said patiently, turning around to look at me from the driver's seat. Stanwich was a town of almost no crime but a large police force, which meant that breaking up teenagers' parties on weekends was what they seemed to spend most of their time doing. And the first sign of a high school party was a ton of cars around a driveway, haphazardly parked. So it was standard party etiquette to park far enough away that you would deflect any suspicion, and walk. But I always parked farther than most people, not wanting to risk it. "Andie. It's fine. You don't have to worry about anything tonight but having fun. And you need some fun."

"It's true," Bri said from where she was sitting next to me. "We voted on it."

"We did," Toby agreed from the passenger seat, as she lowered the visor and flipped up the mirror lid while simultaneously pulling out her makeup bag. We'd all learned years ago that the best way to get Toby out of the house before midnight was not to make her choose one outfit, but to let her bring options so we could vote in the car, and to let her do hair and makeup en route. But since Palmer refused to let her do her eyes when the car was moving, I had a feeling we might be waiting here for a few more minutes.

"You voted on what, exactly?" I asked as I brushed some lint off my shoulder and fought back the urge to sneeze again.

"That we were going out tonight," Bri said. "And we weren't—"

"Letting you out of it," Toby finished as she started to apply her mascara. "No matter what."

"Exactly," Bri said, nodding, and Toby held her hand back for a fist bump without taking her eyes off the mirror. I shook my head, but I could feel myself smile. It was the B&T show, as Palmer and I had dubbed it. Bri and Toby had been best friends since preschool, and were such a unit people routinely mixed them up, even though they couldn't have looked less alike.

Sabrina Choudhury and Tobyhanna Mlynarczyk had come up to me my first day of third grade at Stanwich Elementary, where I was sitting alone at recess, trying to understand the weird game that was being played with a big rubber ball. They hadn't played anything like that at Canfield Prep, where I'd transferred from after a poll showed that people—and the teachers' union—didn't like my dad sending his daughter to a private school. I was feeling like I'd landed in a foreign country, when suddenly there were two girls sitting on my bench, one on either side of me. They had been Bri-and-Toby even then, talking over each other, trying to get me to settle an argument about which member of the boy band of the moment was the cutest one. Apparently, I'd picked the right answer—Wade, the one neither of them thought was the cute one—because from that moment on they'd been my friends. Palmer and I became friends when I'd moved down the street from her when I was twelve, and when ninth grade started, she'd talked her parents into letting her switch from Stanwich Country Day to the public high school. When Palmer met Toby and Bri, they all got along right away, and from then on it was like we'd become the unit we were always meant to be.

"I appreciate it," I said, grabbing Bri's outstretched hand and pulling myself up from the floor and onto the seat next to her. I brushed some dirt off my jeans, very glad I hadn't worn anything white tonight. "But I'm telling you, I'm *fine*."

"We don't believe you," Toby said, looking at me through the mirror as she started doing her lips.

"Can I borrow that?" I asked, and Toby nodded and handed her lipstick to me. "Look," I said, leaning over Toby to get a sliver of mirror. "It has nothing to do with me. It's my dad's thing. He's going to sort it out."

"But what if he doesn't?" Palmer asked, her voice gentle.

"Then he'll take one of the private-sector jobs he's always being offered," I said as I concentrated on getting the line of my lips even. "Or he'll lecture for a while, or go back to being a lawyer, and *then* he'll run again." My dad not being in politics was nearly impossible to picture—it was intrinsic to who he was. "But nothing's changed for me. I'm still going to my program, and when I get back, things will be settled." I capped the lipstick and handed it back to Toby. "We ready to go?"

"Okay, Type A," Toby said as she zipped up her makeup bag. I rolled my eyes at her in the mirror before Toby flipped the visor back up. "What?" she asked, shooting me a grin. "It's from your name. That's all."

"Uh-huh," I said, raising an eyebrow at her, but not disputing that it was true. So what if I liked to be in control of things? *Someone* had to be, after all. We piled out of the van, and I looked around, reorienting myself.

"Whose house is this again?" Toby asked. She straightened the skirt she'd changed into on the drive—I had heard the debate about what to wear, but she'd ignored my shouted-through-the-blanket opinions, even though I knew exactly what clothes she was talking about without being able to see them.

"Kevin Castillo's," I said immediately. It was the first question I'd asked when Palmer had started telling me the plan. I'd been to parties at his house before, which always made me feel a little better. In a new house, I was always looking for exits and escape routes, in case they became suddenly necessary.

"Which means it's going to be good," Palmer said, raising an eyebrow at me. "Remember the party he had in March?"

"Vaguely," I said, starting to smile, recalling an hours-long quarters game and all of us ending up at the diner at four a.m., ordering plates of fries and laughing too loud.

Morgan Matson

"Where's the house?" Bri asked, and I pointed down the street.

"That way," I said.

Palmer nodded. "Like half a mile." Toby sighed and reached down to take off her wedges, but didn't complain. All of us knew the drill. And tonight, especially, not getting caught was crucial.

I'd been to only one party where it had happened. It was freshman year, and it was only the second real high school party I'd ever been to, and I was still thrilled and excited to be there. We were only there because Palmer's brother Josh, who was a senior, had been invited. He'd agreed to let us come if he could disavow all knowledge of us if anyone got mad that freshmen were there. I was drinking a beer from a red Solo cup, like an idiot—I hadn't yet learned any of the tricks I'd later need to employ at parties—when the red and blue lights streamed in through the living room window, bathing every-one in color. For a second the entire party seemed to freeze, but then everyone was in motion, running in a hundred direc-tions, for cars or hiding places, just trying not to get caught. The excitement of being at a senior's party had been eclipsed utterly by a wave of fear so all encompassing I started shaking. If I were caught at a party, drinking underage, it would be very, *very* bad for my father.

I hadn't gotten caught—I'd been yanked out of harm's way at the last moment. But that close call had been more than enough to scare me. My friends knew now that I wouldn't go to a party that looked like a target, and I had all sorts of tech-niques for staying under the radar once we got to the party. And even now, as we walked in a single-file line along the side of the road, I could feel myself on high alert, looking around to make sure there weren't too many cars parked along the road, nobody looking too long at us, nothing that might give us away. I didn't even want to think what it would do to the story if, on today of all days, I was caught at a party. It would be like pouring gasoline on a forest fire.

We'd been walking in silence for a few moments when Toby cleared her throat. "Guys," she said, her tone grave. "At the party tonight, *something* has to happen. This is when the curse gets broken. Because I refuse to spend another summer without a boyfriend."

"I'll be your wingwoman," Palmer volunteered immediately. "We can totally make this happen."

"No," Toby said firmly. "You're fired from ever being my wingwoman again. Last time you tried, everyone asked *you* out, and Tom got really mad at me."

Palmer opened her mouth to protest this, and I just shook my head. "Toby has a point, P."

"It's not your fault you're a blonde," Bri added. I laughed as Palmer's expression turned from disgruntled to embarrassed. Palmer was beautiful, though she seemed to have absolutely no understanding of this fact. She had long, thick blond hair that would be four shades lighter by the end of the summer. She was a head shorter than me, and whip-thin, with the ability to eat us all under the table, and she seemed to laugh more than most people. You wanted to spend more time with Palmer the second you met her.

"I'll take over wingwoman duties," I said. "What do you want me to look for? Are you still into the floppy-haired thing?"

Morgan Matson

"I honestly don't care about looks." Toby said, her voice wistful. "I'll look across a room, the crowds will part, there he'll be . . . and I'll *know*." Bri, Palmer, and I exchanged looks, but nobody said anything. We each had something that was off-limits for teasing, and love was Toby's.

She'd had the misfortune of growing up with a babysitter who regularly brought DVDs of romantic comedies with her whenever she sat for Toby. Toby had eaten them up, and so, from a much-too-young age, she was watching Julia Roberts bargain with Richard Gere and lose her heart in the process. She was watching Meg Ryan scrunch up her nose before bursting into tears and Bridget Jones run through the snowy London streets looking for Mark Darcy. When Toby wasn't around, the three of us talked about it all the time—how this had warped her perception of romance forever. She now expected what she'd grown up seeing—that was what she thought love would be like. She expected guys to lift boom boxes outside her house and talk in declarations about what they loved best about her and she was always—though she denied it—trying to turn Bri into her plucky sidekick.

I had tried to tell her, over and over, that romance in real life was nothing like the movies and that you shouldn't want it to be. That, really, all you needed was a guy who was a blast to hang out with, a great kisser, someone to have fun with. None of the rest of us expected movie-love. Palmer and Tom were practically married, and Bri tended to date seniors for three or four months at a time. But Toby wanted her happily ever after, her last-minute chase to the airport, her declaration of love. Which was why, I was pretty sure, she'd never had a real boyfriend.

She approached every guy wondering if he was the end of her romantic comedy, which invariably freaked them out.

"Just . . . maybe don't put so much pressure on it," I said, choosing my words carefully. "Maybe just have fun?"

"Easy for you to say, Andie," Toby scoffed. "You *always* have a boyfriend."

"Not at the moment," Palmer pointed out.

"But most of the time," Bri jumped in, backing up Toby as usual. "Like, what, sixty percent of the time?"

"More like seventy-five," Toby countered.

"Poor Zach," said Palmer with an exaggerated sigh. "I liked him."

"We should really stop learning their names," Bri said, deadpan, and Toby grinned.

"Totally," she said. "It'll make things easier. I'll just give the next one a nickname."

"Funny." I tried to look at her sternly, but gave up after a minute and started to laugh. The thing was, they weren't wrong. They would tease me like this after most of my breakups, calling me a serial heartbreaker. But it wasn't intentional—it was just the way it always unfolded. First I'd get a crush on someone. This could, in truth, last much longer than the actual dating-the-guy part of things. I wouldn't be able to think about anything else, I'd talk about him constantly, I'd spend way too long getting ready, just in case I saw him. Then we'd start going out—and usually, the first week or so was great. Lots of making out, lots of butterflies in my stomach, lots of giddiness and hand-holding and endless conversations, either in person or on the phone late at night. But, inevitably, after the third week rolled around,

Morgan Matson

he would start wanting more, and I would start getting antsy. Whether it was physical or emotional, it was always more than I felt comfortable with. I could never understand when guys wanted to talk to you about your *feelings*. That was what my friends were for. Why was it impossible to keep things easy? Light, fun, not too serious, and nothing more than kissing.

At any rate, three weeks seemed to be about as long as this had ever been able to last. Whenever my friends brought it up, I pointed to my relationship with Travis Friedman, which had lasted five weeks and change, but I was always told this didn't count, because two of those weeks were over winter break. But this was the way I liked things. I ended it (or he did), I had a few weeks' getting over it and listening to lots of girl-power music and eating ice cream, and then, before too long, I'd start to crush on someone new and would begin the whole cycle over again. It worked for me. And honestly, I'd never understood the point of getting too serious with anyone you met in high school. It was *high school*. Best to keep it light and date seriously in college or med school, with people who were actually going to end up mattering.

"Wait a sec. Why are you even scoping out prospects?" Palmer asked, turned her head to look back at Toby. "What about Wyatt?"

Toby shook her head. "He's not back in town yet."

"He might be," Bri said. "I saw he posted a picture yesterday that looked like downtown."

"Wait, what?" Toby asked as she stopped short, nearly causing a pileup as she dug in her purse for her phone and then frantically started scrolling through it. "That should have been the lead item! Why didn't you guys tell me?"

"I didn't know," I said, holding up my hands and giving her a *don't blame me* face.

Wyatt Miller went to boarding school in Massachusetts during the year, but his family lived here in Stanwich, and he came back for summers. We'd met him last year when he'd been working the beach concession stand, and started giving us free fries and unlimited soda refills. We'd all started hanging out—Wyatt and my summer boyfriend, Nick, had gotten along really well—and it hadn't taken Toby long to develop a massive crush on him. He'd still been with his girlfriend from boarding school then, so nothing happened over the summer. But when Toby saw that they'd broken up right around Valentine's Day, she was sure that her moment had arrived. She'd asked him to our junior prom and was thrilled when he accepted—even though he kept making it very clear that they were just going as friends. At the after-party, when I'd been breaking up with my date—I hadn't loved prom—Toby and Wyatt had tipsily made out. Toby was sure this was proof of his feelings for her, despite all of us gently—and then not so gently—telling her that it was probably just the effect of Jägermeister and power ballads. Toby had tried to keep things going when he went back to boarding school, but Wyatt had reverted to treating Toby the way he treated all of us—totally platonically.

"Oh my god, I think you're right," Toby said, squinting at the brightness of the screen in the darkness, her voice rising with every word. "Why hasn't he gotten in touch? Oh my *god*!"

"Shh," I said, glancing around, not wanting to draw any more attention to us than we had to.

Toby nodded, then looked back at her phone. "Oh my *god*," she said again, in a whisper this time.

"Okay," Palmer said, stopping in front of a white house that I was relieved to see looked like any other house on the block, no sign of a party unless you were really paying attention to what kind of music you could hear faintly coming from it. "Are we ready? Andie?" I nodded and reached into my purse, then handed over my bottle of Diet Coke—three-quarters full—to her. "Any preferences?"

"Anything but brandy," I said, making a face. "That did not mix well."

Palmer nodded and led the way into the house. I knew Kevin enough to nod at in the halls, but I didn't think I'd ever actually had a conversation with him, so I was happy to let Palmer go first. I heard Bri and Toby laugh about something as I followed Palmer inside. I looked around and realized it was like pretty much every other party I'd been to. There were groups of people standing around talking or lounging on the couch, and the dining room table had been commandeered for what looked like a pretty major game of beirut. The kitchen counter was covered with bottles and mixers and a half-filled blender, and through the open doors to the patio, I could see a keg. The people who always headed to the edges of people's yards to smoke were smoking, and I could already see two people standing in the shadows of the living room, talking close, only minutes away from starting to hook up.

Palmer headed directly to the liquor bottles, and Toby and Bri headed outside to the keg as I scanned the room. I hadn't texted him that I was coming, but I had a feeling he might be here. From what I'd heard, he and his last girlfriend had ended things around when I'd dumped Zach, meaning we would both be unattached at the same time, which hadn't happened in a while. I was about to give up looking inside and see if he was by the keg when a girl I recognized from my AP Chem class stepped aside. And there he was, leaning against the kitchen counter, looking bored. Topher Fitzpatrick.

My pulse kicked up, the way it always did when I saw him. I took him in for a moment longer, since I was sure he hadn't spotted me yet. There was a petite girl talking to him. I didn't recognize her, and she was laughing, smiling up at him while he gave her a smile she probably thought was genuine, and an invitation to keep talking. I knew better. But then, by this point, I probably knew him better than most people.

He looked away for a second, scanning the room, and his eyes met mine. I held his gaze for just a second, but it was enough to know my evening had just taken a turn for the better.

"Here," Palmer said as she appeared at my elbow with the Diet Coke bottle, the top firmly on. "It's rum. I mixed it up."

"Thank you," I said, giving her a smile as I took the bottle. It was the only way I let myself drink at parties. If any pictures from the night got posted, the only thing I would be drinking, or even holding in my hand, was a Diet Coke. I knew only too well that all it would take was someone's cell phone picture on their profile, with a picture of me in the background, holding a beer or even a glass with liquid in it that couldn't be identified, and suddenly it would be a story. I unscrewed the cap and took a long drink, feeling the kick of the rum.

"Oh, look who's here," Palmer said flatly, her eyes straying to the kitchen. She sighed and looked at me. "Andie."

"I know." Topher was still talking to the petite girl as he

Morgan Matson

drank from a Sprite bottle that I would bet money didn't just contain Sprite—after all, he was the one who'd taught me well.

"What?" Toby asked as she joined us, sipping a beer that appeared to be mostly foam. Toby had never been great at tapping kegs. She followed Palmer's glance and then looked at me. "The Gopher surfaces?"

"Stop it," I said.

"You know we don't approve," Palmer said in her best serious voice.

I nodded. "Noted." I'd given up defending Topher to them years ago. He could be charming when he wanted to be; he just never seemed to want to be around my friends.

"Speak for yourself," Toby said, taking another long drink. "I think it's romantic. Like Harry and Sally, circling around each other until they can admit how they feel."

Palmer shook her head. "I really don't think that's what's happening here."

"Well, what do you know?" Toby retorted.

"I know you have foam on your nose," Palmer replied.

"Goddamn it," Toby muttered as she wiped it off.

"What's going on?" Bri asked, joining us, holding a cup of her own. She followed Toby's nod and then turned to me, shaking her head. "Andie."

"I heard it all from them already," I said, swirling the contents of my Diet Coke bottle for a second before taking a quick sip.

"Hey," Toby said, flicking me on the arm. "Wingwoman. You're falling down on the job."

"Okay," I said, looking around the party, trying to find someone I hadn't dated, Toby hadn't already rejected, and wasn't someone we'd known since elementary school. "Just give me a second."

"Alden!" I looked over as the party's host, Kevin Castillo himself, headed over to us from the dining room, holding up his hand for a high five, which Palmer returned with gusto. "Glad you could make it."

Palmer nodded toward the table, where the game seemed to have broken up, at least for the moment. "How's it going?"

"Getting killed in there," he said with a groan. "You guys want to help me out? Bri?" he asked Toby. "Or Toby?" he asked, turning to Bri.

"Reverse those," I said as I took another sip of my drink.

Kevin frowned. "Are you sure?" He pointed at Bri again. "It's not Toby?"

"*I'm* Toby," Toby said, starting to look annoyed. This was not all that infrequent, despite the fact that Bri was tall and willowy where Toby was short and curvy, and Bri had long, straight black hair and Toby was a redhead who was always trying to flatten out her natural curls, with occasionally disastrous results. When you spend that much time together, you get mixed up, even if you *don't* look alike—or act anything alike, for that matter.

"We could combine our names," Bri said, turning to Toby and arching an eyebrow. "Tobri. Then we could both answer to it."

"This has *possibilities*," Toby agreed. "Then you could take history for me and get a great grade and I could take calculus for you, and you wouldn't have to keep getting thirty-eights on tests."

"Swap PE for calculus and you've got a deal," Bri said.

"And then all the guys at parties would hit on me, too," Toby said, looking at Kevin Castillo, who turned red. Bri got embarrassed when you pointed it out, but she was undeniably gorgeous, and we'd gotten used to guys hitting on her. "I like it."

"It's a plan."

"Done and done."

Kevin was looking back and forth between the two, like he was trying to catch up. After a second, he cleared his throat and tried again. "So . . . ," he said, still looking at Bri. "Want to play . . . Bri?"

"*Tobri*," Toby said, shaking her head as Bri started to laugh. "Weren't you paying attention?"

"Alden," Kevin said, clearly baffled and giving up as he turned to Palmer, "I need your skills."

Palmer grinned as she looked at all the cups lined up. Growing up with four older siblings—two of them boys—meant Palmer was great at this kind of stuff. She'd been the one who taught us how to tap a keg, pack a bowl, and play quarters, beirut, and beer pong. She could change a tire and throw a punch and had learned how to drive when she was something like fourteen. "Sure," she said with a shrug. "Why not?" She headed toward the dining room with Toby and Bri following, turning back to glance at me when it was clear I wasn't joining them. "Andie?"

"Not right now," I said with what I hoped was a casual shrug. "Maybe later."

Palmer raised an eyebrow at me, and I knew she knew exactly why I wasn't joining her. "Sure," she said, giving me a look that said she still didn't approve but wasn't going to say anything else. I had a feeling that if I hadn't just had the day that I had, Palmer would be giving me a much harder time right about now. "Well, have fun."

"Make good choices," Toby called, in a louder voice than necessary, as I took a step toward the kitchen, pretending I didn't know them. I had expected Topher would still be there, but the kitchen was empty. I thought for a second about going to look for him, but then decided against it and pushed myself up to sit on the counter. I grabbed a handful of Doritos from an open family-size bag and pulled out my phone. I'd find Topher eventually, or he'd find me—and it seemed like the easiest way to let him do that was to stay in one place. I hadn't expected to see a new text on my phone, since most of the people I regularly texted were all here, but there were three, all from Peter.

PETER WRIGHT

> In case any reporters get in touch, you need to say "no comment."
> About ANYTHING. Don't go on record.
> How's your dad holding up?

I blinked at the last one. This was the kind of information that Peter knew, not me. Why would he expect me to know that?

ME

> Not sure—I'm not home.

I knew from experience what his response to this would be, so I started typing fast.

Just out getting a snack with my girlfriends.
If you want to know how he's doing, ask him.

I looked down at the phone for a moment longer, waiting to see if he was going to respond. It made sense that Peter was concerned about my dad—it was his job to be concerned. But if he wanted to know anything about my dad's mental or emotional state, I was the last person he should be talking to.

"Hey there." I looked up and saw that Topher was across from me, leaning against the kitchen island. I wondered how long he'd been there—Toby had once helpfully informed me that I had a "super-weird reading face."

"Hey," I said, locking my screen and setting my phone down, matching the blasé-ness of his tone. We'd established our boundaries three years ago, when this had started, and we'd never had a problem sticking to them. We kept it casual, which let us be in each other's lives without things getting tense or strained. Which I appreciated, since he was the only person who truly understood what my life was like. His mom was in the Senate, and over the last three years she and my dad had given the media one of their favorite narratives—the senator and the congressman, on opposite sides of the aisle but living in neighboring towns, against all odds and Washington politics, forging a friendship. They often rode together on the train back and forth to D.C., and despite the media's tendency to spin, I knew my dad genuinely liked Claire Fitzpatrick. When both she and my dad were home at the same time—which wasn't often—she and her husband would come to dinner or we'd go to their house, and Topher and I almost always found a moment to escape, usually around the time when the subsidies talk started.

"What's up?" I asked as I took a sip of my drink, not letting myself break eye contact with him. Topher—short for Christopher—was handsome in a way I had never gotten used to, not even after three years. It was the kind of handsome—tall, tan, blond, gray-eyed—that you saw in ads for expensive watches and luxury sweaters. There was a kind of polish and control to him that I had recognized immediately.

"Not much," he said, taking a drink from his Sprite bottle, then setting it down and looking at me, his voice getting a little softer. "How are you holding up?"

I shrugged one shoulder. "I'm fine," I said. His expression didn't change much, but I could tell he didn't believe me. "Really," I said firmly. "I'm leaving town for the summer at the end of the week anyway, so it's not like I'll be here dealing with it."

"Oh, yeah," Topher said, nodding. "That pre-med thing, right?"

I nodded, knowing better than to attach any meaning to the fact that Topher had remembered this. After all, it was what we'd both been taught to do. Hang on to dates and details, remember that colleague's daughter's name and where she's going to college. Make sure you know that important donor loves orchids, and if you bring them up, she'll be beyond pleased, and talk to you about them all night. Collect these facts about these people you don't really know, and let them think you do. "You got it."

"So this will probably be the last time we see each other for a while," he said, his voice dropping slightly lower.

"Maybe so," I said, not letting myself look away, starting to smile.

Topher arched an eyebrow at me, and I saw a smile tugging at the corner of his mouth. He pushed himself off the island and crossed to me. He leaned over, casually, every move just so, like he was in no hurry. His lips were right near my ear, but he didn't speak at first, just let out a breath against my skin that made me shiver. "In that case," he finally said, speaking low, even though we were the only ones in the kitchen. He took a lock of my hair and curled it around his finger before he let it drop. "Want to get out of here?"

Topher went first; he seemed to have a sixth sense for when empty rooms were available at parties, and I had an amazing ability to walk into just the wrong room at just the wrong time. He'd told me to meet him in the basement, and now I needed to wait long enough that nobody would see us disappearing together. Topher had established his ground rules early on—we couldn't tell anyone (I'd decided my friends were an exception to this, since I trusted them completely)—and we'd do whatever we could to make sure nobody would find out. I'd established some of my own—nothing but kissing, and everything we did or talked about stayed between us. I also found that I could be honest with him in a way I never was with my other boyfriends. I knew that whatever I told him, he would keep to himself. Our situation was what I'd once heard Peter describe as "mutually assured destruction." We knew too much about each other, and we both had too much to lose for either one of us to say anything.

When we both started dating people, these ground rules

grew to include that we never did anything when either of us was with someone. Which meant we could go months without seeing each other. But it had become something that I'd gotten pretty reliant on.

I looked down at my phone again and realized that it was now safe for me to join him. I crossed through the living room and headed toward the basement, making sure to lock the door behind me.

Sometimes, making out with Topher was like quenching a thirst, and sometimes it just made me thirstier. Thankfully, tonight it was the first one. After we'd been kissing for a while, the intensity faded and our kisses grew slower and more lingering. I broke away and rested my head on his chest, and he smoothed my hair down absently with one hand.

I looked up from the couch where we were lying. This seemed to be more like a converted garage than a basement, with the couch and TV jockeying for space with workbenches and tools. Someone in Kevin Castillo's family was clearly really into cars—there were three in the basement/garage and two more covered with tarps, tools stacked neatly next to them. I looked at the one nearest to us—a red vintage Mustang, and felt a sharp pang, the way I always did when I saw one. My mother's had been yellow, a '65 convertible that had been her pride and joy. But I hadn't seen it in years—I assumed that it had gone wherever all her things had gone, either sold or to storage somewhere. All I did know was that when I moved into the new house, there was no trace of my mother in it.

I turned my back on the Mustang and ran my hand over the

fabric of the couch. "This was surprisingly comfortable," I said, and heard Topher give a short laugh.

"Well, it's no laundry room." I pushed myself up slightly to look at him, and he smiled as he pulled a lock of my hair forward, winding it around his finger. "I was thinking about that night a few days ago, actually."

"Were you?"

"Yeah," he said, nodding. "Just about how lucky we were." This made me sit up a little straighter, and I looked him in the eye, starting to get nervous, worried that he was suddenly changing the rules on me. "Lucky because we didn't get caught," he clarified, and I felt myself relax.

"We really were." It was three years ago, but I could remember so clearly what it had been like—the thrill of my first real party, then the flashing lights streaking in through the window and my utter panic when I realized that not only was I in trouble, but I might have wrecked my father's career. I was desperately searching for an exit in the chaos, and then, out of nowhere, was Topher Fitzpatrick, taking my hand in his. I didn't know him—we went to different schools, and I'd said only about five words to him the year before, at an event at the governor's mansion. But I saw in his eyes the exact same thing I was feeling—the paralyzing fear that comes with knowing just how high the stakes really are. He leaned closer to me to be heard above the noise of people running, panicking, bottles and glasses breaking as everyone tried to get out, and fast.

"Want to get out of here?" he'd asked. I nodded, and he held my hand tighter as we ran through the house. He stopped in front of a door that I would have run past and pushed it open. It was a laundry room, a tiny space with a folding table, a stacked washer and dryer, and barely enough room to turn around. Topher pulled me inside, and we shut the door behind us and stood in the dark and waited.

We weren't discovered right away, and after a few minutes of both of us panicking that cops were about to fling open the door at any moment, we both relaxed a little and found our way to the folding table. We sat side by side next to a stack of fluffy, neatly folded towels, moonlight streaming through the tiny window above the dryer and the smell of fabric softener all around us. And when the panic that I was about to ruin everything had started to subside, I let myself appreciate this situation for the first time—that I was sitting very close to a cute gray-eyed boy in the moonlight.

We started talking, about school, about our parents, about the counter-spin we'd have ready in case we were discovered—that when we'd realized there was underage drinking happening, we'd removed ourselves from the situation immediately—until I realized that enough time had passed that we could probably go out safely. I turned to Topher to tell him this and saw that he was sitting closer to me than I'd realized and was looking at me thoughtfully, like he was studying my face. My heart started pounding hard, but I made myself keep looking into his eyes as he brushed a stray lock of hair from my forehead and then wound it around his finger once before tucking it behind my ear. And then, moving so slowly, he leaned over and gave me my very first kiss.

We'd ended up making out against the stack of towels until the party's host—sounding very annoyed—started banging on

Morgan Matson

all the doors in the hallway, telling people that the party was over and to either help him clean up or get the hell out.

"So," Topher said, as I pushed myself off the table and tried to smooth my hair down. My lips felt puffy and I had a giddy, racing energy coursing through me. I'd just been *kissed*. I couldn't wait to tell my friends. I wondered if I looked any different. I turned to him and saw he looked slightly nervous, like he was bracing himself for something. "This—I mean . . . this doesn't have to mean anything, you know?"

I blinked, realizing that he was scared I would want to turn this into something—like I would expect him to be my boyfriend or something now. "No," I said immediately. "Of course not." I'd never had a real boyfriend, but I'd been watching Palmer and Tom for a month now, and even the idea of that kind of dependency on someone made me feel claustrophobic. "It was fun, though."

Something washed over Topher's face when I said that, like he'd just seen something that he recognized—relief mixed with the happiness of an unexpected discovery. "It was," he said, giving me a smile, "*so* much better than being arrested."

And now, three years later, here we still were. I played with the buttons on his shirt, thinking about it. "I kind of think maybe we should have refolded the towels."

Topher laughed. "You know, I think it warped me. For months I couldn't smell fabric softener without getting flashbacks."

"So what are you doing this summer?" I asked, when I realized I didn't know, and after the silence between us was starting to stretch on.

"Interning," he said with a long sigh. "At my dad's office. Fun times."

"Oh," I said, a little surprised. Topher's dad was a litigator, and while there was nothing wrong with doing an internship with your parent, we both knew it wasn't the best thing for your résumé.

"I know," he said as he ran his hands over my shoulders, smoothing down the fabric of my sleeves. "But I was too late for the good stuff. I didn't start applying until last month, and by then everything was gone. Internships, summer programs— even the volunteering slots had giant wait-lists." He leaned away slightly, like he was trying to get a better look at me. "You took care of this back in March, didn't you?"

I gave him a tiny shrug. "February," I said, holding back what I *really* wanted to say, which was that Topher should have known better. You had to get this stuff locked down early. The good jobs and internships and summer programs, the ones that looked impressive on your applications, the ones that mattered—they went fast. "But I'm sure your dad's office will be good," I said, looking up at him, feeling beyond grateful, once again, that I was heading to Johns Hopkins and that this summer would be the furthest thing from a questionable gap on my résumé.

"I'll let you know," he said, tracing the outline of my lips with his thumb for a moment.

"Oh, yeah?" I asked, propping myself up on my elbow. "Are you going to write me a postcard or something?"

Topher smiled at this. "Every day," he said, matching my tone.

Morgan Matson

I laughed at that and pushed myself off the couch. I left first this time, returning to the party and hoping that nobody could tell anything had happened, that I didn't look different at all.

Three hours later, I yawned as I headed up the driveway to my house, Palmer waving to me out the window of the minivan. Bri had asked me if I wanted to sleep over at her place—Toby was, of course—but I'd said no, mostly because Bri's evil, ancient cat, Miss Cupcakes, seemed to have some kind of feline vendetta against me.

I let myself in and walked across the foyer, turning off lights while running through my checklist in my head. I'd get ready for bed, go over my packing list for Young Scholars one more time, then—I heard a *creak* of the floorboards behind me and whirled around, my heart hammering.

There was nobody right behind me, but in the long hallway that led down to my dad's study, I saw my father standing in the study's doorway, peering out at me. "Andie?"

I let out a shaky breath and took a step closer to him, squinting in the darkness. The only light was coming from the room behind him, stretching out a long thin line against the floor. "Hi," I called, holding one hand up in an awkward wave and then immediately dropping it again. Now, in hindsight, it seemed ridiculous that I was that startled to hear someone else in the house. But I'd honestly forgotten he was here.

My dad took another step toward me, then stopped, both of us pretty much staying at our ends of the hallway. He ran his hand over the back of his neck, blinking at me like he was surprised to see me too. "I hadn't realized that you . . ." He cleared his throat, then started again. "I guess I thought . . ." But this sentence trailed off too, and he pushed his shirtsleeve back to look at his watch. "It's late, isn't it?"

"Um, I don't know," I said, stopping myself before pointing out that he was the one with the watch.

"It's after two," he said, and I nodded, realizing that sounded about right.

"What were you doing up?" I asked, even though this really wasn't that unusual. When my dad was home, he worked late most nights. And the weekends that I took the train to D.C. to stay in the apartment he kept in Dupont Circle—visits that always were accompanied by carefully crafted social media messages about how I was going to see my dad—I sometimes didn't even see him; he was in his office or at meetings the whole time.

"I had to put some things in order," he said, closing his eyes for a moment and rubbing the bridge of his nose. "There's a lot I'm leaving half-done, and I want to make sure that it's taken care of."

I nodded and took a step back toward the staircase. "So . . . ," I started as my dad took crossed his arms over his chest.

"Is this when you normally come in?" he asked, sounding more confused than anything else. "Joy was okay with it?"

I bit my lip hard, to make sure I wouldn't laugh. I'd never really had a curfew to speak of. Ever since I was twelve, there had been a revolving crew of vaguely related people who'd come to stay and help out with me. There had been an actual nanny hired when I'd first come back from Camp Stepping Stone, the summerlong grief camp my dad had sent me to right after the funeral. But when his opponent during that election found out about it, he started using it in his speeches as a way to trash my dad, saying that he would *never* hire outsiders to take care of his children. So the nanny had been let go, and I'd had the first of many distant relatives come to stay. This had ended the controversy, thanks to Peter's spin—my dad was just bringing in family to help out during a difficult time. It was pretty hard to demonize that, the grieving widower doing the best he could, even though his opponent kept trying, which probably contributed to my dad's keeping his seat that fall. They never stayed all that long, these second cousins and stepsiblings' children—they moved into the house or the furnished apartment above the garage, drove me around, and for the most part, let me do my own thing.

Once I was able to drive myself, the job had pretty much become symbolic, there in case someone questioned whether the congressman's daughter was living unsupervised by herself while he was in D.C. The most recent person had been Joy, my dad's stepsister's stepdaughter, but as soon as the scandal had exploded and my dad had moved back, she'd moved out, leaving a note on the kitchen counter telling my dad where to send her last check. But the high turnover of relatives meant I could tell them whatever I needed to when they moved in, and one of the first things I'd told Joy was that I had no curfew.

"Yeah," I said now, taking another step toward the staircase. "She was fine with it."

"Ah," my dad said, nodding.

"Oh," I said, remembering and turning back before I headed up the stairs. We were at opposite ends of the hallway now, and I couldn't make out his expression clearly anymore. "Peter texted. He wanted to know how you were doing."

My dad looked at me for a moment, then sighed, his shoulders slumping slightly. "I'm fine," he said, even though I could hear the exhaustion in his voice.

"Well, you should probably tell Peter that. He seemed worried." My dad and I just stood there until the silence between us started to feel suffocating. "Night," I said, turning away and not letting myself look back, not even waiting to hear if he said it back to me. Then I hit the last light switch, throwing the foyer into darkness, and took the steps up to my room two at a time.

Chapter THREE

My phone rang the next morning at seven a.m.

I rolled over and reached for it, squinting at the screen. I
didn't recognize the number, but it was a Baltimore area code. I
answered immediately. "Hello?" I asked, hating that it probably
sounded like I just woke up.

"Good morning," a woman's voice on the other end said.
"This is Caroline from the Young Scholars Program at Johns
Hopkins. May I speak to Alexandra Walker?"

"Speaking," I said. I held the phone away from me for a
moment and cleared my throat hurriedly, making myself sit up
straight. Just hearing the words "young scholars" was enough for
me to start feeling some giddy butterflies in my stomach. Maybe
she was calling to give me a last-minute reminder, or an official,
day-before welcome.

"Oh." She cleared her throat, and I could hear some papers
rustling on her end. "I'm sorry to call so early."

"I was awake," I assured her, hoping that my voice wasn't
contradicting this as I spoke. "And I'm incredibly excited to
start the program tomorrow."

There was a pause, and I heard the papers rustling again.

"Yes," she said, and then I heard her take an audible breath, the kind you take before something painful is about to happen. "About that. I'm so sorry, but we're going to have to withdraw your acceptance to our program this year."

I froze, and felt myself blink twice. "Excuse me?" I asked, turning the volume up on my phone and pressing it harder against my ear, figuring I must have just misheard her.

"Yes, I'm afraid . . ." On the other end, the papers rustled again, and my heart started to beat very fast, like I'd just downed my daily latte in one gulp. "It looks like Dr. Rizzoli has withdrawn his letter of recommendation. And since we did not have another on file for you, your place went to one of the students on our waiting list."

"What?" I whispered, my hand gripping the phone so tightly my knuckles were turning white. "I don't understand. I mean, this must be . . . There has to be something else I can do."

"I'm afraid there isn't. Your spot has already been reassigned. And I'm sorry for the late notice, but Dr. Rizzoli didn't send us the e-mail until last night," she said. I could hear the relief in her voice, like she'd gotten the hard part over with. She could see the finish line and just wanted to be off this call with me. "Your deposit and your tuition will of course be refunded."

"Wait," I said, not even having anything to follow this but somehow needing to keep her on the phone, to try to figure out some way around this. Because this *couldn't* really be happening. It couldn't.

"Again, our apologies," she said, and I could tell how much

she wanted to wrap this up. "You will be more than welcome to apply for next year's program, of course."

"But—" I said, willing myself to think faster. "I . . ."

"Have a nice day." A second later the call was disconnected and I was staring down at my phone. The whole conversation, completely wrecking my summer plans and possibly jeopardizing my future as a doctor, had taken two minutes and thirty-three seconds.

My heart was still beating hard, and I had a desperate, panicky feeling flooding through my body. I needed to do something. I needed to fix this. Somehow, I had to make this okay again. These things had to be reversible. This couldn't be *over*.

I looked across my room, the early-morning light slanting through my blinds, and saw my suitcase, the one that I'd packed last night, after having practically memorized the "What to Bring" section of my informational documents. Somehow, seeing it there was enough to steel my resolve. I had *packed*. I had made plans and built my whole summer around this. Some woman named Caroline was not going to stop all of that with a two-minute phone call.

I pulled up my contacts and scrolled through them. I didn't have a number for Dr. Rizzoli, only an address from when I'd sent him his thank-you note. This whole thing had to be because of yesterday's press conference. There was no other explanation for why he would suddenly be trying to distance himself from anything to do with my father—in this case, me.

But if he'd sent an e-mail undoing this, he could send another one putting things back into place. There was still some time, after all—the program didn't start until tomorrow. This could all still be okay. I just had to convince him that this had nothing to do with my dad and that he needed to contact the program and tell them the e-mail had been a mistake, sent accidentally from the drafts folder, in an Ambien haze, whatever—I didn't care what he told Johns Hopkins. But he had to reverse this. He *had* to.

And I had a feeling he'd have a lot harder time telling me he couldn't if I was standing in front of him.

I pushed myself out of bed and ran toward my closet.

Twenty minutes later I sat in my car, across the street from the house of Dr. Daniel Rizzoli. He lived on Sound Beach, over by the water. The closer you got to the water, the nicer the houses got—gorgeous and huge and intimidatingly fancy, and Dr. Rizzoli's was no exception. The last time I'd been there, it had been for a fund-raiser for my dad. The house's gates had been flung wide, there had been candles in lanterns lining the driveway, and valets in white coats running around parking cars.

My phone buzzed in the cupholder, and I looked down at it—it was a text from Palmer. She and Tom were going for breakfast at the diner in case anyone wanted to join them. I didn't know why they were up this early, but I also didn't want to get distracted by a text exchange. I had to focus. I put my phone facedown on the passenger seat, then flipped open the visor mirror of my car and gave myself a last look. I'd wanted to look like I was competent and deserving of a recommendation, but not too dressed up, considering it wasn't even eight yet. I'd gone with dark jeans and a button-down, and since I didn't want to waste time doing something with my hair, I'd pulled it into a knot on top of my head. I slicked on a tiny bit more lip gloss, then dropped it in my bag and flipped the visor up.

"Okay," I said, taking in a breath, holding it for seven seconds, then letting it out for ten. It was actually the only thing I'd taken away from Camp Stepping Stone—a way of making your heart rate slow and calming yourself down. I used it whenever I was preparing to do something stressful. But while this was not the most pleasant thing I could imagine doing today, at least I was prepared. I'd turned the radio off and practiced my speech the whole way over. I had answers lined up for all the arguments I could imagine Dr. Rizzoli making. I could do this. I took a breath, opened the door, and stepped out into the sunshine. "Hello, Dr. Rizzoli," I murmured under my breath, practicing. "Good morning, Dr. Rizzoli. Sorry to bother you . . ." I nodded. That was the one. I straightened my shoulders and headed for the house.

I was halfway across the street when I heard the dog.

There was the sound of loud, joyful barking, and I turned around and felt my eyes widen. A large white fluffy dog was galloping down the road, tongue flying sideways out of its mouth, limbs landing in a haphazard pattern that seemed to send it listing to the side and then scrambling for balance every few steps. There was a leash dragging on the ground behind it, the plastic handle scraping along the asphalt with a dull *hiss*, occasionally bumping over rocks, but the dog was alone—there was no indication that there had been a human on the other end at some point. I looked around, starting to get concerned as the dog zigzagged back and forth across the road. This wasn't a busy street, but I still didn't think it was a good idea for this dog to be running loose.

"Here, um, you," I called, gesturing toward myself and feeling incredibly self-conscious about it. "Come here." The dog stopped and looked at me, then sat down right in the middle of the street, which I didn't think was an improvement. "Come on," I said again, gesturing to myself again as I took a small step closer to it. The dog leaped up and ran a few steps away, then sat down again, and I could see his long tail thumping on the ground. Clearly, he thought we were playing a game, and he seemed thrilled about it. "Okay, just stay," I said as I started to move toward him slowly. I was only a few feet away from the leash that was lying on the ground. If I could get ahold of it, I could at least try to figure out what should happen next.

I had very little experience with dogs. We'd never had one when I was growing up, and none of my friends had dogs either. Palmer's family had cats that were semi-feral and came and went as they pleased, and Bri had Miss Cupcakes, evil feline. Nathan Trenton, who I'd dated sophomore year, had a really awesome mutt that I'd loved. Nathan used to complain that I was more excited to see his dog than to see him, and when I'd realized that was true, I'd broken up with him.

I moved carefully toward the dog, whose tail was still thumping on the ground. It was looking right at me, mouth open and tongue hanging out, and I could have sworn that it was smiling at me. I reached out slowly, keeping eye contact as I inched my way closer.

"Birdie!" This was yelled out in a loud, panicky voice, and I turned around to see a guy running up the street, looking around frantically. When he saw the dog, I could see his shoulders slump with relief, even from a distance. He started running faster, and I turned back to the dog, which was when I noticed two things at almost exactly the same time.

One, the dog was getting ready to run again, apparently convinced that his favorite game had taken on a new and exciting layer. And two, there was a car heading down the street toward us, going much faster than it should have been.

I moved without even realizing I was going to. Going on instinct and panic, I ran toward the dog and grabbed its leash in my hand, then pulled him across the road. I felt the dog resist at first, but then it must have thought this was a fun idea, because it started running, first next to me, then past me, pulling me off my feet. I hit the ground just as I heard a screech of brakes and a guy yelling, "Hey!" I saw the car swerve, then head off down the street again, still going too fast.

The dog started covering my face in slobbery kisses, and I pushed it off as I sat up, still holding on to the leash in case he—because I could see now that it was a he—made another run for it. He was big—he had to be at least a hundred pounds, maybe more—with fluffy white hair and a nose that was probably black at one point but was now mostly pink. He had a tail that curled up over his back, black eyes, and stubby white eyelashes. He had not stopped moving for a moment, jumping to his feet, then sitting down and trying to kiss me again, like he was thrilled with the way everything had turned out, his smile still in place.

"Calm down," I said as I released my grip on the leash slightly. I wiped the dirt and gravel off on my jeans, then reached out and patted the dog's head, even though he probably didn't deserve it. His tail started thumping on the ground more rapidly, and he tilted his head to the side, like he was showing me that I should really be petting him by his ears.

"Birdie!" The guy who had yelled before was running up to us, sounding half out of breath. "I'm so sorry—are you— okay? Is he?" He stopped and bent halfway over, his hands on his knees, taking deep breaths.

"I'm fine," I said as I pushed myself up to standing. I was okay—like, I might have a bruise on my hip tomorrow, but otherwise fine. The dog looked up at me with his head cocked to the side, and I had to admit, he was pretty cute. For a moment I felt sorry that he had been saddled with such a stupid name. I mean, Birdie? For a dog? I brushed off my hands and then rubbed the dog's ears once more. His hair was soft and silky, and there was so *much* of it—like if this dog got wet, he'd only be about half this size. I noticed a tag hanging from his green leather collar, a round gold disk with BERTIE in engraved capitals. So that at least made a little more sense than *Birdie*. But not by much. "Here," I said, holding out the leash to the guy, who was still trying to get his breath back. I wasn't going to be rude— that had been drilled out of me years ago, first by my parents and then by Peter—but that didn't mean I needed to be overly polite to a guy who couldn't even keep hold of his pet. Also, I had something I had to do.

The guy straightened up and smiled at me. "Thanks," he said.

I took an involuntary step backward. For some reason, see- ing him from a distance, I'd assumed he was older than me—in his twenties, maybe. But this guy looked around my age. He was

only an inch or two taller than me, which meant he was probably around five ten, and thin, but with broad shoulders. He had
dark brown hair that was cut short and neatly combed and dark
brown eyes. He was wearing a black shirt that read THE DROID
YOU'RE LOOKING FOR in yellow capital letters, which rang a vague
bell, but nothing I could place. I could see that he had two deep
dimples, like parentheses around his smile. They were incredibly
distracting, and I made myself look away immediately. He was
wearing glasses with frames that were straighter on top and then
became rounded, and his smile widened when I met his eyes.

"Sure," I said as I took another step away.

"I—um, I really am sorry," he said, looking down at the dog.
It seemed like he'd gotten his breath back now. "I'm not sure
what happened, but the leash got away from me." He shrugged
and went to put his hands in his pockets, and it wasn't until
Bertie's head got yanked up that he seemed to remember he had
a leash in one of them. I saw that his cheeks, and the tips of his
ears, were starting to turn red. "Um." He cleared his throat, his
voice getting softer with every word. "I'm not great with dogs."

I was about to say something to this—like, what kind of
excuse was that? He clearly owned a dog—when I decided
to let it go. "It's fine," I said, giving him a quick smile before
I turned back to Dr. Rizzoli's house. I had taken a few steps
toward it when I realized that all the dog drama had taken place
in pretty clear view of the front windows. Had Dr. Rizzoli seen
what had happened?

The dog lunged toward me, and I heard the guy say, "Bert!"
as he pulled him back, and then the soft sound of disappointed
dog whimpering. But I was only half paying attention to this.

My eyes were scanning the front of Dr. Rizzoli's house, my hopes starting to nose-dive. All the curtains were drawn. There were no lights on that I could see, no cars in the driveway, and most telling of all, there was a layer of green summer leaves covering the front steps. Either Dr. Rizzoli was out of town, or he hadn't left the house in a while. Why had I just assumed that he would be here, waiting for me, willing to correct the mistake and let me go to my program after all?

I stared at the house, telling myself that I could still do this, that this wasn't over yet. I could get his number and call him and get him to change his mind . . . but even as I was forming this plan, I knew it wasn't going to work. All the adrenaline and righteous anger that had gotten me here was fading, and I was left with the reality of the situation: Dr. Rizzoli had e-mailed Johns Hopkins and gotten me pulled from the program. He'd meant to do that, and he wasn't about to undo it because I asked him nicely.

Feeling like I was about to cry—something I very rarely did, usually only at movies—I turned around and started walking across the street, back to my car, crossing my arms over my chest.

"Uh—so, see you around?" the guy called after me, and I could hear the nervous, hopeful note in his voice. Under other circumstances, I probably would have responded to this. He was really cute, after all, even if he had no idea how to walk a dog. But not today. Not with everything that had been my life currently in pieces at my feet.

"Probably not," I said, keeping my eyes fixed straight ahead as I pulled open my car door. "I don't live around here." I got in and shut the door but didn't start the car yet—mostly because I

Morgan Matson

had no idea what I was going to do now, or where I was going to go.

The guy turned and started walking back the way he'd come, and I looked for maybe a moment longer than I should have, watching as Bertie took off at a run, the guy stumbling a few steps behind, trying to catch up.

I made myself turn away, then picked up my phone. I unlocked it, then stopped. If I let myself think about the bigger picture—like what this actually meant for my future—I knew I would start to spiral out. I needed to think about my next immediate steps. Small pieces that I could manage. I looked down at my phone and saw the text from Palmer was still open—and Bri had responded, saying she'd be at the diner if she could haul Toby out of bed.

I didn't know what I was going to do, but I knew I wasn't going to figure it out without coffee.

ME

I'll be there too. See you in 15.

Then I let out a long breath and started the car. I glanced back once, to see if the guy and his dog were still there, but there was only an empty road behind me.

We had always called it "the diner," though according to the menus, it actually had a name—Glory Days' Diner. I had never heard anyone call it that, though it did explain the high percentage of Bruce Springsteen songs on the mini jukeboxes that sat on the tables in the booths. We'd been going there since eighth grade, and we'd especially spent a lot of time there before we were invited to any parties, when we all wanted to be out of the house on weekend nights but didn't actually have anywhere to go. Now we had the booth we always sat in and knew the waitresses who tolerated us and the waitresses who flat-out hated us and who the nice managers and busboys were.

It was the place we always defaulted to and where we sometimes went to the parking lot to have either screaming fights or giggle fests. I'd made out with guys in the darkness of the parking lot, guys who tasted like milk shakes and French fries. And it was where we'd all gathered the morning after Palmer slept with Tom for the first time, getting every detail over shared plates of pancakes and waffles.

It was early enough that I was able to get parking out front. I climbed the seven steps and pulled open the metal-handled door, walking past the candy machines and the arcade games, one of which, *Honour Quest*, Bri had become obsessed with two years ago. The PLEASE SEAT YOURSELF sign was facing out, so I pushed my sunglasses on top of my head and scanned the restaurant. Our normal booth was taken by a family—screaming kids and parents ignoring them as they read the paper. I looked around for our second-favorite booth and saw Palmer sitting in it alone.

I made a beeline over to her. I was still feeling jangly and on the verge of panicking, but somehow knowing I would be able to talk about it with her was making things seem a little bit better. "Hey," I said, sliding into the booth across from her. There was what looked like a half-eaten plate of waffles and what I was assuming was a vanilla Coke—Palmer's usual—sat in front of her.

"Hi," she said as she looked at me, surprised, her blue eyes wide. "You got here fast. Did you speed?"

"Not exactly," I said, taking a menu from where they were stacked on the table, opening it, then putting it back immediately, realizing I didn't even have to look. I got about four things at the diner, and this was not a place to experiment. There were things that were safe to get—all breakfast foods, mozzarella sticks, burgers, sandwiches. And then there were things that you should never, ever order at a diner, despite the fact that the menu was the size of a small phone book. Palmer loved to dare people, and last year she'd challenged Toby to get the seven-dollar lobster. When it had arrived, it had looked so suspicious that she'd called off the bet immediately, before anyone got food poisoning. "I was over on Sound View," I started. "And—"

"Morning, Andie," Tom said as he approached the table with a smile. Then he looked at where I was sitting and his face fell. "Does this mean I've lost my seat?"

"Afraid so," Palmer said, patting the spot next to her. "Scoot in, babe."

We had a very particular seating arrangement at the diner. Palmer and I sat across from each other, closest to the jukebox, Bri next to me, and Toby across from her. When one of us wasn't there, Tom got to sit across from Palmer, but if we were all there, he had to pull a chair up to the end of the table. He didn't really complain about it, maybe because he understood that this seating arrangement had come before he had. Tom had, over the last three years, pretty much become a de facto member of our group, but he was always really respectful of the fact that we were still a foursome and seemed to have a sixth sense for when we needed girl time.

Tom slid next to his girlfriend, kissed her on the cheek, and then turned to me. "So what's going on?" he asked. He looked down at his own plate, which had about two bites left on it. "Pancake?" he offered, and I shook my head.

I'd known Thomas Harrison—he always did a bit about how nobody could ever tell if he had two last names or two first names—since third grade. I'd never really thought about him all that much. He was the quiet, neatly dressed kid who sat in the middle of the classroom and was in every single play in elementary and middle school—usually the character part, but occasionally the lead. If I'd thought about it, I would have assumed he was gay, based on nothing other than the most superficial of reasons and the fact that I'd never seen him with a girl.

But on the third day of high school, I'd been at my locker trying to figure out what I'd done with my biology book when Palmer had grabbed my arm. "Who is *that?*" she'd whispered, her voice higher than normal.

"Who is who?" I asked, trying to look around Tom Harrison, who was carefully placing his books in his locker, for whoever it was Palmer was talking about.

"*Him*," she'd whispered, her nails digging into my arm, and I saw she was looking right at Tom, her cheeks flushed. They'd started going out a week later, and they'd been together ever since.

"Well," I started, leaning forward, ready to tell them what happened. My mind had been spinning the whole drive over, unable to attach to anything concrete that would help me figure out the next step. I hoped that in the course of telling them, something might hit me. "So this morning my phone rings at

Morgan Matson

seven a.m., and . . ." I stopped suddenly, noticing that while Palmer was wearing normal clothes—jeans and a tank top— Tom was wearing a collared shirt underneath a brightly pattered red-and-white Christmas sweater. The collared shirt wasn't that unusual—Tom usually looked like he was attending something slightly more formal than the rest of us—but the sweater was. "Tom, why are you dressed like a holiday card?"

Tom opened his mouth to reply as Carly, one of the waitresses who tolerated us, appeared at the table, pen already poised above her order pad. "Ready, doll?" Everyone Carly waited on got a nickname. She always called Toby "Freckles," which Toby was less than thrilled about.

"Can I get the number one with crisp bacon and a Diet Coke?" I asked.

"White or wheat?" Carly asked without missing a beat.

"White, just the tiniest bit toasted. Like, more warmed than toasted. And hash browns instead of home fries."

"Gotcha," Carly said as she turned to go.

"And can you make the bacon really crisp?" Palmer interjected, leaning slightly across the table. "Like, more crisp than you would think. Cook it to an amount of crispness you think that nobody would ever want, and bring that out, and it'll be perfect."

"Sure," Carly said, but still in the same tone that she'd taken my toast order, so I wasn't sure she'd actually listened to any of this.

"Thanks," I said to Palmer once Carly had departed.

"I'm just trying to save us all some time," she said with a grin. "Remember the Bacon Incident of last May?"

Tom shuddered. "I do."

I rolled my eyes and reached over for Palmer's water glass to take a sip. "It wasn't an incident," I said, then focused back on Tom. "But why are you celebrating Christmas in June?"

"The holidays . . . just aren't the holidays without a Country Table ham," Tom said to me earnestly. "This year, that's what *I* want for Christmas."

I just stared at him for a moment. "I don't understand."

"It's for an audition," Palmer explained, and I could hear the pride in her voice. It was one of the reasons that they worked so well together. The two of them were beyond supportive of each other, and they both still seemed to think they'd won the lottery by being with each other. If they weren't Palmer and Tom, it would have been pretty insufferable. "In New York," she added.

"Oh," I said, feeling like things were starting to make more sense. Tom had gotten an actual agent when someone had seen him in last fall's production of *You Can't Take It With You*. Now he went into New York City pretty frequently to audition, clutching the headshot we'd all helped him choose. He'd booked some regional commercials, but so far, nothing national. "But why are you dressed like that now?" I asked. "Aren't you hot?"

"A little bit," he admitted, taking a sip of his water. "But I really want to get into character. Like, why does David—I've decided his name is David—care about ham so much? Why does he want a ham for Christmas? Is something else missing in David's life? Probably, right?"

"And the sweater helps you come up with answers to these questions?"

"It can't hurt," Tom said, taking another long drink.

"Anyway," Palmer said, turning to me. "So you got a call this morning at seven a.m. . . ."

"Right," I said. "It's a Baltimore area code, so of course I answer, and—"

"We're here!" I turned to see Bri arriving at the foot of the table, with a grumpy-looking Toby in tow.

Tom sighed. "I've lost my seat again, haven't I?"

"Fraid so," Palmer said cheerfully as Tom slid out of the booth and went off in search of a chair.

"Hi," Bri said as she slid in next to me. "Sorry we're late. I literally had to drag Toby out of bed."

I looked across at Toby, who was now slumped against Palmer, wearing what were unmistakably Bri's clothes, nice ones, looking like she was about three seconds away from falling asleep again. "Hey, Tobes," I said.

"It's so *early*," she moaned, rubbing her eyes. "And why does nobody at this table have coffee?"

"We'll get you some coffee," Bri said, already looking around for a waitress. "You big baby."

"Babies don't *need* coffee," Toby said, burrowing her head into Palmer's arm, who gave her hair a distracted pat. "Because people actually let them sleep."

"You needed to get up," Bri said firmly. "You have to be at work in an hour, and I'm not taking the blame if you fall asleep and crash into a Monet."

I frowned. "Wait, what?"

"Here you go," Carly said, returning with my food and Diet Coke, not even batting an eye at the fact that two new people had

THE UNEXPECTED EVERYTHING   67

arrived at the table, while one had vanished. "Get you anything, Freckles?"

"Coffee," Toby said, sitting up a little straighter. "And waffles?" she asked, looking at Bri. Toby almost never ordered anything just for herself. She always wanted someone, usually Bri, to share stuff with her and was forever asking if we should get something "for the table."

"I'd have waffles," Bri said, nodding. "Can I get a black tea?"

"Coming up," Carly said, disappearing again. I looked down at my plate—I was thrilled to see that the bacon looked practically black—and realized how hungry I was. I had just speared a bite of my scrambled eggs when Tom appeared again, hauling a chair and looking out of breath.

"Sorry," he said, his face now matching his sweater. "I'm back."

Bri frowned at him and gestured to his outfit. "Okay, what's going on here?"

"That's David," I said, as I crunched into a piece of bacon, "and he really wants a ham for Christmas."

"The holidays . . . just aren't the holidays—" Tom started, but Palmer interrupted.

"Tom has an audition this afternoon," she explained, then turned back to me. "But Andie was about to tell us what's going on with her."

"Wait, who wants a *ham* for Christmas?" Toby asked, sounding more awake than she had yet this morning. "I mean, that's just weird."

"Exactly!" Tom said, leaning toward Toby. "That's the question I've been asking myself."

"Andie?" Palmer interrupted, loud, and everyone turned to me.

I set my fork down, took a restorative drink of my Diet Coke, and told them about what had happened that morning. When I finished, my eggs were looking decidedly cold, and Bri and Toby's waffles had arrived.

"But I don't understand how they could do that," Palmer said as she leaned across the table toward me. "Are they allowed to cancel your acceptance like that?"

"Apparently," I said, and I could feel my heart start to race again. "Which means I have *nothing*. No plans. Nothing lined up. I mean . . ." Topher's words from the night before were suddenly ringing in my ears. Everything good had been gone when he'd started looking a month ago. Which meant I was so, so screwed.

"This Dr. Rizzoli guy sounds like a dick," Toby said.

"Totally," Bri agreed.

"I mean," Toby huffed as she angrily speared a bite of waffle. "To not even give you a heads-up?"

"It's not cool," Tom agreed from his end of the table. "Um, are you going to eat all your bacon?"

I pushed my plate across to him, wondering if Tom was really hungry, or if he was trying to get in character as pork-loving David.

"Wait, but that means you get to be here!" Toby said, brightening. "That's great!" I shot her a look, and she shrugged. "I mean, not so much for you. But it's great for *us*."

"It's not great!" I said, my voice coming out louder than I'd expected it to, and the family in our normal booth glanced over at me. "Everything is wrecked. I'm never going to be able to find anything good now, which means there will be this *gap* on

my résumé. During the summer I needed something the most."
I could feel my heart start to pound harder, like just saying these
things out loud had made them more real.

"She's spiraling," Toby whispered.

"I see that," Bri whispered back.

"Andie," Palmer said, nudging my foot with hers underneath the table until I looked up at her, "tell me about the cute
guy with the dog."

"That's not important!" I snapped.

"What did he look like?" Palmer asked, leaning forward,
nudging me again.

"I don't know," I said, not wanting to think about the guy
right now when there were many more important things I had
to deal with. I had a feeling Palmer was just doing this to try
and distract me, so I could calm down, but when she nudged
me harder, this one bordering on a kick, I relented, knowing if I
didn't answer her, she'd just keep on doing it. "Fine. Um—dark
hair. Glasses. His shirt said something about droids. . . ."

Both Bri and Tom looked up at that. "*Star Wars*?" Bri asked,
looking impressed.

"I like him already," Tom said decisively.

"Can we focus here?" Toby asked, raising her voice. "If Andie's
in town, that means we're all here for the summer, for once."

I looked around the table and realized this was true. Last
year Bri had spent all of July visiting relatives in India, terrified
she was going to lose her memory because of the side-effects
warning on her anti-malarial medicine. (We'd probably had
more fun with that than we should have, making up things that
hadn't happened, pretending she should know what we were

70   *Morgan Matson*

talking about, then acting overly concerned when she got confused. (Bri, understandably, hadn't brought us back any souvenirs from that trip.) And the year before that, Palmer had spent the first half of the summer doing a service program, building houses in New Orleans, and come back with a drawl she didn't lose until November.

"You know what that means you'll be here for, right?" Palmer asked me, raising her eyebrows.

It took me a moment, but then I sat up straighter, seeing the first silver lining of that morning. "The scavenger hunt?"

"The *scavenger* hunt!" Palmer agreed, banging her palm down on the table and setting the plates rattling. For the past five years Palmer had organized a scavenger hunt, usually taking place in August, when she felt things needed to be spiced up a little. Scavenger hunts were an Alden family tradition, and as soon as we'd all become friends, Palmer had started organizing her own. I'd missed last year's, when I'd been stuck in bed with the stomach flu, getting photo updates so I could see just how much fun everyone was having. The year before I'd lost by a single point, something that still irritated me whenever I thought about it.

"I'm sorry, are you referring to my greatest victory?" Tom asked with a grin. "How many points did I win by last summer?"

"Nineteen," Toby and Bri said in unison.

"And I've already started working on this year's list," Palmer said, mostly to me. "It's going to be great."

"Okay," I said, nodding. It wasn't like it was making up for missing my summer program, but it was something, at least. "When?" I attributed my loss two years ago to the fact that

I'd spent far too long trying to get the impossible, high-points items, rather than just getting more of the easier, low-points ones. I wondered if I still had the list somewhere, so that I could use it to start refining my strategy.

"Just plan on August for the moment," Palmer said, smiling down the table at Tom. "We have to look at the performance schedule."

"Oh, right," I said, nodding, feeling my stomach sink. "The play." I realized as I looked around that all my friends' plans were set already, and had been for weeks now. Bri, our cinephile, was working at the Palace Movie Theater. Toby was volunteer docent-ing at the Pearce, the art museum in town—which, I now realized, explained Bri's Monet reference. Tom was acting in the community-theater play, and Palmer was stage-managing it.

"So everyone else has a plan," I said, looking around, realizing that for the first time I could remember, I was the one at loose ends, with no solution for this in sight.

"You'll find something," Palmer said confidently to me as she took a sip of her Coke. "It'll all work out in the end." This was Classic Palmer—she was hardwired for optimism and seemed absolutely incapable of not seeing the bright side. All the Aldens were like that. They didn't dwell; they looked for solutions, made some snacks, and kept moving forward.

"Okay," I said, sitting up straight, figuring that maybe I could learn something from her. "I have to fix this." I needed some sort of plan. I didn't even care if it was a good plan right now. Just so long as it was something concrete. "I have to do something. I can't just hang out all summer."

"We always need people to help build sets," Tom interjected from the end of the table. "I mean, it doesn't pay or anything. And some prior set-building experience *is* preferred. But I could put a good word in for you."

"And all the really good internships are gone," I continued, not letting myself get distracted by this. "Same thing with summer programs and volunteering slots."

"Do we need to be here for this?" Toby whispered to Bri.

"So I need to do something else," I said, my fingers itching for a pen so I could start brainstorming. "Something that might not look as good per se, but something I could spin if I needed to . . ."

"I don't think we do need to be here for this," Bri whispered back, and Toby shook her head.

"Told you."

"I need . . ." I looked around the diner, like it might provide some answers for me, and blinked when I saw that maybe it had. There was a bulletin board by the door that I'd never paid much attention to, covered in business cards, missing-pet posters . . . and help-wanted flyers. "Bri," I said, nudging her. "I need to get out."

"Why?" she asked, even as she slid out so I could get past her.

"Can I finish the bacon?" Tom called as I practically ran up to the bulletin board and started scanning it. There was nothing hugely promising right away, but there were a few that looked like possibilities. I pulled out my phone and started taking pictures of the flyers. *Looking for summer tutor—must be proficient in French; COMPUTER HELP REQUIRED WILL PAY $$; Mother's helper needed, 30hrs/week.* None of them would be perfect—and I'd stopped taking French in eighth grade—but it was something. I'd started to put my phone away when my eye landed on one all the way in the corner. *NEED A SUMMER JOB?* the top of it read in twenty-four-point type. I leaned a little closer. *Great Pay! Flexible Hours! Work Experience that will look great on any application or résumé!! Call or e-mail SOON!* There was a phone number and an e-mail address listed beneath it.

I read it over again, wondering if I'd missed what this job actually *was*. But there was no explanation, which actually made me a little wary. It reminded me of that time Palmer's sister Megan was home from college on Christmas break and took what she thought was a job selling knives that actually turned out to be part of an elaborate pyramid scheme.

"Find anything?" Bri asked, and I turned my head to see she was leaning over my shoulder, looking at the bulletin board as well. I nodded, then tapped the vague one in the corner.

Bri read the ad, then frowned. "But what is it?"

"I don't know," I said, pulling out my phone and taking a picture of it as well. "But there's only one way to find out."

Chapter FOUR

"I don't like this," Toby said through my phone as I parked in front of Flask's Coffee and cut my engine.

"Me neither," said Bri. It was two days later, and I was on a conference call with all of them. But since Palmer was stage-managing, she had to pretend she was paying attention to the play. She had one of her earbuds in, hidden by her hair, and could only say "Mmm-hmm" occasionally.

"Mmm-hmm," Palmer said, somehow managing to convey great disapproval in two syllables.

"Guys," I said, glancing through my windshield to the coffee shop. "There's nothing else. This is my best shot."

"I'm pretty sure this is how kidnapping movies begin," said Toby. "And there's that scene where the girl is going to meet the person who's going to kidnap her and her friends are like 'No, don't do it,' but she does it anyway."

"Well, otherwise there would be no movie," Bri pointed out. "But Toby is actually making a point."

"What do you mean *actually*?" Toby asked, sounding offended.

"I don't like that you don't know what this job is," Bri said.

"*Mmm-hmm,*" Palmer agreed.

I let out a breath as I smoothed down my dress. I didn't love it either, but I really was out of options. In the two days since I'd found out I wouldn't be attending the Young Scholars Program, I had tried everything I could to line up something for the summer. I'd been practically laughed out of the career office at school when I'd explained I was looking for something for *this* summer. None of my other leads had panned out—the parents of the kid looking for a tutor realized pretty quickly that my French wasn't up to par; I could handle my own computer, but couldn't code or work within multiple operating systems; and when I'd called about it, the mother's helper gig had already been filled—which I was actually fine with, since I didn't *love* little kids. Finally, I'd called the vaguely worded listing, and the girl who'd answered—her name was Maya—had seemed thrilled to get my call and only too happy to meet whenever was convenient for me, causing my pyramid-knife-scheme sensors to move to high alert. After we'd agreed to meet at Flask's (my favorite coffee shop and the place where I acquired my daily iced latte) and settled on the time, she'd said good-bye before I could find out what, exactly, this job was.

"Look," I said, after pulling the phone away from my ear for a moment to check the time. "We're meeting at a coffee shop. I'll call as soon as it's over. It'll be fine."

"Hmm," Palmer said.

"I don't know," Toby sighed.

"Aren't you at work?" I asked her. "How are you able to spend this much time lecturing me?"

"I'm just being a caring friend," Toby said, her voice rising, "and—" There was a pause, and when Toby came back she was speaking much lower. "Actually, gotta go. Call me later. Don't get kidnapped."

"Me too," Palmer whispered. "Call me."

"Bri?" I asked, after they'd both hung up.

"Still here."

"You don't think I have anything to worry about, do you?"

"Nah," Bri said easily. "Putting a flyer up at the diner is a super-inefficient way to go about kidnapping someone."

"Thanks, B. I'll call you later." Bri said good-bye, and I hung up and took a breath before carefully stepping out of the car. I was wearing one of my best dresses—blue, with a tight-fitting bodice and slightly flared skirt—along with heels and light, tasteful makeup. I'd printed out a copy of my résumé on thick paper stock and was carrying it in a folder so it wouldn't get bent on my way inside.

I stepped inside and looked around. The place was half-filled, mostly with people typing on laptops and groups of moms with strollers. There was a girl who looked like she was in her mid-twenties, but my eyes skipped over her until I realized she was smiling big at me and waving. "Andie?"

I nodded, my hopes plummeting as I made my way over to her table. "Hi," I said, holding out my hand, feeling myself inwardly groan as she stood up to shake my hand. Her blond hair had pink tips, and she was dressed casually—jean shorts, tank top, sneakers. Even though it was the very beginning of summer, she was already tan, with tattoos that peeked out from under her tank top straps and twisted up her ankles like vines.

"I'm Maya," she said, smiling at me, revealing slightly crooked teeth. If she thought anything about the fact that I was either seriously overdressed or she was underdressed, it didn't show. She took a seat, and I sat across from her, trying to hide the disappointment on my face as I took my résumé out of the folder and slid it across the table to her.

She looked at it while she took a sip of her blended drink, the kind with whipped cream and sprinkles that always seemed more like milk shakes to me than anything else. (I kept this opinion to myself around Palmer, though, who was addicted to the mint java chip flavor.) While she was reading it over, I pulled out my phone and sent a quick text to my friends. Normally, I never would have done this during an interview, but it was clear to me already this wasn't an interview that was going to matter.

ME

All fine. Nothing to worry about.

"This looks great!" Maya said, her eyes scanning down my résumé as I dropped my phone back in my bag. She looked up at me and her smile faltered, and she glanced back down at the paper for a second. "Walker . . . ," she said, like she was trying to place my last name. "Didn't I . . . ?"

"My dad's a congressman," I said easily, automatically. "Maybe that's where you . . ." But a moment later it hit me that maybe her recognizing my name was not in the normal way people sometimes did. That this probably had more to do with my dad's scandal having taken over the news a few days ago. "Um," I said, realizing I wasn't sure how to handle this. "I . . ."

"Well," Maya said, giving me a smile that let me know she probably *had* seen my dad on TV but wasn't going to press the issue. "You've got a lot of awesome experience here. I'm surprised you're still looking for a job, actually."

"Yes," I started, then hesitated. "My, uh, summer plans changed at the last minute. So I'm at a bit of a loose end." As soon as I spoke these words, I felt myself cringe. I didn't even know what this job was, let alone if I wanted it, but I knew that you never made yourself seem too available.

"Oh, man, I know all about that," Maya said, not seeming to realize that I'd violated a core interview technique. "Like, I only put up the flyers when one of my best employees quit because she decided to move to Seattle." She took a long drink, then shook her head. "I think she'll be back, though. Do you know how much it *rains* there?"

"So about the job," I said, trying to steer us back to the reason we were both sitting there, which I was pretty certain was not to discuss weather in the Pacific Northwest.

"Right!" Maya said, sitting up straighter. "Of course. So I run a dog-walking and pet-sitting operation I started two years ago. It's primarily me and my fiancé and one other employee, along with some people who fill in on an occasional basis."

"Oh," I said, nodding, feeling myself start to deflate. Not only did I not have any experience with animals, but I couldn't imagine a single college being impressed that I'd walked dogs all summer.

"It's hard work," Maya said, her tone serious. "And it's a lot of responsibility. People are entrusting their pets—members of their family—to our care. Do you have experience with animals?"

"Yes. In fact, a few days ago, I was . . . with a dog." A second too late, I realized what I was doing. I didn't even *want* this job, so why was I trying to impress her? "But—"

"As long as you like animals and are good with them, everything else can be learned," she said, giving me another big smile. "Just like anything in life." She looked down at her watch, then back up at me. "I'm actually going to pick up some dogs for a walk now. Want to come along? You can see if the job's for you."

I hesitated. This was not the job for me. It was even a step below what I'd been thinking I might have to sink to, which was seeing if Flask was hiring baristas. This would be outside, with no air-conditioning, and I had a feeling it would involve dealing with a lot of crap, both literal and figurative. And what was worse, I would have nothing to show for it when the summer was over. Also, I was wearing one of my best dresses and four-inch heels. I was supposed to walk a *dog* in this?

"Unless you have somewhere to be?" Maya asked, raising an eyebrow.

And maybe that's what did it. The fact that I had nowhere to be, no plans, no structure to my summer whatsoever. Maybe it was that even though I *knew*, rationally, I didn't want this job, there was still a part of me that wanted to get it. For whatever reason, I found myself sitting up straight and looking her right in the eye. "I'm totally free," I said. "Let's do it."

"All right!" Maya said cheerfully as she put her SUV in park and smiled at me. "You ready?"

"Um," I said, with difficulty. There was a very large and fluffy dog on my lap. He had clambered into the front seat as soon as we'd picked him up, and he'd sat there the whole ride,

Morgan Matson

shaking slightly, while I'd tried my best to see around him. He had to weigh at least seventy-five pounds, and at first Maya had tried to get him to move to the back, saying apologetically, "I think he's just going to keep coming up, though. Jasper gets scared in cars, don't you, buddy?" Jasper had whimpered then, like he could understand her, and I'd tentatively patted his fluffy black fur, feeling him trembling under my hands.

It wasn't like I'd had a ton of time to focus on the fact that I was slowly losing feeling in my legs, either, because there were three other dogs in the back. We'd driven all over Stanwich picking them up, Maya keeping up a cheerful running commentary as we drove.

"So I have all the keys color-coded," she said, holding up an enormous key ring, the top of each key painted a bright metallic color. "And we keep a log of all the pets—their habits, things to watch out for. It gets a little more complicated when it's pet sitting, but that's a different conversation. Also, sometimes we take groups out for longer hikes, or to the dog beach, but you wouldn't be doing that right away, so don't worry."

"Uh-huh," I said, trying my best to pay attention. But I was distracted by the fact that there were three dogs in the backseat, all of whom seemed to be staring at me. What was she supposed to do if one of them started freaking out or something? Wasn't this a huge driving distraction? "So you normally do this on your own—just you in the car with four dogs?"

"Oh no," she said easily, and I felt myself relax. "Usually it's more like five or six."

"What?" I asked, as Maya cut the engine and hopped out of the front door. Jasper seemed to realize this meant he no longer needed to be afraid, and he lumbered over me to climb into the back. I looked down at my lap and saw it was covered with dog hair and what looked suspiciously like drool. I shook my head, then got out of the car, brushing off my dress.

"Sometimes dogs get walked alone," Maya said. "Dogs that don't play well with others—and sometimes it's down to scheduling. But Dave—that's my fiancé—and I have a philosophy that dogs are social animals. They're happiest when they're with friends. Just like us."

"Okay," I said, even as I was pretty sure this was the opposite of okay. One dog seemed challenging enough. But *six*? I looked around and realized where I was—what I'd missed with my visibility blocked by Jasper. I was right back where I'd been two days ago, just a few streets over from where Dr. Rizzoli lived. I followed Maya around to the other side of the car, wobbling on my heels.

"Here," Maya said, handing me an armful of leashes. "I usually take them off when we drive, because it's a choking hazard if they get tangled. But they tend to rush the door and get really excited when they know we're going on a walk, so you have to be careful and make sure they don't go running when you open it."

I nodded, and even as I took the leashes, I was realizing that I'd let this go way too far. My competitive instinct had kicked in, but this was getting ridiculous. Was there a way to turn this around at this point without being rude? I set about untangling the leashes, trying to work through the possibilities. After a moment I concluded that there was really no way to tell her that she needed to get back in the car, drive me back to the coffee shop, and probably really confuse the dogs as a result. I needed to just get through this, and then I could walk away and never have to tell anyone that I got dressed up to try to be a dog walker. I had a feeling Toby would never let me hear the end of it if she found out.

Maya opened the door, and then there was a scramble, with the dogs all barking at once, everyone trying to get out the door first. I handed her the leashes, she snapped them on collars, and then we were standing on the side of the road, with four dogs trying to go in four directions. I had ended up with Jasper, even though he was by far the biggest of the dogs. Maya had a pug, some kind of shaggy mutt, and something that looked like a small collie. "Are you okay with him?" she asked, as she arranged the leashes so that all three were in one hand. "Jasper always seems to get tangled with the other dogs, so it's easier if he walks by himself."

"Sure," I said, a little uncertainly, wrapping the leash around my wrist once, then once again. I was pretty sure I'd walked a dog before. I had to have, right? I was struggling to remember if I'd ever walked my ex Nathan's dog when Maya started walking and Jasper, clearly not wanting to be left behind, lunged after her. I ran in my heels to catch up, feeling my feet already protesting.

"Great day, right?" Maya asked, looking over her shoulder at me as I caught up with Jasper.

"Uh-huh," I said, barely listening as I tried to get a tighter grip on the leash, but I pulled a little too hard, and Jasper was yanked back by his neck. I was worried that he would be mad and would lunge again, or worse, start growling or snapping, but he seemed to forgive me instantly, just going back to sniffing the ground. I didn't know how this was going to work with all these dogs, if they'd start to fight with each other or something, but they all seemed pretty well behaved, trotting along in a line. One of them would want to sniff a tree or a rock, and the others would either join in the sniffing or simply sit and wait. Jasper, despite his size, seemed pretty easy to control, responding immediately when I pulled back on the leash.

"Here's what I was thinking," Maya said, looking over at me with an easy smile as I glanced up at her briefly before returning all my attention to Jasper. I didn't understand how she was able to do it—wasn't this taking all her concentration? She had three dogs in front of her, after all. "We walk them around this loop, and then there's a little grassy area. It's not quite a park, but the dogs love it."

"Actually," I started, taking a breath to tell her that we should probably wrap this up quickly, since the job wasn't for me, when all the dogs started barking as one. I looked around, wondering if maybe there was a squirrel or something, when I saw there was another dog and owner coming toward us.

"So, here's a moment for a lesson!" Maya said brightly, though I could tell there was a tiny bit of stress in her voice. "When you have a bunch of dogs together like this, they kind of form a pack mentality and can sometimes scare the other dog. Everyone's trying to make friends; they just don't know the best way to go about it."

"Okay," I said, tightening Jasper's leash around my wrist again, feeling my heart pound when the barking got louder as the other dog got closer. I squinted against the sun, which was right behind the dog and his owner, blurring them out. When they came into view a moment later, though, I realized I knew

Morgan Matson

them—both of them. It was the guy and his runaway dog—Bertie—from two days before.

The guy must have recognized me at the same time, because he smiled and held up his hand to wave—the same hand that was holding his leash. His dog clearly saw his opportunity and took off at a run toward us as the guy grabbed for where the leash had been but only got empty air.

"Okay," Maya said now, her voice raised over the barking of the dogs, who were going into a frenzy, all of them straining against their leashes, "I'll try and grab him while you—"

But whatever she'd been about to say was lost as Bertie ran right up to me, barking and tail wagging wildly. He tried to jump up on me, which honestly would have been okay—it would give me an opportunity to try to grab his leash—but Jasper seemed to take this as some kind of threat, because suddenly his bark changed from what had been a *hi, other dog!* bark to a *get the hell away from me and the girl with the leash* bark. In between barks, there was now a low growl at the back of his throat, and the other dogs, sensing this, started to bark as well, with a definite note of *back off* in their voices.

"It's okay," I said, trying to put myself between the two dogs while feeling this was really not where I wanted to be. "Just—"

"Andie," Maya said, and I could hear the anxiety in her voice, even as it was masked by a layer of cheerfulness. "Stay calm and—" Whatever came next was lost in another wave of barking, as she tried to get closer to me while simultaneously holding back her three dogs, who were all straining against their leashes, trying to get closer to the excitement.

I saw the guy finally catch up with his dog, and then

everything seemed to happen at once. Bertie jumped up at me again, just as he grabbed the leash to pull his dog back, and Jasper tried to follow. I held on to Jasper's leash as hard as I could, and he was pulled back, making a kind of gagging cough sound, and I silently apologized to him while I wobbled on my heels but managed to regain my balance, thrilled that I'd somehow remained upright. I looked over and saw that the guy was not so lucky—he was on the ground, trying to push himself up to standing, while his dog made matters worse, running in circles around his feet and tangling the leash even further. All the dogs were barking like crazy now, though I was relieved to hear it was back to happy excitement barking and not angry, territorial barking.

"Hey!" Maya yelled, and then she let out a piercing two-finger whistle. All the dogs stopped barking immediately, and the sudden silence was surprising, like I'd forgotten what it was like not to have that sound track. "Sit," Maya said firmly, and her three dogs sat simultaneously. Maya gave Jasper a stern look, and he sat too. She looked at the other dog, who just wagged his tail back at her. "Sit," she said, but the other dog tried to jump up, like he was under the impression it was opposite day.

"I'm sorry about that," the guy said. He pushed himself to standing, wincing slightly. He straightened his glasses and looked over at me, and his ears turned bright red again. The guy hadn't gotten any less cute since I'd last seen him, and I was glad he was the one who'd wiped out this time, and not me. However, there was now the fact that I was walking dogs in a dress and heels, which I had no doubt looked beyond strange. "Hey," he said. "Nice to, um . . ." But there didn't seem to be anything to follow this, and his cheeks flushed and he gave me an embarrassed smile. I realized I was staring before I made myself look away. Dimples like that should honestly not be allowed.

"You guys know each other?" Maya asked, shooting me a smile.

"No," I said at the exact same time the guy said, "Yeah."

There was an awkward pause that I was about to jump in and fill—it wasn't like it would take all that long, and then we could get back to walking the dogs—when the guy said, "We— uh, the other day. Bertie got loose, but he was rescued by . . ." There was an expectant pause, and I realized he was waiting for my name.

"Andie," I said quickly, then shook my head, since Maya was starting to look impressed. "It wasn't a big deal."

"It was," the guy said emphatically, though mostly to the asphalt, not to me. "I would have been in serious trouble if anything happened to him."

"Bertie, huh?" Maya asked, leaning over to scratch the dog's ears. "Nice to meet you, buddy."

"And I'm Clark," the guy said.

I looked up at him as he said his name. It seemed to hang in the air between us, like I could see it in a cartoon bubble, inked and shaded. I wasn't sure I'd ever met anyone with that name before, and it echoed in my mind for a moment, calling up dark-haired reporters with secret identities and handsome movie stars in black-and-white. *Clark*. I decided it fit him, which I realized a second later was ridiculous, since I didn't even know this guy.

"I, um, thought you said you didn't live around here," he said, and I could tell that he was nervous, his voice fading out at the end of the sentence like a radio station getting fainter.

"I don't," I said, looking down at Jasper and trying to mentally communicate that now would be a great time to start walking again, but Jasper just yawned and scratched his ear with his back paw. "The thing is—" I took a breath to start to explain, then stopped when I realized I didn't know what to say. That I was on a job interview for something I wasn't even sure I wanted?

Maya jumped in when the silence threatened to stretch from thoughtful to awkward. "We're taking these guys on a walk."

"Are you . . . I mean, are you a dog walker?" he asked, crossing his arms and then uncrossing them. "Or do you just have a lot of dogs?" He was wearing another T-shirt with a slogan on it; this one had what looked like a picture of a British phone box, but blue, and it read THE DOCTOR IS IN. This made about as much sense to me as his other shirt had, but I figured Tom or Bri would know what it meant.

"The former," Maya said, surprising me. I guess I hadn't expected super-proper language from her. It seemed to go against the tattoos. "Dave and Maya's Pet Care. I'm Maya."

"Wow, that's—" Clark said, and then fumbled with the leash again as Bertie tried to run in the direction of the pug.

"Try looping it," Maya said, holding up one of her wrists. "It helps you get a better grip."

"Thanks," he said, doing this immediately and then straightening his glasses. "I haven't had a ton of experience . . . you know, with dogs." Jasper jumped to his feet suddenly, looking directly across the road. Since I couldn't see anything, I wondered if it was just a squirrel—or the hope of a squirrel. Either way, I tightened my grip on his leash, just in case.

"We should get moving," Maya said with a smile, as she made a noise partway between a clicking and a kissing sound, and her three dogs jumped to their feet. "See you around," she said cheerfully, and started to head down the street with the dogs.

Clark looked at me, and I met his eyes for a moment, then looked away. Under normal circumstances, I would have been flirting with him—or at least saying full sentences like a competent human being. But under normal circumstances, I wouldn't have been walking dogs in a fancy dress. I wouldn't have been spinning out, with no idea of what I was going to do with my summer. And until I figured it out, I knew I shouldn't be flirting with random dog owners, no matter how cute they were.

So I gave him a quick nod, then tugged on Jasper's leash, and we turned and walked in the other direction. And even though I was pretty sure I could still feel his gaze on me, I didn't let myself turn my head, or even look back.

"Dog walking?" Toby asked, her jaw dropping open. "Like, with actual dogs?"

"Actual dogs," I confirmed as I looked around the museum courtyard, all marble and palms and a gentle, trickling fountain. "It surprised me, too." When Maya had asked me if I wanted the job, I'd only hesitated for a moment before saying yes. After we'd left Clark and Bertie, we'd walked the dogs for another twenty minutes, and halfway through I'd given up and taken off my shoes, holding my heels and walking barefoot on the pavement. Maya slowly gave me more leashes as we walked, until I was handling all four dogs by myself. She'd been cheerful and encouraging, even though I had a feeling that my complete lack of experience with dogs had been evident. But I'd been surprised by how peaceful it had been, toward the end—when all the dogs had done everything they needed to and sniffed every available tree—when we were all walking in silence and I could feel the sun on my arms and shoulders. I realized that I'd been so focused on making sure the dogs were okay—which was minute-to-minute work, with dangers of cars or squirrels or other dogs around every corner—that I hadn't really been able to think about my own situation. And how nice it had been to get a break from the inside of my head.

Toby had seemed thrilled to see me, in person and unkid-napped, and once she verified that I was fine, started complaining about how bored she was. Apparently, it had been a slow day, and since she was still memorizing her docent script, she wasn't able to give any tours, so she had walked around, familiarizing herself with the paintings and sculptures.

"So," Toby said, tilting her head as she looked at me, "is this a formal dog-walking service?"

"Ha ha," I said, glancing down at myself. I'd changed into flip-flops but was still wearing the dress—it seemed easier than going home and changing, and it was going to need to be dry-cleaned anyway.

"I like it," Toby said, gesturing to me with a flourish. "Andie Walker, dog walker."

I hadn't even put that together until now, and I groaned. "Oh no," I said, shaking my head. "That sounds like something from one of your romantic comedies."

Morgan Matson

"Don't knock the romantic comedies."

I looked around the courtyard of the small museum, more than ready to change the subject before Toby could start lecturing me about the merits of *Sleepless in Seattle* again. "Want to give me a tour?"

Toby grinned and straightened her blue blazer. I noticed there was a crest with a *P* on it sewn over one of the lapels. "Certainly," she said, in her most grave and serious voice—it had dropped about an octave—and I had to bite my lip to keep from laughing. "If you'll follow me, miss . . ."

I followed her past the courtyard and into the museum itself, bracing myself as a wave of memories hit me hard. I actually didn't need a tour at all, since I knew the Pearce really well. My mother had been an artist by training and had volunteered there for years, organizing the kids' art program. I'd spent hours there when I was younger, listening to my mom talk through her art-appreciation class, her holiday ornament-making class, her intro-to-sculpture class.

It had never seemed fair to me that I had no artistic talent whatsoever, whereas my mom could conjure whole worlds with just a paper and pencil, or a tiny bit of clay. I'd seen her turn squares of paper into cranes that could fly and packing peanuts into hippos. It was like she was the one person who knew there was a unicorn waiting to be set free from the paper clip. In addition to her framed pieces, which had been all over our old farmhouse, she'd done drawings everywhere—directly onto the walls. She would sketch absentmindedly while she was on hold on the phone—rabbits and huge fire-breathing dragons sharing a beer while a grizzly bear tended bar. Tiny pink mice chasing one another around the walls of my room, keeping up a running commentary about my snoring. An abstract series of lines that turned into waves, that turned into a town, then a city, before the waves came back and everything went back to lines again and then disappeared. That one had been by my mother's bedside, and I'd wondered ever since if she'd drawn it years ago and I'd only noticed it after she got sick, or if she'd done it after her diagnosis. Although her bigger and more polished pieces had been the ones she was proudest of, it was the farmhouse drawings I thought about first when it came to her art. But the fact that my dad hadn't told me we were moving, just had me dropped off from camp at our new house in Stanwich Woods, had meant that I hadn't been able to see them one last time. I hadn't gotten once last glance at the bashful bear peeking around the corner of the study. He'd always been there, so it was like it had never occurred to me to really look at him, not realizing that one day he might be gone.

I hadn't been to the Pearce in years, but most of the pieces were still the same. It was a small museum, only five galleries splitting off from a central courtyard. It housed the collection of Mary Anne Pearce, who had been acquiring for decades and had donated her whole collection—to the apparent dismay of her heirs—to the town of Stanwich, along with a grant to build the museum. She and my mother had been close, and Mrs. Pearce had died the year after my mother did. I remembered seeing her at the funeral and thinking how *wrong* it was, since it was my mom who was supposed to be at Mrs. Pearce's funeral and not the other way around.

One thing I'd always liked about the Pearce was how eclectic

Morgan Matson

it was. Mrs. Pearce had collected based only on what she liked, which meant it was a little all over the place. There were lots of impressionists, some medieval tapestries, modern sculpture, and Roman statuary. But somehow, it all worked.

"And through here," Toby was saying, motioning me ahead, and I realized I hadn't been listening to her, "we have our contemporary gallery. . . ."

"Do lead on," I said, imitating her serious tone as we walked into the last gallery. A guy wearing an identical blue blazer had been leaning against the wall, blocking a description of the work of Mark Rothko, and he jumped when we walked into the room, standing up straight and pulling a white earbud out of his ear.

"Hey," he said, as we passed, his eyes landing on me briefly before returning to Toby. "How's it going?"

"Fine," Toby said with a shrug as she kept walking, not even looking back at him. "Quiet, you know?"

"Totally," he said, raising his voice, clearly trying to continue the conversation, even as Toby kept walking away.

"He was cute," I said to her in a low voice, glancing behind me once to verify this. He was, too—light-brown hair, blue eyes, tall enough for Toby, even with her heels on.

"Gregory?" Toby asked, sounding surprised. "He's okay, I guess."

I took a breath to say something about this—when I saw the wall in front of me and stopped short.

Toby walked a few more steps before she realized I wasn't with her and came to stand next to me. We both looked at the painting in silence for a minute, while I fought down the lump in my throat.

It was a big canvas, taking up most of the wall. I stared at it, drinking it in like I'd never seen it before, when it was probably the painting I was most familiar with—not just in the Pearce, but anywhere. It was of a field at night—overgrown grass and wild-flowers and an explosion of stars above. Twelve-year-old me was in the bottom left corner, lying on my back and looking up, one hand reaching toward the sky. It was incredibly detailed, in a way that still took my breath away. I could see the broken and double-knotted lace on my dirty yellow Converse, which had been my favorite that year. I could see the slight tear in the sundress pocket, the dress that was still in my closet somewhere, even though I hadn't been able to fit into it in years. I could see my crooked bangs, the ones I'd cut that summer myself when I'd gotten annoyed they were in my eyes. The only thing I didn't recognize was my expression, peaceful and smiling at something just beyond the frame.

Because most of the canvas was so detailed, it always felt a bit like a punch in the gut when your eyes reached the right side and realized that the detail faded away until you were looking at pencil sketches on bare white canvas.

My eyes traveled over the picture to the identifying information at the wall, and I swallowed hard as I read it.

Stars Fell on Alexandra (unfinished). By Molly Walker.

Toby put her arm around my shoulders and gave them a squeeze. "It's such a good painting, Andie," she said, her voice quiet. "You know she'd love that it's here."

I nodded, not trusting myself to say anything else right then. She would have too. Her work, hanging in a room with Rothko and Jackson Pollock and Georgia O'Keeffe. Mrs. Pearce had bought the painting from my dad two days after the funeral. At the time I'd wondered if she'd done it sooner if it might have made any difference. If maybe my mom could have held on somehow, stayed to finish it, kept going if she'd known it would end up here . . .

I made myself look away, trying to stop this train of thought. There was absolutely no point to it. This had been five years ago, and I'd long since gotten over it. There was no need to drag this stuff up again. But even so, I let myself lean slightly into Toby. She gave my shoulders another squeeze, and I was beyond grateful for a friend who knew exactly what I meant even when I wasn't saying anything.

After I left the museum I headed to the library. I sat on the floor with dog books stacked all around me—I figured since my learning curve was pretty high, I needed to find out what I could. Just because this hadn't been the summer job I'd expected, I rationalized, didn't mean that I couldn't do it well. And as I left the stacks, I found myself heading away from the checkout and over to the biography section. I walked down the row until I got to the *W*s and stopped in front of my dad's autobiography. I hadn't done this in a while, and I had a feeling I was only here because I'd seen my mother's painting. That it had led me to the only place I could go for answers to impossible questions.

There was a copy of the autobiography on the bookshelf in my dad's study, of course, and there was a copy in his apartment in D.C. But somehow, reading it at home, actually sitting down with his hardback, would have been admitting what I was doing, and so I'd read the whole thing here, in short bursts, standing in the stacks or sitting on the ground, leaning back against the rows of books. It had been written when my mom was still healthy and things were still good—the intent was for it to coincide with the national election that fall, but by the time it came out, everything had changed.

I flipped through it, stopping briefly at the pictures in the middle—my dad in elementary school, his hair combed flat, his front teeth missing; at high school graduation; my parents in their twenties, arms slung around each other, my mom wearing a shirt that said DON'T MESS WITH KANSAS EITHER, her hair long and wild—until I got to the page I was looking for. The paragraph was at the bottom of the page, and I read the words over, even though by now I had them memorized.

I'm very close to my daughter, Andie, and I'm proud of that. One thing I've realized is that just because you have children, you don't necessarily automatically have a relationship with them. You have to work at it, make them a priority, and take the time to get to know them. I love my daughter, and there's nothing that's more important to me than my family.

I stared down at the words, fighting a heaviness in my chest. When I'd first read this, four years ago, it had made me angry, but now it was more like I didn't recognize what the words meant, even though they were about me. The book could have easily been shelved in fiction, for all that it resembled our lives now. But I still found myself returning here and reading this paragraph over again, feeling a little bit like an anthropologist looking at a lost civilization, once really something, but now in ruins and mostly forgotten.

Morgan Matson

I stood in line to check out my dog books behind an older man reading a thick paperback. I shifted my weight from foot to foot, then, out of curiosity, tried to get a look at what he was reading. He caught my eye, and I took a small step back, embarrassed that I'd been so obviously looking over his shoulder. The man turned his book so I could see the cover—from the font and the image, I could tell it was a fantasy book. "You ever read this?" he asked.

"No," I said immediately, since I couldn't actually remember the last time I'd read a novel. Probably something for school this last year, when I'd had to. But even so, out of politeness, I leaned forward, like I needed to check this. *The Drawing of the Two* was written in raised type across the front, and the cover showed two swords clashing, a crown raised above them. *By C. B. McCallister*, was printed on the bottom, in letters almost as big as the title. "Sure haven't," I said, my tone polite but hopefully not one that was encouraging further conversation.

The guy shook his head and huffed. "Don't start," he said irascibly. "This writer hasn't even finished the series. Left us all hanging for years."

"Ah," I said, nodding, my favorite polite but noncommittal answer. Even as I spoke, though, I realized this was starting to sound familiar. The title was ringing a bell, and I was pretty sure I'd caught half of the movie version on a plane a while back. The movie had been okay, there had been a follow-up, and it was supposed to be a series . . . but the author hadn't written the rest of the books. Since I hadn't loved the movie, this hadn't mattered to me all that much, but it seemed like this guy was more invested than I was. "That's too bad."

The guy nodded. "Goddamn kid," he muttered as he stepped up to the checkout line.

I tried not to smile. The writer was probably in his forties or fifties, but maybe everyone younger than you becomes a kid when you get older. Either way, reading a fantasy series had never been high on my list of things to do, so I figured I was in the clear as the line moved forward and I brought my books up to the checkout.

Half an hour later I unlocked the front door and pushed my way into the house backward, my arms piled high with my library books and a pizza box from Captain Pizza balanced on top of them. As I'd left the library, Palmer had texted, asking if I wanted to go to her house for dinner, and I'd considered it. During the school year I ate down the street at the Aldens' at least once a week. But as I stood there in the fading sunshine, I was suddenly feeling, all at once, the events of the day and the blisters that were starting to form from walking dogs in four-inch heels. And I realized that nothing sounded quite so good as picking up dinner, finally changing out of this dress, and vegging out in front of some really bad TV.

I dumped the books on the table in the foyer and headed into the kitchen with my pizza box, then stopped short in the doorway. The fridge was open, and I stared at it for a moment, trying to understand what was happening. Then the door swung closed, and there, standing behind it, was my father, looking irritated. "Oh," he said when he saw me, sounding as thrown as I felt. "Andie. Hi. Sorry—you surprised me."

"Same here," I said, giving him a quick smile as I set the pizza box on the island in the center of the kitchen. There were stools that pulled up to it, and this was where I ate most nights, when I wasn't eating in front of the TV.

I hadn't seen my father at all yesterday—I'd been out trying to find something to do with my summer, and he'd been locked in his study, there when I left in the morning and when I came back at night.

He was frowning now, as he looked at me, like he was just now putting together that something was off. "Didn't you . . . ? When do you leave for your program?"

I could feel irritation starting to bubble up, but I pushed it away. My dad had forgotten I was even *going* to this program, so I really shouldn't be annoyed that he'd forgotten the start date, even though he seemed perfectly able to remember all kinds of obscure details about his biggest donors. "Well, it was supposed to be yesterday," I said. "But, um . . . I'm actually not going."

"Not going?" my dad repeated, staring at me. "What do you mean?"

I took a breath before telling him, planning out what I was going to say. I'd start with the phone call, then what happened with Dr. Rizzoli, and at least I'd be able to follow it up with the good news about my job.

"Why isn't there any food in the fridge?" my dad interrupted, having pulled the door open again, leaning in closer, an irritated look on his face.

I didn't reply, just waited for him to remember that he'd asked me a question and that I still hadn't answered it. He shut the door and pulled open the freezer, then opened the fridge again, his face suddenly brighter in the refrigerator light. "There's no milk or bread or fruit. . . ."

I could hear how annoyed he was getting, and I realized he'd totally forgotten about my program, had moved on to other things. I knew I could interrupt and tell him why, exactly, I wasn't going, and that it was his fault, but I dismissed this plan before I even found the words. I wasn't about to start begging my dad to pay attention to me.

"Well," I finally said, about to answer his food question, which was clearly the most important thing right now. "Joy would sometimes pick stuff up. Or I'd get what I needed. . . ." The fact was, we almost never had that stuff in the fridge. I ate about four things, so it had never been an issue for me to keep myself fed. I took a breath, not really sure if I should point out that he was an adult who was capable of shopping for himself, when I realized a moment later that maybe he wasn't. He had a housekeeper in D.C., along with interns and assistants who probably made sure he had everything he needed.

"I guess I'll pick some things up later," my dad said, mostly to himself, as he closed the fridge. He blinked at me again, like he was surprised to see me still there, his brow furrowing like he was trying to put something together. "So did you have another program lined up? Or are you going to be here this summer?"

"No other programs. So . . . I'll be here." As I said the words, I felt them sink in as, for the first time, I really understood what that meant. I'd been so caught up in getting my new job and feeling like I had at least some semblance of a plan that I hadn't thought about what this would mean exactly. I would be *home* all summer. With my father.

My dad blinked. "Oh," he said, and I wondered if he was coming to the same conclusion I was—that this was not a state

Morgan Matson

either of us was used to. "Well, that's—that'll be nice."

I nodded, not really trusting myself to say anything else. For a moment I thought about telling him how I'd spent my day— walking dogs, getting a job, seeing the painting, reading what he'd written about me, about us, five years ago. But I couldn't even make myself picture it. It felt like trying to imagine a world without gravity, or something equally impossible.

I opened the pizza box, then hesitated. My plan to watch bad TV while eating pizza on the couch clearly wasn't going to happen. I started to turn and get a plate, then stopped and walked back to the island just as my dad opened the fridge again, then closed it. It felt like we were bad actors who'd collectively forgotten our blocking, like what happened to Tom last year during a particular painful performance of *The Seagull*. I maneuvered around my dad, grabbed a plate, then put two slices of pizza on it. Even though I had a thing about crumbs, I was feeling more sure by the minute that I couldn't keep standing there, more aware with every forced sentence just how little we had to say to each other. Especially knowing now that this wasn't something I'd have to endure for only a day or two. This was the *whole summer*.

"Have some pizza if you want," I said over my shoulder as I headed for the back stairs with my plate, taking them two at a time.

When I got to the top, I looked down. I could still see my dad, standing alone in the kitchen, looking really small from this vantage point and like he was a little lost in his own house. I walked to my room, then closed the door and leaned back against it, my thoughts all circling back and back again to the same question.

How were we ever going to get through this summer?

Tamsin glared at her brother as he lounged in the chair at the other end of the table from her, helping himself to the candied fruit. It was so typically Jack—he showed up after almost a year gone doing god knew what (though she unfortunately did know, and much more than she wanted to, with minstrels writing songs about his most outrageous exploits. She'd heard the groom in the stables singing one yesterday morning, and it had stayed in her head nearly all day) and just expected that everyone would be thrilled to welcome him back.

"What?" he asked, shooting her a grin, the one she was sure had worked on every barmaid up and down the southern coast, all innocence and rumpled charm. It wasn't going to work on her, and Jack seemed to realize this as he dropped the smile and tossed a piece of fruit into his mouth, catching it easily.

"Are you planning to stay this time?" she asked, folding her arms. She wasn't sure, to be honest, which answer she wanted to hear.

"My kingdom needed me," Jack said, raising an eyebrow. "Also, I may have been asked to leave Riverdell. Rather rudely, I'll have you know."

"Because I've been the one keeping things going here," she said, trying not to let any emotion come into her voice. "And—"

"And you've done a *wonderful* job," Jack said, his voice dripping sarcasm. "But the adults are here now. You can run off and do your needlepoint."

Tamsin took a breath, about to let him have it—when she realized what she was being offered. Freedom. She smiled as she stood from the table and walked toward the door, faster, until she was almost running.

"Uh—Tam?" she heard Jack call out to her, but she didn't stop, didn't even turn and look back.

She was going to the woods, to the last place she'd seen the Elder.

And she was going to get some answers.

—C. B. McCallister, *A Murder of Crows*. Hightower & Jax, New York.

Chapter FIVE

"How did it go?" Maya called to me from the driveway as I locked the door, then double-checked that it was locked, then checked once more for good measure. It had been four days since I'd gotten the job, and this was my second training day. I was getting more comfortable with the dogs, but I hadn't had to do it on my own yet, without Maya there for backup.

I was still coming to terms with the fact that this was what my summer was going to look like. It was fine, for the most part—I'd blocked the Young Scholars page on my computer after I'd spent one night just looking at pictures from the welcome party, beyond jealous of all the people who got to be there. I'd also been tiptoeing around my father—or maybe it was mutual avoidance, but I hadn't seen him much, beyond occasionally crossing paths in the kitchen. I hadn't told him about my job, and he hadn't asked what I was doing with my days. But then again, I wasn't asking him what he was doing all day either, so maybe we were just respecting each other's privacy.

"It was okay," I said now as I walked down the front steps to join her. Maya was sitting in the back of her SUV, the hatch open and her legs dangling. She'd let me follow her in my own car, and I'd shadowed her when we'd picked up the first dog— Wendell, a fox terrier who clearly thought he was a Great Dane, judging by the way he barked at every big dog who crossed his path. I'd watched Maya work, trying to keep in mind everything she was telling me—how to announce your presence when you come to the door, the way even some normally friendly dogs' protective instincts kick in when a stranger tries to come into their home, how to always crouch down and let a dog sniff you first, never just reach for their collar—while having the distinct feeling that I was missing crucial lessons because I wasn't able to take detailed notes.

I'd been on my own with Pippa, a rotund French bulldog, who had actually been pretty easy to walk. I had a feeling that her owner had scheduled a walk more to get the dog some cardio than anything else, since I found if I paused even a little, Pippa took that as an indication that it was time to rest and flopped down on the ground. But that was the only real incident, which seemed to me to be a good sign.

"Great," Maya said with a grin as she hopped off the back and took the key from me. She clipped it onto an enormous carabiner that held what had to be thirty sets of keys, then flipped through them and selected one, pulling it off and handing it to me. "Ready to do one without me?"

I knew there was only one real answer to this if I wanted to keep the job I had just started. "Sure," I said, with what I hoped was more confidence than I felt.

Maya laughed. "You'll do fine. I'm just a phone call away if anything happens."

Morgan Matson

"Right," I said as I took the keys from her—three on a ring clearly marked GOETZ-HOFFMAN.

"It's a new dog for us," she said. "Dave walked him for the initial temperament test the other day and thought he'd be fine. They're looking to have their dog walked once a day, so this could be a great regular client for you."

I nodded, trying to ignore how hard my heart was beating. I'd been on national TV before. This was just walking a dog. So why did it seem so much harder? "Great," I said, gripping the keys hard.

"I'll text you the address so you'll have it," she said, pulling out her phone. "And the client wanted the dog walked in the afternoon, but they're flexible with time. If they're at home when you pick up the dog, just confirm that they want this to be a daily thing. And you should be all set."

"Great," I said again, realizing a second too late that I'd repeated myself. "I mean, good."

Maya laughed at that, then slammed her back hatch closed and walked around to the driver's seat. "You'll do awesome," she called as she got into the front seat. She started the car and drove away, waving to me out the window.

I closed my hand tightly around the keys—suddenly and irrationally terrified I would lose them and a dog would be sitting at home, unwalked and miserable, maybe having accidents on expensive rugs, and it would all be my fault. I dropped them in the front pocket of my cutoffs and headed for where I'd parked my car on the side of the road.

I'd just gotten behind the wheel when my phone beeped with the address. I glanced down at it, and felt my stomach plunge.

But this only lasted a minute, as I made myself read the address again and realized there was nothing to be concerned about.

MAYA

Hi! The house is at 8 Easterly Terrace.
Call or text with any problems!

I let out a breath, telling myself to calm down, that this was ridiculous. But for just a second, when I'd first seen it, I'd read the address as East View Terrace, which was where our old farmhouse was.

I hadn't been back since the day I'd left for Camp Stepping Stone. And even though I obviously wasn't driving when I was twelve, I could have gotten one of the people staying with me to drive me over there. But I didn't, and the more time that passed without me seeing it, the more I wanted to avoid it. My friends knew this and wouldn't drive past there when I was in the car. Not that it came up a lot—the farmhouse was on the very outskirts of town. But now that I'd gone five years without seeing it, I was certain that I didn't want to. What if the house had been replaced by something horrible and modern? Or—and this was somehow worse—what if it *hadn't*? What if it was exactly the same house, and there was some other family eating dinner under my mother's drawings, getting to see them every day, taking them for granted like I had done?

I punched the address into my phone's GPS, put the car in gear, and headed over there. I was halfway to the Goetz-Hoffman house when my phone beeped with another text. I kept my hands on the wheel, ignoring it, until it beeped four

Morgan Matson

more times, in rapid succession, and I knew that a text chain had started without me. I made a quick right on a side street, put the car in park, killed my engine, and pulled out my phone, hoping it was an actual all-four-of-us conversation and not just Toby texting until someone responded to her. I looked down at my phone and smiled when I saw everyone was on board.

PALMER

> Okay, it seems that being a stage manager
> means watching your boyfriend macking
> on some random college freshman

BRI

> Macking?

TOBY

PALMER

> Toby, that is the opposite of
> helpful right now

BRI

> It was helpful for me. I had no idea
> what you were talking about.

ME

> You've seen Tom kiss lots of
> girls in the other plays, P.

PALMER

> Yes, but that meant I had to see him do it
> only at the performances.
> Now I'm having to live with it. Like every day.

TOBY

> Egad. I see what you mean. 😐
> Or I would, if I'd ever had a boyfriend. 😣

BRI

> Please don't say that you're cursed

TOBY

> BECAUSE I'M CURSED
>

ME

> Seriously, T, you're not cursed

BRI

> Thank you.

I checked the time on my phone and realized that I should probably get going, especially since it was the first time I'd be walking this dog.

ME

> Gotta go—I've got dogs to walk

Morgan Matson

BRI

Am I the only one who think that
sounds vaguely dirty?

TOBY

Yes

BRI

You don't see it?

TOBY

NO. What's wrong with you? 😜

BRI

Andie?

ME

I am no way getting involved in this, guys

PALMER

Call me later?

ME

For sure

TOBY

THE UNEXPECTED EVERYTHING

PALMER

Seriously, Toby, we're about to stage an intervention

TOBY

Wait, about what?? 😳 😳

I smiled as I turned the sound on my phone to silent, knowing this conversation would probably keep going and that when I looked at my phone again, there would be a dozen or more messages waiting for me. I double-checked my directions to the Goetz-Hoffman house, then turned on my engine and headed that way.

I slowed as I reached Easterly Terrace and started looking for number eight. I pulled up in front of a gray shingled house and felt my jaw drop a little. Unlike the houses in Stanwich Woods, which had all clearly been built around the same time and by the same person, this house had character. It was big, with numerous windows all painted white and a round center section that looked almost like a turret, except really wide. There was a circular driveway with an SUV parked in the turnaround near a three-car garage with the doors down. I pulled around the circle and parked next to the SUV. It was beat-up and mud-spattered, with dents along the side, and it looked like it might have actually been used to go up mountains, unlike most of the SUVs I saw around town, which mostly looked like they were bringing kids to soccer practice. I got out of the car, holding on to an extra leash and the key, in case they weren't home. As I walked past the SUV, I noticed it had Colorado plates. There was a lot of tri-state-area spillover in Connecticut—New York, New

Jersey, occasionally Pennsylvania or Delaware. But Colorado? That one was new to me.

I took a deep breath and let it out as I walked up the wide front steps and pressed the doorbell. "Always knock, until you're on a regular schedule and sure someone's not home," Maya had told me as we'd walked Wendell. "People get funny about you walking into their house, even if they've hired you to do just that."

I didn't hear anything, so I waited another second before I started trying the keys. There were three on the ring, but as soon as I tried the top lock, the door opened easily. I stepped inside, waiting to hear the sound of barking, a dog running down the hall toward me. I closed the door, then waited another second, but there was only silence. Maya had so prepared me for dogs being protective of their houses that it was a little disconcerting to be ignored.

"Hello?" I called into the hallway. My voice echoed back to me, and I took another step inside. "I'm, um, from Dave and Maya's Pet Care," I called, suddenly unsure if I should be calling out for a dog or a human. "Who's ready to go on a walk?" I said in my best dog-excitement voice. I was about to call the dog, but stopped when I realized I didn't know his name. I reached for my phone, but hesitated. I knew I couldn't keep texting Maya for every little thing or she was going to regret ever hiring me.

I walked down the hall, still expecting that any second now I'd see or hear the dog I was there to walk. There were framed pictures evenly spaced down the hallway, most showing a couple, a man and a woman who looked like they were in their fifties. Most of the pictures looked professionally taken and framed, the couple usually in black-and-white, in formal wear or more casual, with the beach in the background. I paused briefly in front of what looked like a framed book cover—but it looked old, like from the thirties. *The Most of Jeeves and Wooster*, the cover read, and I looked at it for a moment longer before continuing on.

I walked to the end of the hallway, gripping the leash, still a little disconcerted that I hadn't heard or seen a dog—or even spotted any dog stuff—anywhere. For a moment I panicked, worried I was in the wrong house. But then my rational brain took over, pointing out that if I was in the wrong house, the key wouldn't have worked to let me in. I was about to call out again, but stopped, my train of thought temporarily derailed as I took in what was in front of me.

Books were *everywhere*. Not in haphazard piles—there was absolutely nothing about this place that seemed haphazard—but there were floor-to-ceiling built-ins on all sides of this very large room, and they were absolutely crammed with books. It was the kind of room—big couches, comfy chairs—that you would expect a TV in, but I didn't see one anywhere. All I could see were books.

"Hello?" I could hear a voice, a hesitant one. It sounded like a guy's, and like it was in the same room as me. I whirled around once, then twice, trying to figure out what was going on, until I realized that there was an intercom covered in the same taupe paint as the walls.

"Hi!" I said, walking toward the intercom, then pausing in front of it. Had the guy heard me? I tentatively pushed the talk button. "Hi," I said again, probably louder than I needed to, if this was working. "I'm the dog walker? I'm here to walk . . . your dog," I finished, wishing once again that I knew the dog's name and hoping that Bri had been alone in her opinion that this sounded somehow dirty.

"Oh, right," the voice said. It sounded somehow familiar, but maybe everyone's voice started to sound the same when coming through an intercom. "We'll be right there. Meet you in the kitchen."

I heard a *click* that I assumed meant the guy was gone before I could ask where the kitchen was. But it didn't take long to find it—it was next to the book room, taking up most of the back of the house, with big picture windows that looked out onto the backyard—an expanse of green with a large pool right in the middle. The kitchen was perfectly neat, like maybe nobody had ever cooked in there. But in keeping with the theme of the house, there were also piles of books in here, brightly colored cookbooks lining packed shelves.

"Hi," a voice behind me said. I turned around, my best professional-dog-walker smile fixed on my face, but felt it falter, and my eyes widen, as I realized I knew the person standing across this immaculate kitchen from me. It was Clark, the guy with the white dog, the one I'd run into twice before. He was wearing jeans and a soft-looking plaid shirt, and his short brown hair was slightly askew, like he'd been running his fingers through it. He must have recognized me too, because his eyebrows flew up behind his glasses. "Oh," he said, sounding surprised. "I didn't know that—"

But whatever he'd started to say was totally lost as his dog barreled around the corner, nails scrabbling on the wooden floor, tail wagging furiously, as he headed right toward me.

"Bertie!" Clark yelled, lunging for the collar and missing as the dog jumped up on me, sending me tipping off-balance and back into the kitchen cabinets. "I'm sorry," Clark said, yanking him back as the dog enthusiastically tried to lick my face.

"No, it's fine," I said, feeling like I needed to start asserting some kind of dog-walker authority in this situation. "How are you doing, buddy?" I asked, kneeling down, even though now the dog was taller than I was. I looked up at him and gave his head a gentle pat. "You ready to go for a walk?" "Walk" seemed to be a word this dog knew, as he immediately sat, his tail thumping rapidly on the ground. I reached for his collar, but Bertie immediately bolted, galloping out of the room as fast as he'd come in.

"Whoops," Clark said, looking chagrined. "Um, sorry. I guess I should have . . . It's like he thinks it's a game. Every time I try to get his leash on, he runs away."

"Oh," I said, looking in the direction where the dog had gone, like this would give me some more information. I took a step toward the kitchen door. "Should I—" Before I could say anything else, Bertie barreled in again, stopping in the center of the room, giving us both the dog smile I'd seen that first day with him. His tail was wagging so hard that his whole back half was swinging from side to side. I took a cautious step toward him, but Bertie jumped in the air and ran as fast as he could out the door again.

"He seems to calm down after a while," Clark said. "But you can't say that word. I usually spell it if I have to, like *W-A* . . ." He seemed to realize that he didn't need to keep spelling "walk" for

Morgan Matson

me and stopped talking, looking down at the kitchen floors.

"Right," I said, hoping I seemed like I'd seen all this before and wasn't totally thrown by it. "That, you know, happens sometimes."

I looked over at Clark, who was leaning against the kitchen counter, and was suddenly aware of the strained silence between us. I'd had to interact with only one owner so far, and in that instance, the small talk had been totally handled by Maya and had revolved only around the dog. I looked to where Bertie had gone, like this would give me some indication of when he might be back again. "This is a great house," I said, after trying for a moment to think of something I could say about a dog who wasn't currently present.

"Oh, thanks," Clark said, crossing his arms, then uncrossing them. "Yeah, it's . . . good."

Silence fell again, and I listened for the sound of paws scrabbling on the wooden floors, thinking that now would be a great time for Bertie to show up again. "Lots of books out there," I said, gesturing toward the other room when I failed to think of anything else to say.

"Right," Clark said, nodding a few too many times. "There are."

Silence fell again, and I decided rather than continue to make insipid comments about the house, I was going to wait for Bertie to return.

Clark cleared his throat, then asked, "Uh—it's Andie, right?"

I nodded, a little surprised that he'd remembered. I'd remembered his name, but that was because it made me think of mild-mannered reporters who were secretly superheroes.

The glasses really weren't helping to take away from that either. "Andie," I confirmed. "You got it."

Clark nodded, then took a breath. "This sounds really cliché, and that's not how I mean it," he said, all in a rush. "But you look . . . really familiar. And I know I saw you the other day, but I don't think that's it. . . ."

I nodded, taking a breath, prepared to jump right in. Topher would never tell people where they knew him or his mother from, would just look at them blankly like he had no idea as they stumbled through their polite confusion and leading questions. But I always nipped it in the bud. Even if it turned out that wasn't what they were asking—because I actually knew them from mock trial semifinals, or something—I always led with my dad's job. It was easier, and that was usually what people were trying to pin down anyway. I was on the verge of saying what I always said—*My dad is Congressman Alexander Walker. Maybe you've seen me in his campaign ads?*

But then I remembered the conversation I'd had with Maya and how now, in the wake of this scandal, the thing I'd been saying for most of my life whenever anyone asked about me—a description of my father's job—was no longer relevant, or something I would want people to associate with me now.

I looked over at Clark, who was waiting for me to answer a not-that-difficult question, but then looked away. "Well—" I started, even though I had no clue what was going to follow this. Silence fell between us again, but I was saved from having to say anything else by Bertie flying back into the room. As though we'd discussed it beforehand, Clark and I jumped into action, moving toward the dog from opposite sides at the same time. This seemed to confuse him, and he froze, giving Clark the chance to grab his collar. Bertie, seeming to accept the game was now over, sat down and started enthusiastically licking Clark's ear.

"His stuff is over there," Clark said, pointing to a cabinet while clearly trying to keep Bertie at arm's length and out of licking range. I walked over to it and pulled it open—it was stocked with all manner of dog paraphernalia. There were leashes and extra collars, bags of food and treats, and a monogrammed canvas bag that read BERTIE W. I looked at that for a moment, wondering what the *W* was for if Clark's last name was Goetz-Hoffman, but then realized I had other things to focus on at the moment.

"Great," I said as I set the leash I'd brought down on the counter. I didn't know if dogs preferred their own leashes, but since Clark had shown me the Bertie cabinet, it would seem like he wanted me to use his accessories. I reached for the nearest one, then hesitated. "Is there one he likes best?" I asked. Clark looked at me, blank, and I added, "One that you'd like me to use?"

He shrugged. "I'm not really sure—like I said, I don't know much about dogs."

I nodded, trying not to let any annoyance show on my face. Bertie might have been primarily Clark's parents' dog, but that didn't mean he was allowed to claim total dog ignorance. I knew that Bri would never have said something like that about Miss Cupcakes, and she was certainly no fan of that cat. "This will probably be fine," I said, grabbing a long blue one with B.W. woven into it. Clark's parents certainly seemed into their monogramming.

"So, uh, I didn't think you'd be here," Clark said as I knelt down to fasten the leash to Bertie's collar. Clark was still holding on to it, and I looked up at him and realized just how close together we were. Clark must have realized this at the same moment, because he let the collar go and pushed himself up to standing. "I did the interview thing with—I think his name was Dave?—so I assumed he'd be the one to, you know, walk Bert."

"We sometimes trade off," I said, disappointment making my stomach drop. Why was I upset that he'd rather someone else walk his dog? I tried to tell myself it was because it would mean I'd miss out on getting my first regular client. But as I looked up at him, at his deep dimples and his unfairly long lashes, I knew that wasn't really the reason. "But I can tell Dave you'd prefer he walk your dog. Happy to pass on the message." I gave him a big smile, then looked down at Bertie, trying to mentally convey to the dog that this would be a great moment to start the game up again and make another run for it, anything to add some distraction. But Bertie just looked up at me with another one of his dog smiles, tail thumping on the kitchen floor.

"Oh, no," Clark said quickly, his ears turning red again. "I'm—that's not what I meant. I was surprised, but . . . I mean, it's nice to see you again. I didn't think that I . . . um, would," he finished, a little haltingly, his voice fading out again at the end of his sentence.

I nodded, starting to smile. He *really* was cute. And I liked that he seemed a little bit awkward, like he wasn't sure what to do with his hands right now. I was so used to Topher's slick confidence that I'd forgotten what this could look like. "Right," I said, when I realized I'd been staring at him. I pulled myself

Morgan Matson

together as I stood, looping the leash once around my wrist. "So. Okay. I'll take him around the neighborhood. Usually, when it's just one dog, these are about twenty minutes, unless you want something longer, or a hike."

Clark shrugged a bit helplessly. "I mean . . . twenty minutes sounds good," he said. "Whatever you think."

"Well," I said, gripping on tightly to the leash as Bertie started straining toward the door, whining, like he couldn't understand why we weren't outside yet. "I should get him out."

"Right," Clark said, nodding a few too many times. "And I should get back to work. Or . . . get back to trying to work."

I looked at him and realized how nice it was that he was close to my height. I was always looking up at Topher, feeling like I was getting thrown slightly off-balance. "Yeah," I said, smoothing my hair back from my face with one hand and giving him a half smile. I hadn't used my flirting moves in a few weeks, but they were coming back to me as I looked up at him, then down again. I took a breath, secretly hoping that there weren't any rules against dating people whose dogs you were walking. "So I'll see you tomorrow," I said, raising an eyebrow at him. "And, you know, maybe—" My phone buzzed with a text, and then another one. "Sorry," I said, taking it out of my pocket, figuring it was another endless text chain with my friends. But I looked at the screen quickly and saw that they were from my dad. I didn't see what they were, just that he'd texted three times.

"Everything okay?" Clark asked.

"Fine," I said, dropping my phone back in my pocket and giving him a quick smile. "Just . . . stuff."

Bertie whimpered, louder this time, and lunged for the

door again, causing me to run a few steps to get my footing back. I knew whatever moment we'd maybe been about to have—if there even had been one—was now over. "See you," I said, trying for casual, only to have this undercut by stumbling two more steps after Bertie. I maneuvered us out the front door, hoping that maybe he was still watching us go.

Almost exactly twenty minutes later, I brought Bertie back inside. He hadn't been bad to walk—he kept trying to pull when we first started, but I did what Maya had told me to do with dogs who were pullers and kept the leash reined in tightly. Once he seemed to see what the new protocol was, he was fine on the leash, albeit determined to sniff every tree we'd passed on our half-mile loop.

I stepped inside the house and unclipped Bertie's leash. He ran toward the kitchen, and I followed, a few steps behind, watching as he made a beeline for his water dish—B.W. painted on the side—and started slurping loudly. I tucked my hair behind my ears and pressed my lips together, hard and quick, the way Palmer's sister Ivy had taught us when we were in eighth grade. I looked around, but there was no sign of Clark. And I knew that logically there was no reason for him to still be there.

Even so, I took my time as I hung up Bertie's leash and double-checked he wasn't tracking dirt all over the house. When I started to feel creepy about being in someone's house when my job there was done, I gave Bertie a quick pat on the head, then headed out the door, making sure to lock it behind me.

Once I was walking to my car, I pulled out my phone again and looked down at the texts.

Morgan Matson

Hi—I was thinking we could get dinner tonight.

The Little Pepper? 7 p.m.

The Little Pepper had been an Asian fusion restaurant the three of us had gone to together a lot when I was younger, but it'd been closed for years now, torn down after a fire. It didn't surprise me my dad didn't know it was gone—I was honestly shocked he remembered we'd ever gone there. My dad never talked about our past, except in the campaign stories I'd heard him tell over and over again, until they were just well-polished anecdotes and not memories.

I got into my car and cranked the AC, still looking down at my phone.

ME

Little Pepper's closed.

I hesitated, then typed again.

ME

But we can go to the Crane if you want. It's pretty good.

I put my phone down and prepared to back out of Clark's driveway—I didn't want him to think it was weird that I was just sitting there, hanging out after I'd walked his dog. But a second later, it buzzed, and I picked it up.

ALEXANDER WALKER

Sounds good. Meet there? Or meet at home?

I stared at the last word he'd typed. I knew what he meant, of course. He meant the house we were both currently living in. But whenever I saw or heard that word, I always thought of the farmhouse first. Our house in Stanwich Woods was never the place that came to mind.

ME

I'll meet you there.

I'd gotten a text when I was merging onto the highway, and so it wasn't until I pulled into the Crane's parking lot that I was able to look at it.

ALEXANDER WALKER

Stuck in traffic by East View. There in 15.

I looked at the words on my screen for a moment, trying to get them to them make sense, before I realized that the text had been sent twenty minutes ago, which meant I was probably late.

I hurried into the restaurant, feeling like everything was suddenly backward. I had gotten used to my dad being perpetually ten—or more—minutes late, to the point where I rarely showed up for things with him on time. I'd start getting texts from Peter, or some random intern, usually a minute before my dad would be there, and then get up-to-the-second information about where he was and what he was doing, like he was a plane whose progress needed to be monitored. So it was beyond strange to walk in and see my dad sitting at a table, waiting.

Morgan Matson

"Hi," I said, sliding down into the seat across from him. "Uh—sorry. I thought you'd be late."

"It's fine," my dad said, giving me a quick smile. "No problem."

I reached over and took a sip from my water glass, noticing how strange it was that my dad's BlackBerry wasn't on the table with us—that, frankly, my dad was here at all, not jumping up to take calls or sending e-mails while I texted with my friends or played games on my phone.

"Something to drink?" the waitress asked, and when I saw who it was, I sank a little lower in my seat, holding up my menu to block my face. My friends and I had almost been kicked out of here by this same waitress—Wanda—when she and Toby got into an argument about the complimentary mint bowl and how many was considered a reasonable number to take. It had been a few months, though, so hopefully I was in the clear.

"Iced tea," my dad said, and I piped up, "Diet Coke."

I waited until I was sure she'd left before lowering my menu again. "You okay?" my dad asked, looking at me with his eyebrows raised.

"Fine," I said immediately. "Just fine." I opened my menu, then set it aside immediately, since I always ordered the same thing here. My dad set his menu aside as well, and we looked at each other in silence. I suddenly wished I'd pretended I needed more time with it, just to have a prop in front of me. "So," I said, after we'd gotten our drinks and given our orders and I wasn't sure I could stand the silence any longer, "um, how was your day?"

"Fine," my dad said automatically. It seemed like that was all there was going to be to it, but after a moment he went on.

"Yesterday was the last day I could have any communication with the office. The investigation started today, so I'm officially not working."

"Oh," I said, a little taken aback. I'd realized, in theory, that my dad would have to stop working when he took his leave of absence. But like all good theories, I'd never seen it put into practice. My dad worked all the time; it was just who he was. Even before he'd been a congressman, I used to hear stories about his public-defender days, sleeping on couches and eating vending-machine dinners, standing up for the people nobody else was going to defend. It *looked* like he was still working—he was wearing a suit and a collared shirt, but no tie, which was what he wore when he wanted to seem professional but not stuffy. "So," I said, "um . . . what did you do?"

"I went to the library," he said, "got some books I'd been wanting to read for, oh, the last decade or so. And then proceeded not to read any of them. Did you know that we have a channel that shows classic basketball games?"

I shook my head. "I did not."

"Well . . . we do," my dad said, giving me a slightly embarrassed smile. "I may have watched one from the eighties. One or four."

I smiled at that. "Even though the outcome was decided years ago?"

"Ah," my dad said as he unwrapped his chopsticks, separated them, and set them to the side of his silverware, "but there always seems like the possibility that something might change this time around." Silence fell again, and I was about to take a breath and say something about the decor, or the size of the restaurant, when my dad asked, "So what about you?" He cleared his throat. "I mean . . . how was your day?"

"Oh," I said, "well . . ." I knew I should probably tell him about my job; with Maya trusting me to work on my own, it seemed likely that I wasn't going to get fired. But I didn't want to see his expression when he heard what I was going to be spending the summer doing. I knew I'd have to tell him eventually, but not today, not when I'd just begun to feel like I was getting the hang of it. "It was fine," I said, and without warning, my mind was suddenly back on the text he'd sent. "Um . . . you texted earlier that you were on East View?" My dad nodded. "Were you . . ." I took a breath and made myself ask it. "Were you at the old house?"

My dad looked up at me, his brow creasing. "The farm-house?" he asked, like we had so many other old houses, he needed to clarify. I nodded, not even sure what I wanted his answer to be. There was a piece of me that wanted him to say that he'd been over there. That maybe he went all the time when he was back, and since I had never asked him, I never knew. It would be some kind of proof, at least, that he thought about my mother occasionally, that he remembered the life we'd all had there together.

My dad sat back in his chair, and it was like something crossed his face briefly before his normal expression returned again. "There was traffic on the Merritt, so I got off at the exit by East Loop and drove over here from there," he said, then shook his head, like he was still trying to understand me. "Why would I go to the farmhouse?"

"I . . . just . . . ," I said, reaching forward and taking my own paper-wrapped chopsticks, unwrapping them mostly to have something to do with my hands while I tried to sort out what I wanted to say. "I don't know." I took a breath and realized that even though I might not know exactly what I wanted to say, I was pretty sure I knew where it was coming from—it was like something had been churned up since the press conference. I wasn't sure if it was seeing my mother's painting, or reading what my dad had written, or even if it was just this, the reality of the two of us struggling to talk to each other when there were no distractions to hide behind.

I looked down at the table, wishing I'd never brought it up. Wishing I hadn't asked. I should have known the answer would be something like trying to avoid the traffic.

When Wanda arrived bearing food, we busied ourselves with our meals until there was just the sound of silverware on plates, and it seemed to take up so much time and energy it was hard to imagine how we would have talked, anyway.

We ate in silence until Wanda came back to check on us and my dad told her that we'd love the check, please—we were ready to go, but that everything had been really wonderful, no complaints, just great.

Chapter SIX

"He thrusts his fists against the posts and still insists he sees the ghosts!" the actors on the stage chanted in singsong unison. I was about to ask Palmer what the hell was going on, when the group continued. "He thrusts his *fists* against the *posts* and still *insists* he sees the *ghosts*!"

"What. Is. Happening?" Toby said from her seat next to me, her eyes wide and fixed on the stage, where the cast had begun to jump around in circles, chanting, "Red leather yellow leather red leather yellow leather."

"Vocal warm-ups," Palmer said with a shrug. "You learn to tune it out after a while."

I looked at the stage again. Everyone was now lying on their backs, rolling from side to side, and I could swear they were meowing. "Really?" I asked skeptically.

"You can tune anything out," Bri said with authority from my other side. "I've now seen *Space Cowboy* fourteen times. I swear, I'm not even hearing the dialogue anymore. Yesterday, I watched it just for the cinematography choices."

"What?" Toby gasped, leaning across me to whack Bri on

the arm, but hitting me in the process. "You've seen it *fourteen* times and you haven't snuck me in once?"

"You know I will, at some point. Just let me work there a little longer before I start breaking the one rule they gave me."

"I thought the one rule was to always wash your hands before operating the popcorn maker," Palmer said.

"Well, that, too," Bri acknowledged.

We were all sitting in the back row of the Stanwich Community Theater, where Palmer's stage manager table was set up. The three of us had the day off (more or less—Bri was working the evening movie shift and I had to walk Bertie at four), so we'd decided to hit the beach for the first time that summer. When we'd been figuring out our plans over group text, Palmer had been whining about the fact that she had to stage-manage and how she was stuck alone in a theater all day (with her boyfriend, which Toby had pointed out, but that Palmer hadn't seemed to appreciate). So we'd decided to stop by with lunch from Stanwich Sandwich on the way to the beach. I had not realized that by agreeing to come over with food and hang out with Palmer, I would be watching tongue twisters performed onstage.

"What a to-do to die today at a minute or two to two," the group onstage started chanting, while bending from side to side, apparently done with their meowing. "A thing distinctly hard to say but harder still to do."

"So is this your job?" I asked, as the group continued with this one, saying something about a dragon and a drum. "You just have to sit here and watch this all day?"

"I wouldn't mind," Toby said, leaning forward in her seat and squinting. "That one guy up there is cute. I'm pretty sure. Is he?"

Morgan Matson

"When are you going to get glasses?" Bri asked her for what was probably the millionth time.

"When they stop making me look like an owl," Toby said, still squinting at the stage.

"You could always get *contacts*," Bri said, leaning closer to Toby and putting her finger on her lens, wiggling it around on her eye, causing Toby to shriek and turn away.

"Stop it," she said, though she was laughing. "You know I have a phobia of hands-near-eyes!"

"I wonder why," I said, knowing it was almost entirely because Bri had been doing this to Toby ever since she got contacts in sixth grade.

"Which guy did you mean?" Palmer asked as Toby pointed.

"You think he's cute?" Bri asked, shaking her head. Bri and Toby never liked the same guys, ever. Tom had a theory about why their taste never overlapped, but it involved Venn diagrams and math, and we hadn't let him get very far with it before we made him stop talking.

"Oh, that's Jared," Palmer said. "He's in college. And he has a girlfriend."

"Damn it," Toby said, as she sat back again.

"It's okay," Bri said, patting her arm. "He isn't that cute."

"He *is*. I think. "

"I write down blocking, when it gets set," Palmer said, leaning forward to answer my question. "But my real job comes when we go into tech and performance. Then I have to call all the light and sound cues."

"Look at you," Toby said proudly, nudging Palmer's arm, "sounding like you know what you're talking about."

"Okay!" a bearded man who looked like he was in his forties stood up in the front row. "Good warm-up. We're starting from the top of act two in fifteen."

Palmer jumped up. "Fifteen minutes!" she yelled, as actors started to jump down from the stage and stream up the aisles. "Be back in fifteen, guys."

"He just said that," Toby said.

"I know. But for some reason, it's my job to repeat times loudly."

"Hey, guys." I glanced over and saw Tom walking down the row to join us, looking slightly out of breath. "When did you all get here? Are you going to stay and watch the rehearsal?"

"No," Bri, Toby, and I said in unison, and Tom took the water bottle Palmer handed him, looking hurt. It was nothing against Tom—but I really preferred to watch a play when it was rehearsed and costumed and lit and people weren't wandering aimlessly around the stage clutching their scripts.

"But it's really good," Tom said enthusiastically, pulling his script out from his back pocket. I turned my head to read the title—*Bug Juice*. "It's this total classic, been around forever. But the writers just won a Tony this year for their play about Tesla. . . ." We all looked at him blankly, including Palmer. "We went to see it together, P," Tom said, sounding pained.

"Oh, right," Palmer said quickly, after shooting us a quick look. "That one. It was really . . . great."

"How'd the ham thing go?" I asked, only to see Tom's face fall even further. We really weren't making it a very good rehearsal for him. "Well, you probably didn't want that anyway,"

I said, talking fast. "To get locked into a role like that. You need to, um . . . show your range."

"Totally," Palmer said, reaching up and giving his cheek a quick kiss, then widening her eyes at me in thanks.

"What's happening with cool-T-shirt guy?" Tom asked.

"You mean Dogboy," Toby corrected, turning to me. "Any progress?"

"You guys know his name isn't Dogboy," I said as firmly as possible. Toby had made good on her promise to call the next guy I liked by a nickname, and despite my best efforts, it seemed to be sticking. I'd been talking about Clark a lot to my friends— the way you can when you have a crush on someone you know absolutely nothing about. "Like I've told you before, it's Clark."

Toby waved this away. "Who's named Clark?"

"Well, who's named Dogboy?" Bri pointed out, not unreasonably.

"Clark what?" Tom asked, taking a long drink of his water.

"You know multiple Clarks?" I asked, stalling.

"Maybe," Tom said with a shrug.

"You don't know a Clark," I said, feeling like we were losing sight of logic entirely. "You certainly don't know more than one."

"Only one way to find out." Palmer raised an eyebrow at me like she knew I was hiding something.

"Fine," I said with a sigh as I examined my nails. "He's Clark Goetz-Hoffman."

There was slightly stunned silence from my friends, and then Toby let out a soft whistle. "Jeez. Did his parents really hate him or something?"

"Nope," Tom said, shaking his head. "Doesn't ring a bell."

"I told you," I said.

"So what's happening with you and Clark Goetz-Hoffman?" Bri asked, and I winced, thinking that I actually preferred "Dogboy."

"Nothing," I said with a sigh. It was unfortunately true. Clark had arranged with Dave and Maya for Bertie to be walked once a day, even on the weekends. Maya had offered to take those shifts for me, to give me some days off, but I'd told her I would do them. So I'd been back to his house six more times, but it wasn't like I'd made any huge progress. I hadn't even talked to him yesterday—he'd just waved from the window as I walked down the driveway with Bertie. He was usually there, either when I arrived or left—I'd decided that the Jeep with Colorado plates was his, since it was always the only car there. I'd never seen anyone other than him, though, so it seemed like both his parents must work all day, and that's why they needed a dog walker. I still wasn't clear on why Clark didn't do it, since it seemed like he was home anyway.

In the week or so I'd had to observe him, my theoretical crush had only increased. Clark still seemed pretty nervous around me whenever I picked up or dropped off Bertie, always managing to drop something or talking a little too fast, and for some reason, this made him even cuter. I also had the feeling that if we could talk for more than five minutes, this would go away. He usually stopped dropping things right about the time Bertie would yank me toward the door, having gotten fed up with waiting.

When I looked online for more information about him

Morgan Matson

(since all I knew about him was that he liked the same movies as Tom and was bad at walking his dog, neither of which were turning out to be great conversation starters), I couldn't find anything, no matter how much I googled. Nobody I knew had heard of a Clark Goetz-Hoffman going to school around us. And, like my friends had just proved, that wasn't a name you quickly forgot. I figured that maybe he went to boarding school during the year, or something. Even as I tried to tell myself I was being ridiculous, I'd started spending more and more time getting ready each day, to the point where Maya, when we were doing a key exchange yesterday, had waggled her eyebrows at me and asked me if I had a hot date.

"You should ask him out," Palmer said with the confidence of someone who's been in a long-term relationship for three years. "I mean, what's the worst he can say?"

"He could say no," Toby pointed out.

"And then he could say, 'You're fired. Please don't walk my dog anymore,'" Bri added.

"Right," I agreed. I'd already done my mental pros and cons list about this and had realized how awkward it would be if I asked him out, got rejected, and then had to see him every day. Plus, there was something nice about how things were right now. Theoretical crushes could remain perfect and flawless, because you never actually had to find out what that person was really like or deal with the weird way they chewed or anything.

"I think you should go for it," Tom said, giving me a thumbs-up. "Give him a shot."

Palmer gave him a level look. "Is this just because you want another guy to hang out with?"

"Not *entirely*," Tom muttered, suddenly finding the floor very interesting. "I just liked his *Doctor Who* shirt."

"You can hang out with Wyatt tonight," Bri said, and Toby's head whipped around so fast, I got smacked in the face by her hair. "He said he was going to try and stop by the diner. And there's supposed to be a party at the Orchard."

"Oh, Wyatt's back?" Tom asked, sounding distinctly unenthusiastic. "Yay."

"How do you know that?" Toby asked, leaning across me to get closer to Bri, like proximity would help her understand this. "Did he call you? Did you talk to him? Did he say anything about me?"

"He just messaged me last night," Bri said. "Calm down."

"How could you not have *told* me this? Can I see your phone?" Toby asked, now practically in my lap as she tried to reach across me and into Bri's bag. "Oh my god. What did he say?"

"Here," Bri said, handing her phone to Toby, who stayed exactly where she was, half leaning across me.

"Tobes," I said, trying to nudge her off me.

"Shh, I'm reading."

"See?" Bri asked, shaking her head. "He basically said that he's in town, I told him we might be at the diner tonight, and he said he'd stop by. End of story."

"Wait, I thought you *liked* Wyatt," Palmer said, turning to Tom.

"Of course he likes Wyatt," Toby said, not taking her eyes from Bri's phone—or moving off of me.

"He's okay," Tom said with a shrug. "I just didn't know we

were going to be hanging out with him again this year."

"You were just telling me how much you wanted another guy to hang out with," Palmer reminded him.

"Yeah, but Wyatt's always, like, calling me 'brother,'" Tom said, dropping his voice down into a pretty decent Wyatt imitation. "And he's always hitting me on the back."

"Maybe that means he likes you," Toby said, looking up from the screen for only a second.

"Well, it hurts," Tom muttered.

"Oh, shit," Palmer said, looking at her watch and jumping up. "I totally haven't been paying attention to the time." She nudged Tom. "You've got to get back there, babe." Tom nodded, gave her a quick kiss, and started to jog up the aisle. She turned to us and nodded up toward the director. "I've got to get these actors back in. See you guys tonight?"

"Absolutely," Bri said as she stood and started to gather her things. "Just text us when you're done with this."

"Have fun," I said, waving at Tom and starting to head out of the row, but not before Palmer grabbed my arm.

"You should go for it with Clark," she said, giving my hand a squeeze. "Why not?"

I smiled at her and headed up the aisle of the theater, then out into the bright sunshine of the parking lot, where Bri's SUV, a purple Escape hybrid, was parked. She'd gotten it earlier this year and immediately named it McQueen. "Because it's the Grape Escape," she'd said, smiling proudly when she told us. "Get it?" None of us did, and Bri had declared us all completely lacking in any kind of film education and then made us watch *The Great Escape* and *Bullitt* back-to-back, which led to Palmer developing a huge crush on Steve McQueen. (This then led to Tom getting incredibly jealous of a dead movie star and getting a sixties haircut that looked terrible and took months to grow out.)

I knew that *why not?* was pretty much Palmer's motto, but even so, I found her words echoing in my head the whole time we were at the beach. We spent the afternoon stretched out on towels on the sand, passing magazines and iPods and bags of chips back and forth, Toby endlessly speculating about Wyatt and what she should wear and if she should make the first move, Bri talking her through every scenario, even increasingly unlikely ones, until they were both doubled over laughing. I was only half paying attention, my mind on Clark and whether I should go for it.

I was still debating this as I arrived at Clark's, a tank top and cutoffs thrown over my bikini, my hair up in a slightly sandy knot. He wasn't around when I let myself in, and I managed to catch Bertie on only the second try. I'd developed a technique that involved hiding a leash in my back pocket and not letting Bertie see it until I had a firm grip on his collar.

I walked Bertie around the neighborhood, taking a slightly longer route than usual, trying to figure out what my hesitation was. Why *wasn't* I just going for it? Asking guys out had never scared me before, and it honestly wasn't fear of losing this client. I knew Maya would understand if I told her I was no longer comfortable walking Bertie. And while there was a tiny piece of me that was embarrassed that Clark knew me as a dog walker—about as unprestigious as you could get—it wasn't like he went to my school or we knew anyone in common. If this was going to be a three-week relationship—max—what did that really matter?

Morgan Matson

By the time I was walking back to Clark's house, I'd made my decision. There was really no downside, after all. If I asked him out and he said yes, that would be great. If he said no—because he might have a girlfriend, for all I knew—I'd pretend that I had been asking him to hang out as friends and discuss Bertie. And then I'd get Maya and Dave to take over some of the walks, since I was really just doing this every single day so I'd get to see him. Either way, it would be fine. There was very little risk involved, just momentary humiliation, and I could certainly handle that.

I unclipped Bertie's leash, and he went running into the kitchen, his nails scrabbling on the wood floors. "Hey there, buddy," I heard Clark say as I realized that he was around and this was going to happen. "Did you have a good time?"

I took a long breath, held it, then let it go as I pressed my lips together, already practicing what I would say. When I walked into the kitchen, Clark looked over at me from where he was leaning against the counter. I realized he looked nervous, even more so than usual, shooting me a smile that faded almost immediately. "Hello, Andie," he said, his voice higher than normal. "How are you today? How did it go?"

"Good," I said, heading to Bertie's cupboard to hang up his leash, wondering why Clark was acting like this—like there was a teleprompter he was reading off of that I couldn't see. It was making it that much harder for me to segue into asking him out. I took a breath, reminding myself once again that this *didn't matter*. Why was I so nervous? "So, Clark—" I started.

"I was wondering—" Clark said at the exact same time.

Silence fell between us, nothing but the sound of Bertie

slurping from his water dish as we both waited for the other one to start talking. "Sorry," I finally said, gesturing toward him. "You go first." I really didn't think I could ask him out now, only to have him say that he needed to change the time of Bertie's walk or something.

"Um. I was wondering . . . ," Clark said. He looked around and gestured to the counter behind him. ". . . if you would like a chocolate?" I took a step closer and saw the large box that was sitting there, a very fancy and expensive kind that I recognized. Small boxes had been given out as favors at one of my dad's fund-raisers, and I'd eaten the extras for weeks. "I didn't buy them for you," he said, then blinked. "Not that I wouldn't have," he clarified, talking fast. "I just . . . They were sent here today, that's all. That's what I meant."

"Thanks," I said, fighting the urge to smile as I pulled the lid off the box and grabbed the first one I saw, hoping that it wouldn't be hazelnut. I liked almost every other kind of chocolate, but couldn't stand hazelnut anything. I popped it in my mouth and felt my stomach clench when I realized that it was, in fact, hazelnut. It seemed to be hazelnut-cream flavored with an actual hazelnut thrown in for good measure.

"Is something wrong?"

I shook my head and tried to force myself to swallow quickly and avoid tasting as much as possible. "Fine," I said, when I was able to speak again. "I mean, thank you. That was . . . chocolate."

"So," Clark said, crossing his arms and then uncrossing them and knocking the box of chocolates to the floor in the process. "Oh, jeez," he muttered as I watched them go flying.

"I've got these," I said, chasing down the two that had spilled out of the box and landed near my feet as Clark picked up the still-full box and placed it carefully on the counter. I stepped around him to toss out the two that had landed on the floor just as he took a step back, my hip bumping his, our shoulders brushing. "Sorry." I felt heat rush to my cheeks and told myself that I was being beyond ridiculous. He liked me, right? He had to, otherwise he wouldn't be this nervous. I just had to get this over with.

"So, um," Clark said, adjusting his glasses, "do you ever work nights?"

I felt my smile fade as I realized I might have read this all wrong. I had thought that maybe he'd been working up the nerve to ask me out. But maybe all of this had just been about the dog. "Nope," I said, trying to keep my voice professional and friendly and not reveal anything else I was currently feeling. "But . . . I mean, if there were an emergency or something, I probably would."

"No," Clark said, shaking his head. "I was just . . . trying to get a sense of your schedule." He blinked, like he'd just heard himself, and I could see the tops of his ears were starting to turn red. "Wow, that sounded creepy. I didn't mean that in, like, a weird way. I think I'm making this worse. Oh god." He took a breath, then swallowed hard. "I was wondering, you know, what you do. At night." He stared at me in horror after he said it, like he couldn't quite believe the words had come out of his mouth. "Oh, man," he muttered, closing his eyes behind his glasses for a moment. "This isn't going well."

I had to bite my lip to stop myself from smiling wide. "Hey, Clark?"

"Okay," he said, taking a big breath, and I was pretty sure he hadn't heard me. "Andie. So you've been spending a lot of time with Bertie. You know, taking him on walks, and . . ." Clark's face fell as he realized a second too late what he'd done. Bertie looked up from his water dish, droplets hanging off his muzzle, practically vibrating with excitement.

"You said the *W* word," I whispered.

"I know," Clark said, as Bertie leaped in the air and tore out of the kitchen, only to tear back a second later, look between us, and take off running again. "I just," Clark said, raising his voice to be heard over the sound of a hundred-pound dog running circles around us, "was thinking that since you've been spending time, you know, with Bertie, maybe we should talk about him, and . . ."

Bertie raced out of the kitchen, nails scrabbling on the floors, and I looked across at Clark in the sudden silence. "Hey, Clark?" He looked up. "Want to hang out with me tonight?"

He just blinked at me for a second, then smiled, and I almost had to take a step back from it. It was like all the other smiles he'd given me so far were pale imitations. This one deepened his dimples, pushed his glasses up higher on his nose, and crinkled the corners of his eyes. "Yes," he said, sounding beyond relieved, giving me a half laugh. "That sounds great."

"Awesome," I said, smiling back at him.

"So we'll get dinner," he said. "I'll find someplace good." He slid a notepad and a pen that had been on the counter over toward me. "Want to write down your address and I'll pick you up?"

"Oh," I said, taken aback for a second. I'd assumed we'd do something like meet up at the Orchard or go for coffee. But going out to dinner—and having him pick me up—suddenly seemed really exciting and a lot more grown-up. "Sure," I said, writing out my address. "I guess . . . pick me up at seven?"

"Seven," he said, still smiling. "Seven's great. I love seven. Okay. That's a plan."

"It's a plan," I echoed, smiling back at him, stopping myself before it became a full-on foolish grin, even though that was what I was feeling. I had a *date* tonight. Like, an actual date with a guy coming to the door and picking me up. And I'd technically had to ask him out, but who cared about that? Without meaning to, I found my eyes drifting down to his mouth. By the end of tonight, we might have kissed. I pushed the pad of paper back across to him. "It's in Stanwich Woods," I said, and he nodded but without any indication that he knew what that was. "So just tell the guard at the gatehouse that you're coming to see me and they'll let you in."

"Great," he said, ripping off the top piece of paper and folding it carefully in half before sticking it in the pocket of his light-blue T-shirt. We looked at each other for a long beat, both of us still smiling, and I realized I needed to get out of there before this nice moment turned awkward.

"Well, then, I'll see you," I said, as I started to back out of the kitchen, nearly tripping over Bertie, who was running back in, clearly wondering why neither one of us was chasing him around with a leash, "at seven." I patted Bertie's head, then glanced at the clock and realized that was in an hour and a half. I'd have to get moving.

"See you," Clark echoed, and I gave him a quick nod before I turned and headed out, fighting the urge to do a little hop as I went.

I walked to my car, feeling like finally something was working out this summer. I may not have had a prestigious program to put on my résumé, but I had a date with a really cute boy, and if all went according to plan, we'd be kissing in a few hours. I pulled open the door to my car, already texting my friends.

ME

Date with Clark tonight!!!
Need prep help & reinforcements!!!

Then, not quite able to keep the smile off my face, I started the car and headed for home.

"You look great," Palmer said from where she was sprawled across my bed. I was standing in front of my mirror, fussing with my hair, even though Palmer had already straightened it and told me not to touch it.

"I liked the other dress better," Toby said from my computer screen. I was video chatting with her—and Bri, in theory, though Bri was in the middle of a fight with both her younger sister, Sonia, and her older sister, Sneha, so every few minutes she would storm off-screen, then return a while later looking vexed.

I hesitated, looking at my closet. "No!" Palmer said, seeing where I was looking. "Andie, no. This dress is great. Look, let's ask a boy." She snapped a picture of me before I could stop her and started typing on her phone—sending it to Tom, I assumed, though I wasn't sure if he even counted, since whenever he weighed in, he was always careful to tell us that while we might look fine, Palmer definitely looked better.

Morgan Matson

I turned back to the mirror and smoothed down my hair. Palmer had walked over from her house only a few minutes after I'd gotten home and had been supervising the process ever since. We had gone through most of my clothes together, and we'd decided on a denim dress with flat black sandals and dangly earrings. I felt dressed up, but still like myself, and I had liked the outfit before Toby had weighed in. "What do you mean?" I asked, walking over to the computer.

"Eh," Toby said from my screen with a one-armed shrug. "I just don't know if it's, you know, dynamic enough."

"It's great," Palmer said, glaring at Toby. "Bri?" she called, but Bri didn't appear in her window, and we were just looking at her *Alien* poster staring back at us.

"You think?" I asked, pulling down on the hem and tucking my hair behind my ears.

"Yes," Palmer said firmly. Her phone beeped, and she glanced at it, then held it out to me. "And Tom agrees. He said you look, and I quote, 'not bad.'"

"That's not really a great endorsement," I said, glancing over at my screen, where Toby gave me an *I told you so* look. "Maybe I should try the other dress again?"

"No," Palmer said, turning my computer screen around to face the wall while Toby yelped, "Hey!" "You seriously look great. And we don't have time for you to change again."

I glanced down at my phone and realized she was right. I looked back in the mirror and decided that I looked fine. After all, Clark been seeing me in my dog-walking clothes for a week. "Okay," I said, letting out a long breath and then turning to Palmer. "Let's do this."

THE UNEXPECTED EVERYTHING

She nodded and rolled off my bed, pocketing her phone in her cutoffs. "Bye, Toby," she called, and I leaned over to the screen and waved, seeing that Bri still hadn't reappeared.

"Text me updates," Toby said, giving me a wink. "Have fun!"

We walked down to the foyer together, Palmer leading the way—she knew my house as well as her own. "So," she said, stopping at the door to dig her keys out of her purse, "if it's going really well, bring him to the Orchard later."

I smiled at that, feeling my cheeks get hot at the thought of things going well enough that I'd bring him to meet my friends after the first night. For that to happen, there would *definitely* be some kissing. "Let's just see how this goes."

"Andie?" I turned around to see my dad standing in the hallway that led from his study, squinting at me. He had stopped wearing his button-downs in the last few days, and now he was wearing what he wore at more casual events on the campaign trail or strategy sessions—khakis, a polo shirt, and loafers. I honestly wasn't sure I'd ever seen my father in a T-shirt. I wasn't entirely sure he owned one.

"Yes?" I called back, looking at Palmer and then widening my eyes at her. I had assumed my dad would stay in his study, reading or watching old sports games, like he'd spent the last few days doing. I was going to write a note and leave it on the kitchen counter before I left, but that was as much as I'd decided to do in terms of alerting him to my plans for the night.

"I thought I heard—" my dad said as he walked down the hall toward me, and I felt my stomach sink. I'd hoped he had a quick question that I could shout back the answer to, and then he could have gone back to watching eighties basketball players

Morgan Matson

and their disturbingly short shorts. "Oh," my dad said when he saw Palmer. "Sorry—I didn't realize Andie had anyone over."

"Hi, Congressman Walker," Palmer said cheerfully. A second later, though, when she realized what she'd said, she paled. "I mean . . . Mr. Walker," she added quickly. My dad was still looking at her, so she glanced at me, then tried, "Alexander?"

"Mr. Walker's fine," my dad said, giving her that practiced smile he used when he was working a rope line. "How are you doing, Palmer? How are your parents?"

"Oh, they're fine. Thanks for asking."

"Palmer was just leaving," I said, before my dad could start asking about her brothers and sisters—I could practically see him slipping back into concerned-candidate mode, wanting to show her that he remembered her siblings' names, that he'd held on to tiny snippets of information. We didn't have time for that. It was going to be tight, but I was hoping I could get her out of here—and my dad back in his study—before Clark arrived. I had never ever done the guy-parent introduction thing and I really didn't want to start now. I raised my eyebrows at Palmer, and she nodded.

"I was just leaving," she repeated back, matching my inflection and shooting me a tiny smile. "Talk to you later," she said as she opened the door. I pulled it back for her and she mouthed, *Oh my god!* to me before turning back to my dad, her face composed and polite. "Nice to see you again, Mr. Walker," she called.

"And you as well," my dad said, his voice warm and sincere, like she was just the person he'd hoped to see in his house unexpectedly today. "Please give my best to Mark and Kathie."

"Will do," she said, giving him a tiny wave before she

headed out the door, pulling it shut behind her.

I looked at my dad in the sudden silence of the foyer, trying to figure out how I could get him back to his office without letting him know that's what I was trying to do. Or maybe I could drive down the street and meet Clark at the gatehouse to avoid any possibility of overlap. "So—" I started, just as my dad said, "Are you going somewhere?"

"Oh," I said, then nodded. "Yeah . . . I'm . . . going out to dinner. A friend is picking me up." As soon as the words were out of my mouth, I regretted them. Why hadn't I just said I was meeting someone? I didn't have Clark's number, but if I was out by the street early enough, I could have flagged him down from out there.

My dad nodded, and silence fell between us again. I had just taken a breath to say that I'd see him later when he asked, "Which friend?"

"You don't know them," I said, then heard, from somewhere on the second floor, a clock begin to chime. Was it seven already? I pulled my phone out from my bag and saw that the clock upstairs must have been fast—it was five to. But either way, I needed to wrap this up *now*.

"I don't?" my dad asked, folding his arms, and again I cursed myself for not just saying that I was meeting Toby or Bri at the diner.

"I don't think so?" I said, letting the sentence rise in a question as I started to edge toward the door. "I'd better get going."

"Wait a second," my dad said, running a hand over the back of his neck. He looked distinctly uncomfortable, like he was an actor in a bad play, speaking words he hadn't totally

148   *Morgan Matson*

memorized. "I, uh . . . Should you be going out with someone I don't know?"

I looked at him for a second, trying to decide if the question was rhetorical, or if he actually wanted an answer. Also, I didn't understand why he was suddenly acting like a father in a sitcom. I hadn't asked my dad for permission to go anywhere in years. He either hadn't been around to ask, or if he happened to be home, he'd nod and wave at me, usually while taking a call, as I yelled that I was going out. This had to feel as weird for him as it did for me. "Look," I started, just as I saw a slightly dented Jeep signal and then pull slowly into our driveway.

I tried as fast as I could to think of something, then felt my pulse start to pick up when I realized I no longer knew how to get out of this. But the last thing I wanted was for Clark to be here, in my house, talking to my dad. I hadn't realized how much I liked keeping these worlds separate until it appeared they were about to collide. I looked out to the driveway, wondering what my dad would do if I just left, walked out the door and met Clark before he'd even made it halfway to the porch. But before I could do anything, Clark came into view, and I realized my moment to escape had passed and this was inevitable. I wondered, as I watched him walk up the path and then climb the front porch steps, if this was what pilots felt like when they realized they were going to crash but still had to wait for the impact.

My dad frowned as Clark got closer, then looked at me, his jaw falling open like he'd just figured something out. "Andie— are you going on a date?"

"Kind of," I muttered as I reached to pull open our door.

Our front doors were half glass, and I knew it already looked weird enough that I was standing around waiting for my date—along with my father. My plan had been to pretend to read a magazine in the kitchen, not even coming close to the foyer until I heard the doorbell. You weren't supposed to let your date *know* that you'd been waiting around for them to arrive. You were supposed to be much too busy and interesting for that.

I opened the door, and there was Clark, standing on the porch, hand half-outstretched toward the bell. "Hi," I said, giving him a quick smile, wishing I had more time to really appreciate the fact that he was wearing a light-blue button-down with his jeans, that his brown hair looked like it had been recently combed, and that he was just so cute it was almost unfair. "Come on in," I said, hearing how high-pitched and stressed my voice sounded, which I was pretty sure wasn't making the best first-date impression. "My dad's . . ." I let this trail off when I realized there wasn't an easy way to sum this up, and just stepped back to let Clark inside.

"Hi," Clark said to me, smiling wide, then looking at my father and standing up a little straighter. "Hello, sir," he said. My dad's eyebrows shot up, and I knew Clark had gained some points in his eyes. First impressions were big with him.

"Dad, this is Clark Goetz-Hoffman," I said, just as Clark said, "McCallister."

"What?" I turned to look at him.

"Clark McCallister," Clark said.

"I thought your last name was Goetz-Hoffman."

"You two need a minute to confer?" my dad asked, looking between the two of us.

Morgan Matson

"Sorry," I said, shaking my head, trying to get my bearings. Maybe his parents were divorced and this was his mother's new name or something.

"Alexander Walker," my dad said, reaching out and shaking Clark's hand with his politician's handshake—two pumps, lots of eye contact. Then he paused and turned to me. "That's right, isn't it? Walker?"

"Ha ha," I said, trying to silently tell my dad this was not the time to try to be funny.

"Well, whoever you are, Clark, it's nice to meet you."

"You as well." Clark looked at my dad for a beat longer, frowning slightly, before he turned back to me. "You look great," he said quietly to me.

"Thanks." I took a step toward the door, which was still open. "So we should go. . . ."

"Just a second," my dad said, and I noticed his voice had dropped to his authoritative TV-spot timbre. "You two go to school together?"

Clark glanced at me, then turned back to my dad. "No, sir. We . . . uh—don't."

My dad paused mid-nod. "But you're going into senior year as well?"

"No, um . . ." Clark looked at me again. We hadn't talked about it, but I had assumed that he was going to be an incoming freshman at a college somewhere in the fall, or maybe that he was going into his senior year at a different school from me. "I actually got my GED a few years ago," Clark said, looking from me to my dad as he spoke. "So I'm, uh, not in school."

"You're not?" I asked, not able to stop myself.

"I was going to mention it over dinner," he explained.

"So . . . ," my dad said, and I could practically feel him trying to regroup. "How do you two know each other, then?"

"Andie walks my dog," Clark said, giving my dad a smile. My dad looked at me, not even trying to hide the utterly baffled look on his face, and I knew I was paying the price now for all the times I'd thought about telling him about my job and then had just chosen to avoid the subject entirely. "Well, not *my* dog, exactly," Clark amended after a second. "But the dog who . . . lives in my house." Now it was my turn to stare at Clark, but before I could say anything, he added, "Well, not *my* house, so to speak—"

"Bertie's not your dog?" I asked, feeling my eyebrows fly up.

"Why are you walking his dog?" my dad asked.

"Andie's a dog walker," Clark said, then a moment later, and in the silence that followed, he seemed to read the room. "Was that supposed to be a secret?" he asked, leaning closer to me, his voice barely above a whisper.

"It's my summer job," I said to my dad, crossing and then uncrossing my arms.

"Since when?"

"A week and a half ago."

"But you have no experience with dogs," my dad said, still staring at me.

"I got trained," I said quickly to Clark, "before I started."

"You do a great job with Bertie," Clark assured me. "She really does," he added to my dad.

"Help me understand this," my dad said, turning back to Clark. It didn't seem like this positive report of my job performance had cleared anything up for him. "You're not in school. But you'll be going to college, I assume."

"No, um . . . ," Clark said, glancing once at me before putting his hands in his pockets, then taking them out again. "I . . . well, I'm a writer. So I've been mostly focusing on that. I'm not sure college fits into my plans at the moment."

"A writer," my dad repeated, his voice flat. I was trying very hard not to look quite as thrown by all this as I felt. Clearly, the downside of having a theoretical crush on someone you knew nothing about was the crashing realization that you actually knew nothing about them.

"Yeah," Clark said with a low, nervous laugh. "I write fantasy novels."

"Wait, *what*?" I asked. All of this was moving too quickly, and I really felt like it would have been better to find this stuff out while sitting across from Clark in a restaurant somewhere, or while driving there in his car—not in front of my dad.

"Another thing I was going to mention later," Clark said with another quick smile. I could see, though, that his cheeks were starting to get pink.

"Fantasy novels?" my dad repeated, his voice skeptical.

"Yeah," Clark said with a shrug, his cheeks still flushed. "I mean, I've only written two so far, but . . ."

"And this is what you do," my dad said, still sounding unimpressed. "Rather than going to college."

"Well," Clark said, shifting his weight from foot to foot. "It is kind of a full-time job, especially after *A Murder of Crows* was published. . . ."

"Wait . . ." My dad stared at Clark like he was trying to

understand what was happening. "I've heard of that. Wasn't it a bestseller? Wasn't it a *movie*?"

Clark nodded. "Two," he said, then cleared his throat. "It was supposed to be a trilogy, but I'm a little bit behind on my newest book." I suddenly flashed back to the old man waiting on line in the library with his thick paperback, complaining about the author who hadn't finished his series. What had that writer's name been? Wasn't it something McCallister?

I blinked at him, trying to figure this out. I had assumed Clark was my age, or close to it, though I was now starting to question everything. Because people who were my age, or close to it, didn't write bestselling fantasy books. They didn't have movies based on their books with huge movie stars in them. How was this even possible?

"I published the first one when I was fourteen," Clark said, clearly reading the confusion on both our faces. He gave an embarrassed shrug. "Homeschooled kids have a lot of time on their hands."

"Well," my dad said. He looked as overwhelmed as I currently felt. "I should let you two get going. Andie, be home by . . ." He trailed off, looking at me blankly.

I stared back at him, silently panicking as I weighed my options as quickly as possible. I normally never had a curfew. But if I said something like midnight or one, what if Clark thought I expected to spend all that time with him? I didn't know how to tell him that I had plans after our dinner without being really insulting. But then again, what if the date went really well and I wanted to stay out with him until late?

"Just don't stay out too late," my dad finally said, maybe,

amazingly, understanding some of my thought process.

I nodded, feeling relief start to course through me. "Will do." I looked at Clark, more than ready to stop standing in this foyer. "Ready to go?" Clark nodded harder than people normally do, letting me believe that he was probably feeling the same way. "See you later," I said to my dad as I took a step toward the door.

"Oh," my dad said, like he just remembered something. "I meant to tell you not to answer any calls from numbers you don't know. Peter thinks one of the interns might have 'misplaced' our cell numbers, and reporters might be calling for quotes."

Now it was Clark's turn to look nonplussed. "Reporters?" he asked. He looked at my dad and snapped his fingers. "You're . . . I saw you on CNN," he said. "I thought you looked familiar! Senator—"

"Congressman Walker," my dad interrupted. Then he added, "At least, I used to be."

I could see it in Clark's face, the dawning realization of just *why* my dad looked familiar and why he'd been on CNN in the first place. "Oh, right," he said, his voice quiet. "Sorry—I didn't . . ." He looked at me, and I looked down at my sandals. "I didn't realize," he said quietly, now looking more embarrassed than ever.

"I was going to mention it later," I muttered.

"I'm sorry, but have you two met before?" My dad looked between us and then let out a big belly laugh.

Clark and I glanced at each other, and I felt my face get hot. It was bad enough for both of us to probably be thinking that without my dad coming out and saying it.

"Well, you two have fun," my dad said, starting to head back toward his study, a laugh still lingering in his voice.

I turned to Clark when he was gone. "Should we go?"

"Let's," Clark said immediately.

Twenty minutes later I set my menu aside and looked across the table at Clark at the Boxcar Cantina. It was a Mexican place in town that Tom loved, and so Palmer was always insisting we go there after his opening nights and for his birthday. It was small, and a little bit dark, with candles in brightly colored glass holders on all the tables and a roving mariachi band Palmer always tipped extra so they'd play mariachi "Happy Birthday" for Tom. It had been Clark's pick—he'd asked as we drove over if it was okay with me—and when we'd arrived, I'd been surprised and impressed when he gave his name to the hostess, who walked us to a table, holding our laminated menus.

Now that we were no longer in his kitchen, Clark seemed a lot less nervous—holding the car door open for me, making small talk, taking charge of things in a way I appreciated, since we were on the kind of date I usually didn't go on.

"So," Clark said, setting his own menu aside and smiling at me. "Congress, huh?"

I raised an eyebrow back at him. "Bestselling fantasy novels?"

He laughed, still sounding a little embarrassed. "Maybe we should start over," he said, holding out his hand across the table to me. "Clark Bruce McCallister."

I smiled at that. "Alexandra Molly Walker." I reached across the table and took his hand. His palm was cool against mine, and as his fingers closed around my hand, I felt something run through me. It wasn't a spark, or a shiver, or anything I'd heard described in cheesy love songs. It was more like when someone touches you on a spot near where you're ticklish, that kind of heightened awareness. Like I'd never known there were so many nerve endings in my fingers. I pulled my hand back quickly, even though something in me was telling me to leave it there and also see what would happen if I touched his arm.

"Bruce?" I asked, placing my hands around my water glass, trying to get myself to focus.

"Yeah," Clark said with a shrug. "I thought using my initials for my books made me sound more grown-up."

"Totally," I said, my voice overly serious. "It's *very* distinguished."

He smiled at that and leaned forward slightly, toward me. "So where's the 'Molly' come from?"

I kept my expression the same, but I could feel the low-level anxiety start to build somewhere around my stomach, which was starting to knot. I hadn't expected to be confronted with this—not right now, not right off the bat. "It was my mom's name," I said quickly, giving him a bright smile, thinking that now would be a great time for our waiter to take our order, or bring us some chips, or something.

"Was?" Clark asked, adjusting his glasses, his voice a little softer.

I took a breath, even as I made sure to keep my expression neutral, wishing I had some kind of prop in front of me. I usually didn't have to deal with this. Any reporter who ever talked to me knew, of course. And all the guys I'd dated at school had already known about my mom. This was not an explanation I'd had to give that often. "She passed away five years ago," I said, keeping my voice light, running over the surface of these words, not letting myself get pulled down into the emotion of what they actually meant. To hear me say it, you would think that it was just no big deal. I ended the sentence with a note of finality, the one that every guy I'd dated had understood to mean that I wanted to move on and had happily obliged.

"I'm so sorry, Andie," Clark said, his eyes seeking mine across the table, as I looked over his shoulder, like I was fascinated with the wall decor. "That's terrible. What happened?"

The anxiety that had been in my stomach was now traveling in the express lane up to my chest, causing my heart to pound and making it harder to breathe. "It was a long time ago," I said, hitting the note of finality even harder, wanting more than anything for Clark to understand this.

"So," I said brightly, picking up my menu again, like I was fascinated by the differences in the fajita dishes. "What do you think you're going to order?" I looked back at him, making sure to keep my expression happy and a little blank. But it didn't look like Clark was picking up on this. He still looked sympathetic, but he also looked confused, like I'd just started speaking French and hadn't told him why.

"What can I get for you two tonight?" Our waitress, in a black and pink BOXCAR CANTINA T-shirt, had appeared at our table, pen poised above her order pad.

I had never been so happy to see a waitress, and I hoped that by the time we'd finished ordering, the awkward moment would have passed and we could start having a nice, normal date. "The bean and cheese burrito and a Diet Coke," I said, handing her my menu. "Thank you."

Morgan Matson

She nodded and wrote it down, then turned to Clark. "And for you?"

"I'll take the Reaper-ito," Clark said, and the waitress—her name tag read BECCA—paused and looked at him.

"Did you read the menu description for that?" she asked warily. "Because most people send it back when they realize they can't handle it." I glanced toward my menu, which was currently tucked under her arm, and wished I hadn't given it back quite so quickly.

"I did," Clark said, adjusting his glasses and smiling at her.

"So you know it has Carolina Reapers in it?" she asked, starting to sound annoyed. "That it's the hottest thing we serve here?" Clark nodded, still smiling, and Becca huffed and wrote the order down. "Something to drink?" she asked. "You're going to need it."

"Just a Coke."

"And could we get some chips?" I interjected, starting to get a little worried by the fact that none had appeared at our table yet.

Becca nodded and took Clark's menu. "What kind of salsa?"

"Mild," I said at the exact same time Clark said, "Hot."

"I'll bring both," she said, rolling her eyes as she headed away, leaving us with each other, and slightly strained silence, once again.

"So what's a Carolina Reaper?" I'd never seen a waitress warn someone off a menu item before, not even when Toby had ordered the seven-dollar lobster.

"It's the hottest peppers you can eat," he said, matter-of-factly. "I'm really impressed they actually have it on the menu. You don't see it that often."

I wasn't quite able to stop myself from recoiling. "Why would you want to do that to yourself?"

"I guess you're not so into spicy foods?"

I shook my head and took a sip of my water, like my mouth needed to be cooled down just thinking about this. My friends teased me about it, but I preferred all my food pretty bland. I'd gotten adept over the years at eating around offending sauces and garnishes. My dad was the same way—it had become one of those things reporters write about, how he always traveled with his own supply of bread and peanut butter. My mom had been the one to push both of us out of our comfort zones, to make reservations at Ethiopian and Peruvian restaurants, who got us to try Korean barbeque, soup dumplings, and escargot. But without her, both of us had retreated back to what we liked, and for me that was bean and cheese burritos, extra-cheese pizza, and hamburgers without any vegetables on top. "Not so much," I said, still trying to understand why someone would order something that spicy unless it was some kind of a dare. "But it sounds like you do?"

"Kind of," Clark said, nodding his thanks at the busboy who dropped off two Cokes, a lemon wedge indicating the one that was diet. "It, uh . . . started as a game between me and my dad."

"A game?" I asked, hitting my straw on the table to shuck off the wrapper.

"Yeah," he said, a small smile starting to form on his face. "My dad's really into the idea of mind over matter, that you can conquer your body's reactions through discipline," he said, shaking his head. "So one night when we were all at a restaurant— my mom and my sister too—I challenged my dad to order something with jalapeño in it. And he said he would if I would too. And then it kind of turned into a competition."

"So who won?" I asked, taking a sip of my soda.

Something faltered in Clark's smile for a second, and he pulled his glass toward him. "Still ongoing."

"Well, you'll have to tell him you ate this Reaper thing."

Clark nodded. "Right. Sure."

We both took sips of our sodas in unison, and then silence descended again. It was on the tip of my tongue to ask him something about his family—like how old his sister was or what his parents did—but then I hesitated when I realized that if I asked him about his family, he'd probably want me to talk about mine.

Clark leaned forward, and I racked my brain quickly for some safe topic, something that we had in common. Usually with the other guys I'd been on dates with, there was shared experience. We had bosses or teachers to complain about, friends to gossip about, something mutual to provide help for these early conversations. I realized after a second that the only thing Clark and I really had was the dog. "So," I said cheerfully, cutting him off right as he was starting to speak, "how's Bertie doing?"

Talk of the dog, and his quirks, got us through the chips and into the meal. Whenever Clark would start to ask me something more personal, I would steer the conversation back to safer subjects—Bertie, the restaurant, the weather, the upcoming batch of summer movies. And the food itself became a subject when we started eating. I watched with alarm as Becca placed Clark's food in front of him and braced myself when he took the first bite. But although he turned a little red and it looked like his glasses fogged up the tiniest bit, he soldiered on, and by the time he'd eaten most of his burrito, three of the kitchen staff, two of the waiters, and a busboy were lingering around our table watching him do it.

I offered to split the dinner check, but Clark insisted and paid with a silver credit card. Becca offered him a half-price discount on their DON'T FEAR THE REAPER T-shirt, but Clark passed, and when we got back to his car, he started driving right back to my house. I sat in the front seat of his Jeep, looking at the vacuum lines on the floor mats that indicated it had recently been cleaned, with the growing and undeniable feeling that this had not been a good date. I didn't think it was my fault—I'd tried to keep the conversation light and fun, but it was like Clark had just been going along with it, like he wasn't really having a great time. As I tried to figure out what was different, it occurred to me that most of the time when I was sitting in a restaurant across from a boy, we knew each other better and the date had honestly felt sometimes like a formality before we got to the making-out part at the end.

As we drove along in silence, I realized that things were always so much simpler once you entered the post-make-out stage of a relationship. After you'd kissed someone, it became all inside jokes and cute references, and everything else was over-ridden by the need to kiss the person again. This haze softened everything and made it all easier. But it really didn't seem like that was going to be in the cards for tonight. I was hoping we could get out of this with minimum awkwardness, so we could pretend we'd gone out tonight as friends—friends who, it turned out, didn't have all that much to say to each other.

But it was too bad, I realized, as I looked at his profile, lit up by his dashboard light. He was really, *really* cute. And he seemed nice. But apparently, somehow, that wasn't always enough. (I made a mental note to be sure to tell Toby, since this seemed to run counterintuitive to everything her Rom-Coms had told her.)

Clark slowed, signaled, and pulled into my driveway, and I felt myself let out a small sigh of relief. This strange date was almost over. It was still early—I could regroup, then find out where my friends were and meet up with them. I could still salvage the night, after all.

He pulled to a stop and put the car in park but didn't turn off the engine or make any move to walk me to my door—which I was glad about. This didn't need to get any more uncomfortable than it currently was. "So, thanks for dinner," I said with a big smile, gathering up my purse, hand already hovering near the door handle. "I had a really nice time."

Across the car, Clark looked at me for a moment. "You did?" he asked, sounding baffled.

Oh *god*. I could feel myself getting frustrated. That was just something you *said*, not something you actually meant. Most people understood that. I didn't like going to Tom's sketch comedy shows or my dad's fund-raisers. But that didn't mean I told either of them that. "Sure," I said, keeping my smile in place.

Clark looked at me for a second longer, and by the dashboard light, I could see confusion knitting his brow. "I just . . . ," he said slowly, then shook his head. "I mean, it was like you didn't want to talk to me."

I drew back slightly in my seat. Why were we recapping this? We'd clearly both had a bad time, so why weren't we moving on? I *had* tried to talk to him, all night. He was the one who hadn't wanted to talk about any of the subjects I brought up.

"We talked," I said. I was fine with having a bad date. I was less fine with *discussing* it forever, not to mention incorrectly.

"No," he said simply, shaking his head. "Not about anything real."

I had opened my mouth to reply to this, but stopped with my argument half-formed. Because it was true. I *hadn't* asked him anything real, because I hadn't really wanted to know anything real. I wanted the date I always had—fun and easy and simple. I had no idea how to explain this. But I knew I needed to get out of his car. The way he was looking at me—the way he was talking about this—was making me feel retroactively embarrassed, like I'd spent the whole night doing and saying the wrong things, even though I'd been doing what I always did.

"See you around," I muttered as I opened the door and stepped down to the ground. I was trying not to think about the fact I was supposed to see him *tomorrow* to walk the dog. But he might be calling Maya as soon as he drove away, requesting a different dog walker.

I shut his door, maybe a little harder than I needed to, and walked toward my house even though I had no intention of going inside. I was going to get in my car, find my friends, and start the process of telling them about this, so it could turn into something we could all laugh about. I walked toward my front door, pulling out my phone and waiting for Clark to drive off. I watched as his car pulled into our turnaround, backed out, and turned around so he was now facing the end of the driveway. But the car just sat there, idling, not going anywhere.

I realized after a moment that he was waiting to make sure I got inside okay. There was a piece of me that would have appreciated this under different circumstances. But not tonight. Tonight it was just annoying. I walked up to the side entrance and pulled open the screen door, then took out my keys and pretended to unlock it. I glanced toward the driveway, but his car was still there waiting. Rolling my eyes, I unlocked the door and stepped inside, and only then did Clark drive away.

I pressed on the brakes even though there were no cars behind me and none in front of me, but I had a habit of missing the turn to get into the Orchard and not realizing it until I'd gone about a mile too far down the road, driving along with the sinking feeling that I should have been there by now. And I didn't want to waste that time tonight. I wanted to vent to my friends. And then, once that was done, I wanted to move on. I'd spent the drive over working out my plan. I needed someone to replace who I had hoped Clark would be—someone to help me forget about everything that had happened in the last two weeks, someone to help me turn my summer around. And Clark clearly was not going to be that person, so I would have to find someone else.

As I was about to speed up, thinking I'd slowed too early, there was the old Orchard sign, with its two cherries, letting me know I was in the right place. I swung in, starting to relax the closer I got. At some point, the Orchard had been a functional orchard, but ever since I'd first heard about it—when Palmer's oldest sibling, Fitz, was in high school and we were still in elementary—it had been the town party spot. Not so much in the winter, but in the summers it was filled with people from the three neighboring high schools and the occasional bored-looking Stanwich College student. And tonight it was just the place I wanted to be.

I swung my car into the open field that had been repurposed as a parking lot. I got out of the car, locked it, and walked toward the main part of the Orchard, where picnic tables ringed the open space and off to the side there was usually someone selling overpriced keg beer or cans from a cooler that never seemed to get very cold, despite the ice packed around them. I walked forward, looking around for my friends. I'd texted them when I'd stopped at the gatehouse and had heard from Tom (on Palmer's phone) that they were en route. I was pretty sure I hadn't beaten them there, but if I had, I'd just sit at one of the picnic tables and begin the process of putting this night behind me.

I felt someone nudge my shoulder and looked over to see Wyatt Miller standing next to me, a red Solo cup of beer in each hand and a half smile on his face.

"I know you," I said, nudging him back, our version of a hug, careful not to spill the beers. "Welcome back."

"Thanks," he said, taking a sip from one of them and smiling a little wider at me, and I made myself look away before it affected me. I got used to Wyatt after a few days, but if it had been a while since I'd seen him, it was always a little startling—he was probably the best-looking person I'd ever seen in my life, outside of a multiplex or a cologne ad. He had light-brown hair that he wore a little long and was always pushing back with one hand. He tended to wear threadbare old band shirts, skinny jeans, and Converse, even when it was the height of summer. He was thin, with cheekbones for days, but Toby swore up and down that it wasn't his looks that made her fall for him. She insisted that he had hidden depths, which Tom said must be *really* well hidden indeed. But I could see what she meant—he was quiet (which made it easier for Toby to project all kinds of silent, conflicted feelings onto him), usually observing more than participating. But he had a deadpan, snarky sense of humor that still caught me by surprise sometimes. He played bass in a series of bands at his boarding school (bands that always seemed to be breaking up and getting back together, which was probably inevitable when you lived with people and couldn't escape them). Without even trying hard, I could picture all the girls at Briarville swooning over him during his concerts.

"How's life? What," he said, looking at me directly, like he was about to ask me a very serious question, "is the haps?"

I laughed at that. "You didn't bring your guitar, did you?" It had been the thing Wyatt and I had argued about the most last summer. When he'd had a beer or two, suddenly his acoustic guitar appeared, and even though he was good, in my opinion, that didn't matter. Suddenly, all conversation stopped and the night became about Wyatt strumming chords. Toby loved it, though, and spent way too much time speculating on whether he was writing her a song, despite the fact that nothing really rhymed with Toby.

"Nah," he said, shaking his head. "Thought I'd wait and give you a private concert."

"No." I groaned, then looked over and saw one of his

eyebrows was raised, which was how I knew he was kidding. Wyatt's deadpan made it hard to tell sometimes. "Oh," I said. "Gotcha." I looked over at him and noticed that practically every girl in the vicinity was looking in our direction. "So how've you been, Miller?"

"I should be asking you that, Walker," he replied, as he nodded toward the tables and started to lead the way over. Wyatt always called me by my last name, and even though I rolled my eyes at it, I secretly liked it. "I hear you had a hot date tonight," he said, taking another drink from his cup.

"Not so much," I said, falling into step next to him and spotting where we were going—the farthest picnic table, where my friends were.

"Oh." He shot me a sympathetic look. "Well," he said with a shrug, "always more fish in the sea? Etcetera?"

I nodded. That was pretty much what I'd been thinking the whole drive over here. "Something like that."

Toby saw us coming and jumped up, then started to sit back down again, then stopped in the middle, doing a kind of half-lean thing that I'm sure she thought was natural but actually looked incredibly uncomfortable. She crossed her arms, then uncrossed them, then crossed them again. "I see you found Andie, huh?" she asked, then laughed loudly. After a few moments, she stopped abruptly and took a long drink from her cup, her face flushing as red as her hair.

"I did indeed," Wyatt said, crossing over to Bri and handing her the other cup. In my peripheral vision, I could see Palmer surreptitiously wipe the excess foam off Toby's nose.

"Don't try to change the subject," Bri said, mouthing

her thanks to Wyatt and then pointing at Toby. "This is an intervention."

"How is saying hello to Andie changing the subject?" Toby asked.

"An intervention for what?" I asked, looking around at my friends and starting to relax. I was already feeling better, just being around them. The date was starting to fade into the background a bit.

"Emojis," Tom, Bri, and Palmer said at the same time.

"Andie," Toby said, turning to me, "tell them they're being ridiculous."

"No," I said, laughing at Toby's outraged expression. "You're out of control with them. I heartily approve of this. How do I join this intervention?"

"I've honestly worried sometimes that you've forgotten how to form whole sentences," Bri said, her voice overly serious. "You're my best friend, Tobyhanna. And I'm concerned for you."

"Emojis are fun!" Toby protested, her voice rising. "It's not like I'm the only one who uses them. You all do."

"I don't," Wyatt said with a shrug.

"See?" Toby said, pointing at him in triumph, then frowning a second later when she must have realized this didn't help her argument.

"You need to dial it back," Palmer said as she pulled out her phone. "Like this afternoon, you texted me 'I'm so whale, dancing girl, dancing girl, blushing smiley, nervous-teeth smiley, star, star, pizza.'" She looked up from her phone. "What was that supposed to *mean*?"

Toby didn't respond, just pointedly looked down at the ground, and I wasn't sure if this was because she was being criticized in front of Wyatt, or because the message was actually about him. Judging by the way Toby had glanced in his direction while it was being read, I had a feeling it might be the latter.

"We're only encouraging you to maybe use more text-based communication," Bri said, a little more gently. "You know, for a fun change every now and then."

"Emojis can express everything you need them to!" Toby said.

"Oh, really?" Palmer asked, the look coming into her eyes that I knew all too well. If Toby hadn't been so riled up, she would have noticed it too. It was the look we had all come to fear. When Palmer looked like that, suddenly she was yelling, "Fire drill!" when at a red light, which meant we all had to get out of the car, run around it, and change seats before the light turned green. It was how I had ended up not being able to use the past tense for a whole month of AP History and the reason Bri still refused to eat wraps. Palmer was about to throw down a challenge. "Then I bet you can't go the rest of the summer using only emojis."

"And if I can?" Toby asked, ignoring the fact that both Bri and I were shaking our heads at her. This was Toby's Achilles' heel, and always had been—the moment she should walk away, she dug her heels in more, even when she was given an out, and her stubbornness always came back to bite her.

"Then . . . I'll never give you any grief about your emoji usage," Palmer said, raising an eyebrow. "You can use them to your heart's content. But if you can't, you can't use any for the rest of the year."

Morgan Matson

"You're on," Toby said, and Palmer held out her hand to shake.

"Witness?" Palmer asked, and Tom and Wyatt raised their hands. "Okay, Toby has agreed to text using only emojis for the rest of the summer. And if she can't, no more emojis until next year. If she can, I never make fun of her again."

"What did you just *do*?" Bri asked, staring at Toby. "And why are the stakes so low for Palmer?"

"It's fine," Toby said, though she was starting to look discomfited. "I can totally get what I need to say across to you guys. I mean, it might take some more work, but that's why emojis are awesome."

"Not just us," Palmer said, shaking her head. "Nothing but emojis in all your texts to *everyone*."

Toby paled—it was clear she hadn't considered this. "Wait," she said a little faintly. "You didn't say that. Did you?"

"She did just say texts," Tom said, though I wasn't sure how much this meant, since he would have backed Palmer up in pretty much anything.

"Wyatt?" Toby asked, turning to him, looking more and more worried.

Wyatt shook his head. "Sorry," he said. "Miss Palmer speaks the truth."

"But . . ." Toby looked from me to Bri, like we hadn't been trying to stop her a minute before. "How am I supposed to tell my mom I'm running late for dinner? Or ask someone to cover my shift at work?"

"Be creative," Palmer said with a grin. "I mean, emojis can express whatever you need them to. Someone told me that."

"Fine," Toby snapped, like she hadn't just agreed to these terms. "I can totally do this. Just watch."

"I will," Palmer said, "and don't think we won't be checking your phone to make sure you're not cheating."

"Andie," Bri said, turning to me with the air of someone who knows that a subject change would be wise, "how was your date?"

"Oh, yeah, the date," Tom said, turning to me and smiling wide. "So?"

"Ugh," I said, as the earlier part of my night came back to me, and my friends' expressions immediately changed from excited to sympathetic.

"Oh, no," Palmer said, reaching out and giving my hand a squeeze. "Not Dogboy! I had high hopes for him."

"Dogboy?" Wyatt asked.

"Yeah, well," I said with a shrug. "One of those things."

"Was it a bad date?" Bri asked, scooting closer to Palmer so that I could sit next to her.

"I didn't think it was *terrible*," I said, thinking back to the actual time spent at the restaurant. It would have been fine if Clark had gone along with any of my conversation suggestions. "But then when he drove me home . . ."

"Bad kisser?" Tom asked sympathetically.

"No," I said, shaking my head. "We didn't even come close to that. He just had a really bad time."

"I'm sure that's not true," Palmer said immediately.

"No, he did have a bad time," I said. "He *told* me he did. Apparently, he was mad that I didn't ask him anything about himself or tell him anything about me." A moment after I'd

Morgan Matson

said it, it was like I actually heard what I was saying. My friends looked back at me, slightly frozen expressions on everyone's faces.

"Um . . . did you do that?" Bri asked, hesitation in her voice after a pause in which everyone had become very interested in the ground, or the contents of their cups. "Or . . . not do that?"

"I did what I always do on dates. He was just weird."

"I think it sounds like he called you on that thing you do," Palmer said, and Bri and Tom nodded knowingly.

"What thing?" Palmer, Tom, and Bri all took a breath at once, like they were preparing to detail just what was wrong with me, and I shook my head. I didn't think I wanted to hear it, and anyway, I needed to get to work scoping out new prospects. I shook my head. "Never mind. Let's talk about something else, okay?" I looked around the group, trying to think of anything that didn't involve emoticons or my dating life. "Wyatt," I said, feeling like he was the most neutral person here, as well as the one currently least likely to make fun of me, "are you here for the whole summer?"

"Three whole months," he said, nodding. "I'm going to have to look into the job thing one of these days."

"The coffee place next to the movie theater is hiring," Bri said with a shrug. "I know, because every time I go in there to get lunch when I'm working, they ask if I want to apply."

Tom frowned. "But aren't you in uniform?"

Bri nodded. "Apparently, they think I wear a white shirt and bow tie every day."

"It wouldn't be the worst look on you," Palmer said with a smile.

"Cool," Wyatt said. "As long as I can get a discount, I'm happy."

"Or, um, I could see if the museum is hiring," Toby said, clearly trying to figure out what it was she normally did with her hands. "And then we could hang out." She seemed to regret saying this almost immediately and looked down at the ground, her cheeks turning the same color as her Solo cup.

"Sure," Wyatt said with a shrug. "I'm up for anything." He took a sip of his beer, then turned to Tom. "You doing the theater thing again?"

"Yep," Palmer said proudly. "He's got the male lead."

"That's awesome, brother," Wyatt said, hitting Tom on the back.

"Yeah," Tom said, wincing and moving a little farther away from him. "Um, thanks."

I felt my phone buzzing in my bag and pulled it out, squinting at the screen. My immediate thought was that it was Peter, before I realized that there was nothing for Peter to contact me about any longer. I didn't recognize the number—it came up as being from Colorado. I remembered the plates on Clark's SUV and realized that over the course of the night, I'd never actually gotten around to finding out why he had them. But could he really be calling me? Calling to . . . what, exactly? I switched my ringer to silent, dropped my phone in my dress pocket, and leaned forward to pretend to listen to Tom, while my gaze roamed around the Orchard. There was a kind of cute guy in a baseball cap by the keg . . . and a decent one sitting one picnic table away. . . .

I felt my phone buzz again and saw I had a voice mail from the same Colorado number, as well as two missed calls that must have come through when I was in the dead zone by the Orchard entrance. Suddenly worried that something was actually wrong, I slid off the table, took a few steps away, and pressed the number to call it back. It rang only once before it was answered, the person on the other end sounding out of breath.

"Hello?"

"Hi," I said. "Um, I got a call from this number?" I was ninety percent sure it was Clark, but that didn't mean I had to necessarily let *him* know that I knew that.

"Andie? I'm sorry to call like this—it's Clark McCallister."

"Hi, Clark," I said, still not sure why this was happening. Why was he calling me? And how, exactly, had he gotten my number?

Clark? Palmer mouthed at me, looking incredibly excited. I nodded, then took a step farther away so I wouldn't have to have this conversation with my friends all looking back at me, listening to every word.

"Yeah," he said, and I could hear his voice was high and stressed, much more raw than usual. "I'm so sorry to call you—I just . . . I can't get ahold of Maya, and I had your number from her. . . ."

"It's okay," I said, realizing that this had something to do with the dog and wondering a moment later why I was feeling disappointed. "What's going on?"

"It's Bertie," Clark said, and when he said the dog's name, I could hear something else in his voice—fear. "I . . . He ate something, and I'm not sure what to do. I'm trying to call his vet, but . . ."

"Okay," I said, trying to sound like I had any idea at all what to do. "It'll be okay. I . . . um . . . Did you google the symptoms?" I glanced back to see Palmer looking confused, Toby and Bri not paying attention, and Wyatt looking amused by all of this.

"Must have been a *pretty* good date," he said, arching an eyebrow at me as I turned away from him and walked a few more steps away.

"Yeah," Clark said, and the tone in his voice made my stomach drop. This was, I realized from that one word, serious. "I don't think it's good. Would you—could you come by and see if you can help? I'm sorry to ask. I just . . . He's not doing too great."

"Of course," I said, and even as I said it, a piece of me was wondering what the hell I was doing. But I knew I was going to go. Because it was what Maya, I was pretty sure, would want me to do. And because I knew if I didn't, it would be all I'd think about for the rest of the night. "I'll be there soon."

Chapter SEVEN

Twenty minutes later I pulled into the driveway of Clark's house. There were lights on outside, and most of the lights on the inside of the house seemed to be on as well. It looked somehow more imposing at night, the size of it magnified by the shadows stretching across the front lawn. My friends had seemed very confused about what I was doing, but I hadn't stuck around to explain, just hugged the person nearest to me good-bye (it was Tom; he'd seemed surprised, but pleased) and hurried to my car, then drove a little faster to Clark's than I probably should have.

I knocked twice on the door, but just as a courtesy—with my other hand, I was already pulling my key out of my bag. "Clark?" I called as I let myself in, then headed toward the kitchen.

He stepped into the kitchen doorway before I got there, blocking the light for a moment, then stepping back as I got closer. He was wearing the same clothes from earlier—except now his shirt was wrinkled and his collar askew. His short hair was no longer neatly combed, but looked like he'd been push-ing his hands through it. "Thanks for coming," he said, and it was what I'd heard on the phone, but more amplified, now that

I could see his expression. He was terrified, but trying to hide it, which made whatever this was seem even scarier. "I wouldn't have called—I didn't know what else to do."

"It's okay," I said, following behind him into the kitchen. For a second I had a flash of us, not that long ago, me following behind him through the restaurant as the hostess led us to our table. And now here we were, both in the same clothes, which now seemed somehow disappointed, like the hopes we'd had when we'd gotten dressed had come to nothing. "What's going on?" Just as the words were out of my mouth, the smell hit me, and I stopped short. I'd been picking up after dogs for a week now, so I wasn't squeamish, but this was something else.

"Sorry," Clark said, wincing, as I tried not to breathe in through my nose. "I've been trying to clean up, but he just keeps going."

"Where's Bertie?" I asked, looking around, noticing as I did paper towels covering up various puddles on the kitchen floor. I didn't know exactly what they were and wasn't sure I wanted to know.

"I think he went to the laundry room," Clark said. "That's where his bed is. I've been trying to research what to do online, since I couldn't get his vet on the phone—"

"What happened?" I asked, and Clark pointed to a box on the counter—the box of chocolates he'd offered to me only a few hours ago, when I'd picked the hazelnut and seriously regretted it. It had been full then—I was pretty sure there was even a second layer underneath the first one. The box wasn't full any longer. It was ripped apart, chewed along one edge, and all that seemed to be left in the box were scraps of the black paper wrappings the chocolate had been in.

"I thought I had it back far enough on the counter," Clark said. "But I got home from the, uh . . ." He looked up at me for a second, then at the kitchen counter. "From dropping you off," he said after a tiny pause, "and it was like this."

"He ate them all?" I asked, feeling my stomach sink. I was in no way a dog expert, but I'd watched enough *Psychic Vet Tech* to know that chocolate was terrible for dogs. As in, it sometimes killed them.

"Well, he's thrown up a lot of them by now."

I realized that probably explained the puddles—not to mention the smell. "This isn't good," I said. I was feeling totally out of my depth here, and like there should be someone else—Maya, a vet, an adult—telling us what we should be doing. "Are . . . ? Should we call your parents?"

"We can," Clark said. "But they live in Colorado. And they're really more cat people."

Just like that, I remembered what he'd said to me in the foyer—Bertie wasn't his dog, and this wasn't really his house. I'd been so fixated on keeping the dinner conversation going, I hadn't followed up on any of it.

"It's my publisher's house," he explained, gesturing around him. "She and her husband are getting divorced, and it was going to be sitting empty for the summer, so she offered it to me. Also, I think she wanted someone to watch the dog. Though if she'd known this was going to happen . . ." Clark's mouth twisted in a grimace, and he looked down at the ground.

"Right," I said, trying to get my bearings. This did explain why Clark hadn't seemed to know how to walk a dog when we'd met. "Um . . ." I heard a faint whimpering sound, and

Clark started moving toward it. I followed him to a room off the kitchen I'd never noticed before. It was small and carpeted, with one wall of cabinets—presumably, the washer and dryer were behind them. A huge round dog bed, with a paw-print design and BERTIE monogrammed on it, was in the center of the room, and there were toys scattered all around. But my eye immediately went to the corner, where Bertie was curled in a tight ball, whimpering.

"Oh my god," I said as I crossed over to him. Somehow, the fact that he had taken himself to the corner, that he wasn't on his soft bed, made this that much more worrisome. "Hey, buddy, it's okay," I murmured, running my hand over his white fur, which felt damp, the fluff turned into curls. He was shaking under my touch, violently, almost more like spasms. "You're okay." Bertie stopped shaking for a moment and looked up at me with his dark eyes. His white eyelashes were stuck together in triangles, and the look he gave me was so trusting—so helpless—that I felt something inside me quake. This dog was in serious pain and needed actual help. And what he had was me and Clark.

"He was running around when I got back," Clark said, and I looked over to see him crouched down next to me, tentatively patting Bertie's leg. "I thought he was just happy to see me—he sometimes does that if you leave the room and come back into it. But then it didn't stop. And that's when I saw the chocolate box."

"And you called his vet?" I asked, feeling like we'd very quickly reached the end of what I knew to do with sick dogs.

Clark nodded and handed me his phone—on it, I could see an instruction list, with a vet's name and number. "I called," he said. "But the office is closed, and there wasn't an answering service. I was about to look up emergency vets when you got here."

"And you called Maya?"

Bertie closed his eyes tightly as another spasm shook him. He was making a soft whimpering sound that was breaking my heart.

Clark nodded. "I left a message for Dave, too," he said, spreading his hands helplessly. "But . . ."

"Okay," I said, nodding like I knew what to do. "Okay." I looked down at the dog, wishing I knew more about this. If this were a person, I would have known how to take their vitals and would have felt like I had some idea of how to proceed. But I had no idea how to begin to help a dog. I put both hands on Bertie, smoothing his ears down, wondering if they were always so hot, or if this had to do with the chocolate. "Okay," I said again, aware that just saying the word did not actually accomplish anything, but not sure that I was going to be able to stop doing it.

I pulled out my phone and dialed Bri, since she was the only one I knew with a pet. "Andie?" she said, sounding confused. "You okay?"

"What's your vet's name?" I practically yelled at her. "I mean, sorry," I said after a second. "Just have an emergency here. Where does Miss Cupcakes go?"

"Um . . . I think it's called the Animal Barn," she said. "Or something like that? Want me to call my mom?"

"It's okay." I noticed Clark was already typing on his phone. "Gotta go. Call you later." I hung up, knowing I could explain when we were out of the woods. "Call them," I said to Clark, pulling up the search engine on my own phone, "and if they don't have an emergency vet on call, we'll look one up."

Clark nodded as he held his phone to his ear. I looked around the room, then pulled open the nearest cabinet to me. This seemed to have mostly dog stuff in it, bigger stuff than what was in his cabinet in the kitchen, like blankets and towels. I pulled out a monogrammed blanket and wrapped it around the dog, who was still shivering and shaking. I had no idea if this was going to help or not, but it's what I would have done for a human who was shaking, so I figured it couldn't hurt. "You're going to be okay," I murmured, though even as I spoke, I wasn't sure if I was talking to the dog or to myself.

"Okay, it's ringing," Clark said as he put the phone on speaker and placed it on the carpet between us.

"Animal Barn Emergency," a man said in a clipped, no-nonsense tone.

"Hi," Clark and I both said at the same time. We looked up at each other over the phone and he gestured to me. "Hi," I said again. "So we have an emergency with a dog. He's a . . ." I paused, looking at the dog, realizing I wasn't entirely sure what kind of dog Bertie was.

"Great Pyrenees," Clark chimed in, leaning closer to the phone.

"Right," I said, "and he ate some chocolate, and now he's shaking all over. He doesn't seem like he's doing too well."

"I'm going to transfer you to poison control," the voice said. "They can get more information from you and find out if you need to bring the dog in."

"Thanks—" I started, but the call had already been transferred, and a moment later, Muzak started playing. I looked up, then drew back slightly. We'd both been leaning over the phone, and I hadn't realized quite how close together our heads were.

"They have poison control for animals?" Clark asked as he gently patted Bertie's leg again.

"I guess so," I said, not wanting Clark to know how far out of my depth I was here. I looked over at Bertie as an instrumental version of the Piña Colada song began to play. His eyes were still tightly closed, but he seemed to be shaking less, which I assumed was a good sign. Unless it was a bad one. I ran my hand over the dog's head. But it wasn't like we could even ask Bertie where he was hurting, what he was feeling. How did vets *do* this?

"Hello?" A gentler-sounding woman came on the line, and Clark and I both leaned forward at the same time, coming within a centimeter of bumping our heads together.

"Hi," I said, then took a breath and started to run through what had happened so far. The woman at the poison control center—Ashley—walked us through a series of questions. She seemed to be trying to figure out exactly how much chocolate Bertie had eaten and what kind. Clark ran to the kitchen to get what was left of the box as I tried to describe the chocolate to her.

"It was dark chocolate," I said, but even as I said this, I wondered if it was right. Had it been milk chocolate? I had been so focused on not tasting the hazelnut, I wasn't entirely sure. "I think."

"Milk or white would have been better," she said. "But you'd have real trouble if it were baking chocolate. That's the most dangerous. Dogs can't process caffeine or theobromine like we can. I get this call a few times a week. Their systems just overload."

"Okay," Clark said, running back into the room, holding the pieces of the box in his hands. "It was . . . ten ounces. Dark chocolate."

"And he ate all of it?" Ashley asked, her voice getting sharper.

"All but a few pieces," Clark said, meeting my eye. "What does that mean?"

There was a tiny pause, and Ashley said, "I think you'll be okay. But you're going to need to get this out of his system. You're going to need to get him to throw up—"

"Oh, he's been doing quite a lot of that," Clark said.

"That's a good thing," Ashley said. "He's basically been poisoned, and he needs to clear it out."

"So we don't need to take him to a vet?" I asked, surprised. I'd assumed that the professionals were going to take over at some point. I hadn't thought this was going to be left to us.

"You're going to need to monitor him for the rest of the night," she said. "If he starts seizing, you'll have to bring him to a vet immediately. But otherwise, based on his weight, I don't think he ate enough for this to be truly life-threatening."

"Oh, thank god," Clark murmured, sitting back and running a hand over his face.

"But you need to to get him to drink fluids so he doesn't become dehydrated," she said. "And keep watch on him tonight. If the shaking gets worse, bring him in."

"Got it," I said, looking over at Bertie. "Thank you."

"Thanks a lot," Clark said, leaning forward slightly to reach the phone. Ashley said good-bye, and a moment later, hung up. And then it was just me and Clark and the sudden silence that filled the room now that Ashley was no longer telling us what to do. "So," Clark said, looking at the dog, then back at me. "Now what?"

Since it seemed like Bertie wanted to be in the laundry room, we got settled in there. Clark went to clean up the kitchen, and though I offered to help, I was secretly glad when he insisted on doing it himself. Not only was I not thrilled with the idea of cleaning up the mess in the kitchen, but after talking to Ashley, I really didn't want to leave Bertie alone. While on one hand I was relieved that he didn't seem to be in any serious, immediate danger, the fact that he had come so close to it was terrifying. As was the fact that Clark and I were the ones responsible for making sure he stayed out of it.

Bertie tried to kick the blanket off, and I took it off of him, running my hand over his back. I set it down just to the side of him, in case we needed to have it on hand. I was about to call to Clark, to see if he could bring out Bertie's water dish, when my phone rang.

The caller ID read MAYA, and I picked up immediately. "Hi," I said, beyond relieved to hear from her. Maybe she and Dave were on their way over, and they could take over the dog night watch. I knew neither of them were vets, but they had way more experience with dogs than Clark and I had combined.

"Hi!" Maya said, and I could hear she sounded like she did when she was trying to wrangle her pack of dogs away from an aggressive barker—stressed, but trying to hide it with cheerfulness. "I'm so glad you picked up. I just heard from Clark. It sounds like he's having a problem with Bertie—"

"Yeah," I said, cutting her off before she could tell me what I already knew. "He called me. I'm over there now."

"Thank goodness."

"Told you," I heard another voice say—after a moment I realized it was Dave. I'd only met him once, when I had gone to their tiny office to drop off my tax and payroll forms. I'd expected the male version of Maya—tattoos, cheerfulness, dyed hair—and had met someone who looked like he could have been an investment banker, except for the spare leashes clipped to his belt with a carabiner. "I knew Andie would have this under control. Hi, Andie."

"Hi, Dave," I said, realizing that I must be on speaker in a car—I could hear both of them clearly, as well as the occasional car horn passing by.

"What's the situation?" Maya asked.

I took a breath and filled them in, ending with what Ashley had told us—that someone needed to sit up with Bertie all night. "So . . . ," I said when I'd finished, waiting for either one of them to jump in and tell me they were on their way, that I could go home.

"Here's the thing," Maya said. "We're up in New Hampshire, visiting Dave's mother, who hates me—"

"She doesn't *hate* you," Dave interrupted, and I could hear a sigh somewhere in his voice, like they'd had this discussion a few times before. "She just doesn't understand the tattoos. I did suggest that maybe you could have worn a cardigan."

"Anyway," Maya went on, more loudly than before, "we weren't planning to leave until tomorrow. And even if we left now—"

"Which would *really* not go over well," Dave muttered.

"We couldn't get there for four hours. So . . ." Now it was Maya's turn to trail off, and I had a feeling I knew exactly what she was asking.

"I can stay," I said, after only the slightest hesitation. I knew I wouldn't be able to leave Clark alone with Bertie without worrying the whole time that something had happened to him. And if Maya and Dave weren't going to be here, I seemed to be the only option.

"Oh, thank you," Maya said, relieved. "Andie, you're the best. I'll make sure you get overtime for this."

"It's okay," I said, glancing over at the dog and rubbing his ears. I could sit here tonight with Bertie. It wouldn't be that bad.

"And you and Clark get along, right?" Maya said, not really asking it like a question. "So you guys will be okay."

"Well . . . ," I started, then realized that Maya and Dave (and whoever else might be in the car with them) didn't really need to know that we'd just had a disastrous date. "Sure," I finally said. "It's fine."

"And I'll keep my cell on all night," she said. "So call anytime. Even if it's four a.m."

"Wait, what?" I heard Dave ask sharply.

"Are you walking anyone tomorrow?" Maya continued over him.

"Just one walk. Clyde, Sheriff, and Coco."

"I'll get it covered for you so you can sleep," Maya said. "And thank you again. Call if there's a problem!"

"I will," I said, as Dave and Maya both shouted good-byes over increasing static. "Bye," I replied, but I wasn't sure they could still hear me, and a moment later I heard the dial tone in my ear.

"Hey." I looked up to see Clark standing in the doorway, wearing khaki shorts and a dark-red T-shirt. His hair looked wet and I could see comb tracks through it. "Sorry that took so long," he said, as he crossed the room toward us. "I was pretty disgusting after cleaning up, so I took a quick shower."

I nodded, trying not to get distracted by the way he smelled—like some combination of Ivory soap, fresh towels, and mint gum. Clark, in his more casual clothes, was making me all that much more aware that I was still in the dress, now ridiculously creased, that I'd worn for our date. "So Dave and Maya called," I said, making myself look away from him. I tried to focus on the dog—his eyes were still closed, and he was breathing heavily. "They're in New Hampshire, but they said to call if we need help."

"Oh," Clark said, his face falling. He adjusted his glasses. "So . . . okay." He looked down at Bertie and twisted his hands together, and I could see how scared he was at the thought of staying here alone with him.

"But I can stay," I said, making my voice light and easy, like this was no big deal. "You know, so we can take shifts."

Relief passed over Clark's face immediately, before it was replaced by something closer to worry. "Are you sure?" he asked. "I hate to ask you to do that."

"You didn't," I said. "I offered." A moment later, though, I suddenly worried that he didn't want me there. It would make sense—who wants to keep hanging out with someone they had a bad date with, *especially* when there's no possibility of kissing at the end of it? "But if you don't want me to," I started haltingly, "I mean—"

"No, no," Clark said, so quickly that I knew he wanted me to stay. Probably his panic at being left alone with Bertie was overriding any awkwardness about spending more time with me. "It would be great if you could stay. I mean, if you don't mind."

"Not at all." Even as I said it, I was wondering what I was doing. I pushed myself to standing carefully, pulling my dress down. "I'm just going to get his water dish."

"Great," Clark said, nodding, then looking at the dog. "I'll keep an eye on him."

I headed toward the kitchen, unlocking my phone as I walked. I started to compose a text to my dad, letting him know what was happening—*I had a work emergency. Sick dog needs to be watched over tonight. Will be home in a.m.*—when my phone beeped with an incoming text.

BRI

Andie, you okay? Why did you need a vet? What's happening? We're about to take off here—should we wait?

PALMER

Where even are you? We thought you'd be back by now.

ME

Dog sickness emergency.
So I'm at Clark's—definitely not coming back tonight

TOBY

THE UNEXPECTED EVERYTHING

PALMER

I'm sorry, Toby—what was that?

TOBY

 !!

BRI

Yeah, I'm not sure I entirely understood what you were trying to convey there.

TOBY

I shook my head as I looked at the texts, wondering if Toby was, like me, becoming aware of how hard this was going to be to keep up all summer.

ME

Guys, stop messing with her.
Gotta go—I'll text tomorrow!

PALMER

Send updates!

BRI

Seconded

TOBY

Morgan Matson

Didn't quite get your meaning there, T.

I smiled as I dropped my phone back in my pocket, knowing this might go on for a while. I picked up Bertie's water dish, filled it with fresh water, and then dropped in a few ice cubes, in case that made it more appealing.

Then, carrying it carefully, I walked back to the laundry room. Clark was sitting cross-legged next to Bertie, patting his head every few seconds. "Any change?" I asked as I set the water bowl down in front of the dog. Bertie raised his head slightly, glanced at the water, then closed his eyes again.

Clark shook his head. "The same," he said. "But he's not shaking anymore, so that's a good sign, I think."

I nodded as I sat down on Bertie's other side, tucking my legs beneath me and smoothing my dress down. I met Clark's eye over Bertie's head, and then we both looked away again. I told myself firmly that it would be fine as I ran my hand over the hair on the dog's back. We could just watch the dog. It wasn't like we had to talk or anything.

It turns out there's only so long you can sit in silence and stare at a sick dog. And that amount of time is apparently twenty minutes. "So," I said, when I absolutely, positively couldn't stand the silence for a moment longer. "You're from Colorado?"

Clark looked at me over Bertie and gave me a half smile, the kind you give when you're being polite, not because you're happy about something. I looked in vain for the dimples, but it seemed they only emerged for the real thing. "I am," he said. He didn't say anything else, and as silence fell again, I took a breath to ask a follow-up. I really didn't even care what it was. I'd see who could recite all the state capitals faster. I just couldn't take the quiet anymore. But before I could say anything, Clark went on. "I was born in Steamboat Springs, but when I was eleven, we moved way out to the country, almost to the Wyoming border."

"That must have been cool," I said. I was pretty sure I'd been to Colorado once—I had vague recollections of a white-water rafting trip from when I was little—but when I thought of the state, it was vague images culled from movies and magazines, of endless blue skies, snow-capped mountains, fields of green.

Clark shrugged as he ran his hand over Bertie's head. "In some ways," he said after a moment. He looked up at me and smiled quickly, a more genuine smile this time. "I got to run around in the woods a lot. That was pretty great, because that's basically all you want to do when you're eleven." I must have looked skeptical at that, because Clark's smile widened. "Well, if you're me. But it also got a little lonely. My sister was the only other kid for fifty miles."

"Is that . . . ," I started, remembering something he'd said in the foyer, which now seemed like a million years ago and not earlier that night. "When you were homeschooled?"

"Yep," he said. "Sixth grade onward." I nodded, trying to get my head around that. I couldn't imagine life without school—without my friends, without teachers, without all the daily drama that went along with it. "It really wasn't so bad," he said with a laugh, and I realized, startled, that he'd been able to see what I was thinking. "I got to read a lot. And I was basically done with high school by the time I was fourteen."

"But . . ." I started to ask why anyone would want to do that, then paused when I realized I didn't know the polite way to ask this question. "I mean, was there a reason you guys moved?"

Clark nodded. "My dad wanted some peace and quiet," he said. "He wanted a place where he could focus on his work, uninterrupted."

"What does he do?"

Clark's smile faltered a little. "He's an accountant," he said. He looked down at Bertie and patted his head. "An accountant who wanted to be a novelist." There was something in his voice that I recognized—a way of letting me know I was getting close to something tender, something he didn't want to talk about. I was a little surprised—he hadn't seemed to understand this when I'd tried to give him the same sign at the restaurant, and he was the one who'd been disappointed we hadn't talked about things that were *real*. But I looked a little closer and saw the tightness in his smile, the way his forehead was creasing, and realized that everyone, no matter what they might want to think, has things they don't want to talk about. So I nodded and let silence fall again. But it no longer felt oppressive and horrible, like it had before. Now it felt like a pause in a longer conversation.

"Did you ever have a dog?" Clark asked me after a few minutes of watching Bertie, both of us jumping at the slightest of movements. He seemed to be okay, as far as I could tell. He wasn't drinking his water, but he also wasn't moaning in pain or shaking violently. "Or . . . do you?"

I shook my head. "No on both counts." I reached forward and scratched Bertie's ears, and his tail gave a small, weak *thump*.

"I always wanted one when I was little, but . . ." I stopped short. Even though this was just a small, simple fact, the act of saying it somehow felt scary, like I was dipping a toe into a pond I wasn't really sure I wanted to go into. "My mom was allergic," I said, all at once, like I was ripping off a Band-Aid.

Clark nodded, and I held my breath, wondering if he was going to ask a follow-up question, willing him to somehow know not to. "My parents are cat people," he said, looking back down at the dog again as I let out my breath. "We always had at least three. And for some reason, they always seem to hate me."

"That's like my friend Bri's cat," I said, shaking my head. "In fact, the last time I slept over at her house . . ." I paused and looked over at Clark, wondering if I should go on. After all, maybe he'd just been making idle conversation, not wanting to share stories. Maybe he didn't really want to hear about the unspeakable things Miss Cupcakes had done to my pillow. But he was looking at me, expectant, waiting. So I took a breath and told him the story.

"Okay, here's what it says," Clark said as he came back into the laundry room, carrying a thin silver laptop, his face lit with the glow from the screen. We'd spent the last fifteen minutes trying to get Bertie to drink, without success, and I was getting increasingly worried that he was going to get dehydrated. I saw that there was something on the front of Clark's laptop—some kind of sticker—but before I could get a closer look, he was sitting next to me and holding the laptop out so that it was between us. "They say you can put fruit in the water, or ice cubes. . . ."

"Tried that," I said, looking down at the bowl, where the ice cubes I'd put in there had long since melted.

"Or chicken broth works too," he said, scrolling down the page. He looked at me and adjusted his glasses. "I know there's no fruit in the kitchen, because I'm the one who buys the groceries."

"Chicken soup?" I asked, looking over at the dog, who seemed to be moving his head as far away from the bowl as possible.

"Maybe." Clark shut the laptop, then pulled it toward him before I could get a look at the sticker. "Want to check?"

We walked into the kitchen—after setting up a video call between our phones and placing one in front of Bertie, so that we could see if there was any change in him—and I was relieved to see that, in addition to it being cleaner, the smell from before was almost totally gone. The windows were open, and I could hear the sound of wind and cicadas through them. Clark went around opening up cabinets and peering inside, and I pulled open the fridge, for no reason other than because I was curious what was in there. I realized I wasn't that surprised by the boy-bought groceries as I looked in—there was a take-out pizza box, a pack of cold cuts, and a bottle of ketchup. And that was about it, except for a six-pack of Coke.

"Feel free to take anything," Clark said over his shoulder as he opened up a cabinet. "I know there's not much in there."

"You shouldn't have gone to Alberto's," I said, closing the fridge door. "Captain Pizza is *way* better."

"Good to know." Clark nodded. "I think I just called the first place that came up."

"Any soup?"

"Chicken rice." He held up a can. "Think that'll work?"

"Probably." I figured that if the dog had already ingested enough chocolate to make him sick, he probably wasn't going to be super picky about his soup flavors.

"Okay." Clark put his laptop on the counter and bent down to open up a cabinet underneath the sink. "So if you were a can opener, where would you be?"

I was only half listening, though. I was looking at the sticker on his laptop. It was one of those thin decals that stick right on, so you can still see the silver underneath. I'd seen them before, of course—Tom had a Kermit the Frog on his laptop, and Bri's younger sister Sonia had *The Giving Tree*—but I'd never seen this one before. It took me a moment to even figure out what I was seeing. There was what looked like a castle on a hill, with a very tall spire. Birds circled around the tower, the biggest ones at the corners of the laptop, then getting smaller as they got closer to it. Leaning out one window was a girl with a long braid. She was reaching her hand out to a bird, who was aiming for her, claws extended. I just stared at it, trying to figure out if I was missing something here.

"Andie?" My head snapped up, and I could see Clark looking at me, an open can of soup in his hand—clearly, at some point, he'd located a can opener.

"Yeah." I blinked at him. It was clear he'd asked me a question, one that I hadn't heard at all. "Um, what was that?"

"I was asking if you think we should heat this up," he said. "I don't know—do dogs ever eat hot food?"

"Well . . ." I stalled, not entirely sure myself. "Maybe just warm it." Clark nodded and stepped behind me to open a cabinet and pull down a bowl—all the dishes I saw inside it before the door shut again seemed to be white. "So . . . what is this?" I asked, nodding down at the laptop as Clark poured the soup into a bowl and headed for the microwave.

"My laptop?" he asked, sounding distracted as he punched the buttons, and with a *beep*, the microwave lit up and the bowl started turning around.

"The sticker." I looked down at it again, hoping it wasn't something totally obvious that I was failing to get.

"Oh," he said, just as the microwave beeped again. He pulled out the bowl of soup and brought it quickly over to the counter, dropping it rather than putting it down. "Hot," he said, shaking out his hands. "We might need to wait a sec before giving it to Bert." He ran his hand over the sticker quickly, a small smile appearing on his face. "It's . . . A reader of mine makes them. He sent one to me, and I liked it, so I stuck it on. I guess I was hoping it would give me some inspiration, or something."

I nodded, like this was normal, to hear someone my age talking about their *readers*. "So what is it?"

"Oh," Clark said, and adjusted his glasses quickly. He tilted his head slightly to the side, like he was trying to figure something out. "You're not . . . I assume you haven't read them."

I shook my head. "I don't really read, you know, books." Clark's eyebrows flew up, and it was like he took a step back from me, even though I was pretty sure his feet didn't actually move. "I know how to *read*," I said, seeing the alarm in his expression. "I just don't love fiction. You know, novels."

"If you don't love fiction novels," Clark said, and even

though I tried to fight it, I could feel a smile tugging at the corners of my mouth, "what do you read?" He shook his head, and it was like I could practically feel how baffled he was. "Wait, I'm sorry, but how do you not read books? Like—what do you do on planes?"

"I study," I said with a shrug. "Or watch movies."

Clark blinked at me. "I just . . . I've never met anyone who didn't read before," he said.

"Okay," I said, starting to get annoyed. "I *read*. I have a 4.0." He was still just staring at me, so I explained. "That's a thing we have in high schools with more than two people. It's called a grade point average. . . ."

"Touché," Clark said, and though he still looked rattled, he was smiling. "Okay. So if you haven't read my books . . . or, um, any books . . ." I rolled my eyes at that, even as I was trying not to smile. "It's showing the main character from the first two books, Tamsin. And these are the crows of Castleroy."

"Oh," I said, nodding, like that had explained anything. I looked down at it for a moment, wondering what that must be like—to create something that someone liked so much, they made laptop stickers for you.

Clark dipped a finger into the soup and nodded at me as he tasted it. "It's cool enough, I think." Then he made a face. "And not really very good."

"Does it need some Carolina Reapers?" I asked, surprising myself—and Clark, too, judging by the expression on his face.

"Couldn't hurt," he said, as I grabbed my phone and he led the way back into the laundry room.

Five minutes later I looked up at Clark over Bertie's head.

Morgan Matson

"I think it's working," I said in a half whisper, like the dog could understand me.

Clark met my eye and nodded, and then I looked back at the dog. When we'd put the soup in front of him, he had opened one eye and sniffed toward it, but then had closed his eyes and put his head down again, which had made me get really, really scared. Bertie always lunged for his food bowl when I brought him home. To see him ignoring food was pretty much the only indication I needed of how sick this dog was. Fear was making my stomach clench as I realized we really might need to bring him to the emergency vet. But before I could say anything, Clark, to my surprise, had stroked Bertie's head while moving the bowl closer, so that it was right under his nose. "Hey, bud," he said softly. "Look, it's people food."

There was a pause, in which I held my breath, worried that this was the turn that the poison control lady had warned us about. But then Bertie raised his head slightly, nose twitching. He sniffed at the soup for a few more seconds before starting to eat—cautiously at first, but then with more appetite, and I finally let myself breathe again.

"I think you're right," Clark said, as Bertie finished the bowl, nudging it around with his nose, trying to get more. "Should I heat up the rest?"

"Maybe give it a second." Bertie looked up at me, and I reached forward to scratch his ears. "You did so good," I said, leaning closer to him. "Good—"

But I didn't get to finish that thought, because right then Bertie opened his mouth and threw up chicken soup—and chocolate—all over me.

• • •

"Okay," Clark said, arriving in the doorway of the laundry room, breathing hard. "So I think you're all set. You're—" He pointed behind him, leaning slightly on the doorframe for support while he caught his breath. "Sorry." He shook his head. "I was trying to hurry."

"It's appreciated." I was trying my best not to inhale. Bertie, after tossing his cookies all over me, had gone back to sleep, while I'd frozen, not wanting to move, or breathe. Clark had scrambled to his feet and gotten me a towel, but it soon become clear that the towel could only do so much and that I really needed to change—and probably needed to shower, since my hair had not been spared. I'd told Clark this, and only after I'd said it did I wonder if this was weird—to ask to shower at a guy's house. But then I figured we'd gone so far beyond anything normal tonight that I no longer cared. And more than worrying if it was weird, I needed to not be covered in dog puke. Clark had gone off to get me a change of clothes, and I'd looked at the sleeping dog, wondering just how much Maya's overtime was going to be and if it would come close to making up for this.

"So my room's down the hall," he said, pointing. "Second door on the left. There's a bathroom in there, and I put out a fresh towel and a change of clothes."

"Oh," I said. Somehow I'd figured that in a house this big, he'd direct me to a guest bathroom somewhere. I hadn't thought I'd be in Clark's *room*. Not that it mattered. It didn't mean anything, after all—I was only doing this because I had to. I got up, trying very hard not to look at what had happened to one of my favorite dresses. I would see if I could work a laundry miracle

Morgan Matson

tomorrow when I got home. "Great. I'll, um, be right back."

I walked down the hall as fast as I could, careful not to touch anything on my way. Even the wallpaper looked expensive, subtly patterned and edged in what looked like gold. I tried to casually glance into the other rooms I passed as I walked, but the doors were firmly closed, and I knew this was not the time to go snooping around.

I found Clark's room right away—it was the only door that was open, light spilling out from it into the darker hallway—and stepped inside, pulling the door closed behind me. I knew this wasn't really Clark's room, just the room he was staying in for the summer, but even so, the genericness of it took me by surprise. This seemed like it was probably normally a guest room, since there were almost no personal touches—just a queen-size bed with a cream coverlet, a gray couch in the corner, and a desk tucked under an eave. I started to let my eyes roam around the room, but looked down, remembered the situation at hand, and made a beeline for the bathroom.

Ten minutes later I'd washed my hair and was confident I no longer smelled like horrible things. I wrapped myself in the towel Clark had left out for me, neatly folded, and walked out to his room. I'd balled up my dress and stuffed it into a plastic bag I'd found underneath the sink, trying not to think about the fact that I'd been worried, a few hours earlier, that it had gotten wrinkled on the drive to the restaurant.

I saw that, at the foot of the bed, there were a pair of sweatpants and a T-shirt laid out. The sweatpants were gray and fit well enough, thanks to the drawstring waist. The T-shirt was a dark blue, and across the front, in typewriter font, it read ASK ME

ABOUT THE LUMINOSITY. I just looked at it for a moment, then gave up trying to figure it out and pulled it on.

I knew I should probably head right back out to help with Bertie, but I'd taken a quick shower, and I figured I probably had a few minutes' cover before my absence seemed suspicious. I told myself I wasn't going to snoop, or look through anything—I had a deep aversion to that, ever since I had returned from the bathroom during an interview two years ago to see the reporter poking through my bag—but I told myself it couldn't hurt to just look around.

It didn't take me long to realize that this was different from the guys' rooms I'd been in before. Usually, there was a lumpy, hastily made bed, a pile of stuff in the corner, and clothes tossed around. Even Topher, who was pretty neat, had a room that was just a little in disarray, like he was always kicking off his shoes and tossing off his jacket, leaving someone else to deal with them.

Clark's room wasn't like that. There was a neat stack of books on the desk—a few thick fantasy books, but most of them seemed to be nonfiction, with titles like *Breaking the Block*, *Jump-Start Your Imagination*, *Moving Beyond Writer's Block*, and *Resisting Resistance*. I glanced away from them quickly, feeling like I'd seen something that I probably shouldn't have seen.

Through the open closet door, I could see three shirts hung up, and on top of the dresser, a neatly folded pile of laundry, tilting slightly to the right. The only thing that was slightly messy were two button-down shirts that were laid out on top of the dresser. I couldn't help but wonder if Clark, like me, had gone through several outfits, trying to find the right one for our date.

I turned away, ready to leave his room. I really didn't want to be in there any longer. It wasn't that I felt like I was invading his privacy—it felt like the opposite, like it was invading in on me, showing me a side of Clark that I felt like I shouldn't be seeing, not yet—or maybe never. I never really wanted to know these things about the guys I'd dated—their fears and insecurities. I didn't want to know that Clark had spent time worrying and getting ready for our date. And I didn't want to ask myself why the sight of his neatly folded T-shirts was making me feel something I didn't even have words to express.

I was almost to the door when something on an end table caught my eye. It was a picture in a small silver frame, showing a little boy, around five or six, sitting on the shoulders of someone who was probably his dad. At first I assumed that it was a picture that belonged to the house, family or friends of the couple in all the pictures downstairs. But as I looked at it for another moment, I realized it was Clark. He looked basically the same, just without the glasses. The man—his dad, I was guessing, based on their resemblance—was looking up at him and smiling, while young Clark, midlaugh, stretched his hands up to the sky like he was trying to touch the stars.

I caught my eyes reflected back to me in the glass and suddenly realized what I was doing. I turned off the light and closed the door firmly behind me as I went. I walked back to the laundry room, tugging at the hem of the shirt, feeling weirdly exposed, even though the sweatpants and T-shirt covered more than my dress had.

"Hey," Clark said, giving me a quick smile. "Are the clothes okay?"

"Fine," I said, nodding, wanting to change the subject. I

tucked my wet hair behind my ears, wondering why it suddenly felt like I had my armor down. That like this—in his clothes, without my makeup and with my hair sopping wet—Clark could see more of me than I wanted him to. "How's he been?" I asked as I looked at the dog, who appeared not to have moved since I'd been gone.

"The same," Clark said, patting his back gently. "I got him to drink a little more but didn't give him any more of the soup. I didn't think we should risk it."

"Probably wise," I said as I crossed over to sit on the other side of Bertie—and then, just to be safe, moved a few inches farther away. "So no change?" I asked, picking up my phone and pulling up the Internet, ready to go over the dangerous symptoms once again.

"Wait . . . ," Clark said, starting to reach toward me, but not before I realized that I had actually picked up his phone—and on his screen, I was looking at the last page he'd had open. I blinked as I stared at it. My dad's official portrait looked back at me from his Wikipedia page. "Sorry," Clark said, and I could hear the embarrassment in his voice.

I nodded. I knew I should give him his phone back, but I kept looking down at the screen, at my dad's factual information. I was there, under the personal-life section—*Daughter Alexandra Molly Walker, 17. Wife Molly Jane Walker (deceased)*. "So did you learn anything?" I asked, looking at the photo at the top of the page. It was the one that always seemed to accompany any article about my dad—though I had a feeling it might soon be replaced by the press conference on our front porch. It was a picture of my dad taken five years ago. He was wearing a dark suit, and the president walked next to him. On his other side was Governor Laughlin. You could see me, a few steps behind him, in a black dress, my hair pulled back with a black velvet headband that had made my head feel like it was on the verge of exploding. I'd never worn it again after that day. The picture had been taken by the press that were waiting on the steps of the church after my mother's funeral, and it had made the front page of the *New York Times* above the fold the next day. It was hailed by pundits and journalists as a seminal moment, a return to decency, people reaching across the aisle even in the middle of a campaign, putting aside differences in times of crisis, etcetera. It was seen by almost everyone as a symbol. And almost nobody who talked about the picture mentioned my mother, except in passing, like her funeral was just the setting for this larger, more important moment.

It was the way her whole funeral had felt—like it actually wasn't about her at all. I watched as her friends and her students looked around at the Secret Service agents, at the *president*, and crumpled up the pieces of paper they'd brought with them, looking doubtful, not wanting to get up and talk about my mom—talk about who she'd really been—in front of the leader of the country. And so there hadn't been any great or silly or funny stories about her. The words that were said could have been said about anyone, and the whole thing felt wrong, like I was letting her down. Like we all were.

"Sorry," Clark said, still sounding embarrassed, and I started to feel bad. I closed out of the screen and handed him his phone back as he slid mine over the carpet toward me. After all, it was public information. If I'd had the time before Bertie had gotten sick, I would have no doubt been googling Clark and his books. "I didn't realize your dad had run for vice president."

"Almost," I corrected, though a lot of people made this mistake. "He had to drop out before it was official." I looked down and traced a circular pattern on the carpet.

"How's he handling all this recent stuff?" Clark asked, and I looked up at him, fixing a smile on my face.

"Oh, just fine," I said immediately, reaching for some of the lines Peter had written for me when everything was starting to fall apart. "Obviously, it's a time of transition, which is always hard, but . . ." I looked at Clark, and it was like I suddenly realized where I was. In a laundry room, with a vomiting dog, wearing someone else's clothes, with a boy who was not, to my knowledge, a member of the media. I could, I realized with what felt like a physical shock, tell him the truth.

It went against everything I'd been told my whole life—sometimes explicitly, but more often not. It was just what I'd learned, before I knew I was learning it. Stay on message. Don't tell people what you really think or feel—unless it's been vetted and approved. Keep people at arm's length and your feelings to yourself. And I'd done it, for years now, until it was second nature. And where had it gotten me?

"Well," I said slowly, feeling like I was going against a lifetime of training, "I'm not sure. It's been . . . weird."

Clark was looking over at me, expectant. I knew other guys would have just nodded, maybe said "bummer," and then we would have moved on—gone back to fooling around, or to safe, easy topics. Topher would have known what I meant and not asked any follow-ups, because none would have been needed.

But it seemed like Clark actually wanted to know—that he was waiting for me to go on.

"He's *home*," I said, shaking my head. "Which he never is. And it's really strange to have him there all the time. And he's not allowed to work, so he's been watching ancient basketball games. . . ." My voice trailed off. I wasn't sure I wanted to tell him about the terrible dinner we'd had and all our awkward silences, which were made that much worse because it was like my dad didn't even notice them. "I think he's waiting for the investigation to clear him, so he can go back to work."

There was a small pause, and Clark nodded, then asked quietly, "And what if he can't? I mean . . . if it doesn't come back in his favor?"

This was the very question I had been trying not to ask myself since it happened. "I'm not sure."

"Well, what did he do before?" Clark asked, then smiled. "I didn't get that far on his Wikipedia page."

"He was a public defender." I could hear the pride in my voice when I said it. I had always liked the idea of it: my dad, helping out the people who couldn't afford their own counsel, righting the wrongs of innocent victims—and a lot of scumbags, too, based on the stories I'd heard. "It was actually how my parents met." I couldn't quite believe I was saying this, but the words were out before I could stop them. The story that the media had was that my parents had met while working together, which was technically true, but without any of the details. "She was putting herself through art school working as a police sketch artist," I said, feeling myself smile even as I had to swallow hard. "And my dad was furious that one of her sketches looked exactly like his client, and they started fighting about it."

Clark leaned forward. "Did the guy do it?"

"Stabby Bob?" I asked, and Clark laughed. "Totally. But it was enough to introduce them." At the farmhouse, a framed sketch of Bob—long white beard, tattoos, a gleam of crazy in his eyes—had hung in the entryway, startling almost everyone who came over. I had no idea where it was now. Like most of my mother's art, it hadn't been hung up in the new place. I assumed he was in storage somewhere, no doubt carefully wrapped, but put away, out of sight.

"That's kind of how my parents met too," Clark said, and I felt my eyebrows raise in surprise. "Well, minus the stabbing guy," he acknowledged. "My dad went to audit a dental practice where my mom was working as a bookkeeper. She'd had the books so organized and could answer every question he threw at her, so he hired her away to work for him."

"So both your parents are accountants?" I asked, and Clark nodded. "That must have been rough."

"Tell me about it," he said, shaking his head. Then he looked at me and gave me a smile, like he'd decided something, before going on. "This one time, I think I was eight, they'd sent me to the store and told me to bring back change. But when I was walking back, I saw a new Batman comic. . . ." As Clark went on, telling his story, I realized that I wasn't trying to stop him, or control the conversation, or keep him from asking me something I didn't want to answer. It was like talking to my friends—and I would just have to see where the conversation took me. And so, surprising myself, I leaned forward to listen.

• • •

"Explain it to me," I said. Now that I was, apparently, spending the night in their house, I thought I needed to know a little more about the people who lived there. "Since you're not Clark Goetz-Hoffman."

Clark winced. "That's a pretty terrible name," he said, and I silently agreed. "My publisher is Goetz. Her soon-to-be ex-husband is Hoffman."

"Got it." I looked at Bertie's water dish, at the B. W. that was painted there. "Then what's the *W* for?"

"Oh," Clark said, giving Bertie a gentle pat. "That's his middle name."

I closed my eyes for a moment. "The dog has a middle name?"

"Bertie Woofter Goetz-Hoffman," Clark said, raising an eyebrow at me, letting me know he thought this was ridiculous too.

"Woofter?"

"Yeah," Clark said with a shrug. "It's from a book they liked. The character is Bertie Wooster . . . so it's like a pun."

"Oh," I said, nodding, remembering the framed book cover I'd seen the first day. "So the dog has four names," I said, still trying to get this to make sense.

Clark gave me a small smile. "I don't get it either."

"So you write books," I said, shaking some Skittles into my hand. I'd found a half-full bag in my purse, and we'd been sharing them. We were both starting to get tired, and I'd decided we needed some sugar. "That's so weird," I said, shaking my head. "I mean, you're my age."

"Just a little older," he said, turning so that he was facing me a little more fully, both of us sitting cross-legged on the carpet.

"I'm nineteen." He held out his hand, and I tipped the Skittles into his palm.

"But still," I said around my candy. "That's weird. You have a *job.*"

"You have a job," he pointed out. "If you didn't, you wouldn't be here right now. You'd be off somewhere not reading."

"But you have a *career,*" I said as Clark gestured to me for more candy. "Isn't that weird?"

Clark laughed. "I guess not to me. I've been doing this for five years now, so publishing books is just . . . what I do." As I watched, his smile faded, the wattage of his dimples dimming slightly. "It's what I did, at any rate."

"So you need to give them your third book?" I asked, and he nodded. "Well, when is it due?"

"Two years ago," Clark said, and I felt my eyes widen. "Yeah. That's pretty much everyone's reaction. There are a lot of people who are really not happy with me at the moment. But it's coming together. I just need to finesse some things, pull some threads together."

I nodded. "Okay." I was still trying to process the *two-year* delay. "So do you have a plan? A schedule worked out for when you're going to turn it in?"

I saw something pass over Clark's face, but before I could really see what he was thinking, it was gone, and Clark was giving me a smile. "It sounds like you're pretty organized."

I nodded, taking that as a compliment, even though he might not have intended it as one. "It's the coin of the realm in my family."

Clark stared at me. "The what?"

I realized a second too late what I'd done. It was an expression my parents always used, and I'd used it enough around my friends that they no longer thought it was strange. But I sometimes forgot that not everyone had heard it before. "Coin of the realm," I repeated. "Something that carries the most value."

"Oh," Clark said, nodding, like he was turning the phrase over in his head. "I like it."

"You still haven't answered the question."

"Busted." Clark paused for a moment, like he was gathering his thoughts, then said, "If it were as easy as just getting organized or sticking to a schedule, I'd have done it years ago. But you can't rush these things, even though I know I'm holding things up. Everyone wants the new book. My publishers keep putting it on the calendar. I'm getting pushback from the people who want another movie. . . . At this point, I don't even think it would matter if it was *good*. As long as there was something they could put out."

"But what's the problem?" I asked, beyond glad that medicine didn't have any of these issues. You didn't take an extra-long time to do a heart bypass, or tell someone you weren't feeling inspired to fix their brain hemorrhage. You did your job, that was all.

"Well . . ." He cleared his throat. "In terms of where I am with the third book . . . It's complicated, because in the last one . . ." He paused and looked at me for a moment before saying, "I wrapped up Tamsin's story at the end. Pretty definitively."

"Oh," I said, then paused. "But wasn't she your main character?"

"Ah," he said, pointing at me. "Now you're beginning to see what the problem is."

"Biggest fear?" I asked around a yawn, leaning back against the wall. Clark had gone and gotten us pillows after the Skittle sugar buzz had worn off and we'd both started to crash. I had a pillow behind my head and one underneath me. We'd tried to get Bertie out to a more comfortable location for us—like one with couches—but he'd just curled more tightly into a ball and made a little moaning sound when we tried to move him, so we decided to leave him where he was. Now that most of the adrenaline and panic had left the situation, I was feeling how late it was. It was starting to feel like two a.m. at a slumber party, when everyone is sleepy and a little bit punchy (and usually hopped up on sugar) and you're too tired to tell anything but the truth—that fuzzy half-awake, honest feeling. It was how we'd found out Bri had kissed her second cousin—by accident, she swore—last summer at a wedding.

"Haunted houses," Clark said around a huge yawn, half-muffled by the hand he raised in front of his mouth.

"Oh," I said, a little surprised. But I supposed it stood to reason that if you wrote fantasy novels, you believed in things like ghosts. "Well, I guess that makes sense."

"Not actual haunted houses," Clark said dismissively. "I don't believe in those. I mean the kind they have at Halloween, that you can walk through and people jump out and scare you."

I just looked at him. "That makes less sense."

"My parents took me to one when I was, like, four. Way too young. It scarred me for life." He shuddered, like he was reliving something, then turned to me. "Yours?"

"Driving the wrong way on a highway on-ramp," I said

immediately. I'd been driving Palmer and Bri home last spring, talking with them and not paying attention, and this had nearly happened. I'd had nightmares about it for weeks.

"That is a very logical fear," Clark said, and I realized that even without looking at him, I could tell he was smiling.

"Thank you." I smiled as well, choosing to take this as a compliment.

"Hey, bud," I said softly to Bertie as I stroked his ears. Clark had gone to turn off the lights and make sure all the doors were locked, and it was just me and the dog. His eyes were closed, but they no longer seemed like they were squeezing tight against the pain. He seemed like he was peaceful, his breathing slow and even, though every time there was a pause in his breath, I would start to panic, fearing the worst, until he'd start again, the sound of his snuffly breathing letting me relax once again. "Hang in there, okay? We need you to pull through." I ran my fingers through his fur and then left them on his back for a moment, letting my hand rise and fall with every breath he took, feeling a little more reassured with every one.

"So how old were you?" I asked, as I adjusted the pillow under my head. I had told Clark that I wasn't going to *sleep*; I just needed to lie down for a little bit. We needed to stay awake in case something changed with Bertie, but that didn't mean I couldn't rest for a little bit. Maybe because of the walls-down, sleepover feeling of it all, I'd started asking the kinds of questions you ask at slumber parties—like how old you were when you had your first kiss.

"Uh," Clark said, and I could hear, even through his fatigue, that he was a little thrown by this. Probably boys didn't have slumber-party questions like this, which was really a loss for them. "Twelve, I think?"

"Whoa. You middle-school stud."

Clark laughed and shook his head. "Not at all. Exactly the opposite, in fact. But when you grow up in the middle of nowhere, you take the opportunities you can—like when family friends with cute daughters show up." He looked at me and slid a little farther down the wall, like my proximity to the floor was pulling him down as well. "You?"

"Um." I was now slightly embarrassed, even though I had asked the question. "I was fourteen." In the silence that followed, I hurried to say, "It wasn't like I didn't have other opportunities." I thought about all the middle-school games of Spin the Bottle and Seven Minutes in Heaven that I'd avoided like the plague. "I wanted my first kiss to mean something."

Clark looked over at me, his eyebrows raised. "Did it?"

"It did," I said, thinking about Topher, in a different laundry room, and everything it had started. It had meant something—I just hadn't fully realized then what that something would be.

"There's this thing in the world of my books," Clark said, and I realized it was getting a little bit more normal to hear him talking like this. The same way it had been strange when Tom had been talking about agents and headshots and casting directors and now it was just something we were all able to ignore.

"What thing?"

"This idea that the person who kisses you first gets, with that kiss, a little piece of your soul. And they have a hold over you.

Morgan Matson

Most people don't ever use it against you. But some people do."

I turned this over in my mind, feeling like maybe I would have to read Clark's books now. "So where'd that come from? Is that what happened with your first-kiss girl?"

"No," Clark said, laughing. "She's fine. We're friends online, and I get to see pictures of most of her meals, even though we haven't spoken in seven years." He turned to look at me. "What about you?" he asked. "Ever think about your guy?"

"Well . . . yeah," I said, realizing I was starting to choose my words carefully again. It was one thing for my friends to know about Topher, but I wasn't about to give out details that could identify him. "He—I mean, we still occasionally . . ." I trailed off, not exactly sure how to put this. "We're kind of off and on."

"Oh," Clark said, and he sounded much more awake now. "Are you now? On, I mean?"

"No," I said quickly, now feeling more awake myself. "Are you? On . . . with anyone?"

"No," Clark said just as quickly, and I felt myself let out a breath. "I was . . . My last girlfriend and I broke up at the end of the semester."

"Semester?"

"Yeah. She was a freshman at Colorado College, and I was living in Colorado Springs, so we started dating. But when school ended for the year, she said she wanted to explore life's possibilities. That's a direct quote, by the way."

I made a face, and Clark laughed. "But I thought you said you lived way out in the woods. Near Wisconsin?"

"Wyoming."

"Right."

"That's where my parents live," Clark said. "It ... I moved out last year and got my own place. It just seemed easier."

I nodded, even though I had a feeling there was a lot to this story that I wasn't getting. I was about to remark about how strange it was that he lived on his own, when I realized that was what he was doing now. And if he'd followed the usual path, he'd be going to college. So maybe it wasn't that weird. But even so, I could feel a slight envious twinge in my stomach, thinking about this college freshman girl who had been Clark's girlfriend, whoever and wherever she was. "And now you're here." I yawned hugely again.

"That I am."

I looked over at him in the moonlight. This should have been strange—sleeping next to a cute guy, with a large dog snoring between us—but for some reason, it really wasn't. Maybe because we were both pretending we weren't really going to sleep. Or maybe I was too tired to feel awkward and had used my embarrassment quotient up with the dog vomit.

"Get some sleep," Clark said, even though he sounded like he was going to drop off at any moment. "I'll stay up and watch Bert."

"No, I can," I said, but even I could hear how unconvincing this was, as my eyelids started to close.

"I've got this," he said. The quiet of the night took over the room, punctuated only by Bertie's breathing and the occasional snore. "Night, Andie."

I opened my eyes and looked over at him to see that he was sitting up like he'd said he would be, watching Bert, albeit while covering his mouth as he yawned. "Hey," I said, and he looked over at me, his expression open, absolutely nothing hiding behind it. He'd looked that way at the restaurant, too, I realized now. I just hadn't let myself see it.

"Hey," he said, a question in his voice.

"I just ...," I started. "You asked me before about my mom." Clark nodded, but I could feel how still he'd gotten otherwise, like he wasn't going to do or say anything to stop me. I took a big, shaky breath and made myself go on. "She died of ovarian cancer five years ago. They thought they got it in time. But they didn't." The words hung between us for a moment, and there were tears somewhere behind my eyes, and I knew when I closed them again, they would slip out, that I would be too tired to fight to keep them back.

"Thank you for telling me," Clark said, his voice quiet. Silence fell again, and I was about to let my eyes close, sleep a bit, when he spoke again. "I ... I actually am not just tinkering with my book," he said slowly, and I could hear the hesitation in his voice—like maybe he hadn't told all that many people this. He took a breath and let it out. "I can't write anymore. I haven't written a single word in the last three years."

"I'm sorry," I said softly, and Clark nodded. A comfortable silence fell between us—like this was just the beginning. Like we'd have a lot more time to talk about this. And with that thought running through my mind, I turned onto my side and let my eyes drift closed.

I jolted awake, looking around the room, momentarily baffled as to where I was. There was faint, early-morning sunlight streaming through the window. After a few seconds I remembered where I was—in the laundry room at Clark's house. I picked up my phone to see the time, but when the screen remained black, I realized it must have died at some point during the night. It took a moment for me to notice that I was alone—both Clark and the dog were gone.

I scrambled to my feet, my heart racing. If something had happened to Bertie, Clark would have woken me up. I was pretty sure of that. But that didn't stop me from running toward the kitchen, nearly tripping on the bottom of the sweatpants, which were a few inches longer than I was used to. "Clark?" I called, trying to tell myself not to panic, that things were fine.

I skidded into the kitchen to see Clark leaning against the counter, a small smile on his face, his hair sticking up in the back. "Hey," I said, and Clark nodded toward the corner of the room.

I turned and saw Bertie—standing up, eating from his food dish. Not with the same gusto that he normally did, but it was clear that at some point during the night he'd gotten through the worst of this. I let out a long breath, one I hadn't realized I'd been holding.

It didn't take long after that for me to gather my things and head out. I knew I could have stayed, but I somehow didn't want to push the moment we'd had together. I wanted to go home and think about the night and try to understand it— which was made more difficult because I hadn't had a night like that before, ever.

"So you'll be okay, right?" I asked ten minutes later, as Clark walked me out to my car. I was still wearing his T-shirt and sweatpants and carrying the bag with my dress in it. I knew I was going to have to face it at some point, but I didn't feel up to it quite yet.

Morgan Matson

Clark nodded. "I got a text from Maya last night. She's going to come by this afternoon and check on Bert."

"Oh, good," I said as I made my way across the driveway barefoot. I was holding my shoes, because even though I knew it didn't matter, I also knew how terrible sweatpants and dressy sandals would look together. "I'm so glad he's out of the woods."

We stopped in front of my car. Only now, in the morning light, did I see how haphazard my parking job had been—my car was practically at a right angle to the house.

I opened the driver's-side door and tossed in my purse and the bag with my dress in it, then turned back to him. "Well," I said, then stopped when I realized I didn't have anything to follow this. Clark looked at me, and I looked back at him, suddenly not sure what happened from here.

"Thanks so much for coming over." Clark took a small step closer to me. "I really don't know what I would have done without you."

"I was glad to help." I wasn't even really aware of what I was saying, as I was focused on Clark and the distance between us, which seemed to be incrementally closing.

He reached toward me, brushing my hair back from my forehead gently, letting his touch linger on my cheek for a second. "So," he said, and I held my breath, feeling my heart pound in my chest. "Do you think you might want to, I don't know . . . try the dinner thing again?"

I felt myself smile, big and dorky and taking over my face. "Yes," I said without hesitating. There didn't seem to be any point in pretending I had plans or telling him I'd have to get back to him.

Clark smiled back at me. "Pick you up at seven?"

I nodded. "Sounds good." We looked at each other for a moment, and it was like the very air between us changed. I suddenly remembered all the things we'd talked about, everything I'd told him when my walls were down. As I looked across at Clark in the morning light, I realized I knew him. Not everything, and not perfectly, but I knew who he was. And I'd let him see me.

A part of me was yelling that this wasn't good, that I'd broken all my rules, that I should pull back, circle the wagons, stop this before it went any further. But before I could sort through this or say anything, Clark took a step back toward the house. "I should go check on Bert," he said. "But I'll see you tonight?"

"See you," I said, nodding. And then, even though I knew it was ridiculous, I waited to make sure he got back inside before getting in my car and heading for home.

I didn't linger once I made it back, just headed straight up to bed, feeling the fatigue set in with every step I took upstairs. I plugged in my phone and didn't even change out of the T-shirt and sweatpants, just crawled into bed and pulled the covers over my head to block out the sunlight, hearing the *beep* that told me my phone had powered back on before I fell into a dreamless sleep.

When I opened my eyes again, the sun was bright and filling my room, and I squinted against it, raising my hand, wishing I'd thought to close the blinds before I went to sleep. I looked at the digital clock on my bedside table and saw that it was noon—I'd slept for hours.

I pushed the covers off me—it was *hot* in my room—and swung my legs down to the ground. I stretched my arms over my head as I grabbed my phone from the charger. I needed a glass of water, and then maybe I'd see what my friends were up to. And I had another date tonight. The thought of it made me smile as I took the steps down to the kitchen two at a time. I didn't know if I could get them all on board for wardrobe prep again, but I also wasn't really sure that I needed it. When someone has seen you wearing their clothes, not to mention first thing in the morning, I was pretty sure you no longer had to try to impress them as much with your sartorial choices.

I had just walked into the kitchen, punching in the unlock code on my phone, when I stopped short. My dad was sitting at the kitchen table, his arms folded across his chest. And he looked angrier than I'd ever seen him look before.

"Where the hell," he asked, his voice low and furious, "have you *been*?"

Chapter EIGHT

I blinked at him. "What—what do you mean?" I asked. "I texted you that I had a work emergency—" But my dad was already pushing himself back up from the table, his voice rising.

"I have been waiting all night for you to come home, young lady," he said, pointing angrily at the clock across the kitchen. "And you stroll on in here at seven a.m. without so much as a word?" I hadn't ever heard my dad's voice like this, ever. This wasn't the controlled anger at his debates and press conferences, when he needed to be upset about an issue only to be able to pivot and speak rationally a moment later. This was real.

"I sent you a text," I said, even as my heart was pounding hard, feeling the anxious, jittery feeling coursing through me that had always meant *you're in trouble*. I suddenly felt eight years old again, approaching the table where both my parents sat looking down at me, furious, my report card in front of them.

I pulled out my phone, and only then did I see I had eight missed calls from my dad and four voice mails. There were also about twelve texts from him, starting friendly and concerned, then getting worried, then angry. I scrolled up past these, to the text I'd sent him, ready to show him proof that I'd covered my bases, been responsible. But my stomach plunged as I looked at the screen. There was the text I'd composed—but never sent. I closed my eyes for a second, remembering. I'd written it, but then Bri had texted, and I'd gotten distracted. I'd assumed, this whole time, that it had gone through and that everything here was fine.

"Oh," I said, my voice small. "So . . . here's the thing." I looked up at him, and when I saw how mad he still was, looked back down at my phone. "I wrote a text to you. But it never got sent. But you can see it. Look . . ." I held out my phone to him, but he barely glanced at it. "I'm really sorry," I said, hoping we could move past this. I knew he must have been worried, but it was an honest mistake.

"You think that's an excuse?" he asked, shaking his head. "You think you can come home whenever you want?"

I felt myself frown as I looked up at him. I was sorry that he'd been worried. I'd apologized. It was a mistake. So what was he doing still yelling at me about it? "Look, I said I was sorry. Can we drop it now, please?"

"Drop it?" my dad asked, his face turning steadily redder. "No, Alexandra, we're not going to *drop it*."

Maybe it was the use of my full name—or the way he was suddenly pretending like he was a regular dad, one who'd earned the right to yell at me about curfews, but whatever it was, I didn't think I could stand there and listen to it any longer. Because the fact was, I was usually coming in around now, after spending the night at a party or at one of my friends' houses.

But he didn't know any of that, because he hadn't been here to see it. I started to take a breath and tell him this, but even thinking about it was like getting close to a powder keg. There was so much in there, that I knew if I said anything else, I would explode. "I don't have to take this," I said, shaking my head. I needed to leave, get out of there, try and get my heart rate somewhat back to normal. I was on the verge of saying things I couldn't take back, and I needed to leave before I did. I grabbed my bag and keys from where I'd dropped them on the counter and headed for the side door.

"Where are you going?" my dad asked, sounding more confused now than angry, like I'd done something that had deviated from whatever script he'd been following. I didn't answer, just yanked the door open with hands that were shaking and stepped outside into the bright sunlight. My sunglasses were back on the kitchen counter, but I didn't think it would be advisable to go back and grab them. "Andie," my dad called after me, and I could hear he was back to being mad again—madder than he'd been when I'd come downstairs. "Come back here. I'm your father."

My lip started to quiver, and I bit it hard as I half ran to my car, trying to keep myself from crying, or yelling, or doing some combination of the two. But mostly I wanted to stop myself from screaming back at him what was reverberating inside my head. *No, you're not. Not for years and years now.* I didn't let myself look back as I started the car, put it in drive, and peeled out faster than I should have. I didn't even signal, just pulled out onto the road, hands gripping the steering wheel, knowing without a shadow of a doubt that I'd just made things much, much worse.

Hey. Where are people?

TOBY

PALMER

I'm at the diner with Tom. I think Toby's trying to say she's at the museum until 5?

TOBY

BRI

Hey! I'm working the concession counter at the theater until six. You guys should come by!
Wait, what's with the rainbow?

PALMER

Toby?

TOBY

BRI

I no longer understand anything that's happening.

Well, I need to get out. Meet you guys at the diner.
Sorry if this was a couple's thing.

PALMER

Totally not! See you soon.
Tob, are they PAINTINGS? Is that what you're trying to say?

TOBY

BRI

So I guess you guys aren't coming by?

ME

Can't right now. Will explain later.

I pulled open the door to the diner and scanned the room for Palmer and Tom, smoothing my hair down. Since I'd gotten into my car barefoot, I'd been relieved to find an old pair of flip-flops underneath the passenger seat. However relaxed the dress code was here, I had a feeling they probably weren't kidding about the "no shoes" thing.

Not that the rest of my outfit was great, by any stretch of the imagination. I was still wearing Clark's ASK ME ABOUT THE LUMINOSITY T-shirt and his sweatpants, and I'd now slept in both. A glance in my rearview mirror let me know that my hair had dried puffy on one side and flat on the other and that I had a pillow crease on one cheek. But if I could just hustle into our booth, I would be okay.

I spotted them, in our normal booth, and hustled over. "Hey," I said, sliding across from Palmer and Tom, who were already sitting on the same side, Tom's arm slung around Palmer's shoulders.

"Whoa," Palmer said, drawing back slightly from me, her expression surprised. "I mean," she said, regrouping, "hi, Andie. Um . . . rough night?"

"Is it that bad?" I asked, tucking my hair behind my ears, slinking down farther in the booth. As I did, I caught the eye of a guy sitting across the restaurant and felt my stomach sink as he gave me a smile and a quick wave. It was Frank Porter, who I'd had a microcrush on last year when I heard he broke up with his longtime girlfriend. But he came back to school in the fall so clearly besotted with Emily Hughes that I'd quashed my crush immediately. That still didn't mean I wanted to look awful in front of him, though. He was sitting across from Matt Collins, who was saying something that made Frank laugh, and I turned my back on them.

"You just don't look," Palmer said diplomatically, "you know . . . like yourself." She frowned at my T-shirt. "What are you even *wearing*?"

Tom looked at it and shook his head. "Like you know what the Luminosity is," he scoffed. "Since when do you read fantasy?"

"Since when do you?" I asked, surprised.

"Um, since last year," he said, raising an eyebrow at me. "Palmer told me I had to read something other than plays."

"This is true," Palmer said. She picked up a fry from the plate in front of her, then nudged it toward me. "Want one?"

"So what is the Luminosity?" I asked, relaxing back against the seat. This was what I'd wanted. I didn't want to think about my dad or the fact that the longer I stayed away from home, the more in trouble I was getting. I wanted to lose myself in conversation and French fries and deal with things at home only when I was sure I could handle them.

"It's a part of the novels of C. B. McCallister," Tom said, his voice going slightly pompous and professory. "He's a fantasy writer—"

"Oh, I know," I said, looking down at the shirt, wondering if this was another fan thing of Clark's.

"What do you mean you *know*?" Tom asked, frowning at me.

"Because I know him," I said, basically just to see Tom's jaw drop. "It's Clark."

"Wait, what?" Palmer asked, leaning forward.

"I'm sorry—*Dogboy* is C. B. McCallister?" Tom asked, his voice hitting a register I hadn't heard since he'd been in *A Little Night Music.*

"Clark," Palmer corrected him.

"I thought his name was Gertnz . . . something."

"Me too," I said, as I snagged a fry off the plate and dipped it into the ketchup. "It turns out I was mistaken."

"I don't understand," Tom said, staring at me. "Why didn't you tell us this?"

"I didn't know until last night," I said, reaching across the table to steal a sip of Palmer's vanilla Coke. "I felt the same way you did. Only not as impressed, since I didn't really know who that was."

"I don't either," Palmer said, turning to Tom. "Who is that?"

"Only a master of the craft," Tom said, his voice rising again. "He's . . ." Tom stopped suddenly, his eyes widening at something behind me.

"What?" I asked, taking another fry. Palmer was looking behind me too and had gone very still.

"Um," Palmer said, sitting up a little straighter, "Andie, your dad is here?"

I whipped around in my seat and saw my dad, standing by the hostess podium, his eyes searching the room, not looking any less mad. "Oh my god," I said as anger, embarrassment, and fear all jostled to be my primary emotion at the moment. My dad met my eye across the restaurant and headed directly toward me. Even crossing a slightly run-down diner, he had the air of someone important, someone who knew what he was doing, and I watched a busboy step out of his path to let him pass. Both Tom and Palmer looked baffled, but I realized I had no way to tell them what had happened before he got here. "Sorry about this," I muttered, knowing it was the best I could do under the circumstances.

"Hello," my dad said as he approached the table. He had his friendly candidate voice back, but I realized there was still real anger underneath it. "Palmer, how lovely to see you again so soon. And . . ." He hesitated for only a fraction of a second. "Harrison, as well."

"Tom," Tom said, half standing and extending a hand to my dad. Tom had always been a little dazzled by him, simply because he was on TV occasionally. Even though he was just being himself, and not acting, this didn't seem to matter to

Tom. "Or Harrison. That's fine too. So nice to see you, sir."

"You as well," my dad said, shaking Tom's hand and giving him a smile that crinkled his eyes in the corners, looking for all the world like he was just delighted to talk to him. But then he turned to me and it all fell away. "I need you to get back home," he said, his voice low and not inviting any arguments. "Now."

I swallowed hard and nodded—I knew when I was beaten. I'd known I'd have to go home and face the music eventually, I just thought I'd be doing it on my terms. "I should go," I said quietly to Tom and Palmer, who both nodded. I could see Palmer was asking me silently if I was okay, and I just gave her a tiny nod. "See you guys soon." I slid out of the booth.

"Well, I wouldn't be too sure about that," my dad said, his smile and friendly tone undercutting what he was saying. "Andie's going to be grounded for a while."

I felt my face get hot, and I had to look away from Palmer's expression of sympathy, because it was making things worse. I just hoped nobody else in the diner had heard, especially Frank. It was embarrassing enough to be humiliated like this without the class president seeing it happen. "Bye," I muttered to both of them, then walked toward the front door, keeping my head down, needing to get out of there as fast as possible.

My dad followed behind me down the steps while I looked straight ahead and tried to pretend this wasn't happening. "Let's go," he said, pointing at his SUV, parked on the street next to the diner.

I stopped and looked at him. "But I drove here."

"We'll get your car later," he said as he beeped open his SUV and started to walk toward it.

"But—" I started, about to say that I couldn't just leave my car there. What if something happened to it? But I had run out of ways to stall. I went around to the passenger side of my dad's car and got in.

I buckled in, and my dad started to drive. As he pulled onto the main road that would take us home, I realized it had been a long time since it had been just me and my dad in an enclosed space like this. No menus to hide behind, no way to make an excuse and slip away.

The embarrassment I'd felt at the diner was only growing as I replayed the scene in my mind—my dad showing up, announcing for everyone to hear that I was grounded, like I was still in middle school or something. My dad just showing up—

Something occurred to me, and I turned away from the window to look at my father. He was staring straight ahead at the road, his jaw set in a firm line, his hands clenching the wheel at ten and two. "How did you know where I was?"

"There's a GPS device in the car," he said. "It's part of the security, in case it gets stolen."

"Wait. What?" I asked, suddenly thinking about all the times I'd said I was somewhere that I very much was not. I'd expected my dad to say something like he'd followed me, or he'd somehow talked to one of my friends . . . not that he was tracking me.

"I've never used it before," my dad said, hitting the turn signal harder than he needed to. "I only turned it on when you brought the car back this morning. This is absolutely unacceptable behavior, Andie."

With that, it was like my brief calm in the diner had just been an intermission. All the anger from earlier was coming back, full force. My dad pulled into Stanwich Woods, nodding at Earl, who looked up from his magazine long enough to wave us in. I crossed my arms tightly over my chest as I looked out the window.

"Are you listening to me?" my dad asked sharply as he signaled and pulled into our driveway.

"Yeah," I muttered, shaking my head. "Sure."

"You can't talk to me like that, Andie," my dad said, and I could hear what I was feeling—the anger, the frustration—in his voice. "I am your father, and—"

"Oh, really?" I asked as my dad parked the car in the turnaround and killed the engine. I unclipped my seat belt and got out of the car, slamming the door, then turned back to my dad, who had followed me onto the driveway. I could feel the anger coursing through me like a drug, like I was about to set off the powder keg, with no idea what exactly was inside it. "You're my *father*?" I asked, putting a snide, sarcastic spin on the words. "Really?"

My dad stood with his keys in his hand in front of the car, looking wrong-footed. Inside there was a part of me that was yelling to stop this, just make peace and go inside, but the louder part of me wasn't listening, and I barreled on.

"Then tell me who I went to the prom with this year," I said, my voice starting to shake. "How many times did I have to take the driving test before I passed it? Who was my history teacher last semester?" My voice broke on the word "history," and I could feel the tears lurking behind my eyes, which somehow only made me angrier, my words coming out fast and out of control. "I haven't had a father in five years. So you can't just show up now and start acting like one." I felt one tear fall, then another, and I brushed them away angrily, trying to hold myself together.

"You can't . . . ," my dad said, shaking his head. He glanced at the house, then turned back to me. "I was doing what I had to for our family."

"What family?" I asked, and my father's face crumpled for just a second before he recovered. I swallowed hard, knowing I'd gone too far but also knowing I wasn't going to be able to stop this now. "I have done nothing but make sure I didn't do anything to make you look bad. My whole life. I've been tiptoeing around, always thinking about how anything I do might affect you. And then you mess it all up. Do you know why I'm not in Baltimore?" I asked, my words coming faster and faster, taking on a life of their own, like a runaway train. "Dr. Rizzoli pulled my recommendation. Because of *you*. Do you know how much that wrecked things for me? And it's like you don't even care." I stopped abruptly, drawing in a sharp breath.

There was silence in the driveway—just the chirping of birds in a nearby tree—but it was like I could still hear the words I'd just said echoing between us, like I could still feel the reverberations.

My dad crossed in front of me to the door and unlocked it without saying a word, and I followed. We walked inside, and my dad hung up his keys, then stuck his hands in his pockets. I had no idea what happened now, but it was clear he didn't either, which made me feel somehow even worse. Like there was nobody in charge, nobody even trying to steer this sinking boat of ours.

We looked at each other, and I swallowed hard. For just a moment I let myself think about what my mom would have said if she could have seen us, yelling at each other in the drive-way. How disappointed she'd be in both of us—in what we'd allowed ourselves to become.

"It's not just this summer," I said, tears falling down my cheeks unchecked. "You moved me to this house without even telling me you were going to. I never got to say good-bye to the farmhouse. There's none of Mom's stuff around, we never talk about her or say what we miss—it's like you want to pretend she was never here at all. It's like she never even *existed*." I was full-on crying, wiping my nose with the back of my hand and not even caring. I could barely see my dad any longer. He was just a fuzzy shape behind the tears I wasn't even trying to blink away.

"And you said—you said in your book that we were so close. That you have to work at a relationship and that you're proud of ours." I took a shaky breath, knowing I was coming to the end of what I was going to be able to say. "But it's not like that anymore. It's not, and I don't know why. I don't know . . . what I did."

My dad was staring down at the floor, his shoulders hunched. He nodded, just once, not looking at me, then turned and walked past me without a word. He walked to the end of the hallway, then opened the door to his study and went inside, closing the door behind him with a soft *click*.

I drew in a shaky breath, not sure what I was expecting but feeling somehow that being left alone, after all that, was so much worse than if he'd yelled at me.

On legs that felt wobbly, I walked slowly up the stairs to my room and headed directly for my bed, kicking off my flip-flops and pulling my quilt up over my shoulders. I curled into a ball and closed my eyes tightly, wishing harder than I ever had before that when I opened them, I'd be back in the farmhouse. My mom would be downstairs, and my dad, too, both of them waiting for me, and everything else that had happened had just been a nightmare, the worst kind of bad dream, but nothing that could possibly be true.

But when I opened them, I was back in my beige room, with everything broken in pieces around me. I closed my eyes again and pulled my covers over my head.

Chapter NINE

"Andie?" there was a double knock on my door, and before I even had time to respond, it cracked open an inch. "Can I come in?"

I looked up from where I was still curled on my bed. After a few hours I had made myself get up. I'd taken a long shower and finally changed out of Clark's clothes and back into my own. Even though I'd left my phone on the kitchen counter, I hadn't wanted to leave my room—I wasn't sure what I'd be walking into downstairs. It was like I'd just broken every unspoken rule we'd had, and I had no idea where we went from here—or what it looked like. And maybe it looked just the same, which was somehow the worst possibility of all.

"Okay," I said, as the door swung open all the way.

My dad didn't come inside, though, just stayed in the doorway, standing on the threshold, his hands in his pockets. "Want to get some ice cream?"

At Paradise Ice Cream I looked across the table at my father. We were sitting at one of the wrought-iron tables on the patio with our ice cream—mint chocolate chip for my dad, cookie dough in a waffle cone for me. We'd driven over here in almost silence, talking only about the logistics of where to go, if he could change lanes, if I could see a parking spot.

"How is it?" he asked, gesturing toward my waffle cone with his spoon.

"Pretty good," I said, taking another bite. "Yours?"

"Not bad," he said, scooping up another spoonful. We ate in silence for a moment, and I looked around the nearly deserted patio in the fading afternoon light. It seemed we'd picked a good time to come—it was a little after five. I knew from experience that around seven, post-dinnertime, the line would be out the door. But right now we had the place practically to ourselves. "So," he said, taking another bite, then pushing his cup slightly away from him and looking right at me. "I thought we should talk about this afternoon."

I looked at him and nodded, realizing that after years of knowing my father's speeches by heart, being able to anticipate every turn of phrase, I had no idea what was about to come next.

"I'm sorry, Andie," he said, his voice raw. "I truly am. I don't think I realized . . ." His voice trailed off and he cleared his throat. "If I'd known how you felt, I would have made a change long ago. And of course I *should* have. It's no excuse. But . . ." He sighed and looked out over the parking lot. In the grass along the side of the road, I could see fireflies begin to wink on and off, not many yet, not so you could take them for granted. "My life's been about forward motion," he said, his voice quieter now. "It has to be in government. You have to think about the next day, the next problem, and keep moving forward. And I've been so focused on trying to get back to where I was . . ." My dad let his voice fade as he looked out again, seeing something that I wasn't. He shook his head, then looked at me. "I wish you'd told me about Daniel Rizzoli."

I shrugged and took a careful bite of my cone. I hadn't wanted to do it while he was talking, like I would somehow have been interrupting. "I didn't think there was anything you could do."

"I could have yelled at him for a few hours, though," my dad pointed out, and I smiled for what felt like the first time in a long time. "It might have made both of us feel better." He pulled his ice cream cup closer to him but didn't take another spoonful, just looked at me. "But I still wish you would have told me."

"Yeah," I said, my voice quiet. I wished I could have told him too—wished he was someone that I could tell things to. But I had no idea how to say this out loud to him.

"So," my dad said, pulling a pen from his shirt pocket and drawing one of the rainbow napkins toward him. "I thought we should devise a strategy."

"A strategy," I repeated.

"You were right," he said, clearing his throat as he drew a series of diagonal lines on the border of the napkin—his version of doodling. "I haven't been around as much as I should have. I've missed out on so much. And of course you're upset about it. As you should be. . . ." He stopped and tapped the pen twice on the napkin, then looked up at me again. "So we have a problem." He set down his pen and picked up his spoon again. "And I thought we could devise a plan for how to correct it."

I felt my fingers twitching for the pen that was just out of reach, wishing I had a napkin of my own to figure this out on, or at least get my thoughts more in order. This was actually

Morgan Matson

feeling familiar—it was how my dad had dealt with every problem he'd had to face in his career. He and Peter sat down and devised a strategy for whatever the problem was, whether it was to get a bill passed or push an agenda through, or to win his reelection. And if something wasn't working, they came up with a new plan. It was like they didn't allow for failure, only course correction. I just hadn't known that it could be applied to things like this. "What were you thinking?"

"The way I see it," my dad said, and it was like I could practically hear the relief in his voice as he started to write, like he was able to grab on to some hard-and-fast facts, "we're dealing with a lack of quality time spent, right? So we'll spend some more time together."

"How?" I was noticing, to my surprise, how comfortable it felt to be able to discuss something like this, to break it down into manageable pieces.

"Well," my dad said, writing on the napkin, "maybe we have dinner together every night."

I drew back in my chair. "*Every* night?" I echoed, the words coming out strangled. Most of my friends had dinner with their families during the school year—and I was usually at Palmer's house, having dinner with her family, at least once a week—but this was the *summer*. How was I supposed to go from hanging out at the beach to a party at the Orchard to pool-hopping if I had to be home in the middle of it to have dinner with my father? He looked up at me and I tried to hide what I was feeling, nodding quickly. "Well . . . um . . . sure. That sounds . . . fine."

My dad shook his head. "Andie, we're *negotiating* here," he said with a half smile. "I know you don't want to have dinner with me every night. I ask for more than I know I'll get, you offer less than you know you'll end up with. That's how this works."

I smiled as I flashed back to a memory of a rainy day years ago, on some senator's campaign bus, my dad stumping for him, while he taught me (and three members of the press corps) how to play poker. "Okay," I said, making my voice more serious, trying to take any tells out of it. "Dinner once a week."

"Twice," my dad countered, and I looked up at him and nodded. Twice a week sounded good. Twice a week sounded like something we could handle. "And we'll talk," he said, his gaze level with mine. "You can't just sit there and be a moody teenager."

"Ugh, when am I a moody teenager?" I asked with an exaggerated eye roll, and my dad smiled, like I'd been hoping he would.

"Seriously," he said, tapping his pen twice on the table. "This won't work unless you tell me things. Like that you're going on dates with fantasy novelists."

"Well, I didn't know that either," I pointed out, but my dad was still talking, overlapping with me.

"I need to make up for lost time. So you have to fill me in. Deal?"

"Deal," I said, and my dad gave me a nod. Dinner twice a week. We could do that. "But you have to too," I added, the words coming out fast. It was what I'd realized when I'd been lying upstairs in my room, going over all the things I'd shouted at my father—like how he didn't know anything about me. But I had been retroactively embarrassed to realize I really didn't know anything about him, either. Peter and the press corps and the random rotating interns knew much more than I did. "Tell me things about you. Okay?"

My dad nodded. "It's a plan."

We finished our ice cream after that and started to head to my dad's car with every intention of going home. But Paradise Ice Cream was right next to Captain Pizza, and we both stopped in front of the door as the heavenly pizza smell drifted out. We looked at each other, and without discussing it, headed inside, where we ate slices of cheese (extra for me, regular for my dad) at the counter while the guy tossing the dough showed off for us, only occasionally losing control of the dough when a toss went wild.

When we were walking to his car in the fading daylight, I tried to pick the right moment, when he was distracted by pulling out the keys, to ask about the consequences for the thing that had started all of this—my staying out all night. "So we're good with everything now, right?" I asked, adjusting my purse on my shoulder, attempting just the right amount of casual in my voice. "Like, with the whole thing from last night. We're okay?"

"Oh, no," my dad said, looking across the hood of the car at me. "You are so totally grounded. I thought you understood that. A month, at least."

I started to protest, then bit my lip. This was really bad—that was most of the summer. But I also knew there was the chance he might increase it if I started complaining. "All right," I said with a sigh. I looked over at my dad, who was shaking his head at me.

"Andie," he said, sounding pained, "we *just* went over this. Am I supposed to negotiate with myself?"

"Right," I said quickly, trying to regroup. "Um . . . two days."

"Please," my dad scoffed as he beeped open the car and got into the driver's seat.

"Four days?" I tried, getting into the passenger seat and buckling my seat belt.

"A week," my dad countered, and I nodded.

"But I get to go to work," I said, "and the grounding doesn't start at night until seven p.m."

"Call it six and you've got a deal," my dad said, starting the car. He glanced over at me. "I realize that things might have gotten a little lax with Joy," he said, and I just nodded, deciding that he probably didn't need to know I'd been without a curfew for years now. "But that's going to have to change now."

"There's a new sheriff in town?" I asked. My dad smiled, and it hit me how rarely I'd seen it—not my dad's candidate smile, but the one that was meant just for me.

"You got it," he said. "And punctuality is going to be the coin of the realm." My dad started to shift the car out of park, then put it back and looked over at me. "I don't want you to think . . . ," he started, talking mostly to the steering wheel. "I miss her so much, you know," he said, his voice wobbling. "Every day. Even now I'm always thinking about things I want to tell her. Stuff she'd find funny. I didn't even know what I was doing that first year. It was like someone had turned off the sun. The center of everything was suddenly gone."

"Me too," I said, my voice barely above a whisper, but loud enough for just the two of us in the quiet of the car.

My dad looked over at me and gave me a small smile. I gave him one back, and we stayed that way for just a moment before he looked ahead, shifted the car out of park, and drove us home.

Morgan Matson

PALMER

Andie is all okay? Why was your dad at the diner?
Tom hasn't stopped talking about him,
which is really fun for me.

BRI

Your DAD showed up at the diner?! Wha?

PALMER

Is your car still there? WHAT'S GOING ON?!?

TOBY

ME

All okay! Long story. But will explain.
Oh, also, I'm grounded for a week.

PALMER

Wait, what?

BRI

What'd you do?

PALMER

But why is your car still at the diner?

THE UNEXPECTED EVERYTHING

BRI

Want me to hot-wire it?

ME

You know how to do that?

TOBY

BRI

I MIGHT be able to do it, Toby. You don't know.

I just need a screwdriver, right?

I've seen enough movies that I'm pretty sure I could figure it out.

ME

Um, figure it out on McQueen first

BRI

Can you video chat later? We need explanations

PALMER

Seconded

TOBY

ME

Yes, DEFINITELY. I'll text you guys soon.

Morgan Matson

I had just set my phone down on the kitchen counter when the doorbell rang. I smiled, wondering if it was Palmer. She'd sometimes drop by when she didn't think I was texting back fast enough. I was headed toward the foyer when I heard the door open on its squeaky hinges and realized my dad must have beaten me there.

"Andie?" my dad called, and I increased my pace, suddenly hoping that Bri hadn't gone ahead and tried to hot-wire my car.

"Is it Palmer?" I asked as I rounded the corner.

"Your—um—friend is here," my dad called, and I stopped short. Clark was standing there, carrying a cellophane-wrapped bouquet of flowers and what looked like a CD.

"Hi," I said, confused, trying to figure out what he was doing there, until it hit me all at once. We were supposed to have a date tonight. We were supposed to have a date *now*. With everything that had happened today, I had totally forgotten. "Oh," I said, then stopped when I realized I had no idea what to say after that.

"It's nice to see you again, sir," Clark said, holding out his hand to my dad, sounding nervous, talking much faster than he usually did. "I was just reading up on the education initiative you spearheaded last year. It sounded fascinating."

My dad's eyebrows went up. "Were you really?"

"I surely was," Clark said, and I could clearly tell how much preparation he'd done—which was making me feel even worse that I had forgotten our date.

"Well," my dad said, raising an eyebrow at Clark. "That's impressive. We'll have to discuss it in depth sometime."

Clark smiled, but I noticed he had turned a shade paler. I shot my dad a quick look, and he nodded. "I'll give you guys a minute," he said, heading back toward the kitchen—but not closing the door all the way, I noticed.

I looked at Clark, who was wearing another button-down shirt, green this time, and I could still see the comb tracks in his hair. I looked down at myself—I was wearing cutoffs and a T-shirt, nothing hugely offensive, but not what I would ever wear on a date. "So," I said, taking a step nearer to him. As I did, I remembered this morning, the gentle way he'd brushed my hair back, how close together we'd been. I blinked and made myself focus on the present moment and how much I'd managed to mess it up. "Okay. Here's the thing. Today's been kind of crazy."

Clark nodded, but his eyes traveled to my bare feet, and I saw his smile falter. He looked down at the flowers he was holding, and I saw some of the happiness in his expression fade, replaced by embarrassment. "Oh," he said. "Did you not want to—"

"No," I said immediately. "It's just . . ." I tried, very quickly, to think of the best way to spin this, then gave up and realized I should probably go with the truth. "It turns out I sort of didn't tell my dad I wasn't coming home last night."

Clark's eyebrows flew up. "Uh-oh."

"Yeah," I said, glancing back toward the kitchen. "So I'm kind of grounded." I was embarrassed even to say it. Even though he was only two years older than me, Clark was basically an adult—living on his own, with the freedom to do whatever he wanted. Nobody was grounding *him* or telling *him* what to do. This must have seemed beyond juvenile to him. "I'm really sorry about this."

Clark shrugged. "It's fine," he said, giving me a smile. "I mean, I'm disappointed, but I understand. We'll do it another time. When you're not grounded. When will that be?"

I felt relief spread through me—until he'd said it, I hadn't realized how much I'd been preparing myself to hear him say something polite but vague, which I would have known meant we wouldn't be having another date. "A week," I said with a shrug, like this was nothing. "Not so long."

Clark glanced down at the flowers in his hand, then held them out to me. "These are for you. Sorry if it's totally cliché to bring them."

I looked down into the bouquet, and it was a moment before I could answer him. "No," I said. A guy had never brought me flowers before—unless it was my prom corsage, which I didn't think counted, since I'd had to order it myself and give explicit instructions for where and when to pick it up. These were beautiful—all purples and pinks and the occasional daisy. "I mean, it's . . . really nice." I looked down into the flowers for one moment more, not wanting him to see just how touched I was by them.

"And," Clark said, presenting the CD to me with a flourish. "This is more of a joke than anything else. You don't have to listen to it."

"What is it?" I asked, taking it from him, then recognizing the familiar font on the cover. This one showed a crow and a flaming sword. *A Murder of Crows*, the title read. *By C. B. McCallister.*

"I know you don't read," Clark said, and I raised an eyebrow at him. "But I thought maybe you wouldn't have anything against *listening*. It's the audiobook, so it's like someone telling you a story."

"Ha ha," I said, turning it over and reading the back. I felt my eyes widen. "This takes nineteen *hours*?"

"Yeah," Clark said, not seeming fazed by this. "And those

are just the first two discs. There's like twelve, but I didn't want to scare you."

"Andie," my dad called. I looked up from the CD to see him hovering in the doorway, clearly not sure what he should do—or what I wanted him to do.

"Clark came by to pick me up for a date," I said, trying to get this over with quickly. "Because I didn't know I'd be grounded."

"Ah," my dad said, his eyes traveling down to the flowers in my hand.

"Sir, I just want you to know Andie was amazing last night," Clark said, giving me a smile, as I felt myself freeze.

"Last night?" my dad asked. His voice was still totally calm, but this was the way he sounded in debates when he realized his opponent had just made a mistake.

"Right," I said quickly, trying to jump in before this got any worse. "So here's the thing—"

"When Andie helped out with my dog who was sick," Clark went on. It took all my willpower not to bury my head in my hands. "She was great." He looked from me to my dad, finally seeming to get that something was going on. "Was that a secret?" he whispered to me.

"I didn't know you stayed the night at Clark's," my dad said.

"I told you it was for work," I said, realizing as I did that I should have probably just told him the truth right from the beginning, as opposed to hoping he would never find out.

"It was totally professional," Clark said, jumping in. "Nothing else . . . I mean that wasn't at all what . . ."

"Nothing happened." I looked down at my feet, not quite

able to believe that I was having to say this, to my dad, in front of Clark. "I just went over there to take care of the dog, and then we took shifts staying up to make sure he was okay."

My dad looked at me evenly, his eyes narrowed slightly, like he was trying to see if I was telling the truth. After a moment he must have decided I was, because he nodded slightly. "Okay," he said.

"Okay?" I'd expected a lot worse. I'd expected him to grill Clark and me for details, trying to find discrepancies in our stories, the way he had when he was a lawyer. And the truth was, something *had* happened last night—nothing that I was even sure I'd be able to articulate to him, but something nonetheless.

"I believe you." I'd just started to relax when he went on. "But your grounding just got extended. It's ten days now."

Remembering our earlier conversation and hoping I'd get points for trying, I ventured, "Eight?"

"Know when to fold 'em, kid." My dad shook his head and started to head back to the kitchen. "You can walk him to his car."

"Uh," Clark said. "That's great, except my car is outside that gate thing."

"Why?" my dad asked, sounding baffled.

"Well, there was nobody inside the gatehouse," Clark explained. "There was a note saying they'd be back in five. So I just parked outside and walked. I didn't want to be late." He gave me a tiny smile, and I felt the forgetting-our-date guilt hit me once again.

My dad shook his head. "Andie, remind me to have a conversation with the Neighborhood Council about what passes for security around here."

I nodded quickly. "Totally. So . . . can I still walk Clark to his car?"

My dad looked between me and Clark for what felt like an eternity before he finally nodded. "Fine," he said. He raised his eyebrows at me. "No driving anywhere. And be back before seven a.m. this time."

"Fine," I said grudgingly, and then a second later, added, "I mean, thanks." My dad nodded, then walked into the kitchen again, tapping his watch as he went.

I looked over at Clark as we crossed from the driveway onto the road. It was a long summer twilight, like the sun was fighting to stay around as long as possible, even as it slowly, steadily, got darker.

"So," Clark said, nodding toward the street we were approaching. It was the main street that wound through Stanwich Woods, the one that carried you past the gatehouse and around in a circle, until you returned to where you came from. "Want to show me around?"

I hesitated for just a second. It had seemed like my dad was giving me permission to stay out a bit longer, with his seven-a.m. comment. "Sure," I said as we walked onto the main road, gesturing for him to follow me. "Though there's not all that much to see."

"Well, I doubt that," Clark said, falling into step next to me. We were walking a little closer than I did with most people. I could have reached out and touched him easily, not even needing to extend my arm.

"Welcome to Stanwich Woods," I said, doing my best imitation of Toby's docent voice. "As you can see, *actual* woods were torn down to make it, but at least they acknowledged them with a nifty name."

Clark turned to me, his eyebrows raised behind his glasses. "I guess you don't like it here?"

I looked around as we took the curve in the path. To our left was a pond, complete with tiny, picturesque footbridge and weeping willow hanging over it. The streets were almost empty of cars, and in the houses we passed—all looking vaguely alike—I could see lights on in the windows and families sitting down to eat, people going about their evenings. The streets curved gently, and the wrought-iron streetlights arched over the road from either side, guaranteeing that when it was dark enough, the evening joggers and dog walkers would be able to see just fine. But you couldn't see the stars here like you'd been able to at our farmhouse. "It's fine," I said after a moment of walking next to Clark in silence. Somehow, without even really being able to say how, I knew he'd wait until I was ready to answer him. And I didn't feel the impatience coming off of him the way I sometimes did with Topher when I was taking too long to gather my thoughts. I could somehow tell that Clark would be happy to walk next to me in silence until I knew what I was going to say. "We used to live way out in backcountry," I finally said, by way of explanation. "And then we moved here, after . . ." I hesitated for just a second, then made myself continue. "After my mom," I said quickly, not letting myself linger on any of the words. "And it just seems so fake. Like the idea of what a picturesque village once looked like."

Clark glanced over toward the duck pond, which was free from ducks at the moment. "I don't know. If you ask me, living way out in the middle of nowhere is overrated."

"How far were you from civilization?" I asked as we followed the curve in the road, and I took a tiny step closer to him—so small that even Clark might not have noticed it.

"An hour to the nearest gas station," he said. "Two and change to the closest real town."

"Wow," I said, shaking my head. "That *is* far."

Clark laughed. "Tell me about it. I got to see, like, two movie-theater movies a year."

"Don't tell my friend Bri that," I said, smiling at him. "She'd make you get caught up on your film history, decade by decade."

"Well, that doesn't sound so bad," he said, giving me a shrug. "I've got some time on my hands this summer."

The comment hung in the air between us, and I noticed there was just an edge of bitterness to it.

"So, about your book," I said after a moment of silence in which I tried not to notice how close together our hands were, both swinging by our sides as we walked. Clark didn't say anything, and I was about to change the subject, start talking about something easier . . . but then I remembered how patient he'd been, walking next to me, and I bit my lip, forcing myself to keep quiet as I walked next to him. I didn't know how exactly, but I could tell he was trying to find the right words.

"What I told you last night?" he finally asked, and I nodded. "You're the only person who knows that. Everyone knows I'm having trouble—there are whole websites devoted to it—but I haven't told anyone else how bad it is."

"Your secret is safe," I said, raising my right hand. "Ex–Girl Scout's honor."

"Ex?"

"Long story," I said, feeling like now was not the time to tell him the story that involved Toby, a cooler of ice cream, and Bri massively failing to be an effective lookout. "Another time. But I'm pretty sure the oath is still good."

"I appreciate it," he said. He shook his head, running a hand through his hair and causing the back to stick up funny. "I knew what was implied when my publisher offered me her house. I could stay there for free all summer, but at the end of it, I'd better have a book for them."

We walked for a moment, not speaking, and I was suddenly aware of how loud the cicadas were all around us. I looked at the fireflies winking on and off in the grass while I tried to figure out how best to ask this. "So . . . what's the problem?" I finally asked, knowing that Bri or Tom, who seemed to understand and appreciate an artistic temperament, would have found a gentler way to ask this. But I was having trouble getting my head around it. I sometimes didn't *want* to study, but I did it anyway. You didn't wait for the perfect studying mood to strike you.

I heard a buzzing sound and looked up to see the streetlights all flickering to life above us, going on one by one until you could see more clearly what had been fading in the slowly falling darkness—the bench by the edge of the duck pond, the tree branches over our heads, the details of Clark's face.

"Well," Clark said, and then stopped. It was like I could practically feel him choosing his words carefully, like he wasn't used to talking about this. "Lately I've been thinking that I might be done."

"With . . . writing?" I asked, just as a pair of headlights swung around the curve in the road. We stepped over to the side, and when the car was gone and we started walking again, we were a little closer still, now just inches away, even though we could have walked in the middle of the open, empty road, the streetlights casting our shadows on the ground in front of us.

"Yeah," he said. "I don't think it's this book, or the pressure to continue the series. Or . . ." Clark shook his head. "It's like I don't have any more stories to tell. Which might be the case. Some writers only get a couple. Maybe I just got two."

I looked ahead and realized that we were almost to the gatehouse; it was just beyond the curve in the road—the brighter streetlights and the road beyond Stanwich Woods, where Clark's car was waiting, which would mean this was over. "Want to see a terrible statue?" I asked, quickly crossing the road to take us on a detour away from the gatehouse, hoping he would be turned around and wouldn't realize exactly what I was doing.

"Always," Clark said, deadpan. I led him down the street—was it really a street if it had no houses on it?—that ended with the statue of Winthrop Stanwich, with the small playground and picnic tables to the side of him. Only the main road had streetlights, so as soon as we stepped off it, we were back to only the fading light to guide us.

"But maybe it's not true," I said as we walked down the road to the statue. Possibly it was because it was so empty—this was mostly meant to be a walking path, without even a yellow line painted down the center—but we were walking farther apart now, a person space between us, so that we could turn and see each other. "That you only have two stories in you."

Morgan Matson

"It might be," Clark said, and I could hear the frustration in his voice. "I keep trying, but it's like there's nothing *there*. I've even tried writing other stuff, other than my series, and it's not working. So I'm left with the conclusion that I really might be done."

"But . . . ," I started as we reached the statue. We both stopped in front of it, which was really the only proper reaction to seeing the statue of Winthrop Stanwich for the first time. Palmer's brother Fitz always joked that by the time they were done building Stanwich Woods, they'd run out of money and decided to let the statue building go to the lowest bidder. It was in bronze, and life-size, or close to it. Winthrop Stanwich was depicted as a slightly rotund guy in a high collar, equally high vest, short breeches, and buckled shoes. There was a cape over his shoulders, slightly raised on both sides, which was probably meant to convey his movement but just made him look like a weird Puritan Batman. He had a beard and a monocle—though Fitz had a theory that he was supposed to have glasses before someone saw what was happening and just decided to pull the funding and call it a day. But the best thing about the statue was Winthrop Stanwich's expression. He was reaching out his right hand, first two fingers extended, like he was pointing at something, his expression equal parts happy and confused. At least, that's how I read it. Tom thought Winthrop was angry and attempting to scold someone, and Toby was convinced he was about to break into song. He was like an inkblot, and everyone saw in his expression what they wanted to.

For a while—not coincidentally, when both Palmer's brothers were in high school—stuff kept showing up in Winthrop's hand. It really was the perfect height and position to hang things on, though Palmer's brothers had preferred to leave boxers dangling around his wrist. The Winthropping—it wouldn't have been very hard to find the culprit, since it was down to the Stanwich Woods residents—had subsided somewhat, but every now and then there would be a note in all the residents' mailboxes, asking them to stop putting Santa hats, or Halloween costumes, or just random take-out bags, on Winthrop. But it was ultimately a losing battle, and something else would show up before too long. He was unsullied now, though, pointing to whatever he was pointing to unencumbered.

"Wow," Clark said, shaking his head. "You weren't kidding." He looked over at me, and I felt my eyes straying involuntarily to his mouth. I took a small step closer to him as he looked away, down at his watch. "I should probably get you home," he said, giving me a half smile. "I don't want your dad to hate me."

We walked away from Winthrop, and I turned back for just a second to see him, arm still extended toward something, cape forever billowing in imaginary wind. When we reached the road again, I pointed for us to go left—otherwise known as the longer way around to the gatehouse—praying that Clark had a terrible sense of direction like Toby, and he wouldn't notice this.

"It's just this way," I said, as Clark paused.

He raised an eyebrow at me, a smile pulling at the corner of his mouth. "Really," he said, not exactly phrasing it as a question.

"Uh-huh," I said, walking with purpose now, knowing that what I'd tried to do was completely obvious but not really caring. But I wasn't ready for this—Clark, the falling darkness, walking next to him—to be over yet. We walked in silence, and I noticed that he was right by my side, closer than ever. Even

Morgan Matson

without turning to look, it was like I could feel his presence next to me, aware of every step he was taking. Our hands were both down by our sides, and they were so close to touching, I could feel the tiny breeze made by his arm as it swung, the night air cool on my skin.

"I don't think you can just decide you're done with writing," I said when I realized that Winthrop had interrupted a pretty important topic. "You don't think you could tell me a story, right here, right now?" Clark shook his head, and I knew he was about to tell me why I was wrong, but before he could, I jumped in. "Look, I'll start you off. Once upon a time . . ." I gestured for him to pick this up, but he was just staring back at me, clearly waiting for me to continue. "Once upon a time, there was a guy," I continued, when I realized this was on me.

"A *guy*?" Clark asked with a laugh. "There aren't *guys* in my world. There are Elders and mages and princes and orcs, but . . ."

"But this *isn't* your world. We're just making up a story that doesn't matter, for fun." Clark didn't say anything, and after a moment I asked, "You don't think you can do it? I'm getting us started, and I don't even read." Clark stopped and looked at me, and I could see something in his expression—like he was fighting a competitive instinct. "Once upon a time," I said again, feeling like he was on the verge of joining in, "there was a guy. Named Carl."

"Carl?" Clark said, incredulous. I shot him a look, and he threw up his hands. "Okay. Fine. But it's Karl, with a *K*."

"What difference does that even make?"

"It makes a huge difference," Clark said, with enough authority that I decided to take his word for it. "Okay, and

Karl . . ." There was a long pause, and I bit my lip to stop myself from jumping in, making myself listen to the slap of my flip-flops against my heels, the cicadas in the grass all around us, the occasional crunch of leaves beneath our feet. I was practically willing him to say something, to jump in with the story, to try. "And Karl . . ." He took a shaky breath, then went on, all in a rush, "Karl was a wanted man. He was on the run."

I smiled but tried to tone it down as we rounded a bend in the road. "Because he'd stolen something," I said, "something . . . valuable. With lots of value."

Clark laughed, and it was like I could practically feel him relax next to me. "But he didn't know that he'd been spotted stealing the valuable thing with lots of value. Unbeknownst to him, an assassin named—"

"Marjorie," I supplied, and Clark stopped dead in his tracks.

"The assassin can't be named *Marjorie*. It's bad enough we've got a Karl."

"What's wrong with Marjorie?"

"Assassins aren't named Marjorie."

"Really good assassins probably are. Because nobody would think they were assassins."

Clark inclined his head toward me. "Well played," he said. "So. Okay. Karl and *Marjorie*—"

"Marjorie the super-assassin—"

"Are in the woods, on a moonlit night," he said, the words coming more quickly now. "Karl thinks he's gotten away with it."

"But he hasn't."

"Not even close. Because he's about to meet Marjorie. And she's going to change his life." I took a breath to continue the story when Clark's hand brushed against mine, and all the words left my head.

I wasn't sure if it was an accident, so I kept my hand stretched down by my side, within easy reach, and what felt like a lifetime later, Clark's hand brushed mine again, sending a spark through me that I felt all the way in my toes. He kept his hand touching mine, and then, moving a millimeter at a time, curved his fingers around so that they were resting against my palm, just brushing it, so lightly. Then he moved up, over the curve of my thumb, and ran his index finger over the inside of my wrist in a slow circle. I could feel my pulse fluttering beneath his fingertips, and I had to remind myself that I knew how to breathe, that I'd been doing it my whole life. And then our palms were touching, perfectly lined up, though I could feel how much bigger his hand was than mine, feel his fingertips curving over the tops of mine, despite what Bri had always called my "weird large tree-frog hands." We stayed that way for just a moment, and then, like we'd talked about it before, like we'd mutually picked the time, our fingers interlocked and we were holding hands.

We walked that way, not speaking, our joined hands swinging gently between us, every nerve in my body suddenly awake. I was concentrating on putting one foot in front of the other, because otherwise, all my thoughts would have been focused on the fact that Clark and I were holding hands, that somehow, on this walk, something between us had changed.

"So then what happens?" I asked, when I saw we were approaching the guardhouse again.

Clark looked over at me. "What happens with what?"

"With Marjorie. And Karl," I said, as he slowed and turned to me, still not letting go of my hand.

"I don't know," he said, stopping and looking down at me. "I guess we'll have to wait and find out."

I nodded and looked up at him and knew this was the moment—if I let this happen, whatever this was, whatever it might be, would start. I could feel my heart pound as Clark dropped my hand and moved it toward my waist, brushing the hem of my tank top between his fingers.

Normally, I kissed first. I didn't like the moment before, the wondering if a guy was going to get up the courage to kiss you while you were just standing there, waiting and hoping. I liked to take matters into my own hands, squash that moment and get right into the make-out session. But now . . .

Now, being in this moment, on the cusp of something happening, made me wonder why I'd been rushing through it all these years. Or maybe I hadn't. Maybe I'd just been waiting for this moment, right now.

Clark looked down at me, brushing his hand over my forehead, smoothing back my hair like he'd done before, and I knew this was my last chance to change my mind. And as much as a part of me wanted this, there was another part that knew this would be different from my three-week boyfriends. That it already was.

But I didn't turn away or walk in the other direction or stop the moment from happening. Moving so slowly, he tilted his head down toward me. I stretched up to him, and we stayed like that for just a second, not kissing, not yet, just hovering in the moment before, only a breath apart.

Morgan Matson

And then he leaned forward, or I did, and then his lips were on mine.

We lingered there, our lips brushing gently. And then he raised his hand and cupped it under my chin, drawing me closer toward him, and we started kissing for real.

And my arms were around his neck and then his were around my waist and he was pulling me closer, lifting me off my feet, and when he set me back down, my knees were wobbly, like the ground had gotten less solid in the interim.

It was a kiss that made me feel like I'd never been properly kissed before, and as we paused to take a breath—a minute later? an hour?—he leaned his forehead against mine. I looked up at him, and a thought passed through my brain before I could stop or analyze it. *It's you—of course it is. There you are.*

And as I touched his cheek and his hand tightened on my waist, I leaned forward to kiss him again, knowing as I did that something was ending while something else had already begun.

Tamsin cursed under her breath as she watched the owl sitting on the branch regard her with what she was almost certain was disdain. This was supposed to be the one area where she was showing any kind of natural inclination, and she had been failing miserably all morning.

"You're distracted," the Elder said from the tree stump where he had sat, motionless, for almost an hour now.

"Maybe," Tamsin acknowledged as she watched the owl ruffle its feathers in a distinctly haughty way.

"Does it have something to do with Sir Charley Ward?" the Elder asked, his voice innocent.

"How did you . . . ?" Tamsin started, then gave up, realizing what a foolish question it had been. She had been aware the Elder knew everything, but until that moment she had thought it was restricted to things like the names of all the plants in the kingdom. She hadn't realized it also included knowledge of her first kiss.

"Be careful there," the Elder cautioned.

"It's fine," Tamsin said, turning back to the bird. She would prefer not to discuss Charley with anyone, but especially not someone old enough to be her grandfather.

"It's always a risk," the Elder said, but more quietly now, like perhaps he was no longer speaking to her. "Wherever there is great emotion. Because there is power in that. And few people handle power well."

"It was only a kiss," Tamsin said, focusing back on the owl.

"Oh," the Elder said, shaking this head, "that is where you are mistaken. Believing that such a thing—*just a kiss*—has ever, for even a second, existed in this world."

—C. B. McCallister, *A Murder of Crows.* Hightower & Jax, New York.

Chapter TEN

Almost without my noticing it, the summer started to find its rhythm. I had dogs to walk, I had my friends to hang out with, and my dad and I were finding a little more to say to each other day by day. But mostly, I had Clark.

"So Karl and Marjorie duck into a roadside tavern," he said to me as we walked three hyperactive terriers, all straining desperately at their leashes, like the trees up ahead of us were just so much better.

"But they're going under false names," I reminded him, and Clark nodded.

"Of course. They can't let their real identities be known, not with the bounty on their heads."

"And it's raining."

"Naturally," he said, taking my hand and squeezing it. "It's a proverbial dark and stormy night."

I looked over at him and smiled. "And then what happens?"

It had been two weeks since Clark and I kissed, and things were going well. I had been grounded for the first eight days—dropped down from ten, with some careful negotiation on my part—so he'd started coming with me when I walked Bertie.

We'd hold hands while we walked, stopping to kiss multiple times, or as much as we could with Bert yanking on the leash. Clark would sometimes come with me on other walks, which I always appreciated, since a full day of walking dogs by myself led to me talking way too much to animals who were never going to answer me back.

But even though we hadn't been able to go on another real date that first week, we'd ended up talking on the phone nearly every night, conversations that happened while he took Bertie for his nightly walk and I sat up on the roof and looked out at the stars. I'd never had conversations like that with a boyfriend before, conversations that were easy and free-flowing, hours passing in what felt like seconds.

I was still getting my head around how Clark seemed happy to talk about almost *anything*, including sharing how he felt about things. The only thing he really hadn't told me much about was his father. Whenever we got close to the subject, I could sense Clark's walls—which were so rarely present—start to go up, and I changed the subject quickly.

But I'd begun to fill in the picture of Clark Bruce McCallister in a way I never had with any of my other boyfriends. I knew now that his favorite color was green, that when he was little, he'd wanted to be a wildfire firefighter ("they fight fires *from helicopters*, how cool is that?"), that he talked to his older sister, Kara, on the phone every Sunday, that he still refused to watch *Jaws* because it had given him nightmares for weeks as a kid, that he hated cinnamon, and that he had found a spot, just below my earlobe, that drove me crazy when he kissed it. I didn't know these types of things about any other guy, including Topher, and none of them

Morgan Matson

would have known them about me. It was different with Clark. And one way I knew this, beyond a shadow of a doubt, was the fact that we were getting close to the three-week mark and I had no interest in seeing it end. It was pretty much the opposite, as a matter of fact—it was feeling like something was just getting started.

"And we're doing groups this year," Palmer said enthusiastically, as she pushed up the brim of her sun hat. "Chosen randomly. Which means, since there will be two of you, the challenges are going to be that much harder."

We had been at the beach since nine, and by my count, Palmer had been talking about the summer scavenger hunt for at least forty-five minutes. She'd sent a group text at eight a.m., saying that it was the perfect beach day, she'd already staked out a spot, and we should join her and bring her an iced coffee. Somewhat miraculously, everyone else's schedules had aligned—and I'd shifted some walks around to make mine work as well. We'd spread out on the patch of sand Palmer had been zealously guarding and now had a stretch of blankets and towels and snacks and magazines.

"Sounds good," Toby said, her eyes fixed on the water in front of her. "Absolutely."

"What are you looking at?" I asked, pushing my sunglasses up and trying to see what was in her sight line.

"What do you think?" Bri asked, shooting me a look. In the two weeks since Wyatt had come back to town, Toby's crush seemed to be getting stronger by the day. She had calmed down enough that she was no longer acting strange around him, but she'd taken to spending much too much time on her hair every day and trying to devise increasingly complicated ways that they could be alone together. She was sending us long emoji missives about her feelings, and I don't know if she was getting better at it or if I was just getting used to it, but I'd been able to accurately decipher a message yesterday that detailed her current emotional state, using mostly just dolphins, the weird gourd fruit, and clapping hands. She was so single-minded about this—about him—that I wasn't sure anymore if her crush was really about Wyatt, the guy who had, by my count at the diner the night before, said only fourteen words. There was a piece of me that wondered—though I would never suggest this to her—if maybe she was just used to the *idea* that she was in love with Wyatt without stopping to see if it was still true and if he was really what she wanted.

"I'm just making sure nobody drowns," Toby said, her eyes not straying from the water even when Palmer started to tickle her bare feet.

I looked out to the water and smiled. Clark, Tom, and Wyatt were all on stand-up paddleboards, but not a single one of them was paddling along placidly, like in the pictures hung up in the tiny building where you could rent kayaks, paddleboards, and boats. Instead, Clark and Tom were using their oars as jousting spears, trying to knock each other into the water. And Wyatt was paddling, but sitting down, with one leg over either side, like he'd really wanted a kayak and was doing his best to approximate one.

"Who *rented* those to them?" Bri asked, sounding baffled.

My phone beeped with a text, and I pushed my sunglasses up to get a better look at the screen, then fumbled the phone when I saw who it was from.

TOPHER

> Hey—heard you were staying in town
> You around this weekend?
> Let me know. It's been a while

I looked up from my phone, but Clark was still in the water, and none of my friends seemed have to notice I'd gotten a text. I read the message again, then started typing fast, holding my phone off to the side.

ME

> Hey—I'm around
> But kind of with someone now

TOPHER

> Got it. Let me know when you're free to hang again

ME

> Sure. Yeah.
> Will do.

I set the phone down, then turned it to silent and dropped it back in my bag, trying to figure out why this was bothering me. It wasn't like it was that unexpected for Topher to text me—so why did it suddenly feel like another part of my life had intruded when I didn't want it to? And I didn't want to compare the two, but the proof of how different Clark and Topher were was right in front of me—in the very fact that Clark was hanging out with my friends.

It wasn't like it had been great right from the beginning—and that was my fault. Normally I would have planned it better, but I was in full-on early-make-out haze and didn't think about what it would mean for Clark to meet all my friends at once. This had never been an issue for my other boyfriends, but they'd gone to school like normal people, in regular classrooms with more than just their sister. So when I introduced Clark at the diner, Toby, Bri, Wyatt, Palmer, and Tom were all there, which in retrospect was too much, too soon. Clark barely said a word the whole night, and when he did talk, it mostly seemed to be reciting facts I'd told him about my friends back to them. It didn't help that Tom was almost equally quiet, stunned into fanboy silence at the reality of sitting across from one of his favorite authors. So all in all, not a huge success.

And it wasn't that Clark couldn't talk to people—last week I'd come in from walking Bert to hear him on a conference call with his editor and publisher and something called a "marketing team" as they discussed a cover redesign. Even though I had a feeling he was the youngest person on the call by a decade, he was very much in charge, clearly running things. Which was hard to reconcile with the fact that he seemed really intimidated by my friends—especially, for some reason, Bri and Toby.

"They were kidding, right?" he asked one night as we sat outside Paradise Ice Cream, he with his with mocha almond ripple, me with my cookie dough and a pint of mint chip I was bringing home for my dad. "They don't really want me to call them Tobri."

"They were kidding," I assured him as I helped myself to a bite of his ice cream.

"They do kind of seem to share one brain, though," he said,

Morgan Matson

reaching over for a spoonful of mine. "I swear, they had a conversation without ever saying anything."

I nodded and moved my ice cream out of reach. "They do that. But they liked you. All my friends did."

Clark nodded but didn't seem convinced, and even when I tried to do better the next time, and not present him with five people he'd never met before, just bowling with Tom, Palmer, and Toby, he was nervous and awkward, reminding me of how he'd been in the early days with me.

I was thinking that maybe it just wouldn't work out, but then, a few days after bowling, came what Bri later called "the beginning of a beautiful bromance." I stopped by Clark's to pick up Bert and found Tom and Clark on the couch in the book room, eyes fixed on the TV, which the room did, it turned out, have. (It just looked like a mirror when it wasn't turned on.)

"Hi," I said as I looked between them, trying to figure out how this had happened.

"Hey," Tom said, nodding at me, like it was totally normal for him to be hanging out at Clark's house.

"Hi there," Clark said, standing up and giving me a quick kiss. "Here to get the beast?"

"Uh-huh," I said. I was actually a little disappointed to see Tom there, as I'd been hoping for a little prewalk kissing action. "What are you guys doing?"

"Well," Clark said, nodding at the TV. It was paused, but I couldn't tell what was on it—it just looked like gray and raininess. "Tom doesn't have to rehearse today, so we're watching the Batsmen."

"The what?"

"All the Batman movies," Tom clarified. "We're still debating the plural."

"Batmans?" Clark asked, heading back to the couch.

"Batmen," Tom offered.

"I've got it," Clark said triumphantly. *"Batsman."*

Tom shook his head. "I really don't think that sounds right."

"Well, have fun," I said, as I went off to find Bert. I was having better luck with him when I could sneak up on him with the leash. If he didn't know there was a walk afoot, he didn't have time to play the run-away-from-the-leash game. I waved at them when I left, but they were back to watching, and I wasn't even sure they noticed. I was happy to see it, though, Clark and Tom hanging out. It seemed like a good thing.

I was less convinced when I came by the next day—I was adding Bert into a group walk for the first time—to find Tom and Clark still on the couch, both of them looking a little glassy-eyed. "Are you guys still doing this?" I asked, feeling my jaw drop open. "How many Batmen are there?"

"We moved on from that," Tom said, blinking at me a few times. "Now we're watching the James Bond movies."

I looked from him to Clark, hoping for an explanation. "Why?"

"Well," Clark said, pushing himself off the couch and coming over toward me, "we were talking about whether it was fundamentally wrong for a Brit to play Batman."

"He's the closest thing we American actors," Tom said, clearly including himself in this group, "have to a classic part. He's our Hamlet."

"And then we were talking about how they'd never cast an American to play Bond."

Morgan Matson

"Who's *they*?" I asked, feeling like I didn't have time for this, with four dogs waiting in the car.

"So we started watching them," Tom finished, like this was the only logical explanation. "In order."

"Shouldn't you really be watching the Supermans?" I asked, then paused. "Supermen?"

"See, it's hard," Clark said.

"I wanted to," Tom said, pointing in Clark's general direction. "It's not often you get a real live Clark in your midst. Especially one wearing glasses."

"That's what I'm saying."

"But then we remembered that Superman is kind of lame."

"Bond versus Superman," Clark said, looking over at Tom, then stopping to yawn hugely. "Who wins?"

"Which Bond?"

"Which Superman?" Clark countered.

"Have either one of you slept?" I asked. Bertie trotted around the corner, and I saw my opportunity and grabbed him by the collar.

"Sleep is overrated," Tom said, yawning as well.

"I've got to take him out," I said, stumbling a few steps behind Bertie, who was whining and stretching toward the door.

"I'll call you later," Clark said, giving me a quick kiss, and even though he looked exhausted—his hair was sticking up all over the place and his eyes were bleary behind his glasses—he also looked really happy.

"Sure," I said, giving his hand a squeeze. "We'll talk then."

And while I was glad that Clark had found someone to discuss all the different Doctors Who with, I realized I was also happy for Tom. Watching them crack each other up was making me realize that I hadn't ever seen him with a guy friend before.

"I think they're coming in," Toby said now, her voice going immediately more high-pitched as she dug in her bag and emerged with a lip gloss. She uncapped it, then squinted out to the water, where Clark and Tom were starting to swim in with their boards. "Oh. Never mind. It's just Tark."

I rolled over on my side to face her, already shaking my head. "Please don't give them a nickname."

"I think it's catchy," Bri said. "It sounds kind of badass."

"You have to admit, it's better than Clom," Palmer said, lowering her sunglasses. That had been Toby's first attempt, and I had done my best to quash it.

"It's not about what the nickname is," I said, even though Clom had been pretty awful. "Why are you giving them one at all? Why not one with *my* name and Clark's?" All my friends looked at me at once, and I focused on smoothing out the wrinkles on my towel.

"Hold the phone," Palmer said, sitting up straight and looking at me. "You're really in a couples-nickname kind of a place?"

"I didn't read anything about hell freezing over today," Toby said, shaking her head.

"I'll check online," Bri added.

"Never mind," I said, hoping by now I'd gotten tan enough so they couldn't tell I was blushing.

"Candie," Toby pronounced triumphantly, and I made a face.

"Ark?" Bri supplied.

I shook my head. "Just forget it," I said. "I shouldn't have . . . um . . ." I lost total track of whatever I'd been about to say next, because Clark emerged from the water and started walking toward me, and all ability to verbalize left my head.

I had made it clear to Clark early on that all we would be doing was kissing. He'd been a little taken aback, but seemed okay with it. And for the most part, that was all that had been happening. All our clothes had stayed put, so today was the first day I'd actually seen that Clark was in way better shape than writers of fantasy novels were supposed to be, as far as I'd been led to believe.

"Shouldn't have what?" Toby asked, then saw what I was looking at. "Oh."

"I know," I said, trying not to stare, but then giving up on that immediately. Clark's arms were muscular, his abs were defined, and his shoulders were much broader than I'd realized, now that they were out in the open and not hidden under one of his T-shirts. I was suddenly rethinking my clothes policy.

Clark and Tom walked up to our spot and tossed their boards down onto the sand, both of them talking fast, overlapping each other. "Not cool, man," Tom said, brushing his wet hair back. "You can't just knock someone into the water like that. I could have died."

"How could you have *died*?" Clark asked, laughing.

"Lots of ways," Tom said, "like if I'd inhaled water . . . or if there had been a jellyfish . . ." He trailed off, then turned to his girlfriend. "Palmer?"

"I'm with Clark. I think you were fine, babe."

"It's not my fault," Clark said as he looked around, squinting. "I couldn't see anything. It was an accident."

"Sure," Tom said, coming to sit next to Palmer. "Likely story."

Clark headed toward me, still squinting, and I pulled his glasses out from where I'd been holding them for him in my beach bag.

"This way," I called, holding up my hand. "Walk toward my voice."

Clark made his way over, and I handed him his glasses as he sat down next to me. "So much better," he said when he put them on. He smiled at me. "Like now I can see the most beautiful girl on the beach."

I rolled my eyes behind my sunglasses. "Stop it," I said, even though I didn't want him to. It was the kind of thing I would have found beyond cheesy with any of my exes. But it was different coming from Clark. I leaned over to meet him for a quick kiss, feeling the sand on his arms and tasting the faint flavor of seawater on his lips.

"Sorry to interrupt," Toby said, looking at me and Clark with her expression somewhere between annoyed and wistful.

"What's up?" I asked, gesturing for her to pass me the bag of chips we were sharing.

"I was just wondering if Wyatt said anything about me." Toby handed me the bag and looked back out to the water, where Wyatt was standing on his board, balancing on one foot for a moment before wobbling and falling off. It looked like he was doing paddleboard yoga, which seemed like a terrible idea all around. "Like, when you guys were . . . having guy talk?"

"Sorry," Clark said. It hadn't taken him long to pick up on her massive crush and Wyatt's complete lack of interest.

"I think you need to move on," Palmer said gently, and

Tom, sitting behind her, nodded. "Because you're awesome, and if Wyatt can't see that, it's his loss."

"Maybe he just can't see it *yet*," Toby said, sitting up a little straighter. "It's like this in all the movies. You can't see what's been right in front of you the whole time until it's the right moment."

I exchanged a look with Bri, who just shook her head quickly—telling me to let this go. "Maybe," I said, but even I could hear it hadn't been all that convincing.

"Wasn't there a guy at the museum who liked you?" Tom asked. "Maybe he already can see what's been in front of him. Like, maybe he's already at the end of the movie."

"But I don't like *him*," Toby pointed out, her voice slow and clear, like all of us just weren't understanding this. She shook her head. "I swear to god, I'm—"

"You're not cursed," Bri said without even looking up.

"Who's cursed?" I looked up and saw Wyatt, standing by Bri's towel, holding his paddleboard and dripping wet.

"Nobody," Toby said, giving me a look that I knew meant I shouldn't say anything to contradict her. "Clark was just talking about his, um . . . dragon book."

"Right," Clark said quickly, with a nod. "That's me. Dragons and curses. That's what my books are all about."

Wyatt nodded and then shook the water off his hands so that so that they dripped on Bri's bare back. "Hey," Bri said, looking around and then pushing herself up. "What's going—" She scrambled to her feet. "Wyatt!"

"What?" he said, shaking more droplets on her. "Sure you don't need to cool off?"

"I'm fine," Bri said, laughing as she pushed him away.

I leaned over Clark and turned his wrist so that I could see his watch—it was black and chunky, you could apparently scuba dive with it, and it had taken me a little over a week to be able to tell time on it. "And I should get going," I said with a sigh.

"Already?" Clark asked, and I nodded.

"Duty calls," I said, then arched an eyebrow at him. "What do you say? Want to walk some dogs with me?"

"Seriously?" Bri asked, looking around at all of us. "I'm really the only one who thinks that sounds dirty?"

"I heard it this time," Palmer said, nodding. She frowned at me. "Keep it clean, you guys. There are children here."

"We'll try," Clark said, getting to his feet and—unfortunately—pulling on his T-shirt.

"Did you see my moves?" Wyatt asked Bri as he flopped down in the sand next to her, despite the fact that Toby had moved so far over on her towel to make space for him, she'd forced Tom onto the sand.

"By 'moves,' do you mean falls?" Bri asked. "Because those really were impressive."

Wyatt laughed and made an obscene gesture at her, which Bri returned. "It's because the water was too deep," he said, pushing his wet hair back. "If we were in a pool, it would be different." He looked around at us. "Any of you acquire a pool since last year?"

Tom shook his head, and Wyatt shrugged, like he was letting it go, when Clark said, sounding just a little bit nervous, "I've got a pool."

Everyone looked over at him, eyes lighting up, and I felt my stomach sink. I tried silently to tell him to walk this idea back, pretend he thought they meant billiards, that it was under construction, anything. Because I knew my friends—they were pool-hungry maniacs with no sense of politeness at all when it came to using one.

"Really?" Toby asked, smiling at Clark, then glaring at me. "And why is this the first time we're hearing about it?"

"It's just . . ." Clark hesitated. "I mean, it's not my house. It's my responsibility for the summer, so I didn't want anything to happen to it. . . ."

"Wait," Wyatt said, raising an eyebrow. "You live there alone?"

"Yeah," Clark said, and I fought the urge to bury my face in my hands.

"This," Palmer said, grinning, "is *awesome*."

"Thanks for the invite, brother," Wyatt said, hitting Clark on the back as Tom winced in sympathy. "Party at Clark's tonight?"

"Text us the address?" Bri asked, and I nodded, knowing there was no way to get him out of it now. I glanced at my phone and realized I really did need to get going—one of my dogs, Wendell, had a tendency to gnaw on doorframes when I was running late. I gathered up the rest of my things, pulling my sundress over my bikini and stepping into my flip-flops.

"So I'll see you guys tonight," Clark said, starting to leave, taking the beach bag from me and slinging it over his shoulder. "I'll, um, get some snacks? Like chips, maybe?" He turned to me, and I nodded, reaching out my hand for his and giving it a squeeze as I realized that this was probably the first party he'd ever thrown. "And Toby?" She looked up at him from where she'd surreptitiously been putting on lip gloss. "For every curse, there's a cure. You know that, right?" Wyatt looked over at him, frowning, and Clark added quickly, "It's a thing in my books. You know, with the dragons."

"We should go," I said quickly, feeling the need to avert my eyes from Toby's expression and how hopeful she suddenly looked.

"Tell me their names again," Clark said as he looked at the five dogs in front of us.

"Well, that one's Bertie." Bertie was currently running circles around Clark, who was trying to untangle himself, in what was pretty much a perpetual loop.

"Thanks for that," Clark said, wobbling slightly as Bertie lunged for a squirrel.

"And that's Rufus," I said, pointing to the terrier mix who was chewing his own leg. "Jasper, Pippa, and Wendell."

"Whatever happened to Rover and Spot?"

"I'm walking them later tonight," I said, and Clark laughed. He leaned down to kiss me, and I kissed him back, hoping that the five dogs on their leashes would keep calm for a few moments.

It had taken me three weeks, but I was finally getting the hang of this dog-walking thing. My car now had towels spread over the backseat and was stocked with treats and water and collapsible bowls. I could tell the difference now between a dog sniffing with purpose and just trying to stall and look at a squirrel a little longer. I'd found my favorite brand of plastic bag— orange, biodegradable, from Raiders of the Lost Bark, whose name thrilled Bri to no end. She'd almost lost it when I'd told her about their other business, Temple of Groom. I had learned that my sweetest dog was Waffles the pit bull, and the most ornery one was Trixie the bichon, who looked like the meekest dog ever, just a white ball of fluff, but it was all a facade. She was the alpha and would growl down dogs who outweighed her by a hundred pounds. I'd learned that the big dogs were usually pretty happy to roll with things, while it was the little ones who were the most stubborn. I'd found out the hard way what happened when you were walking six dogs and a cat streaked across the road. I knew that Lloyd always wanted to smell the flowers, but if you let Leon do it, he'd sneeze for the rest of the walk. And I'd discovered that Bertie seemed to have no sense of how time worked—if he saw a squirrel in a tree, he'd run back to that same tree every day, like the squirrel would have been waiting there that whole time. "Bert springs eternal," Clark had dubbed it. But mostly I began to realize that I was good at this. And there was a feeling of accomplishment when I drove back after a walk with a dog in the passenger seat and three dogs in the back, everyone tired and happy and panting out the windows, a feeling I'd *done something* that I'd never felt in any of my internships or summer programs before this.

"Remind me where we were," Clark said, when we broke apart. He gestured for me to give him another leash, and after a moment's consideration, I gave him Rufus—I knew he and Bertie got along.

Our saga of Marjorie and Karl had continued to expand, taking quite a few twists and turns. The fact that Marjorie originally intended to kill Karl had pretty much been quietly forgotten by both of us, and I was always trying to give the road bandits they encountered some kind of ailment that I would then try to get Marjorie to diagnose, despite Clark always vetoing this.

Clark had started today's installment in earnest when we'd picked up Pippa, but almost right from the start I'd had issues with his current direction. "I was telling you that Marjorie wouldn't say that," I reminded him.

"Oh, right. Well, I think she would. It makes sense for the story."

"Ugh," I said. "Not going to happen. She's not going to get up and admit to everyone in a crowded tavern how she feels about Karl." I realized that Wendell was in danger of getting tangled with Pippa and switched him over to my other hand.

"Why not? I think it's important."

"Why does she need to tell everyone how she feels about him? Isn't it enough that Karl knows?"

"Does he, though?" Clark asked, raising an eyebrow at me. "Do you think it really counts unless other people hear it?"

"Of course," I said immediately. "Probably more so."

Clark shook his head, then stumbled a few feet as Rufus and Bertie lunged simultaneously for a squirrel that was running up a nearby tree. "Why do you think people get married with lots of guests there?"

"Probably for the toaster ovens."

"You might be right. But I think it's more than that. I think there's something to saying it in front of people. It's like it means more when you say it out loud, where everyone can hear you."

"Fine," I said, relenting. I was starting to learn when Clark wasn't going to let go of something, and I wanted to get to what happened next. "Marjorie confesses all to random tavern folk." I looked over at him, wondering if I might be able to get something I'd been pushing for now that I'd given in to this. "Can we finally do my thing where Marjorie discovers penicillin?"

"I told you, there's no penicillin in this world."

"But there's mold, right? Maybe Marjorie's just smarter than everyone else."

Clark smiled at me. "You make a good point," he said, pulling me in for a kiss as all around us dogs barked and leashes got hopelessly tangled.

"You okay?" I asked, looking across the table at my dad, who was staring down at his plate, his expression concerned.

"Maybe," he said after a slight pause, picking up a chopstick and nudging a piece of sushi. "I'm not entirely sure what this *is*, though."

I shook my head as I dunked my vegetable tempura in soy sauce. "I can't help you there."

I'd finished walking the dogs and said good-bye to Clark—who seemed to be taking his party-throwing responsibilities way too seriously and had headed to the store to buy provisions and two kinds of dip—when I got a text from my father, asking if I felt like getting dinner. We weren't all meeting up at Clark's until later, and I'd been surprised to realize that, in fact, I did feel like it. Our two-dinner-a-week plan was officially in full swing now that I was no longer grounded. It wasn't like we hadn't been eating dinner when I'd been stuck at home every night, but it had been much more casual—my dad would eat in front of an eighties basketball game, and sometimes I'd join him in his study with my own plate, looking up facts about the game on my phone and irritating him by being able to call what happened next and pretend I was just really good at guessing. Or we'd both be in the kitchen together, me with my organic chemistry textbook (I was trying to get ahead for next year), him with the paper or one of the nonfiction books he was always reading, about things like the history of salt or tires. We would eat in silence that didn't feel strained and talk only if we had something to say.

But when he'd suggested sushi tonight, it had felt okay—it had actually seemed like a good idea. Well, at least until my dad had gotten his food.

"Why did you order that?" I asked, as a waiter came out with two more plates, set them on either side of my dad, frowning down at the rolls still untouched on the plate in front of my father, like he wasn't eating fast enough. I'd gotten what I always got at sushi places, where not liking fish was a definite handicap, but my dad had ordered "Chef Knows Best," which meant he didn't get a choice in anything, but things were brought out to him and he was expected to eat them. In other words, pretty much my worst nightmare.

My dad picked up a roll with his chopstick, then set it down and took a drink of his sake, like he was trying to get up the courage to take a bite. "Well," he said, looking across the table at me, "it was what your mom always liked to do when she had the option."

"Oh." We had started talking about her slowly, in little pieces here and there. But I still wasn't used to it yet. "She did?"

"Yeah," my dad said, picking up the roll again and eating it this time, but taking a long drink when it was over, so I didn't think I really needed to ask him how it was. "She used to say that normally everyone is telling the chef what *they* want. She thought it was nice to switch it up for a change."

I smiled and picked up a carrot just as two more plates arrived, the waiter starting to look seriously peeved. My dad must have picked up on this, as he started to eat more quickly. "So any big plans tonight?" he asked, wincing slightly as he chewed.

"Oh," I said, just to stall. I had a feeling that telling him I was going over to Clark's house, where there would be no supervision, and if Wyatt was involved, there would probably be beer, would not go over so well. "I think I might just have a quiet night at Bri's," I said with what I hoped was a casual shrug. "Watching movies, you know."

"Uh-huh," my dad said as he looked around, then dropped a napkin over the sushi remaining on his plate. He gave me an even look. "So I take it you won't be seeing a certain novelist?"

"Well," I said, stalling. "I mean, who can say, really, what will or will not happen?"

My dad laughed at that, surprising me. "I think you could have a future in politics, kid," he said, shaking his head. "Well, when you do see Clark—"

"*If.* I mean, it's a *possibility*. . . ."

"Tell him I have something I want to discuss with him."

I set down my chopsticks and looked across the table at him. It was one thing for my father to start acting a little more like a dad. It was quite another for him to have the *what are your intentions with my daughter?* conversation. "Um, what's that?"

"It's about his book. He just introduces this whole new

concept—this Luminosity thing—right as the first one ends. I'm going out tomorrow to get the second one."

"Wait, you read his book?"

My dad nodded and laid his chopsticks across his plate. "I thought I should check them out. It really is impressive that he's a published author. It's quite an accomplishment for someone your age."

I nodded, figuring it might be best not to point out that Clark had actually written the first one when he was three years younger than I currently was. "So was it good?"

My dad looked at me in surprise. "You haven't read them?"

"I'm getting around to it," I muttered as I took a drink of my Diet Coke, not sure if I could explain why I hadn't yet. I was pretty sure the reason (well, one of them) was that when Clark and I were just hanging out, it was like I could forget he had this whole other life, where he was a professional author with a job and a tax return, who lots of people on the Internet were mad at.

"It was great. And it's not the kind of thing I usually read." My dad looked at me for a moment, then raised his eyebrows. "What would you think about having the next dinner at home?"

"Sounds good."

"And why don't you bring Clark," he went on, so smoothly that I realized I'd just walked into his trap. There was, after all, a reason my dad had been successful in politics for most of his professional life. "If you're spending time with him, I would like to get to know him."

I quickly scrolled through possible excuses but realized my dad had skillfully painted me into a corner—I couldn't say that

Clark was busy, because he'd left the date open. Knowing when I'd been bested, I nodded. "I'll ask." I thought of something and looked up at him, eyes narrowing. "Is this actually because you want to get to know him, or because you want to ask him about the Luminosity thing?"

My dad shrugged as he signaled for the check. "You know," he said with a smile, "two birds, one stone."

Three hours later I sat on one of the lounge chairs by the pool, with Bertie, who had seemed thrilled by all the unexpected company, flopped across my legs. I'd never spent much time around Clark's pool—the only time I'd ever even been in his backyard was when Bertie had managed to make it outside during his favorite game, Run From the Lady with the Leash. But now that I was out here, I could see it was lovely—landscaped and carefully designed, with lounge chairs placed at exact intervals. The lounge chairs were white and beige striped, which matched the striped towels that were rolled up in baskets placed around the pool deck. Basically, this looked like the kind of pool people had when they never used their pool, which was certainly not the case now.

Wyatt had spent most of the night floating around on a pool raft, looking like he wasn't planning to move a muscle, lulling everyone into a sense of complacency, and then had started a stealth-dunking campaign. He would begin a conversation with you, and then just when you'd let your guard down, he would dunk you unexpectedly. After he'd gotten me twice in a row, I'd gotten out. Wyatt now seemed determined to dunk Bri, despite the fact that Toby was pretty obviously putting herself in his path. Clark was sitting in the hot tub, and Tom and Palmer were currently making out on the diving board.

My phone buzzed on the lounge chair next to me, and I picked it up, frowning when I saw it was from Toby.

TOBY

I looked over to where she was standing by the overstocked food table, but she was not meeting my eye, and I had a feeling she didn't want people—people meaning Wyatt—to know we were texting about this.

ME

You're sad because Wyatt's not dunking you?

TOBY

ME

I'm sorry, T.

I looked up from my phone and over at Toby, and she gave me a small, sad shrug before she walked to the other side of the pool with a handful of chips, dangling her feet in the water near where Wyatt was currently floating on his back, her expression wistful.

Morgan Matson

After a few moments, I saw Bri look around for her. She swam over, pushed herself out of the water, and sat next to Toby on the edge of the pool. After a second I saw Toby smile and shove Bri's shoulder, and Bri shoved her back, both of them laughing now.

"Hey," Clark said, grabbing a towel from the towel basket, and I enjoyed my second look at his abs in one day as he walked over and sat on the lounge chair next to mine, since Bertie was taking up the remainder of the free space on mine. "Do you think people are having fun? Is there enough food?"

"It's great," I assured him. "I just hope you realize what you've done."

"What's that?"

"You know how you're never supposed to feed stray cats, because then they'll never leave?"

"Or put a salt lick out for deer," he said, nodding.

"Right," I said. Clark looked at me blankly, and I nodded out to the pool, where Palmer was now cannonballing into the water and it looked like Toby and Bri had teamed up to dunk Wyatt. "You've fed the kittens. You've salted the deer."

"What?"

I pointed at the pool. "A parent-free house with a pool? They're never leaving now."

"Well," he said after a moment, leaning toward me and closing the space between our lounge chairs. "Will you be here too?"

"I will. I'm not leaving you alone with these freeloaders."

"So then maybe it's not the worst thing," he said.

"Well," I said, like I was really thinking about this, "maybe not."

Clark smiled at me and leaned in for a kiss, at just the right angle for Bertie to enthusiastically start licking his face.

"So does it come up in book two?" my dad asked as he rinsed off a plate and handed it to Clark, who carefully put it into the dishwasher. "You can't just drop something in like that and not have it pay off, right?"

"Well," Clark said, reaching for another plate, his voice coming out hesitant. "Do you really want me to tell you?"

My dad looked at him, and I could see the struggle plainly written on his face. "No," he finally said. "I'll just wait."

"I think it'll become clearer in the second book," Clark said, transferring glasses to the top rack one by one. "It seems to, for most people."

"Oh, good," my dad said, brightening as he turned the water off.

I watched this from the opposite side of the kitchen island, still not quite believing what was in front of me—my dad and my boyfriend, getting along. My dad had grilled hamburgers, Clark had brought a cheesecake for dessert, and we'd eaten out-side on the back porch. My dad had given Clark a hard time at first, which he had partially deserved, since he'd gone out of his way to memorize obscure policies my dad had put through and minor floor-debate victories, as though they were common knowledge. So of course my dad had pretended he wanted to talk in detail about these, asking Clark more and more ques-tions, until I finally took pity on him and intervened.

But after my dad had finished torturing him, they actually seemed to get along well, which I had not been expecting—and it meant I could put aside the talking points I'd prepared in case of awkward silences or lulls in conversation. I'd learned my dad loved John Wayne movies, and apparently Clark's grandfather had as well, so they had that in common. And unfortunately, my dad told Clark about the time I'd tried to run away from home when I was four and had walked all the way to the neighbors' house, knocking on the door and asking if I could live with them instead, because my mother was refusing to let me have the cookies I wanted. I should have known I wasn't going to get out of this dinner without an embarrassing story told about me, and I was secretly glad it wasn't the one about the time my mom brought me to my dad's first swearing-in and I had a full-on tantrum on the floor of his office.

And now, cleaning up from dinner, they were talking about Clark's books, making me realize that I really needed to read them—if only so I wouldn't be left out of any more conversations.

When all the dishes were cleared and the dishwasher was running, my dad gave me permission to "walk Clark to his car" but with a look that told me I wasn't fooling anyone. "You know, it took you two hours to walk him to his car last time. So maybe you two need to increase your cardio or something?"

"Right," I said quickly, grabbing Clark's hand and pulling him toward the door, wanting very much to no longer be having this conversation.

We walked together in the moonlight, his arm slung around my shoulders and my fingers threaded through his, the pulse in his fingertips beating against mine. "I think that went well," he said after we'd passed out of view of my house, like Clark didn't want to talk about it until then, like my dad had supersonic hearing.

"I think it did," I agreed, still a little shocked by this.

"Um, except for all that Secret Service stuff. Do you think he meant it?"

I bit back a laugh. My dad had started off the evening clearly trying to get in Clark's head, happening to "casually" mention that he knew some of the VP's Secret Service agents well, and did he know they were trained in all kinds of deadly force, not just firearms? "He was just messing with you," I said, leaning my head on Clark's shoulder. He kissed the top of my head, resting his chin there for a moment before we walked on. "So," I said, turning my head and looking up at him. "Where were we?"

"Wasn't there a tavern brawl?"

"Isn't there always?" I replied, and he laughed.

I came back home a little over an hour later, Clark dropping me off in the turnaround, where we weren't quite able to resist making out for another twenty minutes or so.

I let myself back in the house, half expecting that my dad would be in his office, watching the classic movie channel or reading a book. But he was sitting at the kitchen table, a half-eaten piece of cheesecake in front of him.

"Hey," I said, smoothing my hair down. I hesitated, then crossed the kitchen toward him.

My dad looked up and smiled at me and pushed his plate slightly toward me. I decided more cheesecake was an excellent idea and grabbed a fork before sliding into the chair across from him. I speared a bite, realizing suddenly how nervous I was. What if my dad had been being his candidate self all night, pretending to get along with Clark while secretly hating him? I tried to tell myself it didn't matter what my dad thought, knowing all the while that it did.

My dad was just calmly eating his cheesecake, like he had nothing to say, and I decided I wouldn't ask. I'd just wait for him to tell me what he thought of Clark, but it wasn't like I needed to know or anything. This lasted exactly one more bite before I blurted out, "So what did you think of him?"

My dad rotated the plate slightly, looking for the perfect bite, before he said, "He seems like a very nice young man. A little mistaken as to where *Stagecoach* fits in with Wayne's filmography. But we can't have everything."

I rolled my eyes at that, not wanting to let my dad see just how relieved I was. "You freaked him out with all that Secret Service talk," I said, rotating the plate back toward me as I cut off a piece with my fork. "I think he thought you were serious."

"Who says I'm not? Though I suppose I didn't need to say 'Secret Service,'" he mused. "I could have just mentioned some of my old clients. Some very bad people would love to do me a favor."

I looked up at him, remembering something that had been in the back of my mind ever since the night of Bertie and the chocolates. "Hey, what happened to the drawing that used to hang in the foyer? The one of Stabby Bob?"

My dad looked at me, surprised. "What made you think of him?"

"I was, um . . ." I took a breath. "Clark asked me how you and Mom met."

Something passed over my dad's face then, sadness mixed with something happier. "Did I ever tell you she wanted to invite Bob to the wedding?"

"No way." I hadn't ever heard this before and was starting to smile, even though there was a slight tremble to it.

"She did. She thought he deserved to be there, being the reason we were introduced."

"So did he go?"

"Well, he was serving fifteen to twenty by then. So no." I smiled at that, and neither of us said anything for a moment, but it was like I could tell we were both thinking about my mom. Like just a little bit of her was here in the kitchen with us. My dad cleared his throat, then said, "I can try to find him for you if you want. The drawing," he said quickly, maybe seeing what I was thinking. "Not Stabby Bob."

I nodded. "That would be good." I took a breath, wondering if this was the moment to ask him the question that I'd never stopped wondering about—what he had done with my mother's Mustang. I hadn't asked, five years ago, when it didn't come to our new house with us, and I just hoped that he had saved it rather than sold it off to someone. I was getting ready to ask him about the car, when my phone buzzed in my pocket.

TOBY

Toby clearly wanted to know how dinner had gone, but it was easier these days to call or video chat with her rather than text her. But then it buzzed again, and I saw Palmer was texting now too.

Morgan Matson

HOW DID IT GO?

"Let me guess," my dad said, picking up the cheesecake plate and pushing himself back from the table. "Bri?"

"Toby," I said, shaking my head. "And Palmer, too." My phone buzzed again. "And now Bri."

"Well, I'll leave you to it," he said, placing the plate, with at least three good cheesecake bites remaining, in front of me. Then he patted my shoulder quickly, just once, before he turned and headed down the hall to his study.

I watched him go, then picked up my fork, settled back in my seat, and wrote back to my friends.

Chapter ELEVEN

I looked down at the dog sitting in front of me, a smallish sandy-colored mix of some kind. This was a one-time walk; his owners usually spent the summers away but were back in town for just a day or two and needed him to get some exercise. The dog looked back up at me, his tail thumping on the ground. "Okay," I said, smiling at him as I made sure his leash was clipped on tightly. "Ready for this?" I paused when I realized I'd blanked on his name. But in my defense, when I'd gone to pick him up, it had been a pretty chaotic scene. The dog had been running around barking happily, seemingly trying to get himself as underfoot as possible. Classical music was blaring and a girl who looked a year or two younger than me was doing a series of very complicated pirouettes in the kitchen, while a guy who looked like he was probably her brother sat nearby with a thick law textbook, seemingly unfazed by all of this, muttering about torts. It was a girl around my age who'd taken charge, giving me the dog's leash and instructions for where to walk him.

"Sorry about all this," she said loudly, trying to be heard over the music, as she gestured behind her. "We usually spend the whole summer at our lake house, but my sister has an audition for a dance company in New York tomorrow, so . . ." She shrugged, and I tried to hide my surprise, since the twirling girl looked like she couldn't have been more than fifteen. But I'd taken the dog and said I'd be back in about half an hour. Now I knelt down to see if his name was engraved on his tag, but there was just an *M*, and his owners' phone number.

"Okay, M," I said, as I straightened up again, hoping that when I brought him home, I could give a report on how the dog did without having to use his name. "Let's do this."

The dog trotted forward, tail wagging, and I started walking him down the long, steep driveway toward the road. As I walked, I pulled out my phone, telling myself I just wanted to listen to some music, pretending that was the real reason right up until the moment I scrolled to my brand-new audiobook section. I'd transferred the discs Clark had given me to my phone two days ago but hadn't listened to them yet. It seemed like the time had come.

I took a breath and pressed play, and the sonorous voice of a very famous British movie star filled my ears.

"If it had not snowed on the second day of the Aspen moon," he intoned, and I noticed, not for the first time, how *everything* sounded better with a British accent. "The life of Tamsin Castleroy would have been quite different. . . ."

I turned up the volume as I walked along with the dog, trying to pay attention so I didn't miss anything, as I listened to Clark's story.

"Wow," Maya said, looking at me with her eyebrows raised. She glanced down at the pile of dogs at her feet. It was the three terriers again, the ones that were normally so hyperactive that my arm was always sore afterward from having to pull back against the leash the whole time. But now they were flopped on the wooden floors of the tiny office Maya and Dave ran their business out of. I had been walking them nearby and figured I might as well stop in with them, since I needed to get a set of keys for a new dog, and this way I could pick up my paycheck. All the dogs looked exhausted, and Tofu—normally the most hyperactive of them all—was starting to fall asleep in front of me, despite the fact that another dog was currently sitting on his head. "It looks like they really got a workout."

"Yeah," I said, busying myself by folding up the extra plastic bags I kept in my back pocket, avoiding Maya's eye. "There were . . . um . . . lots of squirrels today." Maya nodded, and it looked like she believed me. My explanation was almost as rational as the truth, though—that I was currently devouring Clark's books, and the dogs I walked were feeling the direct effects of it.

Once I'd gotten the hang of listening to the audiobook, it hadn't taken long for me to get swept up in the story of Tamsin, a rebellious princess who captured the attention of the Elder, the mysterious, Yoda-like figure who lived in the woods on the outskirts of her kingdom. There was a prophecy, and since Tamsin fit the description, many—including herself—believed she was the chosen one, the one who would unite the kingdoms torn asunder by a hundred years of war. I had my doubts about this, and the Elder did as well. But he started to teach her anyway, as Tamsin's roguish brother, Jack, kept the kingdom more or less (oftentimes less) afloat, honing her abilities, especially her talent for communicating with birds. The first book had ended on a cliffhanger, as Tamsin and the Elder were forced to flee the kingdom, pursued with an invading army at their backs. I'd downloaded the second book immediately and was already about halfway through it.

I was listening to it constantly—in my car, in my room, before I went to bed, my phone propped on my nightstand and a sleep timer on so I wouldn't miss anything. But the place I really loved to have the story told to me was while I was at work. There was something wonderful about being outside, moving, keeping an eye on the dogs in front of me while the rest of me was swept up in the story. As a direct result of this, all my dogs were getting much longer walks than normal, since I hated to stop in the middle of a really great part. The walks that were normally twenty minutes had turned into epic walks that took us all over town, and as a result, most of them were getting pretty wiped out.

"Well, it sure looks like they had fun," Maya said as she bent down and scratched Banjo's ears. Banjo immediately flipped onto his back and looked at her expectantly—he was a fool for belly rubs.

"Definitely," I lied, since I honestly couldn't have told her. Tamsin had been captured by the book's great villain, locked in a tower, and separated from the Elder, so the amount of fun the dogs were having had not been my primary concern.

"So here are the keys for the Wilson house," she said, handing them to me. "You got the e-mail Dave sent you?" I nodded. Dave was beyond on top of this—making sure I had dog information and addresses and instructions, most of it laid out on spreadsheets.

"I should probably get these guys back," I said, looking at

the time on my phone and realizing that I should have had them back an hour ago and was going to have to hustle if I wanted to bring them home before their owners returned from work.

Maya nodded, but then looked at me thoughtfully. "You've been doing a great job here, Andie," she said. I looked at her, surprised. "I mean it. I think you really have a talent for this."

"Dog walking?"

"Working with animals," Maya said, looking at me steadily. "Not everyone does. Certainly not all the people we've hired have it. But you do."

I nodded, trying to process this. At the start of the summer, I would have said that it was just walking dogs, that anyone could do it, but now I wasn't so sure. Especially after Toby came on one walk with me and spent the whole time freaking out every time Bertie sniffed a tree. Maya gave me a smile as she clipped her carabiner filled with keys back onto her belt loop. "So . . . ," I started, not really even sure what I was asking her. "Did you know you always wanted to do this? The whole dog and cat thing, I mean?"

"Oh, *no*," she said, shaking her head. "Not at all. I was actually in business school, getting my MBA. That's where I met Dave."

"Really?" The question was out of my mouth before I could stop it, and I hoped I didn't look as shocked as I felt.

"I know," Maya said with an easy laugh, not seeming insulted by this. "Hard to believe, right?"

"So what happened?"

Maya smiled as she bent down to scratch Banjo's belly, and the dog's back leg started twitching like crazy. "At the end of the day, I decided I wanted to do something that made me happy."

Morgan Matson

She gave the dog one last pat before standing up again. "And it's working out so far."

I nodded as I clipped the Wilson keys onto my own key ring. Maya handed me my paycheck, we said our good-byes, and I stepped out into the late-afternoon sunlight, three dogs moving sluggishly behind me. But even as I tried to get the dogs to move, Maya's words were staying with me. The idea that you could rethink the thing you'd always thought you wanted and change your plan—it was almost a revolutionary concept. That you could choose what would make you happy, not successful. It was the opposite of everything I had long believed to be true. I looked back at the office for a moment, Maya's words still echoing in my head. Then I gave Freddie a pat on the head and pulled the dogs back out onto the sidewalk.

ALEXANDER WALKER
Andie, you okay?

ME
Fine.

ALEXANDER WALKER
It just sounds like you're crying. At 3 a.m.

ME
I'll keep it down.

ALEXANDER WALKER
What's wrong?

ME

I just finished Clark's second book.

ALEXANDER WALKER

Oh boy.

ME

HOW COULD HE DO THAT?

ALEXANDER WALKER

I think there's ice cream in the kitchen.
Meet you there in ten?

ME

Better make it five.

"What's going on?" Clark asked as I glared at him, taking the stairs to the diner two at a time, my arms folded tightly over my chest.

"I'm not talking to you," I said, pausing at the ever-deserted hostess stand, looking around the restaurant, and seeing Palmer and Tom sitting a booth over from our normal one. I started to head over to them, Clark following close behind me.

"You're technically talking to me right now," he pointed out, and I just glared at him again.

"Hey!" Palmer said as we arrived. Tom slid out from where he'd been sitting across from her and walked around to sit next to her, doing an abbreviated version of his usual complicated handshake with Clark.

"Hello, *Palmer*," I said pointedly to her.

Morgan Matson

"Um, hi," she said, looking from me to Clark, clearly sensing something was going on.

"Perfect timing," Tom said, drumming his hands on the table. He nodded at the mini jukebox at the end of the table. "Because I put my money in, like, half an hour ago, and now you two will be here for my song."

"What's happening with you guys?" Palmer asked, mostly asking this question to me.

"Well, Andie's not talking to me," Clark said as he got a menu from where they were pressed against the wall with the ketchup and saltshakers. "I don't know why."

"Oh, yes, he does. He knows what he did."

Palmer and Tom both looked at Clark. "What did you do?" she asked.

"He killed Tamsin," I said, glowering at him, while across the table from me, Palmer's jaw dropped.

"You *what*?" she gasped.

"Fictionally," Clark explained hurriedly. "It's not like she was a real person."

"Clearly not, to you," I huffed.

"You bastard," Tom said, now glaring at Clark as well.

"Wait, why are *you* upset?" Clark asked, sounding baffled.

"Because it's all coming back to me now," he said, shaking his head at Clark. "Really, *how* could you have done that?"

"Yeah," I said, turning to him. "Was it all just a big joke to you or something?" After I'd eaten my way through a half pint of cookie dough ice cream, trying to deal with my grief about this, I'd left a series of predawn texts on Clark's phone that had started sad and then had gotten more and more

THE UNEXPECTED EVERYTHING

angry when I realized that all of this was his fault and he could have prevented it if he'd wanted to. When he'd picked me up to go to breakfast, I'd crossed the line into refusing to speak to him.

"Hey, remember when I said I wanted you to read my books?" Clark asked. He shook his head. "I regret that now."

"You read a book?" Palmer asked, looking impressed.

"I did try to warn you," he said. "I told you I wrapped up her story at the end of the second book."

"I thought you meant you gave her a happy ending. *Not* that she died a terrible death in the highest tower."

"I'm just impressed you read a book," Palmer said.

"Technically, I listened to one," I admitted.

She considered this for a moment. "Still counts."

"So what now?" I asked Clark, deciding that the time had come to start speaking to him again, especially because there were things I needed to know. "What happens in the next book? And when do you think it'll be done?"

"Yeah," Tom said, turning to Clark as well. "When will it be done?"

Clark looked at both of us and then dropped his head in his hands. "Not you guys too."

TOPHER
    Hey.

                                                                ME

                                            Hey—how's it going?

TOPHER

Can't complain. You around this weekend?

ME

So here's the thing.
I'm dating someone.

TOPHER

Damn—you're a total heartbreaker this summer.

ME

Ha ha, no. It's the same guy as before.

TOPHER

Oh.
Really?

ME

Yep

TOPHER

Well. That's new.

ME

It really is.

"Let me see if I can do it," my dad said, looking down at the six dogs I was holding, three leashes in each hand. His brow furrowed as he looked at them. "Fenway, Bertie, Leon, Duffy, Crackers, and . . ." His voice trailed off as he stared at the Pomeranian in front of him. "I don't know that one."

"Bella," I said, and my dad nodded. "But that was really close. I'm impressed."

"You get good with that when you can't ever forget a donor's name and you get brand-new colleagues every two years," my dad pointed out.

I'd been heading out on an afternoon walk when my dad had wandered into the kitchen and asked if he could tag along. I'd hesitated before agreeing—what if he saw the reality of what I was doing and was disappointed that it wasn't more impressive?—but had said he could come. Which meant that I'd already suffered through at least three "take your father to work day" jokes. "Ready?" I asked, intending this to be for my dad, but all the dogs looked up at me, tails wagging furiously.

"I can take some," my dad said, then took a small step back as he watched the two biggest dogs, Bertie and Fenway, lunge forward. "Uh, maybe not all of them."

"Here," I said. I separated out the leashes for Bella and Crackers and handed them to him. "Let's go."

We started walking, taking up most of the street with all the dogs. I'd gotten better at scouting new routes, looking for really quiet streets with ample trees and bushes. This was a new route, but I was already liking it—and so were the dogs, judging by the amount of ecstatic tree sniffing going on.

"Do you remember," my dad said, his words coming out hesitantly, "that stuffed dog you used to have?"

I stared at him for a moment, trying to remember which

one he was talking about—at one point my stuffed animal collection had been vast. But a second later, there it was. My dad had given it to me when I was something like six, a small black stuffed dog that came with its own leash. I remembered how thrilled I'd been to get it, how I had carried and dragged it with me everywhere for a while.

"Yeah," I said, looking over at him. "Of course."

"I was just thinking that maybe it was good practice for this," he said, nodding at the dogs and their leashes.

"Was that a Christmas present?" I was searching my memory, trying to recall the details. It was like one day the dog had always been with me, but I couldn't call up how it had gotten there.

"No," my dad said, looking offended. "Don't you remember? I had to go to that summit in London, and brought it back with me. It wouldn't fit in my carry-on, so it rode next to me on the plane."

I smiled, fighting down a lump in my throat. How had I forgotten about this stuff? It was like I hadn't let myself remember it in years and years—that my dad had been more to me than the last five years. That at one point we'd been really close, and the dog he flew across the ocean with had become my favorite because it was from him.

We walked without speaking for a few minutes, as I concentrated on making sure leashes weren't getting tangled and that everyone was getting along. It was a beautiful day out—sunny but not too hot, and the street we were on was tree-lined, the sunlight filtering through the leaves. "So what do you think?"

My dad reached over and scratched Bertie's ears, then patted him on the top of his head. "I think . . . ," he said, looking around at all the dogs in the sunshine, and then smiled at me. "I think you picked a pretty great way to spend your summer, kid."

"Yeah," I said, tugging on the leashes in both hands, more relieved than I'd realized I would be to hear this. "It has its moments."

TOPHER

    So who is this guy?

ME

You don't know him

TOPHER

    Try me

ME

His name's Clark. Do you know any Clarks?

TOPHER

    CLARK?

ME

Told you

TOPHER

    What, did he time travel here from the 1930s?

ME

Ha

Morgan Matson

Well, call me when you're free again.

Or have your old-timey boyfriend send a carrier pigeon.

ME

Talk to you later, Topher.

I dipped my toes into the hot tub and looked over at the very intense Ping-Pong game that was going on between Palmer and Clark on the lawn. Wyatt was in the pool, Toby was perched on the edge near him, and Bri and Tom were both floating on the oversize rafts Clark had bought last week, shaped like donuts and pretzels. None of this was a new or unusual sight because, as I'd predicted, my friends had pretty much moved in.

We still went to the Orchard and other people's parties, and movies when Bri could sneak us in for free, and there had been a week when Palmer had been determined to try out all the mini golf courses in a fifty-mile radius, and Wyatt had hit a hole in one into the clown's mouth and we'd all gotten free ice cream. But most nights, no matter what we did, we ended up back here, hanging out in the pool, watching movies on the couch, or lying on the lounge chairs under the stars. We'd even spent the Fourth of July there, everyone lying on floats in the pool and watching the fireworks we could see overhead from the official town celebration. Well—everyone else had watched the fireworks. Clark and I had taken turns sitting with Bertie in the laundry room, since Bertie hadn't realized all the explosions were just for pretend and had spent the night trembling and whimpering.

"Hey." I looked down and saw that Bri had floated up to the edge of the hot tub in her pretzel. She nodded over to where Toby was, and I could see in her expression that she was worried.

"She's fine," I said, though without a ton of conviction in my voice. Toby was wearing a new bathing suit, and she'd gotten her hair blown out straight, which was why she'd avoided getting in the water all night. She was wearing much more makeup than you normally did if you were going to be hanging out and swimming, and there was a kind of fixed desperation in her smile as she watched Wyatt in the pool.

"I don't know," Bri said as she pushed off the wall and steered her pretzel closer to Toby.

"So, Wyatt," Toby called in what I'm sure she intended to be a casual voice, but just came out strangled. "Wyatt," she repeated when he still didn't look over at her.

"Sorry," he said, giving her a quick smile, but not making a move to go any closer. "What's up?"

"So," she said, her voice coming out too fast and rehearsed, as she smoothed her hair down with one hand, "I was thinking about how you were saying you needed a new band name? And I came up with—"

"That's okay," he said with a shrug as he started to swim into the deep end. "We decided it might be better to just be unnamed. More mysterious, you know?" He ducked under the water, and I watched Toby's smile falter.

It didn't get any better over the next hour—Toby moving around the pool, clearly trying to be closer to wherever Wyatt was and Wyatt either not noticing or avoiding her on purpose,

Morgan Matson

but either way, barely talking to her. Palmer had won the last three Ping-Pong games and decided to quit while she was ahead, and we'd been lying on loungers next to each other while Tom and Clark tried to dive through the hole of the donut raft, often with disastrous results.

"I've got this," Tom said as Bri steadied the donut in the water for him. "I'm just visualizing my victory. And—"

Clark didn't let him finish, just pushed him in, and Tom belly flopped spectacularly, sending water flying.

"My hair!" Toby yelled, scrambling to her feet—and I could see she'd been squarely in the splash zone.

"Hey!" Tom said as he resurfaced, sputtering. "Not cool, man. I could have died."

"Did you have to do that?" Toby snapped, glaring at Tom. "Really? I was trying to keep my hair dry—it's the one thing I wanted, and you guys just—you just . . ." Toby's voice broke, and as I watched in horror, she started to cry.

Bri was out of the pool lightning-fast, putting her arm around Toby's shoulders and steering her toward the house. I looked at Palmer, who nodded and helped pull me to my feet.

"Um . . . I'm sorry," Tom called, sounding baffled as to what was happening.

Palmer and I found them in the kitchen, where Toby was sobbing into a paper towel and Bri was rubbing her back. "Sorry about your hair," I said, even though I knew it wasn't about the hair.

Toby started to smile, but then gave up the attempt partway through and shook her head. "It's so stupid."

"It's not," Bri said immediately.

"I just keep thinking that one of these days he'll look over and really see me, you know?" She wiped under her eyes, where mascara had started to streak down.

"I know," Bri murmured, pulling her in for a hug. I mouthed *She okay?* to Bri, who gave me a small smile and nodded. *I've got this*, she mouthed back.

An hour later, things had calmed down somewhat. Toby had pulled herself together and had done a spectacular swan dive into the water, clearly giving up on her hair for the night. After a serious game of sharks and minnows earlier that had ended with Palmer doing victory hand stands in the shallow end, I was on a lounge chair with Clark. He was sitting behind me, and we were wrapped up in the same towel. Bri and Toby were sitting on the edge of the deep end together, feet dangling in the water, laughing. Palmer was floating on her back while Tom treaded water next to her, saying something that made her smile.

"Did I tell you?" I asked, shaking my head as I leaned back against Clark.

"You told me," he said, leaning down and kissing a spot that I'd never even thought about before, but drove me crazy whenever he came near it, right on the edge of my shoulder. Over the course of many hours of making out, my formerly rigid boundaries—just kissing, and nothing more—had gotten a little fuzzier. Clark wasn't the one pushing me—though he seemed thrilled every time we ventured just a little further from my self-imposed limits. It was mostly me—everything was just feeling so good and so right that I was having more and more trouble remembering why I'd decided that was all I could do.

"They're never leaving," I said, shaking my head. "Don't say I didn't warn you."

I felt rather than heard Clark laugh behind me, and I leaned my head against his neck and closed my eyes for a moment—breathing it all in. The faint smell of chlorine on his skin, the way I could feel the pulse in his neck beating against my cheek, the soft terry of the towel around us. I looked up and saw the stars, and despite what had happened before, I felt really peaceful—Clark was next to me, I could hear my friends' laughter so close, and I knew for a fact that there was an unopened bag of chips inside in case we got hungry later. It felt like a really perfect moment that nothing could ruin.

"Hey," I heard Wyatt say, and I raised my head to see that he was sitting on a lounge chair across the pool from me, near Bri and Toby, and he had his guitar with him. "You guys mind if I jam out?"

"Sure," Toby immediately replied, tucking her hair behind her ears. "Of course."

"No," I said, struggling to get up, only to have Clark tighten his arms around me. I could already hear him laughing as he held me back. "He's doing it again," I protested, turning to look at Clark.

"I know," he said, smiling down at me.

"You promised. After last week's twelve-minute original composition, you *said* you'd let me shut him down the next time."

"I said that," Clark admitted as, across the water, Wyatt started to strum a chord.

"How is he going to learn this isn't okay?" I asked, giving up and letting myself fall back against Clark, who kissed the top of my head.

"Next time," he promised. The music started to drift toward us. It wasn't bad, though I'd never admit it. Clark held me a little tighter, and I leaned back against him, threading my fingers through his. "Next time for sure."

"I'll believe that when I see it," I said, leaning my head back against his.

Clark kissed my neck, and I felt a shiver run through me. "So you're free tomorrow, right?" he murmured, his lips close to my ear. "For your surprise?"

"Uh-huh," I said, trying to make myself focus. Clark had asked me last week to make sure the day was clear, but he'd refused to tell me any more of what we were going to do. I'd kind of been hoping it would involve Clark's empty house, the two of us, and an uninterrupted afternoon, and had let my mind drift toward this possibility more than it should have. "No clues?"

"Don't worry," Clark said, wrapping his arms around me and pulling me close. "I think you're going to love it."

"I can't believe you went *mountain biking*." Toby laughed as she shook her head.

I raised my head slightly, but every muscle in my body protested, and I lowered it again. It was two days since Clark's big "surprise," and now, in Toby's bedroom, I was still feeling the aftereffects. I'd spent the night before—when everyone else had been playing a very high-stakes game of chicken in the pool—sitting in the hot tub. "Clark's from Colorado," I explained. Even talking hurt. Even *breathing*. Needless to say, I had not been a fan. It was a sport for crazy people, and I was never going to do it again. "They think things like that are normal."

"I wouldn't do it," she said definitively.

"You totally would," I said, mostly to her ceiling, since it hurt too much to lift my head. "Don't you think you would in a second if Wyatt asked you?"

When she didn't respond after a moment, I forced myself to sit up, inch by painful inch. "Tobes?" I called before I'd sat all the way up, hoping she was still in the room and I hadn't just been talking to myself. But she was there, twisting her hands together, in the way I'd learned long ago meant she was upset about something. "You okay?"

Toby bit her lip, then came over to the bed and flopped down next to me. "I talked to Wyatt," she said, her voice quiet as she pulled at a loose thread on her comforter.

"Oh," I said, my heart sinking as I realized from her tone that this wasn't good news. Otherwise, I would have heard about it immediately, with lots of big-smile, star, clapping-hands, and heart emojis.

"Yeah," Toby said, pulling at the thread harder now. "I figured that you guys had been telling me to forever, and what's the worst that could happen? So I asked him if he wanted to hang out sometime, just the two of us."

"And?"

"And at least he didn't pretend not to understand what I was talking about," Toby said with a sigh. "He just said that he thinks I'm great, but he's interested in someone else."

This made my sit up straighter, and a second later I regretted it immediately, as my abs felt like they were on fire. "I'm so sorry, T," I said, trying to reach out to hug her but giving up when I realized it wasn't going to happen.

THE UNEXPECTED EVERYTHING

"Yeah." Toby sighed as she gave me a sad smile.

"What did Bri say?"

"Just that it's better to know. And she's right. Now maybe I can start to get over him."

"Who's this girl?" I asked. This honestly had shocked me, and I figured it had to be someone he worked with, since Wyatt was hanging out with us every night. Unless—and this seemed like a real possibility—it was just what he'd told Toby to let her down easier.

Toby rolled over onto her side and looked at me, her expression anguished. "I don't *know*. I didn't really feel like I could ask. So then we had the world's most awkward hug, and I pretended I was getting a text and told him I had to leave."

I took a breath, to suggest getting ice cream, or coffee, something to take her mind off of this, when I realized maybe she didn't want to be distracted from it. That maybe this wasn't something she wanted me to try to fix. Maybe she just wanted me to be here. "Hey," I said, nudging her with my foot, which was one of the few things I could move without searing pain, "so what are you thinking?"

Toby gave me a slightly trembly smile, then took a breath and started to talk. I just lay there next to her, as the afternoon light starting spilling across the room, and listened.

Morgan Matson

Chapter TWELVE

"Are you guys ready for this?" Palmer asked, clapping her hands together. She was standing next to the statue of Winthrop Stanwich in the fading sunlight, and she was practically bouncing up and down.

It was the last week in July, which meant it was finally the night I'd been looking forward to all summer—the night of the scavenger hunt. We were all there—me, Clark, Tom, Palmer, Bri, Toby, and Wyatt. Toby was sitting next to me, while Bri sat on the nearest picnic table, and the boys seemed to be trying to figure out who could get injured the fastest, as they swung, standing up, on the playground swings.

Palmer grinned and pulled out three sheets of paper, which she fanned out and held up. "Three teams of two," she said. "Same items on all of them. You guys have two hours."

"What do we win?" Toby asked, looking only mildly interested. Ever since the Wyatt rejection, she'd been a little more quiet and sad, like she was a dimmer version of her usual self. I watched her look over at him as the boys jumped off their swings and came to join us, but then immediately look away again. In contrast to the rest of the summer, she'd been avoiding being alone with Wyatt whenever possible.

"You win eternal glory," Palmer said excitedly. She pulled out a battered trophy on a pedestal, shaped like a cup. "And this trophy." When none of us responded, she smiled. "Okay, and here's a sweetener. Winner gets to choose the terms of their prize. Within reason."

"What does that mean?" I asked.

"What do you want?" Palmer countered. "Like for example, if Toby wins, and she wants it as her prize, I drop our emoji bet and she can go back to texting for real again."

Next to me, Toby had gone very still. "Really?" she asked, suddenly sounding much more awake than she had for the past week. "You mean it?"

"So like, if we win, we could make the winning team pay for all our meals at the diner for the rest of the summer?" Tom asked.

"Or we could play guitar without anyone complaining?" Wyatt asked, widening his eyes at me.

"Both sound fair," Palmer said with a grin. "You guys ready to learn your teams?"

"Wait," Toby said, and I saw she was looking over at Bri. "We don't get to choose?"

"The cup chooses," Palmer intoned. She dropped pieces of paper into the cup and swirled it around. "Well, I mean, technically I choose, but you get the idea." I had just looked at Clark, when Palmer pulled the first two names from the cup. "Clark and Tom," she pronounced as Bri and Toby said, "Tark!" simultaneously.

"Next," Pamer said, reaching into the cup. I saw Toby look

around at the four of us who were left, her expression growing worried, and I had a feeling the last thing she wanted was to be paired with Wyatt.

"Bri and Wyatt," Palmer said, and I could practically feel Toby relax next to me, turning her head away when Wyatt walked up to Bri, holding up his hand for a high five, saying something that made Bri laugh. "And that leaves Andie and Toby," she said, dropping the papers back in the cup.

"We're going to crush this, right?" I asked, smiling at her, secretly hoping this was what Toby needed to get out of her funk.

"Right," Toby said, blinking at me. Then a look of fierce determination came over her face, and I had a feeling that the possibility of being able to text for real had raised the stakes for her. "I mean, yes!" She took a step closer to me. "Seriously, Andie," she said. "My boss doesn't understand emojis and thinks I'm making fun of him when I text. I *need* this."

"So this is like a quest, right?" Clark asked, looking thrilled, while next to him, Tom did a series of limbering-up exercises.

"Kind of," Tom said as he bent from side to side, then started running in place.

"Can we call it a quest?" Clark asked, his voice getting a little higher, the way it did when he got really excited about something. "I've always wanted to go on one of those."

"Here we go!" Palmer said, placing three papers down on the table in front of her. Then she backed away, turning her palms like a croupier to show us they were empty. "Best of luck to all teams. You have two hours. Your time starts . . . now!"

We all ran for the table, and Toby grabbed our sheet and ran away with it, gesturing for me to go with her. Tom grabbed a sheet and dashed off, and I looked at Clark. "Good luck," I said, raising an eyebrow at him.

"May the best team win," Clark said, and then pulled me in close to him, dipping me into a Hollywood-style kiss. I giggled, but my laughter soon faded as I started kissing him back for real.

"Hey!" I broke away and looked over to see Toby standing in front of me, waving the paper in my face. "Come on. We're wasting time. And you're fraternizing with the enemy!"

"But the enemy's so cute," I said as Clark pulled me back up to my feet and gave me one more quick kiss before running off to join Tom, glancing back once and waving to me.

"That might have been part of their strategy," Toby said as she snapped her fingers in front of my face. "Get you all distracted and then they get to sweep in and take the win. Well, not on my watch. I'm not losing my chance to start using actual words again."

"What do we have?" I looked at the list Palmer had typed up.

COTTON BALLS 1 POINT

THIS LIST, NOTARIZED 20 POINTS

BLUE GUM BALL 4 POINTS

ARTICLE OF FORMAL WEAR (MEN'S OR WOMEN'S) 10 POINTS

FIREFLY 12 POINTS

BURNT SIENNA CRAYON 5 POINTS

HAT THAT'S NOT A BASEBALL CAP 7 POINTS

BELL 1 POINT

BOOK 1 POINT

CANDLE 1 POINT

A SQUARE YOU EAT 5 POINTS

Morgan Matson

SOMETHING IN A JAR 5 POINTS

SOMETHING ALIVE 7 POINTS

SOMETHING WITH A BOAT ON IT 5 POINTS

AN ACTUAL BOAT 10 POINTS

SOMETHING HOT 3 POINTS

SOMETHING COLD 3 POINTS

DICTIONARY 3 POINTS

PICTIONARY 6 POINTS

SOMETHING THAT LIGHTS UP 7 POINTS

ITEM THAT STARTS WITH Z 9 POINTS

COIN FROM BEFORE 1980 5 POINTS

DINER MENU 10 POINTS

BUSINESS SLOGAN WITH A PUN 5 POINTS

PIZZA WITH THREE TOPPINGS 5 POINTS

NAPKINS 2 POINTS

BOTTLE OF SODA 2 POINTS

ICE CREAM SAMPLE SPOON 3 POINTS

THRILLER DANCE, FROM BEGINNING TO END 12 POINTS

I stared down at the items on the list, thinking about the strategy I'd been refining. I wouldn't make the same mistake I did last time by going for the big-ticket items. This wasn't about getting everything on the list. This was about getting the most points and winning Toby her texting freedom back—not to mention freeing me up from trying to figure out what three dancing girls, a cat, and a frowny face meant.

"Okay," I said, reading the list once, then once again. I watched Bri and Wyatt take off toward his truck and Tom and Clark start to run for Clark's SUV.

"What's our plan?" Toby asked, running her hands through her hair.

"I think we go with home-court advantage," I said. Toby just looked at me blankly. "My house is down the street," I clarified, and she started nodding. "I say we go there, get what we can, and we're already ahead of the game. . . ." I reached into my pocket for my keys, but it was empty. I frowned, starting to get a bad feeling as I reached into my other pocket. "Oh, no."

"What?"

I turned in the direction Clark had run, but of course, he and Tom were long gone. "Clark took my keys," I said, suddenly understanding the dip kiss. I was trying to stay mad at him, but I was actually just impressed with his technique. I hadn't seen it coming. "We need to take your car."

"Bri drove me," Toby said, her eyes getting wide. We both turned to Palmer, who was sitting on top of the picnic table. "Palmer, we need your car," Toby said, running up to her. She grabbed Palmer's purse, then started shaking the contents of it out onto the table.

"Tom drove me," Palmer said, frowning at the pile of her possessions Toby was currently rifling through. "Looks like you guys will have to figure out something else." Palmer held up her phone so that we could see the timer counting down. "One hour and fifty minutes, guys. Tick-tock."

Toby and I looked at each other, and I realized there was just one thing to do. I pulled off my flip-flops and nodded down the road. "My house," I said, taking a breath. "Ready to run for it?"

. . .

Morgan Matson

"DAD!" I screamed as I barreled into the house, Toby at my heels. A second later, I realized how that sounded. "Everything is fine!" I yelled a moment later. There was no need to give my father a heart attack.

"No, it's not!" Toby yelled, though a little less loudly than me. "We need help!"

"What's going on?" my dad called. A moment later he hustled into the foyer, where we were trying to catch our breath. The run we'd done to get to the house had been enough to remind me that walking large dogs, while nicely toning my biceps, had not actually done much to improve my running ability. He took in the sight of us, and his expression grew more alarmed. "You two okay? Hi there, Toby."

"Hi, Mr. Walker," Toby said, still breathing hard, her face pretty much the same color as her hair.

"We're doing a scavenger hunt," I said, handing my dad the paper, which had gotten more than a little wrinkled during our dash to my house. "Were you doing something?" I asked, suddenly noticing that my dad's reading glasses were sticking out of his shirt pocket.

"No, just looking at something for a friend," my dad said as he glanced down at the paper, absently smoothing it out. His eyebrows raised. "This is a pretty challenging scavenger hunt."

"Palmer," I said by way of explanation, and my dad nodded. "And we have to win."

"We really do," Toby said, the gleam back in her eye. "It's *essential*."

"And Clark stole my keys, so I might need to borrow your car."

"He did?" my dad asked, starting to smile. I frowned at him, and his expression grew more serious. "I mean, of course he shouldn't have done that to you. But I didn't think he had it in him."

"We need to move!" Toby said, clapping her hands together. "Let's go!"

"Okay," I said, leaning over to look at the list, which my dad was still holding. "We need to see what we can get here before we go elsewhere," I said, eyes scanning down it. "Cotton balls," I said, and I pointed upstairs. "My bathroom."

"On it!" Toby yelled as she ran for the staircase.

"I can get you a bow tie or cummerbund so you can get your article of formal wear," my dad said, reading off the paper, and I looked at him, surprised. "If you want me to help, that is."

"Yeah," I said, after only the tiniest of pauses. It wasn't that I didn't—I just hadn't imagined that he'd *want* to help, or be a part of this at all. "That would be great."

"That might be all we have here," my dad said, pulling out a mechanical pencil from his pocket and starting to make notes on the list, using the hall table as a desk. "I can look at my change and see if I have any from before 1980." He looked up at me and tapped his pencil twice on the paper. "Do you think that *includes* 1980?"

"Probably better not to assume," I said. My dad nodded and started making more notes. I looked down at the paper and shook my head. "I don't think I have a burnt sienna crayon," I said. "But I can grab a book and a hat that's not a baseball cap from my room."

"Andie!" Toby yelled from upstairs.

My dad looked at his watch. "Let's reconnoiter in five," he said, and I nodded, then bolted up the stairs.

"What?" I asked as I walked through my room to the bathroom. After this many years, I knew she would have no compunction going through my things, so I wasn't sure what she needed. "Did you get the cotton balls?"

"Got them," she said, pointing to the bag on the counter. "But . . . what's this?" She opened up my bathroom cabinet, which was stacked high with pretty much every feminine product you could imagine—tampons, pads, Midol, and *lots* of all of them. "What, is there like a shortage or something?" she asked, laughing. Then her expression grew more serious. "Wait, is there actually a shortage? Do I need to stockpile too?"

"No," I said, resisting the opportunity to mess with her. "My mom bought them for me when . . . when she found out she was sick."

"Oh," Toby said, her expression changing immediately. She looked at me without speaking, searching my face, and I knew she was trying to see if I wanted her to talk about it, or to drop it. She'd do either one in a heartbeat. I knew that from experience.

And normally I would have left it at that. But I'd never told anyone this—maybe not surprisingly, it had never come up before. "Yeah," I said, my throat feeling a little tighter than usual. "She was worried I wouldn't have any when I needed it. And she didn't want me to feel embarrassed about asking my dad to buy them for me." I looked at all the stacked boxes, most of which I hadn't touched in years, once I was able to start shopping for myself. But I'd never even thought about throwing them away. My mother had bought them for me. She'd gone to

CVS and picked them out so that she could help me even when she wouldn't be here.

"That's really nice," Toby said quietly, giving me a smile, and I nodded.

"Girls!" my dad yelled from downstairs. "It's been five minutes!"

Toby paled. "It has?" She grabbed the cotton balls and bolted for the door. Then she stopped and turned back to me. "Unless you want to talk," she said, voice rising in a question.

I shook my head and pointed to the door. "Scavenger hunt!"

Five minutes later we were in the car—all of us, with my dad behind the wheel. "Seat belts?" he asked as he backed out of the garage.

"Check," Toby said, from where she was sitting in the middle of the backseat, leaning forward.

I hadn't anticipated that we were formally adding a member to our team, but we'd been all set to go—having dropped all the items we were able to grab from the house into a big canvas bag—when my dad had handed me the keys to his sedan and then frowned. "Do you know how to drive a stick shift?"

I did not, and I was pretty sure learning to drive stick took more than five minutes. And since we still wanted to have a fighting shot at winning this, my dad had offered to drive us. We'd decided on the first stop, and I was trying to figure out our plan for the rest. "I think we should get the pizza toward the end," I said, making a note with my dad's pencil as he pulled out onto the road, going a little faster than normal. "We can get the napkins, the ice, and the soda at the pizza place too." I thought of something and looked up. "Do you think this is just Palmer's way of getting us to pick up dinner?"

"We don't have time for speculation," Toby snapped, frowning at her phone. "I'm trying to learn the Thriller dance here."

"I thought we agreed to skip that one because it was time-inefficient."

"Well, it's a mute point anyway, because my phone just died," she said, dropping it into her bag.

"A *mute* point?" my dad asked, glancing over at me.

"I know," I said, shaking my head at him. "Believe me, we've all tried to tell her."

"Can I use yours?" Toby asked, leaning forward and holding out her hand.

"Sure," I said, handing it over while still reading over the list, waiting for a sudden flash of insight that would help me figure out what item we could get that started with *Z*. The only thing I could seem to think of was "Zamboni," even as I tried to tell my brain there had to be other words that started with that letter. "Oh, but do me a favor and text Clark? Tell him I'm mad at him about the keys and he's not going to get away with it."

"I think he did get away with it," my dad pointed out, as he slowed for a stop sign, but then immediately gunned the engine again. I had a feeling he was enjoying this. "You're just going to have to figure out how to get him back."

"Okay, how's this?" Toby asked, handing my phone to me.

"What is this?" I asked, turning around to look at her.

"What?" she asked. "I said that we were mad, that we wanted the keys back, and if he didn't do it, he was dead."

"But what's with the sneaker?"

"Toby," she explained in a patient voice. "Toe-bee. Come on, Andie, think about it."

"But this is my phone," I pointed out. "You're texting as me. I think you could use actual words and still win the bet."

"Oh," Toby said, suddenly looking nervous. "I . . . I'm not so sure about that."

"Why can't you text with actual words?" my dad asked as he sped through a yellow.

"Palmer's betting Toby she can't go the whole summer only using emojis," I said, shaking my head. "We tried to talk her out of it."

My dad glanced down at my phone, then threw Toby a sympathetic look in the rearview mirror. "Well, I think that's very clever," he said to her, and Toby smiled as she took my phone back from me. "Maybe you should have tried harder," he said to me in an undertone.

I fought back a smile as I looked down at the list. "Well, if we win this, she's in the clear again," I said. I glanced into the backseat. "Tobes, how are we on time?"

"Hour and a half. We're going to need to move."

"On it," my dad said, grinning as he sped up. We screeched to a stop in front of the diner five minutes later, and I turned to Toby.

"Ready?" I asked, and Toby yelled, "Break!" and bolted from the car, not waiting for me to follow.

"Be right back," I said to my dad as I unbuckled my seat belt.

"I'll keep the car running."

I ran full-out toward the diner, taking the steps two at a time. Most of the other items on the list could be acquired at a variety of places—or at least more than one—but for Diner Menu, I was pretty sure Palmer meant one of the actual, fake-leather-bound menus, not the paper ones for to-go orders. We'd also discussed that this might be our best chance to pick up a Blue Gum Ball from the candy machines in the waiting area. As I pulled the door open, I saw Toby was already feeding coins into the candy machine and cranking the knob. "Just check the dates," I reminded her as I continued in to the restaurant. "Anything before 1980, don't waste on the gum ball!" Toby gave me a withering *I know* look, but I noticed that she started checking her coins.

I approached the hostess stand, which was deserted as usual, even though the restaurant was pretty full, mostly of families crammed into the booths. I glanced under the hostess stand, where I'd seen extra stacks of menus in the past. But was I actually going to be able to just steal one? This immediately became a mute point, though, since the podium was empty. I looked around the restaurant, and spotted Carly sitting at the nearly-empty counter, with a stack of menus and a bottle of Windex in front of her.

I headed straight over, grateful that she was working and not one of the waitresses who hated us. I knew we would have had no luck at all with them.

"Hi there!" I said in my friendliest voice, as Carly looked up from where she was cleaning the menus—Windexing and then wiping off with a towel.

"It's self-seating right now," she said, giving the appetizer page a wipe-down. "Anything that's open."

"No, it's not that," I said, taking a breath. I needed to be charming and ingratiating, or we didn't have a chance. I realized that I hadn't had to do this in a while, since I hadn't had to go to any fund-raisers or meet with potential donors. It was like trying to flex a muscle I hadn't used in a long time. "I was just wondering if possibly we could just borrow one of these menus for an hour or two? We'll bring it right back. And you can even give me one of the ones you haven't gotten to yet, and I can clean it for you!" I smiled brightly at Carly, who just looked at me and gave the menu another spray.

"This about the scavenger hunt?" she asked, nodding before I'd had a chance to answer. "They already beat you in here. Clark and . . ." Carly frowned, and there was a long pause—a much longer pause than was normally needed to come up with someone's name. "Phil?" she finally asked, sounding very unsure of her answer.

I tried to keep my face steady, and resolved not to tell Tom that Carly thought his name was Phil. It would probably just add insult to injury that she knew Clark's name, even though he'd been going there for six weeks, but not Tom's, who'd been going there for three years. "Right," I said, nodding. "Guess they beat us here. But . . . do you think we could have one too?"

"Sorry," Carly said, snapping a menu shut and adding it to the stack. "I made a promise."

"But . . ." It wasn't like the diner, as far as I knew, had a one-menu-per-scavenger hunt policy. If she could give Clark and Tom one, why not one to us?

Morgan Matson

"Also, they gave me forty bucks *not* to give you one," Carly said, raising an eyebrow at me. "So no can do."

I silently cursed Tom, since I was pretty sure this had been his idea—learned, no doubt, from Palmer's sister Ivy, who had won numerous Alden family scavenger hunts with only one item, having spent the whole scavenging time shutting down other people's chances. I took a breath to try and persuade Carly, but she'd just spun her stool so that her back was to me. Clearly, I wasn't going to get anywhere with her—not unless I could somehow find eighty dollars to bribe her with.

I walked out to the candy machines, where Toby was fuming. "No luck?" She just pointed down, where I could see her purse was half-filled with gum balls—none of them blue.

"I've gotten like eight yellows and four reds," Toby said as she checked the date on her quarter and dropped it in the slot. "Usually all you can get are these stupid blue gum balls!"

"Well, maybe Tom and Clark got to all of them first too," I said, shaking my head. Toby opened up the little metal flap and pulled out a green gum ball, then frowned at me.

"What do you mean?" she asked, throwing the green one into her purse. "Where's the menu?"

"The guys gave Carly forty dollars not to give us one."

"What!" Toby straightened up to face me. "That's just unfair. Your stupid boyfriend with his stupid dragon money!"

The outside door swung open and my dad stepped in, looking between me and Toby. "You ladies doing okay?" he asked, glancing down at his watch. "Because we should probably get going."

"Clark's bribing people not to give us menus," Toby said, looking at me like this was somehow my fault.

"We don't know that," I said. "Let's not cast aspersions. It could have been Tom. Or, as Carly calls him, Phil."

"And none of these are blue," Toby said, picking up her purse, which made a *click*ing sound. She sighed. "Let's just move on. They won this round."

My dad glanced into the diner and frowned. I saw a look in his eye, one I recognized. I knew my dad really did care about helping people and making a difference. But he was also great at campaigning. And this was the look he had when he was behind in a debate, when pundits were calling the election, and not in his favor, when all seemed lost. It was how he looked just before he started to fight back. "Not so fast," he said as he started to walk into the restaurant.

Toby blinked at my dad, then looked at me. "What does that mean?"

I didn't answer her, just watched my dad stride up to Carly, his important-person walk still making people in the restaurant look up and take notice. "Hello," I could hear him saying, his voice carrying across to me easily. He held out his hand for a handshake, and I noticed Carly take it, suddenly sitting up a little straighter. "I'm Representative Alexander Walker. I was hoping to talk to you about a time-sensitive matter."

I looked back at Toby. "It means we're getting a menu."

Five minutes later, we were all running out to the car together, my dad clutching two leather-bound menus with a smile on his face. "How did you do that?" I asked as we ran, the contents of Toby's bag clinking as she walked.

My dad beeped open the car and we all got in, nobody

wasting any time. "I just told her," he said as he started the car and screeched out of his parking spot, "that I was thinking about hosting a campaign fund-raiser there and wanted to see what kind of options they had available."

"And she believed you?" I asked.

My dad nodded to the menus he'd dropped on the dashboard. "Enough to give me those," he said. "I just need to return them tomorrow. Along with a signed picture for their wall."

"Awesome," Toby said, leaning forward between our seats as far as her seat belt would allow. "Onward!"

TOM

Did you have success at the diner?

ME

"What's with the elephant?" I asked, taking my phone back from Toby as we ran up the steps to Captain Pizza. We'd called in our order on the way, and I was just crossing my fingers that, even though it was a Friday night, they would actually have our pizza ready on time. I saw, next door, my dad striding into Paradise Ice Cream, where he was going to try to get the Ice Cream Tasting Spoon, despite the fact that they weren't disposable at Paradise but actual spoons that you dropped into a mason jar to be washed and reused. We were getting tight on time, but with luck, we'd be leaving the pizza parlor with three items checked off the list—Pizza With Three Toppings, Bottle of Soda, and Napkins.

"Because elephants never forget," Toby said, like this was the most obvious answer in the world, as she yanked open the door. "And I'm not going to forget either."

"We got the menus," I reminded her as we ran up to the counter. The restaurant was half-filled already, and I hoped it wasn't going to affect how fast they were getting to-go orders out.

"Even so," Toby said darkly.

"Hey!" a blond girl in a CAPTAIN PIZZA shirt said as we approached the counter. DAWN, read the lettering in military typeface on her T-shirt. "Can I help you?"

"Picking up for Walker," I said as I glanced down at the clock on my phone. "Large pie with toppings on three-fourths of it, and one-fourth plain." I had been the one placing the order, so this had been my attempt to try to get some pizza I could actually eat, since I wasn't going to touch the sausage-mushroom-onion combo that Toby swore to me was actually really good.

"And we need a bottle of soda," Toby said, slapping her hand on the counter while I silently tried to tell her to take it down a notch. "And napkins! All the napkins you have!"

"Okay," Dawn said, looking a little freaked out as she turned to look at the to-go boxes stacked above the oven.

"I've got the soda," a voice behind us said, and a girl with short dark hair came out from where she'd been sitting in a booth. She wasn't wearing a Captain Pizza uniform, and it took me a moment to recognize her as Emily Hughes.

"Hi," I said immediately, then hesitated. I knew who she

was, and I was pretty sure she knew me, since I'd been in AP Physics with her last year. But I mostly knew her because everyone knew who Emily Hughes was—she was half of the school's golden couple.

She smiled back at me. "Oh, hi, Andie," she said. "How's it going?"

"We're kind of in a hurry?" Toby said.

Emily just laughed. "Sure," she said, crossing behind the counter and heading to the refrigerated cases. "What kind of soda?"

"Any kind!" Toby yelled, as I said, "Diet Coke?"

"Pie's up," Dawn said. She slid it across the counter to me. I handed her a twenty, and she turned to the register to ring me up. As she did, I noticed the back of her shirt read, CAPTAIN PIZZA . . . YOU BETTER MARSHAL YOUR APPETITE!

I looked at Toby, then nodded at the shirt, and saw her eyes widen. This could easily take care of Business Slogan with a Pun. "Um, so," I said as I took back my change from Dawn and dropped a dollar in the tip jar, "do you guys sell those shirts here?"

"These?" Dawn asked, glancing down at herself and making a face. "Why would you want this?"

Emily placed the two-liter bottle of Diet Coke in front of me and came to stand next to Dawn, leaning her elbows on the counter.

"It's . . . ," I started, trying to think of some excuse that would make sense, but finally decided we didn't have time for me to come up with anything rational and that I should probably just to go with the truth. "We're doing a scavenger hunt, and we need something that has a business slogan with a pun," I explained.

"Ah," Dawn said, turning to Emily. "So you're trying to check items off a list?" she asked, nudging her. "What's *that* like?"

"Ignore my friend," Emily said to us, rolling her eyes. "She's inhaled too many pizza fumes today."

"We don't sell the shirts," Dawn said, bending down under the counter. "But we hired his guy who lasted, like, one day and then quit in a huff last week." She held it up, turning it around so I could see. The name on the front read T.J., and on the back was printed, CAPTAIN PIZZA . . . YOU GET THE GENERAL IDEA! "I could give it to you if you want. I'm pretty sure he's never coming back."

"That's awesome," I said, and next to me, Toby nodded and grabbed the shirt out of Dawn's hands. "Thank you so much."

We were halfway across the parking lot, heading for the car, when I saw my dad walking out of Paradise Ice Cream, a pint in one hand and his car keys in the other, whistling in a way that I'm sure he thought was nonchalant but actually wasn't. "Got the ice cream," he called to us in a loud, far-too-cheerful voice, glancing once behind him. He started walking fast down the steps, and I didn't understand what was happening until the door to Paradise opened and an annoyed-looking girl stepped out.

"Hey!" she called, as my dad started walking even faster. "Sir? You're not supposed to take the sample spoons!"

I looked at my dad, feeling my jaw fall open as he tossed the keys in my direction. I caught them with one hand, which surprised me so much I almost dropped them again. "Unlock the car," he said to me, now breaking into a run. "I think we should get out of here."

The girl was still standing in the doorway glaring at him,

Morgan Matson

phone held out in one hand, like she was debating calling the police. I unlocked the car, and Toby and I got in just a second before my dad did. He handed me the pint of ice cream, I handed him the keys, and he started the car and roared out of the parking lot. "You *stole* the sample spoon?"

"Well, she didn't want to give it to me," my dad said, glancing into the rearview mirror once, like he was making sure the Paradise security team wasn't giving chase. "I offered to pay her for it," he said, slowing down a little now as he must have realized that he wasn't actually involved in a high-speed pursuit. "Here," he said, pulling a spoon out from his shirt pocket, then glanced behind him at Toby. "Did we get the pizza?"

She nodded. "And a slogan with a pun in it," she said. "So I think we're in pretty good shape." She leaned forward, motioning for me to give her my phone. "How are we on time?"

"We have thirty-five minutes left," I said. I looked at the list. "We need a place where we can get a lot of little stuff, because some of them have big points value, for some reason."

"I know where to go," Toby said, leaning forward between the front seats. "Mr. Walker?"

"Talk to me, Toby," he said, and she grinned.

"Take the right up there," she said. "And step on it."

Six pretty harrowing minutes later, my dad screeched up at the entrance to the gas station/mini-mart and swung into an open parking space with a spin of the wheel. I had a feeling it was going to be hard for him to return to regular driving after this, and not driving while pretending to be James Bond.

"Are you sure you don't want help?" I asked, turning to look at Toby.

"No," Toby said, hand already on the car door handle. "This one is all me."

I nodded, even as I snuck a glance at the clock. We only had half an hour left, and we still had to make it back to the Winthrop statue, but Toby felt she had something to prove and was insisting on doing this alone.

"How long did she say she needed for this?" my dad asked a minute later, looking straight ahead through the glass doors, where we could see Toby dashing up one aisle and down another, then doubling back to the first one. While there were a few people pumping gas, there was nobody in the mini-mart except the guy behind the counter, which, judging from how crazy Toby was looking from out here, was probably a good thing.

I glanced down at the time I'd set on my phone. "She said she only needs seven minutes." I wasn't sure she was going to make it, since she was still running around the store and she had only three minutes left.

"I'll take that action," my dad said, raising his eyebrows at me.

"You think she can't do it?" I asked, as we both watched Toby come to a standstill, apparently distracted by the maga-zine display.

"If she can't, I get to pick what we watch on Sunday," my dad said. "If she can, it's your pick." I looked at Toby, who was back in motion, and nodded.

"Deal." We shook on it, and I looked back at the mini-mart, willing Toby to move faster. My dad and I had fallen into the habit of having lazy, stay-around-the-house Sundays. We usually seemed to both wind up in my dad's study, where I'd pretend to read my textbooks and he'd pretend to read his latest historical biography while we basically just watched TV all day. Last week my dad had decided to be proactive about it, and had DVR'd a John Wayne marathon. I'd rolled my eyes, but it actually hadn't been that bad, though I was looking forward to getting him back with a marathon of my own.

I glanced down at the countdown clock on my phone, then turned it over, knowing if I didn't I'd just stare at it the whole time. I leaned back in my seat and looked around, suddenly realizing where we were—at the mini-mart almost on the Hartfield border. I glanced over at my dad, wondering for a second if he knew. My mom had always said it was our secret, but I was a kid then, so I'd never actually been sure.

I took a breath, then said, "Did Mom ever tell you we used to come here?"

My dad just looked at me. "Where?" he asked, sounding confused. "The gas station?"

"Not really," I said, closing my eyes for just a second and remembering. My mom gently shaking me awake, the smile on her face as I struggled to bring her into focus. "Andie," she'd whisper. "Want to go have an adventure?"

"It was when you were working in D.C.," I said, the words coming slowly. I'd never talked about this to anyone before. It had been something just between my mother and me, all those magical nights where time seemed to stop, and for a little while it was like we were the only people awake in the world, like the stars were shining for us alone. "I never knew when it was going to happen. She said it was when life was getting too ordinary."

"That sounds like her," my dad said, a smile tugging at one corner of his mouth, his voice quiet.

"She'd wake me up," I said, smiling just remembering it, how it somehow felt exciting just to be out and driving around in a car in my cupcake pajamas. "We'd drive all over in the Mustang with the top down. And we'd always end up here."

We both sat quietly for a moment, looking into the window of the store, as Toby wandered down an aisle, stopped, consulted the list, then started moving again.

"We used to get candy and hot chocolate," I said, remembering what it had been like to drive home, the wind whipping though my hair and my hands around the warm paper cup. "She always said that it was something you didn't necessarily need to know about."

"I'm glad you told me," my dad said, his voice still quiet, a tiny hitch in the back of it somewhere. We weren't looking at each other now; we were both looking straight ahead, and I knew that was making it easier. "She really could make anything magical, couldn't she?"

I nodded. It was one of the things I'd taken for granted when it was just my life, but now that it was gone I could see how amazing and rare it had been. "She could," I said, still looking ahead, feeling my throat get tight. "It's like anything could be an adventure, even just driving around in pajamas."

"You know how much she loved you, right?" my dad asked, and two tears fell down, one from each of my eyes, without me even realizing they were going to. "She thought you hung the moon. She'd be so proud of you."

I brushed the back of my hand over my face and took a shaky breath. "Yeah?" I asked, thinking that she probably would have been—with my grades, and my goals, and my other summers full of productive things.

"Absolutely," my dad said, his voice still cracking a little. "This thing with the dogs? She would have loved that. She would have done a series of oil paintings of them all by now."

I gave a laugh at that with half a sob mixed in, because I could see in that moment just how true it was. My mother would have loved that I was outside all day, that I was having fun. I would have come home every day and told her about the canine misadventures, and she would have done different voices for every dog. "What happened to the Mustang?" I asked after we'd sat in silence for a moment, even though it didn't feel like bad silence—it just felt filled up.

"I'm not sure," my dad said, looking down at the steering wheel. "I could find out if you want."

I nodded. "Yeah," I said. "That'd be good."

"Here!" The backseat door was flung open and Toby tumbled inside, carrying two overstuffed plastic bags. The inside lights flared on and it suddenly seemed very bright. I leaned forward, brushing my hand over my face again, hoping it wasn't totally obvious that I'd been crying. "I'm here. Did I make it?"

"Oh," I said, turning over my phone to look at the timer. I had totally forgotten about it. I'd forgotten, frankly, about the scavenger hunt. "Um, no. Missed it by a minute and a half." I looked at my dad, who was starting the car with a grin. Now that I was getting pulled out of this moment I'd had with my dad, it was all coming back to me—the side bet we'd placed on Toby, which meant he got to choose our next movie. "Just no more John Wayne?"

"I make no promises," he said. He turned and looked at me, gave me a small smile, and I gave him one back, and even though we weren't technically speaking, it felt like we were saying the same thing. Then he put the car in gear and pulled away from the mini-mart.

Sixteen minutes later he screeched to a stop, pulling to the side of the street in front of the Winthrop statue. "We made it," he said, exhaling and shooting me a smile across the car.

"Let's move, people," Toby said, clapping her hands and then scrambling to pick up the items that were scattered all over the backseat. "Andie, can you see anyone? Did everyone else beat us here?"

"I see the guys," I said, unbuckling my seat belt and leaning forward to look. While we'd been gone, Palmer had clearly been busy—the picnic table was now divided into three sections, and she'd put signs up, marking which team each section belonged to. Clark and Tom were setting up a truly impressive pile of stuff, and I felt a twinge of alarm. From a distance, at least, it looked like we would be pretty evenly matched, if not behind them. "But I don't see Bri or Wyatt anywhere."

Toby stepped backward out of the car, hoisting an over-stuffed canvas bag on each shoulder, and slammed the door closed with her foot. "I'll get us started," she said, already running toward the table. "Hurry!"

I grabbed my stuff and hustled out, shutting the door behind me. I started to follow Toby toward the picnic table, but then stopped and turned back to the car, where my dad was watching the proceedings through my open passenger-seat window. "Um," I said, not really sure what to say. I suddenly wished this weren't ending in just a few minutes. For a while there, it was like we'd been part of the same team. "Thanks," I finally said, and my dad gave me a smile.

"Good luck," he said, shifting the car into drive. "Just don't stay out too late celebrating our victory."

"Knock on wood!" I called as I started to run toward the table, and his car pulled out, now moving at a much more normal speed as it headed in the direction of the house.

"Two minutes," Palmer called out as I stumble-ran up to the table.

"Okay," I muttered. I dropped my bags and started hauling stuff out of them. Tom and Clark were at the opposite end of the table; the middle was Bri and Wyatt's, and it was still totally empty. "Have they not shown up yet?" I asked. Palmer shook her head.

"We don't have time for this!" Toby yelled, much louder than she actually needed to. "Who cares where they are? If they're not here, it's one less team we have to beat."

"Oh, you think you're going to beat us?" Tom asked, from where he and Clark were organizing the items on their end of the table.

"That's why I said it," Toby shot back.

"Easy there, you two," Clark said, looking over at me. "How'd you guys do?"

I took a breath to answer, and Toby snapped her fingers in my face. "No fraternizing!" she yelled, her face turning alarmingly red again. "We have to see where we stand."

"One minute," Palmer said, and I pulled out the list.

"Okay, we have pizza," I said, giving it a check mark. "A menu. Something with a boat on it. A square you eat," I said, looking at the Rice Krispies Treat Toby had picked up in the mini-mart. "Something Hot, Something Cold. Items of Formal Wear. A Coin from 1972 . . ."

"Ugh," Toby said as she nudged it to the center of the table, touching it with one finger. "Think how many decades of germs are probably on it."

"Soda, napkins, the pun, cotton balls . . ."

"The bell, book, and candle," Toby said, pointing, "The sample spoon . . . and I kind of know the Thriller dance . . ."

"How many points is that?" I asked, biting my lip as Palmer started the ten-second countdown.

"I'm adding," she said, looking at me, and I could see she looked as worried as I felt. "How many do you guys have?" she asked, just as Palmer yelled, "Time!"

I let out a long breath, and Toby held up her hand for a high five. "Go team," she said.

"Hey," Clark said, reaching out his hand for mine. "Don't be mad about the diner. It was all Tom's idea."

"It was," Tom said as he circled the table, clearly trying to see how our pile stacked up to theirs.

"And my keys?" I asked, trying to stay mad but sensing that it was a losing battle.

"Oh, that was all me," Clark said as I relented and took his hand, and he raised mine to his lips and gave it a quick kiss.

"Okay," Palmer said, clapping her hands together and grinning at us. "How'd you guys do?" She looked around. "And where are Bri and Wyatt? They're totally disqualified by now."

"Who cares about them?" Tom asked. He straightened up from where he'd been counting our items. "Who won?"

"Just give me a second to tally," Palmer said, pulling out her own copy of the list.

"You guys caught a firefly?" Toby asked, from where she was staring at the guys' pile. "Seriously?"

"And that counts for three extra," Tom said, walking over to his side of the table. "Something Alive, Something in a Jar, and Something that Lights Up." I felt my heart sink as I looked over at Toby. It was looking more and more likely that the guys had won this.

"And . . . it's a tie," Palmer said, setting down her sheet of paper, eyebrows shooting up. "You both have eighty-four points. I'm not sure this has ever happened before."

"Wait, what?" Tom asked, frowning down at Palmer's paper. "How is that possible? I spent like ten dollars getting all the blue gum balls!"

"Well, we did waste a lot of time catching that firefly," Clark pointed out, sliding his arm over my shoulder and pulling me in close to him.

"Rookie mistake," Palmer said, shaking her head.

"Also, Carly thinks your name is Phil!" Toby said gleefully, apparently a believer in kicking someone while they were down.

"Congratulations to both teams," Palmer said as she opened up the pizza boxes. "Who's hungry?"

"But nobody *won*," Toby said, frowning at the guys' items, clearly counting them again silently.

"But Bri and Wyatt definitely lost," Clark pointed out. "So there's that."

"Oh, right," Toby said, brightening, as she grabbed a piece of pizza and a napkin.

"Honestly," I said to Palmer, taking a cheese slice after checking that no other toppings had migrated onto it. "Was the pizza your way of getting us to bring dinner?"

Palmer shrugged. "I just know how hungry these things can make you," she said, giving me a tiny wink.

We ended up pushing the items to the side and sitting around the picnic table, mostly hearing about Tom's failed attempt to convince a notary to work after-hours. I was recounting the story of my dad suddenly going rogue and stealing spoons when headlights cut across the grass and a moment later I recognized Wyatt's truck.

"Finally!" Palmer said, setting down her crust. She looked at her watch. "Do you think they thought they had *three* hours, not two? Are they really going to play that card?"

"I bet you they got them all, though," Tom said despondently as he rolled the empty jar between his palms. "Just someone tell them that we really did have a firefly. Clark, we never should have set it free."

Bri and Wyatt climbed out of the truck and I watched, expecting them to go around to the back and start unloading the bags of their stuff, come running up to the picnic table full-speed. But they just continued on toward us, walking a few feet apart, both of them empty-handed.

"Hey," Toby called as they got closer. "Where have you guys been? And where's all your stuff?"

"Car broke down when we were on the way to the diner," Wyatt said, pushing his hair back with one hand. "I had to call Triple A and get a jump."

"Yeah," Bri said, shaking her head. "They took forever to get there too."

Morgan Matson

"Are you okay?" Toby asked Bri, eyes wide. "Were you, like, stranded on the side of the highway? That's how almost every serial killer movie starts."

"We're fine," Wyatt said with a laugh. "Totally un-murdered."

"So you weren't able to get anything?" Palmer said, putting her hands in her back pockets and then taking them out again, a slight hurt tone to her voice that I almost never heard.

"We really wanted to," Bri said quickly, looking at Palmer and then away again. "But . . ."

Palmer nodded and started cleaning up, putting empty plates and crusts into the pizza box, spending time making sure she got the lid on just right. "So who won?" Bri asked, her voice a little more cheerful than usual, and I wondered if she was picking up on the same thing I was—that Palmer was disappointed, that the fact they hadn't participated at all was draining some of the joy from the whole thing.

"Tie," Toby and Tom said in unison.

"Really?" Wyatt asked, as he loped over to the table and started looking at what was there. "Wow, they just gave you these diner menus?"

"Please tell me there's some pizza left," Bri said.

"Only if you want weird toppings," I said, opening up the box that was in front of me, the one that still had a few passed-over slices in it. Wyatt, no doubt drawn by the prospect of food, came to stand next to Bri as I tried to figure out what three toppings Clark and Tom had gone with. "So I think this is . . . pepperoni, jalapeño, and . . . pineapple?" I asked, staring at the slice and feeling myself recoil. "Ugh, why would you guys do that to yourselves?"

I glanced up and saw Wyatt nudging Bri as she tried to take a bite of the terrible-sounding pizza and Bri turning away, taking her pizza, and going to sit next to Toby.

"So," Wyatt said, sitting down on the bench and taking a slice of his own. "What did we miss? We need details."

"So tell me something," Clark said to me a few hours later. We were lying on a blanket in the back of his SUV, taking a brief kissing break, the back door open and a breeze intermittently blowing through the car.

After we'd brought the items back to our own cars and cleaned up the impromptu pizza party, and Wyatt and Clark had affixed Tom's bow tie around Winthrop's neck, everyone had scattered, and Clark and I had headed to his house to "watch a movie." Even if there were a movie playing, it would simply be in the background, a pretense for fooling around. We'd been doing this for a while now, so even the pretending to need the movie was starting to get old. But Clark had just gotten to the gatehouse when he'd slowed, then put the car in park. We looked at the time, did some quick calculations, and realized that if I was going to make it back for my curfew—which, since my grounding, I did try to stick to the general vicinity of—we were going to lose most of our time getting to his place and then back to mine. So after a brief discussion, Clark had turned the car around and we'd returned, parked to the side of the road near the statue of Winthrop, beneath the section with no streetlights shining in on us.

Clark's second row of seats was already down from hauling the mountain bikes, and I was glad they weren't currently there, taking up precious space. Clark had raised the back and we'd stretched out there for a few minutes, looking up at the stars though the open door, listening to the low hum of the cicadas in the grass.

"What's that?" I asked. He must have gotten some sun today—the skin on his neck was warm, and I rested my lips there for just a moment before putting my head on his chest. I felt the soft cotton of his T-shirt under my cheek and just breathed in that Clark smell I loved so much but hadn't yet adequately been able to describe to my friends. It was just *him*, and it made me feel wide awake and really peaceful, all at the same time.

"You guys," Clark said, turning to face me a little more fully, moonlight and reflected streetlight falling across his face. His glasses were carefully folded and placed against the window, and he reached for them now and slipped them on, then smiled when he saw me, like I'd just come into focus. "Your friends. This is what you guys do."

I looked at him. "I'm going to need more than that," I said after a second of trying to figure out what he was talking about. "I thought you were supposed to be good with words."

"Sorry," Clark said, giving me a quick, embarrassed smile. It faded, and I realized in that moment that this was actually something more serious—probably not something I should be teasing him for trying to ask about.

"No, tell me," I said, propping myself up on an elbow. "What do you mean?"

"Just . . ." Clark gestured to the bag propped by the wheel well, the one that contained half of the scavenger-hunt items, including eight blue gum balls that were all his. "You guys. You do things like this. It's like the coin of the realm with you." I smiled at that. "You create quests—"

"Scavenger hunts."

"You hang out together all the time. You have these games and inside jokes and nicknames and adventures. . . ." Clark looked down at his hands, and I got the feeling he was weighing every word before he spoke, trying to find the one that would let me understand what he was feeling.

"Well, not all the time," I said, not wanting him to get a false impression of things. "During the school year, there's a lot more homework and a lot more of Tom attempting to grow a beard so he'll get cast in the Chekhov play."

"I guess I just . . . ," Clark said as he adjusted his glasses. "I've never had a group of friends, so I didn't . . ." He shook his head. "I didn't know it could be like this."

"Oh," I said quietly, finally understanding what he meant. I didn't want to tell him that it wasn't always good, or wasn't always like this, because the fact is that most of the time it was. I'd sometimes look at other people at my school—the girls who seemed to thrive on drama and were always fighting with their friends, the ones who didn't even seem to *like* their friends that much—and know just how lucky I was. But I wasn't sure that was what Clark needed to hear at the moment. "Well," I said, as I moved closer to him, laying my head back down on his chest and hooking my foot over his, letting our legs tangle together. "Maybe you missed having a group before," I said. "But you're part of one now."

Clark didn't say anything for a long moment, and it was like

I could practically feel him turning over these words, thinking about their implications. Finally, I felt him kiss the top of my head and rest his chin there. "How about that."

"So next summer," I said, "you're going to want to refine your strategy early. If you want a chance of winning, that is, because—" It was like my brain caught up to what I was saying just a moment too late. Clark wouldn't be here next summer. He'd be back in Colorado, or he'd be somewhere else, but he would not be in Stanwich, doing a scavenger hunt with my friends.

"Oh," Clark said, pulling away a little so he could look at me and dashing my hopes that he had just not been paying attention to the last thing I'd said. "Um. Are you—"

"Never mind," I said quickly, feeling like this was a conversation I really didn't want to have. We had been having a nice moment, and the last thing I wanted to do was spoil it. I stretched up to kiss him, wishing I could rewind the last minute and delete it. "We're good."

We had to get moving not long after that. Clark finally gave me my keys back, and we kissed good-bye when he insisted on walking me to my car, even though it was only parked a few feet from his. After we'd kissed as long as we could without me really being in danger of staying out past my curfew, Clark got into his car and kissed me one last time through his open driver's-side window, and I watched him drive away, his taillights growing fainter until he rounded the bend in the road and I lost them. Then I headed home, yawning.

I let myself in, and stopped in the kitchen for a glass of water. As I was drinking it, I saw a note taped to the kitchen TV, in my dad's neat, slanted handwriting.

Well?

DID WE WIN?

I smiled at that, then looked down at the phone in my hand. I normally just texted my dad when I got home, so that even if he was sleeping, he could see the time stamp. But I was pretty sure I'd seen a light on as I'd driven up to the house, and as I glanced down the hallway, I saw that there was a light on in my dad's study and that the door was cracked open.

I walked down the hall and knocked once before pushing the door open all the way. My dad was lying on the leather couch in his study, reading some papers that he was holding above his head. He pushed his reading glasses up and smiled when he saw me.

"Hi," I said, leaning against the doorway, giving him a small smile back. "I'm home."

Chapter THIRTEEN

"So Karl and Marjorie are on the run," I said, as Clark, lying next to me on the couch, pointed the remote at the movie we'd been totally ignoring, silencing it. "But," I said as I ran my fingers through his hair, "Karl doesn't know Marjorie's sold him out. Told the highwaymen about him."

Clark tossed the remote in the general direction of the coffee table and started kissing down my neck. "Oh, are there highwaymen now?"

"Of course," I said, twirling my fingers in his hair, leaning in to kiss him. "Every good story has them."

"And so I asked Bri what I should do about Wyatt now, since he told me about this other girl he likes, and she had like *nothing* to say," Toby said as she paced in front of me in the gallery that was mostly impressionist, except for the unicorn tapestry and the Warhol.

"Hmm," I said, trying my best to focus on her, but finding that every few seconds, my thoughts were straying back to Clark. His eyes, his lips, his hands . . .

"Andie!" Toby said, waving her hand in front of my face. "Are you even listening to me?"

"Of course," Clark said, as I rolled on top on him on the couch. We'd removed the side and back pillows, since they kept getting in the way. We hadn't yet moved things into his bedroom—I think we were both a little too aware of the implications that might come with that—but we had pretty much turned every couch in his house into a bed equivalent. "Marjorie doesn't know that Karl has some plans of his own."

"Oh, yeah?" I asked, in between kisses, as I slipped my hands under the fabric of Clark's T-shirt and pulled it over his head. Ever since I'd seen his abs on the beach, I tended to need constant verification that they were still present and accounted for. "And what might those be?"

"She needs to let it go," Palmer said as she glanced away from the stage and to me. I was slouched down in the theater seat, my feet propped on the seat back in front of me. I'd mostly come to the community theater for the free air-conditioning between walks, and had found myself pulled into the Toby-Wyatt conundrum. "And Bri agrees with me. He told her how he felt, and now it's just getting super awkward."

"Right," I said, nodding. There was part of me that agreed with Palmer. But most of me was thinking about the fact that I'd get to see Clark in less than two hours, and my pulse was already racing just thinking about it. "Totally."

"Oh my god." I looked over to see Palmer shaking her head at me. "Alexandra. You are so far gone."

• • •

I was beginning to understand what Palmer, and even Bri, had been talking about now. My boundaries, the ones I'd once clung to so fiercely, had long since vanished. Now I was the one moving us forward, while Clark would stop, his eyes searching mine in the darkness, asking me if I was okay. If I was sure. And with every new threshold we crossed, it was getting harder to remember just why I'd clung to all those rules in the first place. When I could think about it clearly—always after the fact, my brain no longer gone fuzzy at the sight of Clark and the feel of his hands on me—I would realize that it wasn't a coincidence it was happening now. It was *Clark*. I trusted him, and I knew him, and it made me wonder, every time we stopped, just why we weren't going forward. And as I started to care very little for anything that wasn't the two of us, alone in the darkness, it fell to Clark to pick up the slack.

"Your curfew's in thirty minutes," Clark said, breaking away from kissing me, his voice breathless, as he squinted at his digital watch, the glow from the tiny screen the only light in the room.

"Such a long time," I said, running my fingers over his arm, which was propped above me.

"Your dad got super mad last time," he reminded me, even as his head started to dip down toward mine.

"He got over it."

"We'll have to find your bra."

I waved this away. "Details."

"And my shirt."

"You shouldn't ever wear one of those," I said, running my hand over the ridges of Clark's abs. "Why cover this up?"

"Fine," he said, pushing some buttons on his watch; they made a little *beep!* sound, like he'd just programmed the world's tiniest microwave. "Ten more minutes. But then I have to drive you home."

"Sure," I said, stretching up to kiss him as he wrapped his arms around me, pulling me close, my skin against his. "Sounds like a plan."

"I think she's getting over him, don't you?" Bri asked me from across the diner booth.

I started to nod, then hesitated when I realized I had no idea who she was talking about. "Um, remind me again?"

"Toby," Bri said in the extra-slow way my friends had taken to speaking to me these days. "Getting over Wyatt?"

"Oh," I said, reaching to snag one of the mozzarella sticks we were sharing. I knew I hadn't been totally paying attention recently, but even I knew this didn't sound right. "I'm not so sure about that." Bri nodded and looked down at the paper place mat in front of her, like she was studying one of the ads for the local businesses printed on it. "You okay?"

"Yeah," Bri said, taking a mozzarella stick of her own. "I just was hoping that Toby was moving on. It's not good for her, especially when he told her he wasn't interested."

"I think she just needs time," I said with a shrug.

"Or," Bri said, sitting up straighter, "I need to fix her up with someone!"

I winced. Bri liked to think she was a great matchmaker, but she was absolutely terrible at it. After we'd all been burned a few too many times, we'd made her swear that she was done with it.

Morgan Matson

"What about the oath you swore that you would never do that again? Remember, the one you took after the mullet guy?"

Bri waved this away and shook her head, looking determined and now much more cheerful. "These are extreme circumstances," she said. "Trust me. It's a great idea."

"Hold on," Clark said, sounding half out of breath as he fumbled with one hand behind him, trying to find his bedroom doorknob.

"Holding," I said, and I leaned down to kiss him, even though I knew I was making the situation worse. We'd been on the couch when I'd decided that I couldn't stand it any longer—I was getting a crick in my neck, and the fabric of the cushions was scratching my skin. It just seemed crazy that we were putting ourselves through that when there was a perfectly good, unused bed right down the hall.

We hadn't stopped kissing as we walked, and even though I knew it was probably slowing us down. Clark was half carrying me, my legs wrapped around his waist, as he finally opened the door and stumbled for a few steps inside. I kissed him again, and we stayed that way for a long moment before he set me down and I looked around, taking in his room for the first time since the night of Bertie and the chocolate. It looked the same—the neat stacks of clothing, the carefully made bed. Although I did notice that the books on writer's block seemed to have vanished from the top of his desk.

I looked at the bed for a long moment, letting my mind go places it probably shouldn't. As things with us had progressed, our discussions over the last two weeks about taking things to the next level had gone from "if" to "when." Which was exciting and scary and overwhelming and pretty much all I could think about.

"You okay?" Clark asked, squeezing my hand. I squeezed his back and made myself look away from the bed, making myself remember that this random Tuesday would not be the night. I had to get my head around it a little more first, talk to my friends, and actually do my hair, as opposed to just twisting it into a knot like I'd done tonight. I wanted it to be totally special.

"Hey," Clark said from behind me as his slid his arms around my waist and kissed that one spot on my shoulder. He pulled me closer against him, and I swore I could feel the beat of his heart against my back. I turned to face him, and he ran his hand over my hair, his fingers trailing down my cheek, stroking along my jawline so gently, like I was something precious. He leaned down to kiss me, and I kissed him back, and then we were kiss-walking across the room, until we fell down onto the bed together, and then there was only his lips and his hands and our breath, falling into a rhythm until I couldn't think about anything except him, and us, and now.

"Talk," Palmer said, pointing her Twizzler at me. "Andie. Details."

I rolled over to look at her, holding my hand up to cut the glare. We were sunbathing on Palmer's roof, all four of us. Our schedules had aligned for the afternoon, and it wasn't until we'd set up there, with towels and snacks, that I realized it had been a while since it had been just us—no boyfriends or crushes or Tom. And how much I'd missed just the four of us hanging out. "What?" I asked, even though I was pretty sure I knew. And it was one of the reasons I'd wanted to hang out with them

Morgan Matson

today—I needed some girl talk, and to figure out what I was feeling, in a way I never seemed to be able to except when we were together.

"Come on," Bri said, pushing her sunglasses on top of her head. "You and Clark. Spill."

I wasn't quite able to stop myself from smiling as I smoothed out the edges of my towel. This, truthfully, was a new experience for me. My friends and I all knew every detail of what the others had done with guys—but I usually didn't have anything to contribute to this conversation. I'd been keeping things vague with them and letting them believe I was still safe within my old boundaries.

"Wait, what?" Toby asked, as she paused in applying her spray-on sunscreen to her legs. She turned to me, her expression incredulous. "Don't tell me the queen of first base is actually doing something."

"She totally is," Palmer said, nodding with authority. "You don't lose that many IQ points if you're just kissing someone."

"First of all," I said, busying myself with smoothing out imaginary wrinkles in my towel, "why does first base get such a bad rap? It's like the most important base."

"This is true," Bri said, nodding. "And I know it's true, because in every movie, the first baseman is always really cute."

"I'm just saying, wait until you try the other bases," Palmer said, waggling her eyebrows at us.

"No," Toby said, holding up her hand. "Please no. Every time you talk about sleeping with Tom, I end up picturing him naked."

"You might be surprised to know—" Palmer started, raising an eyebrow as Toby waved her hands in front of her face.

"Seriously, stop it." She shuddered. "And now I'm seeing it," she said, shaking her head. "And I can't unsee it."

"All I'm saying," Palmer said, turning to me, "is that the other bases are just more *interesting*."

"Mmm-hm," Bri said, taking a long drink of her soda.

"Yeah," I murmured without thinking, replaying the night before in my head.

"Wait, what?" Toby asked, suddenly sitting up straight. She raised her sunglasses and looked closely at me. "Are you . . . and Dogboy . . . ?"

"Clark," I said automatically.

Bri shook her head, starting to smile. "Andie, you are so busted," she said. "I need details *now*."

"Wait a sec," Palmer said, eyes wide. "You guys haven't done it yet, have you?"

Toby's head whipped over and she stared at me.

"No," I said, shaking my head. "But . . ." This was, after all, what I'd wanted to talk to them about. But also, once I talked to them about it, once I said the words and they became part of our conversation, I knew this would become real in a way it hadn't been before. "But we're talking about it. Like . . . happening-in-the-next-two-weeks talking about it."

"Oh my god," Palmer said, grabbing my arm and smiling at me. "That's so huge."

"I can't believe you thought I would have done it without telling you," I said, shaking my head. "Did you really think I would have forgotten to mention something that big to you guys?"

"I don't know," Bri said, her voice muffled as she dug in her bag for something. "Sometimes people don't always tell each other every single thing. I mean—"

"Wait," Toby said, talking over her as she looked around at all of us. "So this means all you guys are off, like, rounding the bases and I'm still in the dugout. I'm the person selling Cracker Jack in the stands."

"This metaphor is getting weird," Palmer murmured to me.

"You and Palmer are leaving me and Bri behind," Toby said as she dropped her sunglasses down again and Bri started looking through her bag once more. "But after this, nobody can go off and have experiences without me. I'm falling way too far back."

"So what's the plan?" Bri asked, looking up from her bag. "Have you guys talked about it?"

I nodded, then hesitated. Something had been bothering me more than I ever would have let Clark know. "It won't be his first time, though."

"He's done it?" Toby asked, looking shocked. "Way to go, Homeschool."

"Yeah," I said, taking a drink of my Diet Coke, which was mostly just crushed ice by now, then started to tell my friends about it. I'd suspected he had—he seemed to know a lot about the Colorado College dorms for someone who wasn't spending a lot of time there. But when we crossed the line from "something that might possibly happen someday" to "something that's actually going to happen in the foreseeable future," Clark had told me about his ex-girlfriend and that they'd been pretty serious for a while. This had led to a night I wasn't necessarily proud of, in which I'd googled "C. B. McCallister girlfriend Colorado

College pretty" trying to get a visual on what his ex looked like, without success.

"Whoa," Toby said, looking at me closely when I'd finished recounting the story, complete with embarrassing failed Internet stalking. "You *really* like him. Otherwise, you would have told us everything already, whether we wanted to know or not. And you wouldn't care about his ex this much."

I looked down at my cup, shaking it, like I could somehow get some more Diet Coke to emerge from the ice, wondering why I suddenly felt so much like I was going to cry.

"Andie," Palmer said, her voice gentle and much quieter than usual, as she leaned closer to me, "it's okay if you like him. It's *good*."

I nodded, even though I could feel that my lip was starting to tremble. This wasn't even what I was getting upset about. It was something bigger, and so scary, that I was mostly avoiding thinking about it and hoping it would just go away. "I know that," I said. "But . . . he's leaving at the end of the summer." I hated even saying it out loud, though it had been circling around in my head ever since I'd realized it the night of the scavenger hunt. Usually, end dates like this didn't bother me. Usually, I loved them. But this was different. *Clark* was different. And I was starting to realize why all my three-week relationships had been so easy to get over—there was nothing at stake, so there was nothing to lose. And I knew that if we took this next step, if we went there, it would be that much harder when he headed back to Colorado.

And it wasn't like it was a surprise to me. I had known, almost from the beginning, that Clark would be leaving when the summer was over. His life was back in Colorado, in an apartment in Colorado Springs that was currently sitting empty, though he had hired someone to collect his mail and leave a different light on every time, in the hopes of making it seem like he'd never left. I'd known this, of course. So why was it suddenly feeling like brand-new information?

I looked up and saw my friends all had identical sympathetic expressions on their faces, and I looked away from them and reached for the Doritos. "Let's talk about something else," I said, hearing how falsely cheerful my voice sounded but going on anyway.

"Really?" Palmer was looking at me like she was debating whether or not to let me off the hook.

"Really," I said firmly enough that she nodded and motioned for me to share the Doritos.

"We could talk about Toby's *date* this week," Bri said, brightening.

Toby slumped back on her towel. "I'm still not happy about any of this," she said. She pointed to me and Palmer. "You two are my witnesses."

"Maybe it'll be good," I said, propping myself up on my elbow to look at her. "Maybe this is how the curse gets broken. Maybe this is how you stop selling the Cracker Jack."

"I don't think so," Toby said with a sigh.

"You don't know that," Palmer said cheerfully.

"It's that weird guy from the projection booth," Toby said flatly.

"Oh," Palmer said more quietly.

"Craig is a nice guy," Bri said firmly. "And he knows a ton about movies."

"Cause that's always the first thing I look for," Toby muttered.

"You can at least give it a shot," Bri said.

"Or you could just flirt with Gregory," I said, thinking about how every time I was at the Pearce he was going out of his way to try and talk to Toby, who barely acknowledged him. "I can tell he likes you."

"Ooh, from the museum?" Palmer asked. "He's totally cute-ish!"

"Ugh," Toby said, rolling over onto her stomach, clearly done with all of us and this conversation. "I'm going out with what's-his-face from the movie theater, okay? So just leave me alone."

"You know his name," Bri said, nudging Toby's leg with her foot. "Don't pretend you don't." Toby nudged Bri back— though it looked like it was maybe more of a kick.

"Hey!" Bri said, half yelling and half laughing. She reached out to retaliate as Palmer threw her empty Sprite bottle at them.

"You guys, we are on a *roof*," she said. "No fighting until we're on the ground!"

We all descended through Palmer's room when it started to get dark out and then congregated on her gravel driveway, talking— but not saying good-bye, since I knew I'd be seeing them in a few hours, except for Bri, who was working concessions at the evening show and was trying to bribe us with popcorn to come and hang out with her.

"But it's really not *that* bad," she was saying as she and Toby walked to her car. I'd walked over from my house, but was feeling sun-stunned and lazy enough that I was considering asking them for a ride.

"That's what you said before we actually saw the movie," Palmer reminded her as Toby flung her stuff into the backseat. "Not falling for that one twice."

"Andie?" Bri asked hopefully.

I shook my head. "But text when you're done and we'll tell you where we are."

"Fine," Bri said with a sigh as she got into the driver's seat. But a moment later she stood up again and turned to me. "Oh, I almost forgot. The woman you work for—does she handle cats, too?"

"Yes," I said a little warily, since I was well aware of the cat under discussion. Maya and Dave mostly did dog walking, but there were a fair number of cat-sitting clients on the roster as well.

"Good," Bri said, shoulders slumping with relief. "Text me her info, would you? My mom needs someone to bring Miss Cupcakes to the vet and I almost lost a finger last time."

"Sure," I said, pulling out my phone and doing it while it was still fresh in my mind, saying a silent apology to Maya. "Done."

"Thanks," Bri said, getting into her car. I could already hear her arguing with Toby about something, indignation mixed with laughter, as they pulled out of Palmer's driveway and headed out, Bri waving out the window as they went.

I shouldered my canvas bag—the slight prickling of my skin letting me know I might have missed a spot or two with the sunscreen—and started to head toward my house, only to find Palmer falling into step next to me. "Come on," she said, nodding down the road. "I'll walk you home."

I looked down at Palmer's bare feet with their flip-flop tan lines. "Shoes?" Palmer waved this away, and we started walking together, almost in the center of the road.

"About Clark," Palmer said, after we'd been walking in silence for a moment or two, and I knew suddenly this was the reason she'd wanted to walk me back—apparently she hadn't actually let me off the hook at all. "Don't fixate on the fact that he's leaving."

"But . . ." We walked in silence for a few more steps. We'd totally passed my house by now, but neither of us had even paused in front of it—we were both aware, without having to talk about it, that this was just a ruse to keep talking. I knew that Palmer would wait until I was ready to speak again, and it gave me the space to get my thoughts together a little more. "What if we take this huge step together, and then . . . ?" I let the sentence trail off. I didn't even want to think the words required to finish it.

"Just because the summer's over doesn't mean you guys have to be," Palmer pointed out. "Even if he goes back to Colorado, planes do exist. You guys could figure it out."

I shook my head, not really able to take this in. "I just feel like I should have planned for this."

"Here's the thing," Palmer said. "You've been really happy this summer." I looked over at her, and Palmer went on. "Like, the happiest I've ever seen you. And it's also the first time in forever you've had no plan. You've been enjoying the right now. I don't think that's a coincidence."

"I know. But . . ."

"So maybe just keep doing that. After all," she said, raising an eyebrow at me, "this is a problem for Future Andie to solve."

I smiled at that. "Well, Future Andie is *way* smarter than I am."

"She totally is. She can handle this."

"I just wish I knew what was going to happen next."

Palmer nodded, then after a moment, said, "But you never really know. I mean, look at what happened with your dad."

I nodded, thinking for a second about the summer I'd wanted to have, but almost couldn't get it to come into focus. A summer at Johns Hopkins would have meant not meeting Clark, which was getting harder and harder to imagine—like trying to picture a world without electricity. "You know some things, though," I pointed out as we approached the Winthrop statue, and like we'd discussed it before, started to turn around and head back to my house. I thought about my friends, about how through all the crushes and boyfriends and bad kisses and horrible dates we'd had, the four of us had been together, constant and unshakable. "I know you guys are always going to be around."

"Well, naturally," Palmer said, bumping me with her hip. "That's just a given."

Chapter FOURTEEN

"See?" my dad asked, gesturing to the screen with his bagel. "Not so bad, right?"

I squinted at the TV, where John Wayne was walking across a dusty town square with the loping gait that I was unfortunately getting all too familiar with. "It's okay," I said, leaning back against the soft leather of the armchair and picking up my everything bagel with cream cheese. Despite the fact that it was almost two on a Sunday, my dad and I were just now getting around to eating breakfast, while he called in the terms of our scavenger-hunt bet and was making me watch *Rio Bravo*. "It's better than *Blood Alley*, at any rate."

"Yeah," my dad acknowledged with a grimace. "That one was probably a mistake."

I tucked my feet up underneath me. It was an overcast, cloudy day, with occasional showers, which made watching the movie feel somehow much cozier. It was exactly how you should spend a rainy day—though I might have been able to do without the John Wayne aspect of it. But as I watched, I found myself getting more engrossed in the story, almost against my will—Wayne and his newly deputized deputies holed up in a jail cell as a standoff with a militia took shape and the men forced to be in the same room together started telling stories and airing old grievances. At one point, one character sang a song, and then immediately after, another character sang a song, which made me wonder if they were just trying to extend the running time, or if everyone in the fifties knew that this was when you were supposed to take a popcorn break. It helped that the actors were good singers, though it did stretch logic a little—if you could sing that well, would you really be in a dusty jail in Texas? Wouldn't you have been in vaudeville or something?

"Those guys could really sing," I said, when the singing portion of the movie appeared to be over and everyone on-screen seemed to suddenly remember that they were actually in mortal danger.

My dad looked over at me from where he was lying on the couch. "Those guys?" he repeated, sounding surprised.

"Yeah," I said, pointing to the screen. "Those two. They were good."

My dad sat up and paused the movie, then turned to face me fully. "They *should* be able to sing," he said, a concerned expression starting to take over his face. "That's Ricky Nelson and Dean Martin."

My dad said these names like they were supposed to be somehow significant to me, and I just nodded. "And they're, um, good," I said, starting to regret I'd ever said anything.

"Oh my god," my dad said, shaking his head. He pointed to my phone. "Get Sabrina on the phone," he said, in the kind of voice I'd heard him use in his D.C. offices, the tone that sent interns scurrying to do whatever he needed done.

"Um," I said, even as I reached for my phone. "Why?"

"Because she needs to hear about this," he said in a tone that absolutely didn't invite discussion.

I called Bri, put the phone on speaker, and hoped she wouldn't answer. When she did, on the third ring, I took a breath to start talking immediately, but Bri beat me to it.

"Andie," she said, sounding happy to hear from me. "Hey! I'm . . . I'm actually really glad you called."

"So here's the thing," I said, jumping in so that she would know my dad was on the line and wouldn't start talking about how hungover she was, or my plans to sleep with Clark at some point in the undefined future, or anything. "Um, I'm here with my dad. He wanted me to call you. . . ."

"Wait, what?"

"Hi, Sabrina," my dad said, moving over to speak into my phone. "Alexander Walker here."

"Hi, Mr. Walker," Bri replied politely, but I could hear the confusion in her voice.

"We have a situation here. We're watching *Rio Bravo*—"

"*Excellent* choice," Bri said, all the confusion gone now that we were talking movies.

"And my daughter apparently has never heard of Ricky Nelson *or* Dean Martin."

"Andie," Bri said, sounding scandalized. "What's the matter with you?"

"What?" I asked, looking from my dad to the phone, feeling the need to defend myself. "What's the big deal?"

"I'm sorry about this, sir," Bri said, chagrined. "I'll take care of it."

"I just thought you should know," my dad said, looking at me and shaking his head. "It's a failure on my end too, of course."

"Okay, that's enough," I said, picking up my phone and taking it off speaker. "It's just me now," I said to Bri as I headed out of the room.

"Not too long," my dad called after me as he picked up some papers that were stacked on the coffee table. "We're watching *The Searchers* after this!"

"Oh, that's such a great movie." Bri sighed as I closed the study door behind me and walked a few steps down the hall.

"Come over," I said immediately. "I think we have some bagels left."

"No, thanks," Bri said, and I could hear the disappointment in her voice. "I'm on concessions for the five thirty show."

"You're working so much lately," I said. Bri didn't respond, and a moment later I felt bad for bringing it up—but more and more these days, it was getting harder to see her. She was either working at the Palace, or texting at the last minute that she wouldn't make the Orchard or pool hangouts because she had to close up the theater.

"Yeah," Bri finally responded. "I'm really sorry about that. Things are just . . . kind of crazy. At work."

There was something in her voice that made me stand up straighter. Since Bri almost never told you what was bothering her until she was ready to, you had to learn to pick up on signals. And I had a feeling Toby would have sensed something from the very beginning of this conversation. "Is everything okay?"

There was nothing but silence on the other end of the

phone. With every second that passed, I was getting more sure that there was something going on with her, even though I had no idea what it could be.

"Actually—" Bri started, just as my dad yelled, "Andie! Are you coming?"

"Ignore him," I said into the phone, hoping somehow that she wouldn't have heard him.

"It's fine," Bri said, and her voice was brisk and composed again. "I'm fine. I promise. I was just . . ." The sentence trailed off, and when she came back on the line, her voice was much more upbeat. "I'm fine," she said again, "just have to get ready for work. I'll talk to you later, okay?" Before I could say anything else, she'd hung up, and I was left looking down at the contact picture that filled the screen, of Bri and Toby either arguing while on the verge of cracking up or having their laughter interrupted by a fight, I'd long since forgotten which. I held the phone in my hand for just a minute more, wondering if she was going to call back, before giving up and returning to the study.

Three hours later I'd finished my second John Wayne movie of the day and was feeling emotionally depleted. "Man," I said, as my dad turned off the TV and reached again for the stack of papers, pulling his reading glasses out of his pocket. "Didn't John Wayne ever make a comedy? A musical or two?"

My dad looked at me evenly over his reading glasses. "Don't make me call Sabrina again."

"I withdraw the question," I said, stacking up my breakfast plates and preparing to take them into the kitchen. I watched my dad reading for a few moments, making marks on the paper with his mechanical pencil, before I asked, "So what is that?" This was how I had been used to seeing my father—always working, always reading, head half-buried in a stack of papers or fixated on the news. Seeing him like this again was making me realize just how long it had been since I'd seen him in work mode.

"This?" he asked, looking down at the sheaf of papers in his hand, and I nodded. "It's for a case," he said, looking back down again. "An old friend in the public defender's office asked me to take a look at something."

"Oh," I said, leaning back against my chair, trying to figure out what this meant. My dad had not been talking at all about what he was thinking about doing with regard to his job, and for the most part, it was something I'd almost forgotten about. It was like we were both on summer vacation, and none of the real rules for either of our schedules seemed to apply anymore. This was probably made much easier by the fact my dad wasn't allowed to have any contact with his office, as it really did seem like that whole part of his life had just faded out. "Are you . . . ?" I started, then bit my lip, not sure exactly what I was trying to ask him, or what I wanted him to reply.

"I'm just looking at something for a friend," my dad said easily, seeming to understand what I was trying to get at. After a moment, though, he set the papers aside and took off his reading glasses, turning to face me more fully. "It is something I've been thinking about, though," he said. He cleared his throat and rolled his pencil between his palms before he asked, "What would you think about that? If I didn't run again in the fall?"

"What about the investigation?" I asked, thrown. As far as I'd understood things, we were still waiting for the results to come back. I hadn't known my dad not running for reelection in November was even in the cards.

"Even if it comes back in my favor," he said. "I don't know. It's just been on my mind lately."

I looked at him for a moment, then looked back down at the stack of plates once again, trying to get my thoughts together. It hadn't been that long ago that I couldn't picture my dad without his job. But now it was getting harder to remember when things hadn't been like this, our lives overlapping. It was in the way my dad knew to make sure that the fridge was stocked with Diet Coke, the way I knew his paper-reading hierarchy—national news, sports, business, comics (he was especially invested in the family hijinks of the Grants in *Grant Central Station*). It was how when he'd been running late to dinner at the Crane last week, he'd called and asked me to order for him, and I'd done it without needing to ask him what he wanted. It was last Sunday, when Clark had come for dinner and then Tom and Palmer had stopped by afterward to hang out and we'd all ended up playing Pictionary, my dad teaming up with Tom and Clark, the three of them strategizing and taking it way too seriously (and winning, not that I was bitter). It was this, now, watching movies on a rainy Sunday and not wanting to be anywhere else.

"So if you didn't run," I said slowly, trying this idea out, "you'd be here?"

"I would." My dad looked across at me. "What do you think?"

I looked down at my hands for a moment, twisting them together, trying to gather my thoughts. The idea that this summer wouldn't just be over as soon as news came from Washington was something I really hadn't let myself think about before. I cleared my throat before I spoke. "It would be okay with me. If you were around, I mean."

"Good," my dad said, tapping his pencil once on the coffee table.

"After all," I said, making my tone faux serious, "Palmer might do another scavenger hunt. And we'd need you for backup."

"Well," my dad said, matching my tone, "I wouldn't want to miss that." He smiled at me, then settled back against the couch and picked up his papers again.

I'd planned to bring the plates to the kitchen, take a shower, and get ready before Clark came over for dinner. But I found myself curling back up in the chair. I just wanted to sit there, in the quiet, with my dad working, letting myself imagine, for the first time, what October or February could look like. No train rides down to D.C., no Peter. Being able to tell someone who was actually interested, and not being paid to listen, how my day had been. And so, even though I knew I should probably get moving, that Clark was on his way over, I stayed there, perfectly still, letting myself picture it, playing it out in my head like a movie—seeing what, just maybe, could be.

The rain didn't let up the next day. It just got heavier, which meant all my walks were much shorter than usual, and my car was now covered in muddy paw prints, despite my best efforts to keep the seats covered in towels. Since the shorter walks left me with unexpected time on my hands, Clark and I ended up getting lunch at the diner and then going to the Pearce to hang out with Toby, who was, to put it mildly, not looking forward to her date that night. She'd been sending incredibly long text messages about it, and I was spending most of my time trying to figure out what she was actually trying to say with the emojis. We found ourselves walking through the Renaissance room listening to Toby complain about what a weird name Craig was and wondering why Bri wouldn't just let her mourn the loss of her Wyatt crush in peace.

When a group came in for the tour that Toby had forgotten she was scheduled to give, she hustled out to the front entrance, leaving me and Clark alone to wander around the museum. Which, I realized, wasn't actually the worst way to spend a rainy day. We walked around, making up backstories and names for the people in the paintings as we walked.

When we reached the gallery where my mother's picture was, I knew I could have steered him away, or told him I was museumed out, or something. But I didn't; I took his hand and led him to where my mom's painting was. I'd told him about it, here and there, but he'd never seen it before. And even though anyone who paid the Pearce's entrance fee could see this picture, standing next to Clark as he looked at it, I was feeling somehow exposed—like he was seeing something I usually kept to myself.

"So?" I asked, keeping my voice light, like I really didn't care about the answer, even though my heart was pounding hard in my chest.

"It's great," Clark said, looking at the painting for a moment longer before looking at me, and squeezing my hand. "It's really wonderful, Andie. Your mom was so talented."

"She was," I said, looking at the way the stars seemed to glow against the canvas, the way you could somehow feel the wind that was blowing through the trees.

"So what are you looking at?"

"I don't know," I said. "I think there was meant to be something else there," I said, gesturing to the bare section of the canvas, the faint etchings of pencil lines that I'd spent way too long trying to make sense of. "But I don't know what it was."

Clark nodded, eyes still on the painting. "So did you pose for this, or . . . ?"

I shook my head. I hadn't ever known where the inspiration for the painting had come from, only that my mother had started working on it late one night when she was sick, before my dad had quit the campaign and moved home again. "I don't know where it came from," I said, and as I did, I felt the hollow realization in my stomach that because I had never asked her about it when I had the chance, now I would never know.

"Because you're definitely looking at something," Clark said, almost more to himself, as he leaned closer to the picture again. "Right? I mean, look at your sight line."

"I know," I said, shaking my head. "But I don't think we're ever going to know what it is."

"Well, maybe not," Clark said after a moment, his words coming slowly, like he was still putting something together. "Was this supposed to be somewhere? That you know of?"

"It's the field behind our old house," I said. I had recognized it as soon as I'd seen my mother start sketching it out. You could see the top of our roof in the distance and the remnants of the tree house my dad had tried to build for me before he'd admitted it was outside of his capabilities and I'd admitted that I actually hadn't wanted a tree house. "Why?"

"Because I have an idea," Clark said, raising his eyebrows at me.

Twenty minutes later I sat in Clark's passenger seat, feeling my heart beat harder the closer we got to East View. When Clark had suggested going to my old house to see if we could find out anything, I'd been ready to tell him that I didn't want to go back there, that I'd avoided it for five years. But I didn't tell him that. Instead, I'd found myself agreeing and giving him directions. I wasn't sure why, but I didn't want to have to hide from it any longer. And Clark seemed so convinced that we'd find our answer to what was happening in the painting that I found myself wondering if maybe this could be true. The closer we got, I found myself anticipating every turn, every landmark, even though I hadn't been down these streets in five years.

"You'll be coming up to it on the left," I said as he signaled and turned onto our street.

"Gotcha." The rain started to come down harder, and he increased his wiper speed.

I turned to face the window, feeling like maybe I was ready to do this after all. That it probably had been ridiculous to avoid it for all these years.

"Where is it?" Clark asked, looking out to the side of the road, then at me.

I started to answer, but it got caught somewhere in my throat as I stared out through the rain-streaked window. I somehow couldn't get my brain to understand, to process what was right in front of me. I looked around, wondering if there was any way I'd taken us down the wrong street, if we'd turned too early . . .

But even as I thought it, I knew that wasn't the case. Clark pulled to the side of the road, and I got out of the car as soon as he put it in park, not even caring about the rain, and walked

Morgan Matson

across the street, to the spot where the farmhouse had been.

But it wasn't there.

There wasn't *anything* there. Just the plot of land, slightly overgrown, though I was pretty sure I could still see where the foundation had once been.

I was getting soaked; the rain was running down my face and I wasn't even moving to wipe it away. So the house had been torn down. My dad had sold it; I knew that much, so maybe it had been here for a while before it was knocked down? I looked around, as though I was going to get some information from the deserted street, but there wasn't anything. Just an empty space where our house, my whole world when I was a kid, had been. And now, unless you'd known, you wouldn't even stop to slow down and look at it. You would never have known anything was there at all.

I waited for the devastation to come—the tears, the feeling that things were falling apart. But it didn't.

I looked around through the rain, at the place where our house had been, and realized that it was just a piece of land. That was all it had ever been. It was the fact that the three of us had lived there together that had made it special. But now when I thought about home . . .

A series of images flashed through my mind. It was my dad in the kitchen, heating me up a slice of pizza, along with one for himself. It was walking back and forth with Palmer between our two houses. It was running up and down the stairs like crazy people as we gathered scavenger-hunt supplies. It was sharing a piece of cheesecake with my father. It wasn't the farmhouse, not anymore.

"Hi." I turned to see Clark standing next to me, raising his voice to be heard over the rain. He looked at the empty lot, then at me, his brow furrowed, and I could see just how much he was regretting this. "Andie, I—"

"Car," I said, taking his hand and walking back across the street toward it, feeling like there wasn't any need for us to get even more soaked. I climbed into the passenger seat, and Clark got behind the wheel a few seconds later. When he shut the door, it was like someone had turned off the volume—with the rain gone, it was suddenly very quiet, and much warmer.

"I'm so sorry," Clark said immediately. "I didn't realize—"

"It's okay," I said. I gave him a half smile. "Really."

"Really?"

I nodded. "Yeah." There was just the sound of the rain, then I said, "I always thought I didn't want to come back here. I've been avoiding this place for five years. And in the end . . ." I looked back at where the house had been once more. "It would have been better to do this years ago. I was making it so much harder for myself when it didn't have to be." What Bri had said to Toby about Wyatt flashed into my head. "I think it's better to face it," I said.

Something passed over Clark's face, and he looked down at the steering wheel.

"I do wish I could have gone back inside before it got knocked down, though." Clark nodded, and I knew he probably assumed it was for sentimental reasons. I paused for only a second, listening to the rain hitting the window, before telling him what I'd never told anyone. "I always thought maybe my mom left something for me in there."

"Like what?"

I shrugged and turned my back to the empty space where the farmhouse had been. "I don't even know," I said, realizing as I did that it was the truth. I'd never gotten further in my head than "something left for me in the house." I'd just wanted some proof—beyond my mother buying out the feminine-care aisle of CVS—that she'd left something for me, something so that I could pretend, at least for a moment or two, that she was still with me. "Just . . . something." I gave it one last look, then turned to Clark. "We can go now," I said, giving him a smile. "I'm good."

Clark squeezed my hand, then started the engine, and headed back toward the center of town. I kicked off my wet flip-flops and propped my feet on the dashboard, settling in for what I knew would be at least a half hour's journey. I looked over and saw that he was gripping the steering wheel hard, his hands flexing against it and a muscle working in his jaw, like he was struggling with something. I started to say something, then realized that maybe I should wait for him to speak, just like he'd waited for me. I pressed my lips together and made myself sit in silence, and when I was almost sure I couldn't take it any longer, Clark cleared his throat.

"I was just thinking . . . what you said? About how it's better to face it?"

"Yes," I said slowly. You can almost feel it coming, when someone needs to say something to you and you don't want to spook them. It was the same way I felt whenever I picked up Fenway, the most jittery dog I walked. Any sudden movements and he'd go skittering under the bed, seeming to forget every day that it was nothing to be scared of, nothing but a walk, and that he was always happy once I got him out the door.

Clark let out a long breath, like he was steeling himself for something. And I somehow knew that there was a reason he was telling me now, when we were driving, when he didn't have to look directly at me, when there were other things to focus on. "My dad," he said, and I watched as his hands gripped and flexed against the wheel again before coming to rest at ten and two. I just nodded, even as I felt my breath catch in my throat. Since the first night we'd talked, I'd known there was a story there, but Clark hadn't offered up any more details and I hadn't known how to ask about it.

"What about him?" I asked, when Clark's silence stretched on, and I started to worry that maybe he was waiting for me to say something. Clark paused at a red light and gave me a ghost of a smile before looking back at the road.

"He's never read any of my books," Clark said, his voice quiet. I blinked, just trying to understand this for a second. How was that even possible? "He always wanted to write," Clark went on, before I could ask. And I knew, right away, that this wasn't a story he'd told a lot—or ever. There was no easy cadence here, or practiced gloss. It felt like Clark was finding each word for the very first time. "He was doing the accountant thing to have some stability, but it was always supposed to be temporary. Until his real job could begin." I nodded, the light changed, and Clark drove on. "But he never sold anything. Never even got an agent to take him on. But since I could remember, he was working on what he considered his masterpiece—this sci-fi epic."

"Sci-fi?" I asked, surprised. Clark had mentioned that first night that his father was an aspiring writer, and I'd always assumed he wrote fantasy, like Clark.

"Yeah," Clark said, with a half smile. "He doesn't really get what I do, I don't think. . . ." His voice trailed off and he cleared his throat. "Anyway, he was really happy when I started working on my book. I think I only did it because I saw my dad writing every night, and it became something we were doing together. The McCallister men and their books. My mom used to joke about it. . . ." A smile flitted across his face but was gone almost as soon as it appeared. "So when I finished, my dad had lists of agents to send it to. I didn't think anything was going to happen—I don't think he did either. But then the book sold."

Clark hit his blinker, and I realized we were heading toward the diner. I didn't know if Clark was hungry, or if he was going there out of habit, but either way was fine with me. I'd had enough driving-around talks with my friends to know that sometimes you just needed somewhere to go, some destination so that you could keep the car moving and the conversation going.

"He was really happy for me at first," Clark said, and the faint trace of hopefulness still in his voice was breaking my heart. I wanted to slide across my seat and wrap my arms around him, kiss him until he had forgotten all about this, but I knew that neither one would actually be helpful right now. "And he thought that it would be good for his book too. But my agent didn't want it. And he couldn't sell it anywhere, this book he'd been working on for ten years. And then my books started to do well. . . ."

"And he wasn't so happy?" I filled in, feeling my anger at Clark's dad starting to rise.

"Not so much," Clark said, and though he was keeping his tone light, I could practically see the effort involved with it. "He used to say that he was planning on reading my books, getting around to it any day now. But we've stopped talking about it, really, and I've accepted now that he's just not going to read them."

"What about your mom?"

Clark shrugged as he made the right onto the street that was the shortcut to the diner's parking lot. "She stays out of it mostly," he said. "She keeps the peace, changes the subject if it looks like we're going to start talking about something that could be upsetting." I nodded, trying to ignore how familiar that sounded. "It was why I moved out this year." Clark pulled into the parking lot, which was half-deserted. He swung into an open space and cut the engine but didn't take the keys out yet, and I didn't unbuckle my seat belt or do anything that might stop him from continuing.

"Was it just too hard?"

Clark looked over at me and gave me a sad smile. "No," he said. "That's the thing. We were getting along great. But it wasn't until I realized why that I knew I had to leave."

I blinked at him, trying to figure out what this was without having to ask him. Before I could formulate the question, Clark went on quietly. "It was because I realized he was happier when I wasn't succeeding. Because we've never gotten along better than when I couldn't write."

I drew in a sharp breath as the impact of this hit me— what Clark had been going through for the last three years. "I'm really sorry," I said when I realized that there was nothing else I could say—what I really wanted to say about his dad might be better saved for another time.

"Thanks," he said, looking down at the steering wheel as he shrugged. "It's just hard." We sat in silence for a moment, and then Clark said, his voice quiet, "Your dad read my books right away. Because we were dating, and he wanted to know more about me."

"Maybe the first one," I said, "but the second one was because he liked the story."

Clark gave me a faint smile. "But he did it for you. I mean . . . I wish my dad were more like that," he said, his voice getting softer with every word. "You're just really lucky."

I sat there, listening to the rain beat against the car windows, and realized he was right. It was something I would never have believed at the beginning of the summer. But it was true now. I couldn't imagine my dad ever stepping in my way to try to block my path, or wanting anything but for me to be happy.

"I know," I said, my voice quiet.

I reached my hand over to cover his, and he threaded his fingers through mine. We just stayed like that, neither one of us making any move to get out of the car as the rain fell all around us. I rested my head on his shoulder, and he tipped his head down to rest against mine, and I sensed he was feeling what I was—that there was no need to talk just then. That what we'd said, and the rhythm of Clark's heartbeat, and the sound of the rain, in that moment, was enough.

Chapter FIFTEEN

Clark had started writing again.

He didn't tell me right away, but I knew something was different. I'd come by to get Bertie and he wouldn't be there to greet me, Bertie already wrangled into his leash. He'd emerge a few minutes later, a faraway look in his eye, his mind clearly on other things, and he'd head out to the walk forgetting essential things—his keys, his sunglasses, the dog. He always seemed to be typing things into his phone or scribbling things down on scraps of paper. When I finally asked him if he was writing—as carefully as possible, since I didn't know the rules of writer's block, and whether you could call it back by saying its name, *Beetlejuice* style—he told me that he was. He seemed thrilled but wary, not wanting to tell anyone any details about it, something that was driving Tom bananas.

But maybe he needed to say out loud that he had an idea and it was worth exploring, because after that Clark dropped the pretense and started to work for real. This meant that while he sometimes would take a break to walk Bertie with me, mostly when I picked up the dog now, I would come into the dining room, where he'd set up his office, and give him a quick kiss, but wouldn't even stop to talk.

I knew the idea had real potential when he let his publisher know he was writing—apparently, she'd called when he was working, and didn't have his defenses up—and she was thrilled. He'd told me one night when we were all hanging out by the pool that he'd even agreed to a reading and book signing in New Jersey in a few weeks and had asked if I'd go with him.

"I haven't done a bookstore event for years, because the first question you always get is about the new book and what it's about."

"But you can answer that now," I said, giving him a smile that I hoped looked sweet and innocent. "Like, what would you say, exactly, if someone asked you now?" Clark shot me a look, and I protested, "Tom wants to know too, you know. He promised me twenty dollars if I can get you to tell me the plot."

"Andie," Tom called from where he was sitting with Palmer on the side of the pool, "remind me to tell you the definition of the word 'secret' one of these days."

Despite our best efforts—including my dad at dinner—Clark hadn't given up any real details, though from the few comments he'd made, I was pretty sure that the new book was about Tamsin's ne'er-do-well older brother, Jack.

But I was beginning to understand just how spoiled I'd been, having a boyfriend with no job and no responsibilities, one who was usually happy to walk dogs with me or hang out all day. Now I had a boyfriend who spent most of his time working feverishly on a new book, his hands flying over his laptop keyboard, like if he didn't get the words down, they might disappear and not come back again. I was glad that he was working, mostly because he was so happy about it—relieved and terrified and excited all at the same time. But it did mean my summer of Clark having nothing but time on his hands was over. Since he'd started working some nights, we'd been scheduling our dates.

And there was one date in particular that we'd both blocked off. It was this coming Saturday, and I'd marked the date off in my phone with no subject, just a series of exclamation points. It was the night that we'd decided we were going to take things to the next level. It had been my decision. While Clark let me know in no uncertain terms that he was more than okay with this, I didn't feel any pressure from him. This was what I wanted, and now that we had a date marked off, I wasn't so much scared as I was really excited.

Since I knew that if I had nothing to do all day, I would just obsess about what was going to happen that night, I'd packed my schedule full. I had early-morning walks, and then Toby and I were going to Mystic Pizza for lunch—we'd all slept over at Bri's the week before and had a Julia Roberts Rom-Com fest, and when I'd found out that it was an actual pizza place just an hour outside Stanwich, I'd made plans to go immediately. Toby was equally insistent on going, though I suspected mainly because she wanted the T-shirt. Bri and Palmer were busy, so it was just the two of us on a mini road trip. That would take up most of the day, so hopefully I'd be able to go home and get ready and not have too much time to let my thoughts run away with me. Clark had planned a date for us, but he wouldn't tell me what it was, just that it was a surprise, and—I'd made him swear to it—didn't involve either mountains or bikes.

DAD

>Hey, hon. Make sure to get some gas
>on your way home from Clark's.
>I don't want you to run out on the way to Mystic.

ME

>>Sure. But what do you mean "Clark's"?
>>I'm at Palmer's. We're watching educational television.

DAD

>Don't make me GPS the car again.

ME

>>Gas. Sure.
>>Clark says hi.

DAD

>Get me a summary of his new book and all is forgiven

ME

>>I'll see what I can do

>>Clark says if you promise no
>>Secret Service agents he'll think about it

DAD

>Tell him he's got a deal.

"Hey," I called on Saturday afternoon as I kicked off my flip-flops in the entryway and dropped my bag by the door. I glanced at my phone, then picked up my pace. I just needed to take a quick shower. One of my dogs today had been Rosie, who always insisted on sitting on my lap and putting her head out the window while I drove, which meant I was pretty much covered in dog hair and drool—the last thing I wanted before going to eat lunch, especially because I had a feeling Toby would be making comments about it the whole drive up to Mystic. "I'm home," I called as I headed into the kitchen. My dad's car was in the garage, so I assumed that he was either in the kitchen or in his study. "Okay. I looked into bringing you back pizza, and I'm just not sure . . ." The rest of my sentence died halfway to my lips.

Peter was standing in our kitchen, leaning against the counter, a mug in his hand, looking like he'd never left.

"Andie," he said, looking over and smiling at me, which was almost as off-putting as seeing him there in the first place. "How are you?"

"Fine," I said, looking from Peter to my dad, who was standing across the kitchen from him, trying to figure out what was happening. My dad wasn't wearing what had become his summer uniform of jeans and a T-shirt (he'd grown particularly fond of the Captain Pizza one we'd gotten on the scavenger hunt). He was wearing a crisp button-down and khakis, and his hair was sharply parted. It was like the father I'd spent the summer with was gone, and the one who was usually there had just come back. "Um . . . how are you?"

"Oh, can't complain," Peter said, and I noticed that his BlackBerry was put away, both hands around his mug, like he was giving my father his undivided attention, which worried me more than anything else.

"Peter dropped by so we could talk over some things," my dad said, and I noticed Peter look from me to my dad, surprised, and a second later I realized why. My dad never would have explained any of this to me before. I wouldn't have been in the need-to-know loop.

"Come on, Alex," Peter said. "Way to bury the lede! I came here because the results of the internal investigation are going to be announced after the summer recess, and it came down in our favor. Your father is going to be cleared of all suspicion of wrongdoing."

"Oh," I said, my eyes darting to my dad, who gave me a smile. "That's good."

"*Good?*" Peter echoed, shaking his head. "It's great. It's what we expected to happen, naturally," he added after a moment, his tone growing more serious. He looked over at my dad. "Marshall and Stuart are fired, of course. How they ever thought they could get away with something like this . . ."

My dad's phone rang on the counter, and I looked over at it, almost surprised to hear the sound again. I watched it light up and then fall silent again. A second later the ringing started up again, and my dad picked it up and switched it to silent.

"Not a good idea," Peter said, shaking his head. "All the donors are going to come back around. Best not to alienate them."

"Pete," my dad said, shaking his head. "It's just a lot to take in."

"No time for hesitating. You know that better than anyone. This will be officially announced after the recess, and before it is, we've got to get back in work mode. I'm sure you're more than ready to get back to real life," he said, glancing around the kitchen, clearly unimpressed. "We should talk about this speech."

I just stared at my dad, who was nodding and taking his mechanical pencil from his shirt pocket. "What speech?"

My dad was already reaching to take the paper that Peter was holding out for him, and I took a step back so I wouldn't be in the way. "Erickson wants me to headline an event with him in two weeks," he said, clicking his pencil twice and frowning down at the paper.

"The governor of New York, Erickson?" I asked, and my dad nodded. "But I thought he hated you."

"Nobody hates anyone for too long in this game," Peter said, glancing up from his screen for just a second before looking back again. "Nobody can afford it. And Erickson can't look like he's alienating powerful congressmen before an election."

"But . . . ," I said, still trying to figure out what was happening. "I thought . . . Are you going to run again?"

My dad looked at me just as Peter said, "Of course he is. We have to do some polling, test the waters, but after the official announcement, there's no reason to delay." He looked up at my dad. "Alex, I think we might actually be able to come out of this stronger. You took responsibility even though you weren't at fault and stepped aside for the greater good . . . and now you're coming back vindicated." He smiled wide, which I only ever saw him do on election night. "This is the kind of stuff that's going to set us up nicely on the national stage." He paused, then started typing into his phone rapidly, like he had been away from it for as long as he was able.

"But . . . ," I said, remembering the conversation we'd had in his study. Was that just over? Totally forgotten about, knocked down like our old house?

Morgan Matson

"So we should get to work," Peter said, heading out of the kitchen. "Alex, I'll just get us set up in your office. We have the speechwriters on a conference call in ten."

"Speechwriters?" I echoed, feeling like things were happening too quickly.

"You have to get in front of these stories," Peter said, probably to me, even though he was speaking to his BlackBerry screen. "Otherwise, you lose your ability to shape the narrative. I'll meet you in there." He headed down the hall to the study, eyes still on his screen.

"So," I started. I wanted to ask my dad about the movie day we'd had planned for tomorrow, my revenge for when he'd turned last Sunday into a Dean Martin fest, including the original *Ocean's 11*. Since it was my pick, I'd gone with the newer one, mostly just to see his reaction when it started playing. But I knew it wasn't just about movie night. I wanted to know what this actually meant.

"You know how Peter can get," my dad said, looking up at me for a second before frowning down at the paper again. "He showed up here today and is already going full steam."

"Right," I said. I tried to tell myself that nothing had really changed yet, that things were still okay. "I, um, need to go pick up Toby. So I should probably get going."

"Great," he said, eyes still on the paper. "I'll see you around later. I assume you're out with your friends tonight?" He didn't wait for my response before heading into the other room. "Not too late, okay?"

A moment later I could hear him talking to Peter, and the sound of CNN's theme music. The TV in his office, which we'd mostly used to watch John Wayne fight bad guys, was now back to what it usually was doing, keeping him plugged into everything that was happening in Washington.

I stood alone in the kitchen for a moment, trying to get my bearings, telling myself I shouldn't be surprised, not really. But even as I tried to believe this, it didn't change that I felt like someone had just pulled the rug out from under me, and then, for good measure, the floor.

My phone buzzed, and I pulled it out of my pocket.

TOBY

I looked down at this, shaking my head. The end of this emoji bet could not come fast enough as far as I was concerned.

ME

We can't have pizza—because you forgot you had to work?

TOBY

Morgan Matson

It wasn't a big deal—it was the kind of thing that happened all the time. But I could have used the drive up to Mystic to clear my head and talk through what was happening.

ME

It's okay—we'll do it another time.

I closed out of Toby's text and pressed the button to call Clark. If I couldn't talk to Toby, maybe I could talk to him. Not that he would be able to do anything, but talking it through might help. I wanted to hear his voice, but my call went right to voice mail, and I realized he probably had it turned off—because he was working.

Because he had a job, one that he would also be going back to once the summer ended. Just like my dad was going to do.

In just a few weeks, when everything was going to change.

I could feel myself start to get the panicky, spiraling feeling I hadn't had since the start of the summer. I had thrown out my plans and my schedule and had just been going with the flow all summer—taking Palmer's advice and not thinking about the future. But that hadn't meant the future had gone away. I'd just been ignoring it. I hadn't considered the fact that everyone else was treating this summer as temporary. It was like I was just now realizing that I'd spent the last few months in a bubble, thinking it was real life. But it wasn't. And I never should have let myself forget that.

When my phone rang a second later, I tried not to be disappointed that MAYA was coming up on the caller ID. It wasn't like Clark was psychic, after all, able to know when I needed to talk to him the most. "Hey, Maya."

"Andie!" she said, and I could hear the stress in her voice. But I wasn't that surprised—if nothing was wrong, or if there was a scheduling change, she would have texted me. "Hi! Quick question—are you busy this afternoon? Around one?"

"No," I said automatically, since I'd cleared the afternoon to eat pizza in Mystic, which was now very much not happening. "Need me to do a walk?"

"Well . . . kind of," Maya said after a pause, which should have been my first clue that something was up. "I did a drop-off at a vet, but can't make the pickup and was wondering if you could do it."

"Oh," I said. "Sure. Which dog is it?"

"It's actually a cat," Maya said, and I could hear how hard she was trying to make this sound fun and exciting, but not even coming close to pulling it off.

"Oh, no," I said, since I had a feeling I knew exactly which cat we were talking about. "Is this Miss Cupcakes?"

"Oh, you know her?" Maya asked, and I could hear the relief in her voice. "Thank goodness. So you know what you're in for." I tried to get myself to think fast, wishing I hadn't so definitively told Maya that I was free, but before I could come up with anything, she was pointing out that the hard part of the job was already done, since she'd had to corral the cat and get her into the carrier, and all I'd have to do was pick her up and bring her home. It was so logical, I really couldn't argue with it. And since I had nothing else to do that afternoon, I'd agreed.

And it truthfully wasn't that bad, picking Miss Cupcakes

up. The strangest thing, I realized as I brought her carrier into the kitchen, was being in Bri's house without anyone else there. I pushed open Bri's front door and stepped inside, holding in front of me, at arm's length, Miss Cupcakes's carrier, which contained a very angry Miss Cupcakes. "Look, you're home," I said, setting the carrier on the ground while trying to keep my hands away from the airholes, which I'd learned the hard way Miss Cupcakes was very skilled at getting her claws through. "Okay? Stop being such a jerk." As though the terrible cat could understand me, she started yowling, the carrier rocking back and forth. I reached over to unlatch the door, keeping the rest of me as far away from it as possible, and once it was open, took a huge step back. The cat shot out of the carrier, hissing, and disappeared into the kitchen. I let out a breath, thinking, for the umpteenth time that day, just how much I preferred dogs.

I'd texted Bri earlier to see if she was going to be around but hadn't gotten a response back, which made sense, since she'd told me she had plans. Even though I'd been in her house more times than I could count, being there alone was making me feel like an intruder. I closed the latch on the empty carrier, then wrote a quick note to go along with the letter from the vet that they'd given me when I'd picked her up.

I started to head toward the front door when I heard a sound from upstairs.

"Hello?" I called, figuring one of the Choudhurys was home after all. "I have your cat!" I called, then a second later, realized it made me sound like I'd kidnapped Miss Cupcakes and was demanding a ransom. "She's fine," I added when I didn't get a response. I waited, ears straining, but didn't hear anything and tried to tell myself that it might have been my imagination, or the house settling, or something. I had just reached for the doorknob when I heard it again—the sound of low laughter and footsteps coming down the stairs. I looked around, trying to decide if I should stay, or make a run for it, when I heard someone say, "Well, of *course* you do," and I realized it was Bri.

I started to walk toward the front stairs, figuring I'd meet her halfway, when I heard someone else. I'd just assumed Bri was on the phone, and it took me a second to recognize the voice. It wasn't until I saw them on the stairway together—pressed up against the wall, arms around each other, kissing—that I even began to get what was happening. And even then I somehow couldn't get my brain to understand what I was seeing, though it was right in front of me.

Because Bri was kissing Wyatt.

Chapter SIXTEEN

I dropped the keys I'd been holding, and they clattered onto the wood floor. Bri jumped and broke away from Wyatt, her eyes widening when she saw me. "Andie," she said, blinking at me. "What—what are you doing here?"

"I was bringing the cat back from the vet," I said, saying these words because they still belonged to a universe that I understood, with logic that I could follow. "I . . ." I stared at them, wondering if there was any way I could have misunderstood, trying to come up with some other explanation for what I'd just seen. But Wyatt's hand was still tangled in Bri's hair, and her cheeks were flushed, and Wyatt's shirt was on inside out. There was no pretending that she'd been giving him emergency mouth-to-mouth, or anything other than what this was. Wyatt was looking from me to Bri, like he was trying to figure out what happened next.

"Right," Bri said, taking a step away from Wyatt and smoothing her own shirt down, like she was trying to regain some of her composure. "I guess I just thought . . . I didn't realize you would be the one bringing her back."

"Last-minute thing," I said, and Bri nodded and then looked down, and I wondered if she'd just felt what I had—that I'd reached my limit of talking about things other than the elephant in the room.

"So I think I'll head out," Wyatt said to Bri, after the awkward silence had stretched to the breaking point, and I watched them have a fierce, silent conversation that ended with Bri glancing at me and nodding. Wyatt leaned forward, and was clearly about to kiss her, but stopped at the last moment, looked at me, then pulled back and gave Bri an awkward half hug/pat-on-the-head combo. Wyatt hurried past me like he was fleeing the scene of the crime, slamming the door behind him as he went.

I looked at Bri, who wouldn't meet my eye, just turned and started walking up the stairs again, her steps heavy. "Come on," she said over her shoulder. "We should talk."

"You *think*?" I asked as I followed her up the stairs to her room.

"I know," Bri said, looking down at her hands, which were twisting together. "I *know*, Andie."

"But . . . ," I said, trying to get my head around this. "What is even going on? I mean . . ." I looked at her, wanting her to jump in, somehow explain things so that I could understand them. "How did it happen?"

Bri let out a long breath and looked up at me. "The night of the scavenger hunt," she finally said, and I felt my jaw drop open.

"Wait," I said, shaking my head. I had been ready to hear that this had been a one- or two-time thing, that she now realized was a huge mistake. "The scavenger hunt was *weeks* ago. You guys have been . . . this whole time?" Bri nodded and pressed her lips together hard. "Did it happen when Wyatt's car broke down?" Bri just gave me a look, and much too late, the penny dropped. "His car never broke down," I said, feeling like an idiot for not putting this together sooner.

"No," Bri said, her voice quiet. "We were starting to do the list when he told me how he felt. And I hadn't wanted to admit it, but . . . I'd been feeling the same way too."

I closed my eyes for a second, still trying to get this to be a reality I could deal with—that Bri and Wyatt had been together, in secret, for half the summer.

"Oh my god," I said, sinking down to the floor, feeling like my legs were not really up for holding me at that moment. My eyes strayed over to her bed—it was messy, the sheets rumpled, and I knew for a fact that Bri made her bed, hospital corners and all, every morning. "Are you sleeping with him?"

Bri just looked at me—I could see the answer clearly written across her face. *"Bri."* I suddenly thought of the day on Palmer's roof, how quiet she'd been when we were talking about guys and bases, keeping this secret from all of us. Keeping it from Toby. "What about Toby?" I asked, feeling like this just kept getting worse.

Bri shook her head and let out a short laugh, the kind with no humor in it whatsoever. "Right," she said, and I could hear her voice was tight, and higher, the way it was when she was getting emotional and didn't want to show it. "Because *of course* this is about Toby."

I just looked at her. "Well . . ."

"It's *always* about Toby!" Bri yelled this, her voice reverberating in the room.

"That's not true."

"Isn't it?" she asked, her voice still raised. "You found out I'm sleeping with Wyatt and your first thought was about Toby.

Not me. I don't get a morning at the diner where we all get to talk about it. I don't even get to be with him in public, because of Toby. Because we need to protect her." Bri brushed her hand across her face. "Nobody ever cares about making things easier for *me*. It's always about Toby. It's like I can't even see myself sometimes when I'm with her, and I just . . ." Her voice trailed off, and she sat down on the bed, pulling her knees up underneath her.

I pushed myself off the floor and walked over to sit next to Bri on the bed. "Okay," I said, hearing the question in my voice. I felt like I was so without a plan and so beyond anything we'd ever experienced that I had no idea what to do from here, how we should proceed. My first, automatic thought was that it should be Toby here, doing this, before I realized how crazy that was. "So tell me about it."

Bri gave a trembly smile as she looked at her hands. "It's . . . He's . . ." She looked up at me. "You know he's the first thing I've had that's mine? Just mine? In, like, a decade? And it's good." She took a shaky breath. "It's great. He's so different when you really get to know him. He's actually really funny, and he's got such a good heart. And he gets me," she said, more quietly now. "He sees me. I make him laugh, and . . ." Her smile got wider. "We just . . . work."

"I'm glad for you," I said. "I am," I added quickly when she shot me a look. And I was—I was thrilled that Bri had fallen for someone she really liked. But there was almost no way to separate this from *who* it was she had fallen for. "It's just . . ." I knew I didn't have to say it. The underside, the shadow, of everything Bri was saying was that Toby was out there, not knowing any of this.

Morgan Matson

"I never wanted to hurt her, Andie. That's the last thing I wanted."

"I know that," I said, my voice quiet.

"But . . ." Bri pushed herself off the bed and paced over to the window. "They never even dated. It's not like he's her ex, or anything. She has this crazy crush on him, but Wyatt *told* her that he's not interested. And still she has this claim on him. And at some point . . ." Her voice faded out, and she bit her lip.

"What?" I asked, keeping my voice soft, thinking back to Clark, in the car, in the rain.

"At some point," she said, then took a big breath. "It was like I was putting my happiness on hold for something that only existed in Toby's head." She stared at me with something like horror. "Oh god, I have to tell her the truth, don't I?"

I let out a long breath. "Well . . ." Sitting between us, the elephant in the room, was that this had been a secret. That the only reason I knew—the only reason we were having this conversation—was because I'd caught them. That this might have been a different conversation if she'd told Toby before anything had happened with Wyatt. But now . . .

I played this through to the end, and it hit me. Just what this meant, really. For all of us. Because there was no way we got out of this, as a group, still okay. Even if Bri and Wyatt came clean now, I didn't see Toby getting over this any time soon. If she found out by accident, it would be the same thing—but probably worse. There was no way out of this, unless . . .

Unless Toby never found out.

I pushed myself up to standing and walked over to the couch in Bri's room, the one that was parallel to the bed, and felt something inside of me click back into place. Peter's words from this morning were echoing in my head. We had to shape this narrative and figure out a plan while we still could. This was still fixable.

It *had* to be fixable. The four of us had to be okay. My friends had been the one thing I could always count on, and with everything else beginning to spin out of my control, I needed us to stay together. My dad might have a foot out the door, but I wasn't about to let us fall apart.

"Bri," I said, leaning forward. "Tell me how you see that playing out. You telling Toby you've been sneaking around all summer and lying to her."

Bri's chin trembled slightly as she pulled at a thread on her comforter. "I . . . ," she started, then shook her head.

"Exactly," I said, not looking away from Bri. "So . . . what if she doesn't need to know? What if she doesn't have to go through all that?"

Bri blinked at me. "Andie?"

"Who does it benefit for her to find out?" I asked, making my voice as calm and reasonable as possible. "You've been keeping this a secret all summer. What's a few more weeks?"

"What do you mean?" Bri asked, though the expression on her face told me she knew exactly what I meant.

"I mean," I hesitated, then made myself say it. "Have you guys talked about what is going to happen when Wyatt leaves?"

"No," she said, and I could hear her start to get defensive. "Have you and Clark?"

I swallowed hard. "No," I admitted, feeling my heart clench, the way it always did when I had to think about this. "But," I said, trying to focus on Bri as I told myself that ours wasn't even close to the same situation, "do you think that this is . . . like, a long-term thing?" I winced even as I said it and braced myself for her to throw the same question back at me, one about Clark that I couldn't come close to answering.

Bri looked down at the floor, and I could see her lip was trembling and I felt horrible for putting her through this. I told myself firmly that this was for the best—not only for Bri, but for all of us. "I don't know," she finally said, in a half whisper.

"That's okay," I said, sitting down next to her. "And it's understandable. You guys are still figuring it out. But since you're not totally sure it's going to be a long-term thing . . ." I let my sentence trail off, hoping that Bri would fill in the blanks.

"What if Toby finds out that we were both keeping this from her?" Bri finally asked, looking up at me. "And Palmer, too. How do you see *that* playing out?"

"I think it's better than the alternative," I finally said. "Don't you?"

I held my breath while I watched Bri struggle with this. She had to be able to see it. Because the four of us, together, was everything. And we had to stay that way—we had to do what we had to to make it happen.

"Okay," Bri finally said, nodding once.

"It's for the best," I said, feeling relief flood through me. "For all of us."

"You're sure about this," she said, not exactly phrasing it like a question.

I nodded, quashing any small voices of doubt that were trying to tell me that I was doing this all wrong and that there was more going on here than just Bri and Wyatt. This was the only way we were going to make it out of this unscathed. And so I nodded and looked Bri right in the eye. "I am."

Bri nodded, and I felt a weight start to lift off my shoulders. It was all going to be okay. I had the same feeling as when you duck at the very last second and miss something you would have walked right into—realizing just how close you came to danger. And then the relief that followed when you realized you were safe, that everything was going to be fine.

"What do you think?" Clark asked, as he swung his car into the parking lot of the Boxcar Cantina. "I thought it might be nice . . . kind of romantic . . ." He adjusted his glasses, and I saw how nervous he was about his surprise.

"It's great," I said, leaning across the car and giving him a quick kiss. We hadn't been back here since the night of our first date, and I liked that we were going back now, when everything between us was different, on the cusp of another first.

I started to get out of the car, but Clark practically ran around to my side and opened my door for me. "Thanks," I said, stepping down and taking the hand he offered me. Clark closed my car door and then slid his arms around me.

"Hi," he said, pulling me close.

"Hi," I said back. He leaned down and kissed me, and I kissed him back, until we were pressed up against the side of the car, both of us breathing hard, and my pulse was galloping in my throat. "Um, do we really *have* to have dinner?" I asked, and Clark laughed. But I was only partially kidding. There was a piece of me that wanted to tell him we should skip it, just get back in the car and head straight back to his place.

Morgan Matson

"So," he said as he took my hand in his and we walked up to the restaurant, "how was your day?"

"Oh," I said, feeling myself start to come back down to reality as I thought about the day—starting with Peter showing up in our kitchen and ending with walking in on Bri and Wyatt. I didn't want to tell Clark that everything was fine—he'd be able to see through me, anyway—I just didn't want to have to think about these other things tonight. Tonight was about us. I'd been looking forward to it for weeks, and nothing was going to wreck it. "Well—" I started, just as we reached the hostess podium, and took my opportunity to avoid answering the question.

While Clark gave her his name, I felt my phone buzz in my purse and pulled it out.

TOBY

PALMER

Yes! Tonight's the night!!

TOBY

PALMER

I think Toby wants a picture of what you're wearing.
Me too.

THE UNEXPECTED EVERYTHING

I smiled as I read these, then sent one of the pictures I'd taken when I was getting ready, mostly because I'd had a feeling this conversation would happen. I was wearing one of my favorite dresses and the fanciest underwear I'd ever owned—Bri and I had bought it together last week, and it hadn't even occurred to me then to wonder why she was also getting some for herself.

PALMER

You look amazing!!

TOBY

ME

Thanks, you guys.

PALMER

We can meet up at the diner and discuss tomorrow over waffles!
Keep tradition alive and all.

TOBY

I felt my smile fade as I looked at the screen. For a moment I wished I was back where Palmer and Toby were, not knowing any of this—not knowing that Bri had gone through her first

Morgan Matson

time without telling any of us, without talking to us about it, without doing the diner recap. And the thought of that just made me sad—not just for Bri, but for all of us.

ME

Right. Totally!
Talk to you guys later.

"Andie?" I looked up to see Clark standing by the hostess, with menus tucked under her arm, and I dropped my phone in my bag as I hurried to join him. We were seated at a table just one over from where we'd been on our first date, and I had a feeling that Clark had done something to arrange it.

"So where was your dad tonight?" Clark asked, as I glanced at the menu and then set it aside, knowing I would get the exact same thing I'd gotten before. "He wasn't lying in wait and telling me that he knows people who know people. Is he feeling okay?"

Clark clearly meant this as a joke, and I gave him a small smile. "He's good, actually," I said, making my voice much more upbeat than I was currently feeling. I didn't really want to go into it, telling Clark how it had felt seeing Peter standing in our kitchen, seeing my dad slip back into his old mode like it was nothing, like our summer hadn't even happened. If I told Clark about it, it became the truth in a way I wasn't sure I wanted, not tonight. So I smiled at him brightly across the table. "It turns out that he's going to get cleared of any wrongdoing. So he should be back to running for reelection in the fall, everything back to normal soon." I took a sip of my Diet Coke, needing to avoid Clark's eye and the way he always seemed to be able to read me.

"But . . . I thought he wasn't going to run again. I thought he told you that."

"Well, it seems like he changed his mind."

"I'm sorry, Andie," he said, his voice low and soft. He leaned toward me, and I felt myself, without meaning to, draw slightly back.

"It's fine! It's what was probably always going to happen, right?"

Clark just looked at me for a long moment, his brow furrowing. "Are you okay?" he asked softly. "You seem . . ."

"What?" I asked, not meeting his eye as I folded up the top of my straw wrapper.

"I don't know," he said after a long moment. The waitress came and took our order—Clark got his Reaper-ito again—and when she'd left and the menus had been cleared away, Clark looked at me across the table, his eyes searching mine.

"Anyway," I said, looking around for the chips, "that's what happened to me today. How was your day? What did you do?" I was trying to get back to where I'd been just a few minutes ago, but I could hear that my voice wasn't quite right—it was a little shrill, and I was talking faster than usual.

"It was okay," Clark said. "I worked this afternoon, and then . . . um . . . got things ready for tonight." He smiled at me, and I looked down at the table and wished, more than anything, that I was back in that same place with him.

"Neat," I said, my voice coming out too high. "Awesome."

"Andie." Clark leaned across the table and took one of my hands in both of his. "If you're nervous about tonight, it's okay. And—"

"No," I said, wishing I could shake this off once and for all.

It wasn't Clark's fault my day had gotten so totally derailed. "I'm not. I mean, a little bit. But it's not that."

"Then what is it?"

I looked at him and realized that while I knew I didn't have to tell him about Bri and Wyatt, I wanted to. I didn't want to keep something that big from him. And maybe if I talked about it, the thoughts that had been swirling around in my head ever since I left Bri's house would settle down a little and I could enjoy what was supposed to be one of the most important nights of my life.

"Okay," I said, letting out a breath. "But you can't tell anyone. All right?"

"Of course," Clark said easily.

"I mean it," I said, not breaking eye contact with him.

"Yes," Clark said, his tone growing more serious, clearly picking up on how I was feeling. "What's going on?"

I took a breath and started to tell him. By the time I was through, our chips had finally arrived, but neither one of us had touched them yet.

"Jeez," Clark said when I'd finished, letting out a low whistle.

I winced. "I know."

"This . . . I mean, this can't end well, right?"

"Well," I said, letting go of his hands, "I mean . . . Bri and Wyatt have been keeping it together all summer. So if they can get through this until he goes back to school, they'll be fine. That's what I told her to do, actually."

"Wait, what?"

"It just makes sense," I said, breaking a chip in half, not even because I really wanted it, but because I wanted to have something to do with my hands.

"Why were you telling her to do anything?" Clark asked, sounding mostly baffled.

"Because it was going to wreck everything," I said, hearing myself get defensive, "and it was the logical thing to do."

Clark just looked at me. "So is Bri just going to keep this secret from Toby forever? Are you?"

"Do you really think they're going to be able to make a long-distance thing work?" I asked, knowing full well that I wasn't just talking about Bri and Wyatt. "Especially since they haven't even talked about it?"

The sentence seemed to hang between us for a second, and I pressed my nails into my palms, not even sure what I wanted him to say.

"Yeah," he finally replied. He cleared his throat and looked down at the table. "That's . . . I mean, I guess it's a complicated situation."

I nodded, trying not to let the disappointment I was feeling show on my face. What had I wanted Clark to say? That we were different, that we'd find a way to make it work? That he'd at least thought about this, like I had?

I took a long drink of my soda, wishing more than anything that we'd just left when I'd wanted to in the parking lot. It suddenly felt like Clark was getting farther away from me across the table, like there was a gulf between us, even though he hadn't actually moved. "Well," I said, giving him a tight smile, "it was the only thing to be done. If you'd been there, you would have understood."

"Okay," Clark said, and silence fell between us once again. I looked across the table at him and tried to imagine the rest of the night playing out. Suddenly, all our plans, all Clark's

Morgan Matson

preparation, my fancy underwear . . . none of it felt right anymore. This wasn't how I wanted the night to kick off. I couldn't even imagine recapping this in the diner in the morning, that we had been awkward and sniping at each other over dinner, not saying what we really meant. None of it was going the way I'd wanted it to. And it wasn't fair to do this to Clark, since he had just been yanked into this. "Clark," I said, swallowing hard. "About tonight. I think maybe it's not the best night for it."

I looked up at him, and he nodded. "Yeah," he said, and while I could hear disappointment in his voice, he didn't sound surprised. "I think maybe another night would be better."

"But soon," I said.

"Yes, absolutely soon," he said immediately, and I laughed. Our food arrived, and when Clark started eating his burrito, the kitchen staff gathering to watch again, I sent a text to my friends, telling them that our plans had changed, there was no need for waffles, and I'd talk to them tomorrow.

By the time we were done with dinner, things were feeling better. Not like the evening could still be salvaged, but somewhat back to normal. We were feeling like us again, at least.

"But I am worried about you," Clark said, once the plates were cleared. He reached across the table and squeezed my hand. "How are you doing with all of this?"

For a moment I thought about telling him how I was really feeling—like things were spinning out of my control and all I knew to do was to hold on as hard as I could, and try to keep everything together. But the moment passed, and I just gave him a smile, even though I was pretty sure he would see through it. "Of course," I said. "I'm fine."

Hey! Running a few late to pick up Bert. Be there soon.

CLARK

That's fine!
Whenever.
Um.

ME

What?

CLARK

So I have to tell you something

ME

What is it?

CLARK

I told Tom
About Bri and Wyatt

ME

What?!
Clark!!

CLARK

You were acting so strange about the whole thing
Not like yourself at all and I didn't know if you were okay.

I just wanted his take on it.

But it's okay. He promised not to tell

ME

You really think he's going to be
able to keep this from Palmer?

CLARK

Maybe?

ME

I don't.

Wait, hold on, he just texted

TOM

Andie! What the hell?!

ME

I know

TOM

I mean . . .

ME

I know

TOM

You know I have to tell Palmer

ME

NO

Tom, seriously, you cannot

CLARK

What's he saying?

ME

Oh, just that he has to tell Palmer

CLARK

But he promised he wouldn't!

ME

He hasn't yet, but it seems likely

CLARK

I'll talk to him

TOM

Hello?

ME

Sorry. Clark's mad at you

TOM

What did I do? I didn't even want to know
any of this. And now I'm keeping secrets from my
girlfriend?

Morgan Matson

ME

How do you think I feel?
You can't tell her. Tom, SERIOUSLY
It's bad enough you and Clark know

TOM

What's that supposed to mean?

PALMER

Hey. What's going on?

ME

Nothing. Why?
What do you mean?

PALMER

What?

ME

Did you talk to Tom?

PALMER

About what?

ME

Nothing. Just . . . checking.

PALMER

Want to see a movie later?

THE UNEXPECTED EVERYTHING

ME

Maybe! Can I let you know?

CLARK

Okay, now Tom's mad at me

ME

But is he going to keep it secret?

CLARK

He says he can

ME

He also said he could do a British accent
You didn't have to sit through the production of
My Fair Lady like the rest of us

TOBY

ME

Hi! What's going on?
Anything happening?
Anything you want to share?

TOBY

Morgan Matson

ME

You're bored at work?

TOBY

ME

That's great

Toby

??

ME

No, I just meant that it's good it's
not something more serious, that's all

PALMER

Movie? Bri thinks she can get us in free
And that it's not just a ploy to get us
to hang out with her this time

ME

Want me to see if Clark can come?

PALMER

Idk, I was thinking maybe just us
I feel like I haven't seen Bri lately

ME

She's probably just busy

With her job

CLARK

Tom might be mad at you now

ME

I know that

CLARK

No about something else

(sorry)

TOM

Oh, so now I can't act, either??

You said you LIKED my Henry Higgins

ME

I did!

TOM

SURE.

ME

CLARK!

CLARK

I'm sorry! I needed an example

Morgan Matson

ME

Stop telling Tom everything!

PALMER

Movie?

ME

Sure. Fine. Sounds good
And let's not ask the guys
I'm currently mad at Clark

PALMER

What'd he do?

ME

Nothing
He just

PALMER

What??

ME

He won't tell me what his new book is about

PALMER

I'll get Tom to find out—I bet he can

ME

I'm beginning to agree with you

THE UNEXPECTED EVERYTHING

TOBY

ME

Awesome, you're in?

TOBY

PALMER

Okay, I'll see you tonight

I have to go talk my boyfriend off the ledge

Suddenly he's worried about his British accent??

ME

Actors.

Weird, right?

CLARK

Can I see you tonight?

ME

Seeing a movie with the girls.

Tomorrow?

Morgan Matson

CLARK

    It's a plan.

    And I am sorry about telling Tom.

    I just needed to get some perspective.

                                                    ME

                                        I get it.

                                  I'll see you tomorrow.

                                          Xx

"So do you guys have an arrangement with management or something?" Toby asked as she leaned across the glass case in the lobby
of the Palace Movie Theater, looking down at the candy. "That the
only movies you can get us into for free are the bad ones?"

    "I didn't think it was that bad," Palmer said from the other
side of the lobby, as she looked at one of the coming-attraction
posters. "I liked the dog."

    "I don't think that's the best indication of a movie's quality,"
I said, looking around from my spot behind the counter, next to
Bri. We were the last ones there—after the show ended, Bri had
swept up and we'd helped by pointing out where she needed
to sweep. All the moviegoers had gone, and after Craig the pro-
jectionist exchanged an awkward greeting with Toby (their date
had not been a success), we had our run of the place.

    I looked at Bri doing her last checks of the theater, locking the
front door so nobody would wander in and making sure everything was turned off, I was impressed that she was hiding her secret
so well. But maybe she'd gotten used to it over the last month, or

we just hadn't been paying attention. But as I looked around at all of us hanging out, Palmer and Toby none the wiser to what was going on in our midst, I began to really feel like this might be okay. That we'd get through this, Wyatt and Bri would fade out, and nobody needed to get unnecessarily hurt in the process.

"What do you guys want to do now?" Palmer asked, heading over to me and Toby, while Bri did actual work, taking inventory of the popcorn kernels and condiments. "Diner? Or we could go to the Orchard?"

"Orchard," Bri and Toby said in unison.

"Oh," Palmer said, looking crestfallen. "But . . ."

"If you want food, P, just get something to go," I suggested.

Palmer pointed at me. "I knew there was a reason we keep you around," she said, pulling out her phone and taking a few steps away.

"Order me French fries!" Toby yelled after her, then turned to me. "Think she heard me?"

"I think she heard you," I said, laughing. "I just don't know if she listened to you."

"Okay," Bri said, setting her clipboard down. "Done."

"Can we leave?" I asked over Toby, who, rather than walking up to Palmer, was just yelling, "French fries!" at increasingly louder levels.

"Almost," Bri said. "I just have to make sure that everyone's out of the bathrooms and that they're not a complete disaster."

"How long?" I asked, taking out my phone. "I'll see if Clark wants to meet us at the Orchard."

"We should be good to leave in ten," Bri said, picking up her phone to check the time, then leaving it on the counter as she headed for the bathroom. "And tell Toby I want in on her fries."

I started to text Clark as Toby reached into her bag for her own phone, then sighed as she looked at the screen. "My phone's dead," she said, dropping it back in her purse.

"Why is your phone always dead?" I asked, shaking my head at her.

"Give me yours," Toby said, grabbing for it, and I held it out of her reach.

"Wait a sec," I said. "I'm texting Clark."

Toby rolled her eyes at me and then reached for Bri's. "Because you *never* talk to Clark," she said, already scrolling through Bri's apps.

"Okay," Palmer said, coming back to join us. "Food'll be ready in ten."

"Did you get my French fries?" Toby asked.

"Did you *want* French fries?" Palmer asked, sounding extra confused. "Why didn't you say something?"

"Palmer!" Toby said, then looked up to see Palmer's expression. "Oh," she said, smiling. "Gotcha. I just—" Bri's phone dinged with a text update just as I finished writing my text to Clark. "Oh, Wyatt texted," Toby said, squinting at the screen, and I looked up at her and felt my stomach plunge.

"Maybe you shouldn't see that," I said, quickly reaching for Bri's phone, but Toby took a step away, still reading, her brow furrowing. "Tobes, just use mine," I said, desperately trying to get in front of this, holding my phone out to her.

"I . . . ," Toby said, and now I could see that she was scrolling up, reading Bri's text messages, her hand shaking and her eyes filling with tears. "I don't understand what . . ."

"What are you talking about?" Palmer asked, looking at me

as my pulse started going double time. This was happening. It was happening right now.

And there was absolutely nothing I could do to stop it.

"Done!" Bri said triumphantly, emerging from the bathroom smiling at us. It faltered, then faded, when she saw Toby. "What's going on?" she asked, and I saw her eyes dart from her phone to Toby's face and then to mine. I gave my head a tiny shake.

"Why is Wyatt texting you?" Toby asked, her voice was trembling. "Why is he telling you that he misses you and it's been too long and he needs to see you tonight?"

"Wait, what?" Palmer asked, her jaw dropping open. She looked at Bri. "Is this a joke?"

"I . . . ," Bri said, looking at me, then back to Toby. "Okay, so . . ."

"You've been hooking up with *Wyatt*?" Toby asked, her voice rising. "My Wyatt?"

"He's not yours," Bri said softly, and I closed my eyes for a moment, wishing that we'd talked about how to handle this if Toby found out. How had we not had a contingency plan in place?

"What?" Toby asked, looking like she'd just been punched in the stomach.

"He's not yours," Bri said, and I could see she was blinking fast, the way she always did when she was starting to cry but was trying to fight it. "You guys made out *once*. It's not like you two were even together—"

"Seriously?" Toby asked, shaking her head. "You're seriously saying that?"

"Okay," Palmer said, looking at me, clearly wanting backup. "Let's—"

"Here's the thing," I said in my most soothing voice, taking a step forward. "I think we all just need to take a breath and focus here. If we just—"

"If there was nothing wrong with what you were doing with Wyatt, why didn't you tell me?" Toby asked, still gripping Bri's phone. "Why keep it a secret?"

"Because I knew you'd do this," Bri said, her voice breaking. "I knew you wouldn't get it."

"So you've just been lying," Toby said, and I could tell that she was still struggling, on some level, to understand what was happening. "You've been lying to all of us all summer."

"It was for the best," Bri said a little desperately, shooting a look my way. "And it was . . . for all of us. For our friendship . . ." She looked at me again, like she was waiting for me to jump in and fix this. "Andie, tell her."

Toby whipped around to face me. "You knew about this?"

"I only just found out," I said. "But—"

"You kept this from me?" Toby asked, her voice breaking. "You lied to me?"

"And me," Palmer said, shaking her head. "How could you do that?"

"I was just . . . ," I started. "It was the only thing that made sense. There was no reason for Toby to get hurt if it could be avoided."

"Oh my god," Palmer said, shaking her head in disgust. "Don't try to *spin* this, Andie. Are you kidding me?"

"That was not your call to make," Toby yelled at me, her face getting red.

"I just wanted us to stay friends," I yelled back, and Toby let out a short mocking laugh.

"Well, that worked out *really* well, didn't it?"

"Toby—" I started, looking around the group, at all the people who were currently furious at me, willing myself to think fast enough, to figure out how to fix this.

"You were supposed to be my best friend," Toby said to Bri, and I could see that she was crying now too, tears she tried to wipe away with angry swipes across her face.

"I am," Bri said, looking up at Toby, her voice anguished.

Toby shook her head and dropped Bri's phone on the counter. "No," she said quietly, sounding shattered. "You're not." She walked across the lobby, yanking the glass door open and then pausing once she got outside, looking around for a moment before turning right and walking toward the parking lot, her shoulders hunched.

Bri looked down at her phone on the counter, then swallowed hard as she picked it up and put it in her back pocket. "You guys should probably go," she said, her voice cracking.

"Bri—" Palmer said, but Bri was already talking over her.

"Really. I just want to be alone, okay?" Palmer and I looked at each other, and I knew we were both weighing the same thing—trying to decide if she really meant it, what we should do in this totally uncharted territory. "Please," Bri said before either of us could come to a decision. "Please just go."

Palmer gave me a tiny nod, and I took a step toward Bri—not sure what I was even going to say but feeling like I couldn't just leave like this, without a word. But Bri crossed her arms tightly over her chest and looked down, giving me every indication that she meant what she said—that she wanted to be alone.

Palmer walked toward the door first, and I followed, still

a little unable to believe that this had happened, was still happening, right now. It was like a slow-motion car accident that nobody was doing anything to stop. I followed Palmer out the door, out of the air-conditioned theater and into the hot, humid night, the cicadas sounding even louder than usual somehow.

"Toby was my ride," Palmer said, and I nodded.

"I'll drive you." It felt like we were trapped in a bad play, neither one of us saying what we really wanted. We started to walk to the parking lot, and I looked back one more time to see Bri, looking lost in the empty theater, her hands over her eyes, her shoulders shaking.

I made myself look away, and Palmer and I walked to my car, not speaking to each other while she canceled her diner order and I texted Clark to let him know about the change of plans. I unlocked the car and Palmer got in, slamming her door hard and then turning to face the window. I looked over at her as I started the car, practically feeling the anger and resentment coming off her in waves. We didn't say a single word on the way back to Stanwich Woods. Every time I'd take a breath to say something—I didn't even know what—Palmer would turn away from me more in her seat, until she was totally facing the window and all I could see was her back.

When I went through the gatehouse, Jaime barely looking up from his novel to wave me in, Palmer said, "You know, Tom's been acting really weird."

Normally I would have made a joke here, asking her *how can you tell?* or something along those lines, but I knew this was not the moment for that. "He has?"

"Yes. Like he's been hiding something." She turned to face

me. "He knows, doesn't he? You told Clark, and he told Tom."

I nodded, swallowing hard. I was almost to Palmer's house, and even though the street was deserted, I put on my blinker to turn into her driveway. "But—"

"So not only were you keeping a secret from me, you were making my boyfriend lie to me."

"I had to tell someone," I said. "I was doing the best thing I could think of to keep us together and I just wanted to know—"

But she was already unbuckling her seat belt, shaking her head as she got out of the car. She slammed the door hard and walked fast across her driveway, not once looking back at me.

When I got home, my dad wasn't waiting up to talk to me. I could see the light was on in his study, but I didn't make a move to walk down the hall. What could he possibly do in this situation? And I didn't want to tell him about what had happened. Because even if he had advice that was helpful, I couldn't let myself get used to it—because who knew if he'd be here the next time I needed him.

I shut the door to my room behind me and leaned back against it for just a moment. I pulled out my phone, hoping against hope that there would be a text chain going, everyone admitting that they were sorry, and that we could all move past this. But there was nothing. I started to send a message, then stopped when I realized I had no idea what I would say. I selected just Toby's name and started to write, trying not to see the last time we'd texted, when she'd been excited about the movie.

Toby, I'm so sorry.
Are you okay? I'm worried.

I looked down at the screen, waiting, hoping she would respond. After a full minute I set my phone down on my night-stand and started to get ready for bed, even though it was only a little after ten. I felt like I was moving underwater as I brushed my teeth and washed my face, then turned off my light and got into bed. I'd just rolled over onto my side when my phone *ding*ed with a text message.

TOBY

I waited to see if there would be more, but nothing else followed. I didn't know what I was supposed to say to that—had no idea how I was going to make any of this right, or if that was even possible. I looked at my phone, glowing in the darkness of my room, for a long moment.

Then I turned it off.

Tamsin looked across the shadows of the dungeon at the old man who always sat huddled against the stone, the one whose voice was like the rattling of bones, the one who hadn't seen sunlight in fifteen years. He'd asked her to describe the sun when she'd first been thrown in here, which she had thought was ridiculous. Who could forget what it looked like when light dappled across leaves in the forest? She could recall them so easily—the early-morning light, so cool and blue and not yet warm; the way sunsets in Castleroy seemed to linger, putting on their best show before disappearing for the night.

But now, though it had been only three months, she was beginning to understand better. She'd forgotten about warmth, forgotten that once, she'd been lucky and free and able to raise her face to the sunlight, closing her eyes and breathing in the day. Once, she never could have imagined herself in a place like this. Now she was having trouble remembering that she'd ever been anywhere else.

"The Elder is dead," she said out loud for the first time. As soon as she said it, she knew it was true. He would have come for her if he hadn't been. He would have done something. She would not have still been in here if he could have prevented it. "I'm all alone."

The old man in the corner turned to face her, moving inch by inch, until she could see his face, the whites of his eyes gleaming in the light of the flickering torches. "We're always all alone," he said, his voice cracked and worn.

Tamsin shook her head. She knew that wasn't true. She had years of proof to the contrary. "No," she said. "Not always. Not even often."

"Oh," the old man said, with a sigh that seemed to come from the depths of his being. "I forget you're still young yet." He coughed then, a dry, rattling sound. "Sometimes we get a little bit of a facade. We think we have people. Family, friends . . . but in the end, it's just you and the darkness. Everyone leaves eventually, my young friend. It's better, really, to learn it early. This way, you can save yourself some disappointment." He sighed then and slumped back against the wall once more. "Because believing you're not alone is the cruelest trick of all."

—C. B. McCallister, *The Drawing of the Two*. Hightower & Jax, New York.

Chapter SEVENTEEN

I stood in the back of the Stanwich Community Theater, clutching my iced latte and a blended java chip drink for Palmer. I'd been at Flask's, getting my usual, when I'd found myself blurting out Palmer's order as well. I decided, there in the coffee shop, that I'd bring it over to her as a kind of a peace offering and hope she'd forgive me, so that we could start to sort this out. Because the longer my phone stayed silent, the longer there was no communication on our group text, the more worried I was getting. Toby and Bri were both equally stubborn, and I didn't want to know what would happen if more than a few days of this standoff went on. I was afraid that at some point this would just become our reality. This had to change, and I knew I couldn't do it without Palmer, especially since Toby wasn't mad at *her*, as far as I knew.

But now, standing at the very back of the theater, looking at Palmer sitting at her stage manager's table, her bright hair glowing in the dimness of the room, I was starting to get nervous about my plan. I ran my thumb over the condensation on my cup as I walked down the aisle to the row where her table was set up, telling myself not to be ridiculous. This was *Palmer*.

I shouldn't be nervous about talking to Palmer. But that didn't change the fact that I was.

I hesitated at the end of her row, shifting my weight from foot to foot, waiting for her to notice I was there. But her eyes were fixed on the stage, where Tom was being yelled at by the actress playing Camp Director Arnold. I walked down the row, hesitating for a second before taking a seat next to her and placing her drink in front of her. "Hi," I whispered.

"Ready follow spot forty-seven," Palmer said, but under her breath, like she was saying it to herself. "Forty-seven, go." She looked over at me, then turned to face the stage again.

"Palmer," I said, leaning forward so that I would be in her line of vision. "Come on."

"Ready sound forty-eight," she said, half under her breath, her eyes moving between the stage and the marked-up script in front of her, making tiny check marks with a pencil. "Forty-eight, go."

"Hold!" The bearded director stood up and started making his way to the stage, shaking his head as Tom and the actress moved downstage to talk to him.

Palmer looked over at me, then sighed and put her pencil down. "I can't really talk," she said. "I'm practicing calling the show." She looked at the drink in front of her, and it was like I could practically sense her struggle before she picked it up and took a sip.

I took a sip of my own, to give me some courage, then blurted out, "I'm so sorry, Palmer."

She looked back at the stage, where the director was now standing next to Tom, gesturing big, while Tom nodded and scribbled notes in his script. "What are you sorry about?" she asked, not looking at me. "That you lied to me about what was happening with Bri and Wyatt? That you asked my boyfriend to keep lying to me?"

"You don't think I wanted to tell you?"

"But you told Clark," Palmer said, looking at me evenly.

"I did," I said quietly, knowing there was no way out of this. "But we have to fix this, P."

"Yeah," Palmer said quietly, reaching for her drink but just holding it for a moment and rolling it between her palms. "But I don't know if we can."

I sat back in my seat. This was what I'd been worried about, when I'd even allowed myself to go there. But hearing her say it was something else. The fact that she wasn't seeing the best and looking on the bright side was almost more than I could take.

"What are you saying?" I asked, my voice coming out unsteady. "That we're all just done? Friendship over?"

She took a long drink and then set her cup back down. "I don't know."

"Okay!" the director yelled, walking back down to the auditorium from the stage. "We're picking it up from Duncan's line, people. Let's go!"

"I have to do this," Palmer said, picking up her pencil again and flipping a few pages back in her script binder.

I nodded and shouldered my bag but didn't leave yet. I still didn't know where we stood, and the thought of leaving with things so unsettled was making me feel panicky. "So," I started, then hesitated. "Are we okay?"

Palmer looked over at me for a moment before looking back at the stage. "I'm not sure," she finally said.

I nodded, swallowing hard. "Okay," I said as I stood up. I paused there for just a moment when I realized there was nothing else to say. I walked up the aisle, to the back of the auditorium, looking at the stage one last time, where Tom and the camp director were starting the scene over again, having made their adjustments, trying to get it right this time.

The afternoon dragged on, one of the worst of the summer, time seeming to crawl. I ended up just driving around aimlessly, from Flask's to the beach to the Orchard, but no place felt right, and I didn't stay in any of them for more than a few minutes. I couldn't go home, because Peter was there. I couldn't hang out with any of my friends. Two of my constants had vanished, and I was getting more agitated with every hour that passed. I didn't know what my life looked like if we weren't all still friends. It was a reality I couldn't even fully grasp. For the last five years, it had been the four of us, what I had always believed to be an unshakable unit. The thought of not having them—the thought of some reality I might have to accept where I didn't have them—was making me feel like I wanted to scream, cry, and throw up, all at the same time.

These feelings were reaching a boiling point when I pulled into Clark's driveway to walk Bertie. I was angry and on the verge of tears, always a dangerous combination. A tiny voice in the back of my head was whispering that I should just leave, come back later, that I was spoiling for a fight and in no condition to see anyone, much less Clark. But I ignored it and got out of the car, heading up the walkway and letting myself in the side door.

"Bert," I called as I stepped inside the house. The dog was

standing in the kitchen, giving me his biggest doggy smile. His tail was wagging so hard his butt was shaking back and forth. "Now, Bertie," I said, in a tone that was intended to let him know I meant business. "I don't want to do this today."

But Bertie didn't seem to pick up on any of this, and as I took a step closer, he did a little leap into the air and galloped out of the room. When Clark did Bertie's inner thoughts—in a voice Bri had told me sounded like a decent Jimmy Stewart impression—he always said, "The game, Andie. It's afoot!" when Bertie jumped like that and went running off. Normally, this routine cracked me up, since Bertie always seemed so pleased with himself, like he was sure he was getting something over on us. But today it was just irritating me.

"Stupid dog," I muttered as I walked into the kitchen, getting his leash from the cupboard and making sure I had enough plastic bags with me, then slamming the cupboard door harder than I needed to.

"Hi, you," Clark said, standing in the kitchen doorway. He had the rumpled, unfocused look that I had learned meant he'd been writing all day, his eyes bleary behind his smudged glasses.

I made myself look away from him, back down to Bertie's leash, which I was coiling in a loop. "Hey."

"How are you doing?" Clark asked, walking over to me. He wasn't asking it in the rhetorical way, where you don't even really expect an answer. He asking it in the careful way you ask people who've just suffered a loss or undergone a trauma. After all, he knew the bare bones of what was happening—I'd texted him the situation that morning.

I shrugged, then shook my head. "Not so good." Clark

reached out for my hand, but I took a step back from him and picked up Bertie's leash. "I have to take him out," I said, looking away from Clark. "Bertie, *now*," I yelled, willing the dog to listen to me just this once.

"Hey," Clark said, taking a step toward me. He wrapped his arms around me, and for a moment I leaned against them and let my eyes close. There was a piece of me, a big one, that just wanted to let everything out. To hug him back, to cry on his shoulder, to tell him everything and talk about it together— things always seemed a little better once I'd talked to Clark about them—and he'd tell me that everything was going to be okay. But that thought jerked me out of the fantasy, as appealing as it was. Because everything very possibly *wasn't* going to be okay.

I broke away from him and picked up Bertie's leash. I saw a flash of hurt cross Clark's face, but I made myself look away from it. I took a breath to yell for Bertie again at the moment he came barreling into the kitchen, nails scrabbling on the wooden floors. Clark reached out for him and so did I, and we managed to corral him between the two of us. I snapped on his leash, then straightened up. "See you in a few," I said, realizing that it would probably be best to put some distance between us, just so I could try to get my emotions under control and stop this powder-keg feeling that was getting stronger by the minute.

"I'll come with you," Clark said, giving me a full-dimple smile. "I could use a break anyway."

I didn't know how to tell him that I wanted to be alone, especially since I wasn't sure that *was* what I wanted. After all, I'd been alone all afternoon and had hated it. So I gave him something between a shrug and a nod and headed out the front door, half running behind Bertie, who was straining as hard as he could against the leash. We stepped outside, and I was about to pull out my keys, but Clark was already locking the door with his set. I saw him reach down for my hand and quickly transferred Bertie's leash to that hand. I was feeling that if I really let Clark touch me for too long, if I let myself feel everything I was feeling, I would be venturing into dangerous territory, where if I started to cry in front of him, I wasn't sure when I'd stop.

"So what's been happening?" he asked after we'd walked for a few seconds in silence, Bertie bounding ahead, trying to sniff four things at once, then doubling back to smell what he might have missed. "Any change?"

"No," I said, feeling the weight of the word even as I said it, like a bowling ball dropping into my stomach. I took a shaky breath, then let it out. "I'm not sure," I started, then had to make myself go on, say the rest of the sentence. "I'm not sure we're going to come back from this."

Clark looked over at me, a furrow appearing between his brows. "Of course you are," he said, but I could hear the worry creeping into his voice as well. "I mean . . . you guys are best friends. You're not going to fall apart over this. You'll get past it."

"We might not, okay?" I snapped, and my voice was sharp and spiky. I bit my lip. "I'm sorry," I said, looping Bertie's leash around my wrist and then unlooping it. "I'm just . . ." *Taking it out on you* flashed through my head before I could stop it.

"So," Clark said, looking over at me, and I could see the same realization I'd been having all morning was dawning for him, as well, and he looked just as happy about it as I was. "It's just over? All of us this summer? It's just—gone?"

I could hear the hurt in his voice, and I knew that he was also losing his friends. But he'd known them for two months, not years and years, and there was a piece of me that didn't want to accept that he would be hurt by this too. I shook my head, not trusting myself to speak just then. Bertie stopped by his favorite tree, and Clark stopped as well, reaching out for my other hand.

"Andie, I'm here. It's okay."

I looked up at him, at the sunlight filtering through the trees and landing across his face, and I wanted to tell him everything I was feeling. I wanted to have someone I could talk to about this, someone who would face this—however it turned out—alongside me. But I couldn't rely on Clark to help me, just like I couldn't rely on my dad. Clark was leaving in just a few weeks, and I never should have let myself forget that, not for a moment. Both of them were heading out the door any minute now. I couldn't tell Clark what I was feeling, couldn't get used to him in my life like this, because at the end of the summer he would leave, and then I'd be truly alone.

"I don't know why you're so upset about this," I said, even though I knew it wasn't fair. "I mean, you're going to leave in a couple weeks anyway."

Bertie, done with his tree, started walking again, and I looked over at Clark, expecting him to be angry or hurt. But he was giving me a small, nervous smile, putting his hands in his pockets and then taking them out again. "Actually," he said, then took a deep breath, "I wanted to talk to you about that."

"Talk to me about what?"

"Me staying here." My head snapped up, and I stared at him,

pulling back against the leash harder than I needed to, sending Bertie stumbling back a few steps.

"What . . . ," I started, then shook my head. "What do you mean? Here at the house?" As far as I'd understood it, Clark's arrangement with his publisher has been just for the summer. I was sure of it.

"No," Clark said. "I mean . . . not going back to Colorado. I was thinking about going to Stanwich College. Taking some classes. I e-mailed the dean about it last week. I really should be in college now anyway. And that way . . . I could stay around here." He gave me a shy half smile, and there was such open, aching vulnerability in it that I had to force myself not to look away. "So . . . what do you think?"

He was nervous. I could hear it in his voice. A part of me wanted tell him what great news this was, let myself be happy about it. This was what I'd wanted, wasn't it? An answer to what was going to happen to us at the end of the summer?

But another part of me—a bigger part—felt myself pulling away, backing up, slamming all the doors tightly. Because it was one thing for Clark to be here for a season. But this was already the longest relationship I'd ever had. Did I really think I was going to be able to keep this up for months and months longer? I'd already managed to wreck the best friendships I'd ever had— of course I would wreck this, too. At some point he'd see who I really was, and then it would be over and I'd be worse off than I was now. So I pushed down what I was really feeling, all the hurt and hope and fear, and reached for anger instead.

"Were you even going to ask me about this?" I asked, walking a few steps away from him, pulling Bertie's head up from where he'd been straining to get to a particular rock, knowing I wouldn't be able to say these things if I had to look at Clark's face.

"I . . . thought you'd be happy," he said. "I thought the other night, when you brought it up . . ." I could hear the confusion in his voice, but I made myself push on anyway.

"Maybe I just want someone to ask me what I want, for once. Maybe I just want someone to consult me before there's another huge change that impacts me." I started walking faster. I was feeling reckless and angry and like I was just going to keep going down this road I was pretty sure I didn't even want to be on.

"I thought that's what I was doing," Clark said, shaking his head. "I was talking to you about it." Clark stopped walking. I stopped too, and Bertie took the opportunity to start sniffing our shoes, weaving in and around our legs. "So . . . you don't want me to stay?" I could hear how hurt Clark was, how he wasn't even trying to hide it, wasn't masking his feelings and running away from them like I was.

We looked at each other, and it was very quiet, no cars on the road, just the birds in the trees, a far-off lawn mower, the dog snuffling at our feet. I could feel that we were at a threshold, that things could go different ways from here, but that a gauntlet had been thrown, and we wouldn't, at this point, be able to go back to where we'd been twenty minutes before. That things had changed, were changing, right now. That a decision had to be made.

And even as I looked at him in the sunlight, with his face that had become so precious to me, with his kindness and his humor and his patience, with him holding his heart out to me

Morgan Matson

so bravely, I felt myself backing away. Him—this—everything it would mean to continue with this was too scary. It was too much. I would hurt him in the end, and he would hurt me, much worse than either of us were hurting now. So I made myself say it, knowing that, deep down, it was probably the truth. "I don't think it would work out."

"What are you saying?" Clark asked, his eyes searching mine, like he could find the truth in them, find what I was really feeling behind the walls I was putting up as fast as I could.

"This was always supposed to be for the summer, right? That's what I thought." I looked away from him, down at Bertie, so he wouldn't see the tears that were forming in my eyes.

"Andie, this isn't you."

"It is, though," I said, fighting back the sob that was forming somewhere in the back of my throat. "Our first date?" I asked, and he nodded. "*That* was me. We can pretend to be different people for a few months, but . . ." I flashed to my dad, back in his work uniform like nothing had happened, like the entire summer we'd spent could just be erased. "In the end, people don't change who they are." I could hear the conviction in my voice as I said this, and as I looked across at Clark, I saw that he was finally starting to believe me.

Bertie flopped down on the ground between us, his head resting on my feet and his tail on Clark's, but despite how close we were, I could feel a gulf splitting open between us, widening and widening with every passing second.

"Do you really believe that?" he asked, and I knew this was his last shot. His last attempt, my final chance to change our course.

I nodded, swallowing hard. "I do."

Clark looked away, down the road. When he turned back to me, I could see that he was suddenly farther away from me now, even though he hadn't actually moved. There was a distance in his eyes that hadn't been there a moment before. "It's probably for the best," he said, his voice still raw but getting more composed with every word. "I mean, I have a lot of work to do. I should probably focus on my book now anyway."

I nodded, wondering why it hurt me so much to hear him say it when this was my idea and I was the one bringing it about. "Right," I said, nodding, hoping what I was feeling wasn't clear in my voice. "Sure."

I pulled Bertie to his feet and we started walking back toward the house, more space between us than before—we were practically on opposite sides of the road. Neither of us was speaking, and Bertie was walking between us, happily sniffing, not aware that anything had changed. For him, things were still the same—sun and grass and things to smell—while Clark and I were standing in the rubble of what only minutes ago had been our relationship.

The silence seemed to get more oppressive with every step, until I was sure I wouldn't be able to handle it for much longer. It was like the silence in the car after our first disastrous date, but exponentially worse, since I knew him now—knew who he was, how much he'd meant to me, and exactly what I was walking away from.

When we reached the driveway, I stopped, having reached my limit. "Here," I said, holding out Bertie's leash to him, glad that I had my keys in my pocket and that he had his own, and

Morgan Matson

we didn't have to continue this into the kitchen and have what had the potential to be the world's most awkward good-bye. Clark took it from me, and Bertie didn't even seem to notice the handoff, just sat down and started scratching his ear with his back paw. "I'll tell Maya someone else needs to start walking him now."

Clark just looked at me for a moment and gave me a smile with no happiness in it. "It's not necessary," he said. "I can walk Bert. I mostly just called Maya because I was hoping to see you again."

It felt like someone had reached into my chest and squeezed my heart, and this continued as he turned away and walked toward the house, Bertie trailing behind him. As I watched them go, my throat got tighter, like it was getting harder to breathe. Was this really how it was going to end? Without saying anything else, without even getting to hug Bertie one last time?

"Clark," I called, when he was almost to the door. He turned back to me slowly, keys still in his hand, his expression wary. "What happens?" I blurted, before I could stop myself. "With Karl and Marjorie?" It was such a small thing compared to everything that had just happened, but it was a world we had built together, and I needed to know.

Clark looked at me for a moment, then unlocked the door. I thought for a second he was going to ignore me, but then I saw him unclip Bertie's leash and let him in before he turned and crossed the driveway toward me, stopping when there were still several feet between us. "You really want to know?" he asked.

"Yes."

"Well, Marjorie kills Karl."

I drew in a breath—it felt like someone had just pressed on a bruise. "What?"

"Oh, yeah," Clark said, his voice certain, like this was the only answer, like there was no other way this could go. "She finally remembered that she was an assassin. She was just pretending to be someone else, but in the end, it wasn't who she was."

Clark's voice was cold and dispassionate, and I had never heard him speak that way before. When I thought about the gentle way he'd talked to me when I'd first arrived at the house, not even an hour before, I knew that he sounded this way because of me—that I was the one who'd done this to him. I bit my lip hard and felt tears, the ones that had been lurking behind my eyes, threaten to emerge. "No," I managed, shaking my head, but before I could say more, Clark was continuing on.

"And then Marjorie dies too," he said, folding his arms over his chest. "After she kills Karl. The king's men kill her in a tavern. They can't have her talking. It's best to just erase the evidence, so it's like it never happened. The end."

"You can't just do that."

Clark looked at me for a long moment. "I just did," he said, then turned and walked back up the driveway, then into the house, letting the door slam behind him.

I walked to my car, and my hands were shaking so hard it took two attempts to get my key in the ignition, and it wasn't until I'd gotten the car started and driven two streets away that I pulled over and really let myself cry.

Morgan Matson

Chapter EIGHTEEN

Maya looked at me from across the table at Flask's, concern on her face that didn't seem to match her purple and pink hair. She pushed aside her blended coffee drink—pumpkin spice. It was the last week of August, but apparently, as far as Flask's was concerned, that meant it was fall. "How are you doing?" she asked, leaning toward me.

"I'm fine," I said automatically, taking a drink of my iced latte, since this was just what I said now.

It was what I told my dad when I passed him in the kitchen or the hallway. We weren't doing our Sundays in the study with movies anymore, and we hadn't had a dinner, just the two of us, since Peter had appeared in the kitchen. My dad was busier now, but he was still suggesting places we could eat and threatening to make me watch more Westerns. But I had a feeling he was just going through the motions. And even though he kept telling me he hadn't decided if he was running again, I could read the writing on the wall. So I found a way out of everything he proposed. I told him I was busy, that I had plans with my friends, that I had to work. I didn't want to fall back into the habit of spending time with him like he was going to be around, when clearly he had one foot out the door.

It had been two weeks since my friends and I had imploded, two weeks since Clark and I had broken up, and it felt more like months. For the first few days I was texting everyone—both on our group thread and individually—but when the silence became deafening, I stopped. The silence of my phone just underscored how alone I was now. I could sometimes get Tom to text me back, but never for very long. He was clearly worried he was being disloyal to Palmer and quickly told me he had to go. I'd gone to the opening night of *Bug Juice* alone, sitting by myself in the back row, looking around for my friends but not seeing them, barely paying attention to the play as I scanned the theater for Clark, sure I saw him dozens of times before the guy would turn his head and I'd realize it wasn't him—and then feeling like an idiot for thinking it could have been. But the whole show had run smoothly, and I'd been so proud of Palmer, sitting in the sound booth, pulling it off without a hitch.

I'd told Maya I had to stop walking Bertie, and to make up for it—and to distract myself from my friendless state—I'd been taking on as many clients as she could give me. I was out of the house every morning early, with extra leashes and plastic bags and treats, and didn't return until early evening, tired and sunburned. And then at night I'd work my way through my organic chemistry textbook, trying not to notice how little I was interested in it any longer, telling myself firmly that this was normal, that nobody liked organic chemistry.

"Really?" Maya asked, her brows knitting together. "Because I'm worried you've taken on too much. I can take over some of these walks, or Dave can. It's summer, after all. You should be out having fun with your friends."

I had to bite my lip to keep from wincing. "Right," I said hollowly. "My friends." I busied myself with carefully folding the Flask's paper napkin into a perfect square.

"Well," she said with a shrug, leaning back in her chair, "make sure you go have fun tonight. Dave and I are doing payroll, which is a blast. So have a good time before you have to worry about things like that."

Maya and I headed our separate ways shortly after that, but what she'd said kept returning to me throughout the evening, while I ate my take-out dinner alone and then tried (without success) to get through a chapter in my O-chem study guide.

And it was Maya's words, coupled with severe boredom and loneliness, that led me to reach for my phone and scroll through my contacts until I got to Topher.

ME

Hey. You around?

TOPHER

It's about time.

I pushed open the door and stepped inside the party, smoothing my hair down and looking around. Topher had told me he would be here later—a friend of his from school was throwing this party. He'd neglected to inform me the friend's name, just dropped a pin on the address, so I was hoping that nobody would ask me what I was doing there before I could find him.

Topher's "later" could mean many things, and he never seemed to get any more specific—in fact, usually the opposite—when you pressed him for clarification. So I'd gotten ready, then stalled for an hour before heading over, hoping I'd waited long enough, but not really caring all that much if I hadn't. Even though this party looked just like dozens of parties I'd been to, I was out of the house, which was enough for me at the moment. I didn't see Topher—or anyone I recognized—but I wasn't worried about that, not yet. If Topher still hadn't shown up in an hour, it would be a different story, but I could cross that bridge when I came to it.

I caught my reflection in a hall mirror as I headed back to the kitchen, and smoothed down my skirt. It had just felt wrong, getting ready to come here tonight in silence, with no video commentary, no Palmer sprawled across my bed vetoing outfits, no text chains about what I should wear. And it was equally strange to walk in with no group around me, trying to pretend I belonged there and knew where I was going. I found myself looking around for my friends automatically, even though I knew they probably wouldn't be here and wouldn't be talking to me if they were.

I made my way into the kitchen, where an array of bottles and red cups were scattered along the countertop, and pulled the Diet Coke bottle out of my bag. Now that I was pretty sure my dad was running again, I figured I couldn't be too careful. It was also, I realized as I opened the bottle and took a long drink, not a bad idea for me to just stick to soda, since I was at a party, for maybe the first time ever, with no backup.

My eyes drifted out to the back patio, where there was a

pool half-filled with people and what looked like a guy passed out on the diving board. And there, sitting in an Adirondack chair, was Topher. For a second I thought about trying to catch his eye, wait for him to notice me, do this same routine we always did. But only for a second before I left the kitchen and headed outside.

I walked up to his Adirondack chair, where he was leaning back, a bottle of Sprite in one hand, listening with a faint smile on his face as the guy in the chair next to him was leaning forward, saying something about galaxies.

"For years, man," he was saying, gesturing vaguely up to the sky and spilling some beer on his own arm, "they've thought the galaxies were just fixed, done, boom, that's it. These perfect orderly systems, right?"

"Who's 'they'?" Topher asked, in a way I knew from experience meant he didn't really want to know but had just seen a flaw in an argument.

"Astronomers!" the guy said, gesturing again, sending more beer flying. At this rate, he'd be out before he was done talking. "NASA people. You know. They weren't even studying some of them any longer because they thought all that was done eight billion light-years ago. But then they started noticing stuff."

"Really." Topher was looking away, not even listening to the guy anymore, but that didn't seem to be stopping him.

"Yeah," the guy said. "Galaxies don't start perfect. They start crazy disorganized, and they change over time." He looked at Topher, waiting a beat, clearly expecting more of a reaction. "Doesn't that, like, blow your mind?"

"Sorry," Topher said, finally noticing me, or at least

acknowledging that he noticed me. "My friend just got here."

"Hi," I said, giving the guy a halfhearted wave.

"Want to hear this crazy thing about galaxies?" the guy asked, leaning forward again, clearly glad to have found a potential new audience.

"She's good," Topher said, giving him a nod. "Thanks, though." The guy seemed to notice then that he'd lost most of his beer while gesticulating, pushed himself up, and headed off toward the keg, still murmuring under his breath about star formations.

"Hey," I said, adjusting my purse on my shoulder, then folding and unfolding my arms.

"You made it," Topher said, looking up at me. "I was getting worried."

I nodded, starting to feel weird standing while he was sitting and making no move to get up, so I took the galaxy guy's seat, settling back into it and looking over at Topher. "Really," I said, not phrasing it as a question.

Topher gave me a sleepy smile. "Sure," he said, in a way that was designed to let me know he was lying and that this was supposed to be funny, that he'd forgotten about me. I gave him a half smile as I crossed my legs. I could feel it happening, this pattern we always fell back into, but for some reason it didn't feel like it normally did. It was feeling more like the time Bri accidentally took my shoes after a sleepover and I had to wear hers all day, aware with every step of how they didn't fit me right. I took a drink of my Diet Coke, waiting for this feeling to pass. It had just been a while since I'd seen Topher, that was all. Things would go back to normal soon.

"So what's been happening?" I asked, after we'd sat in silence for a few moments. I somehow knew that Topher wouldn't be the first to break it, that he'd wait for me to get the conversation rolling. Once, these kinds of games had made every interaction with him feel somehow exciting, but tonight they were exhausting me, and I was struggling to remember what the point of them was.

"You know," Topher said with a tiny shrug. "Doing the intern thing. Beyond thrilling." He looked over at me and frowned. "Wait—what did you end up doing again?"

"Dog walking," I said immediately. Topher just stared at me. "Some cats, too, but mostly dogs. Walks and hikes."

"Are you serious?" he asked, a laugh somewhere behind this. "You've really been walking dogs all summer?"

"Yep," I said, nodding. I knew that a month ago I would have lied, or at least spun it, told him that I was working in an assistant capacity in a small independently owned business, in the service sector. But the last thing I wanted to do was to diminish what I'd spent the summer doing. "It was actually really great," I said, realizing it was true as I said it, seeing, all at once, Clark and Bertie, and Maya and Dave, and walking with two leashes in each hand and the sun on my shoulders, driving back with a dog on my lap and a head sticking out of every open window.

"Well," Topher said, looking a little discomfited by this, like I'd just gone off script on him. "I'll take your word for it." We lapsed into silence again, and before I could think of something else to say, he asked, "So it's finally over with *Clark*?" Topher asked, putting a snide spin on his name.

"Uh-huh," I said, not saying it, but really thinking that people named Topher weren't exactly in a position to throw stones.

"So what happened?"

I shook my head, then made myself shrug, trying to force myself back into this role I'd played so often before. Totally over whoever it was I'd been dating and ready to move on with Topher. "It doesn't matter," I said. "It's over."

Topher took a sip from his Sprite bottle, eyes still on me, like he was trying to figure something out. "That lasted a while," he finally said.

"Well," I said, giving him a smile I didn't even partially feel, "now it's over." I looked at him for a moment. Even though we were sitting on outdoor furniture by a pool, Topher looked, as always, beyond cool and composed—like he could have been in an ad for cologne, or Adirondack chairs, or Sprite. "You?" I asked, hoping I knew the answer. I had a feeling Topher wouldn't have told me about the party if he was seeing anyone, but I wasn't entirely sure. "With anyone?"

Topher's smile widened as he shook his head. "Not at the moment."

I nodded and gave him a smile in return. This was why I'd texted him, after all. "Want to get out of here?"

The bottom bunk of the little brother of the host—I still didn't know what his name was—was not the most romantic spot in the world. But when Topher had done a quick recon around the party for our options, this was all that was left. He'd suggested his car—which I knew from experience was a massive SUV

456   *Morgan Matson*

with a middle row of seats that folded down, allowing plenty of room to stretch out—but I somehow found I didn't want to leave the party with Topher, didn't want to feel the fresh air against my skin as we walked to wherever he'd parked, waking me up and making me think about what I was doing. So the bottom bunk of a room that seemed decorated in some kind of dinosaur-space mash-up was what we were left with. It also wasn't totally dark—when Topher hit the lights, dozens of glow-in-the-dark constellations and a T. rex night-light came to life.

And as Topher eased me back onto the astronaut sheets and we started kissing, I told myself that this was what I'd been missing all summer. This was who I was, like I'd told Clark, and I never should have veered away from that. I should have stuck with the routine, the one that had been working for me for years now. Trying anything else just hurt that much more when it invariably ended.

And I tried to tell myself this was good as I tangled my fingers in Topher's hair, trying to lose myself in our kisses, which could normally make everything else in the world totally disappear. But it was like I was too *aware*, somehow, of everything that was happening, unable to shut off my thoughts, which were spiraling, the opposite of what I wanted them to be doing.

I slipped my hands under Topher's shirt, and he broke away and looked down at me, and in the night-light glow, I could see his surprise that I was breaking my rules. I tried to pull his shirt up, only to have him say, "Ow!" and realize a second too late that he was wearing a button-down.

"Sorry," I said, stretching up, starting to undo his buttons, fumbling with them in the dark. "I'll just . . ."

"I've got it," Topher said, taking it off himself, and I stretched up to kiss him again before reaching down and pulling my own shirt off, tossing the tank top in the direction of my purse. "Yeah?" he asked, sounding surprised but not at all displeased as he smiled down at me.

"Sure," I said, then added quickly, "I mean, yeah." I pulled him down toward me, and even as we kissed, my skin against his for the first time, I couldn't lose myself in the moment, couldn't shut off the sense that something wasn't quite right. I opened my eyes, realizing at once what it was. There was no laughter here, no playfulness. No Karl-and-Marjorie-getting-busy-in-a-barn narrative tangents, no Clark making me laugh about how my bra clasps had all been designed by the same people who made bank vaults, since they were impossible to open.

This, now, just . . . felt like it always did with Topher. Like it could have been three months ago, or any other time in the last three years. Which until now had been fine. It had been what I'd thought I wanted. But now I knew there was something else. Something better—something more.

And before I could distract myself, or stop the thoughts from coming, I was missing Clark so much, it hurt to breathe.

I moved back and sat up, pushing Topher away as I tried to get my thoughts in some kind of order.

"What?" Topher asked, blinking at me. "What's the matter?"

"I'm not sure," I said slowly. I knew what it was—but not how I could put it so that Topher would understand. "I just . . ."

"Is it that guy?" Topher asked, shaking his head as he sat back from me. "Seriously?"

I looked across the narrow bed at him. The disdain in his

voice would have been enough a few months ago that I would have denied it. But I realized, all at once, that I couldn't have cared less about that any longer. "Seriously," I said, nodding.

Topher let out a short laugh, still looking at me like he was expecting me to go back to who I'd been, start making sense again. "What, were you like in love with him or something?" he asked sarcastically, phrasing it so that the only answer to this was no.

"Yes," I said without even thinking about it, but knowing as soon as I said it that it was the truth. It had been the truth for a while now, but I hadn't let myself see until this moment. "I was." I took a breath and made myself say it. "I am."

"Oh," Topher said, sounding utterly thrown. "Um . . . okay."

"Yeah," I said with a small laugh. I sat up a little straighter and pulled the sheet up in front of me, tucking it under my arms, my fingers tracing, for just a second, the pattern of the Little Dipper that was printed there. I looked over at Topher and knew that this—whatever we'd been doing for three years now—was over. That it was better to have what I'd had with Clark than something like this. I might stay safe with Topher and never get hurt, but that also meant I'd never feel anything real. "Sorry I didn't realize it until right now."

"You *love* him?" Topher asked, sounding not cool or dismissive or sarcastic, but for the first time in a long time, genuine. I could hear the hurt in his voice, but also the confusion underneath.

"I do," I said, nodding. I wasn't sure what, if anything, I was going to do with that information. But for tonight, knowing it felt like enough. "So I think, you and I, we're probably . . ."

"Yeah," Topher said, pulling on his shirt and buttoning it up. "I figured that." I pulled on my tank top, and then we just looked at each other for a moment, across the comforter with rocket ships printed on it. "I sometimes wonder," he finally said, his voice soft and maybe the most genuine I'd ever heard it, all games and stratagems gone, "if maybe in the beginning, I'd just . . . if we'd actually . . ." He reached forward and brushed his fingers through the ends of my hair slowly, like he knew that soon he wouldn't be able to do this. "Never mind," he said, shaking his head, some of the briskness coming back into his voice. He looked away from me and adjusted his cuffs, and when he looked back, I could see the little authentic window he'd shown me was now closed.

Topher headed back down to the party after that, and I waited two minutes, more out of habit than anything else, before following him. I let myself out the front door and walked to my car, which I'd parked half a mile up the road. It was a breezy night, the humidity cut by the wind, and I took off my flip-flops and held them in one hand as I walked barefoot, tipping my head back to look up at the sky.

I remembered the stick-on, glow-in-the-dark stars that had been all over the walls of the kid's bedroom—the ones that looked pretty good until you had the real thing to compare them with, and then they just looked like pale imitations. I thought about the guy outside, and his galaxy theory, and as I looked up, I wondered which of these stars—the ones that seemed so permanent and fixed—weren't actually done changing quite yet.

The Elder shook his head, feeling the weight of each of his years, the wisdom he had that nobody seemed to be able to hear. "You have to *try*," he said, his voice barely above a whisper. He closed his eyes, just for a moment, then opened them and forced himself to go on. "You have to take your chances. Go and attempt and see what happens. And even if you fail—*especially* if you fail—come back with your experience and your hard-won knowledge and a story you can tell. And then later you can say, without regret or hesitation . . . 'Once, I dared to dare greatly.'"

—C. B. McCallister, *The Drawing of the Two*. Hightower & Jax, New York.

Chapter NINETEEN

Two *beeps* from my phone sent me bolting upright in bed the next morning, fumbling for it and sending the stack of precarious things on my nightstand crashing to the floor. I squinted at my phone, trying to get my eyes to focus, willing it to be texts from my friends. Maybe Toby and Bri had figured out a way to move past this, and Palmer had decided not to be mad at me any longer, and . . . I felt my shoulders slump when I saw what was actually there, two calendar reminders that had popped up.

Dad—campaign event/New York. 12 PM

Clark's reading!!!! New Jersey 3 PM

I looked at these, and at the exclamation points by Clark's, realizing that with everything going on, I'd forgotten about both events and had certainly not put together that they were happening on the same day. As far as I knew, I was not expected to be at my father's event—Peter hadn't said anything and neither had my dad, so I figured I was in the clear.

I flopped back onto my bed, then looked at my calendar for the day—which was totally open. I must have cleared it with Maya for Clark's reading. Now, the thought of having the whole day ahead of me open—especially with my revelation from the night before—was not appealing in the least. I pulled up my texts and started to write Maya, asking her if there were any walks I could take over today—I'd even deal with a cat—when my phone screen turned black. I'd run the battery down.

My first thought was that I'd have to tell Toby that I could no longer make fun of her for this, before I remembered, once again, what had happened. I pushed myself out of bed and went downstairs, yawning, in my sleep shorts and the ASK ME ABOUT THE LUMINOSITY shirt of Clark's that I'd never gotten around to returning.

"Morning," my dad said as I stepped into the kitchen. He was hovering around the coffeepot, but in a way that made me think he wasn't actually having coffee and had instead been waiting for me to come down.

"Hi," I said, rubbing my hand across my eyes as I went to the fridge in search of orange juice. He was wearing a button-down shirt and a suit jacket, but no tie—his *I'm professional but not stuffy* outfit he always wore when campaigning in the summers. His hair, though, was as sharply parted as ever. "So," I said, after taking a long drink and waiting for my brain to start waking up, "You have that campaign event today?"

"Kind of," my dad said, giving me a shrug. "It's the governor's campaign. He just wanted to me to say a few words."

I nodded as I took another drink of my juice, convinced that even after all these years, I would never understand how politics worked. The governor and my dad had privately hated each other for years, but maybe he was trying to get a piece of my dad's redemption arc. It was all going to start unfolding at a press conference on Monday, with Peter laying out every step of it.

"But there's actually something I wanted to show you," my dad said, smiling at me, and I realized he really had been waiting for me to get up.

"Okay," I said, looking around the kitchen.

"Outside," my dad said, walking toward the side door. "Ready?"

"Sure," I said, setting my glass down, utterly baffled as to what this could be. I honestly wasn't sure there was anything I wanted, unless standing on the driveway would be Palmer, Toby, and Bri, all having made up, having forgiven each other and me, along with Clark and Bertie, everything somehow fixed and okay. I stepped outside, and the heat hit me like a slap in the face. "Ugh," I said, wincing. It was boiling already, and humid, like I'd just walked face-first into a hot shower.

"Yeah," my dad said, grimacing at me. "It's going to be a hot one today."

"*Going* to be?"

"Okay, let's go to the garage," my dad said, talking fast, sounding excited. I had a sudden Christmas-morning flashback of both my parents sitting on the couch watching me open my biggest present, waiting to see my reaction. But it wasn't Christmas, and it was nowhere near my birthday. So what was this, exactly?

I followed my dad to the garage door, which was closed, and looked around, in case I was missing something. But a second later my dad pulled out the garage door opener from his pocket and took a breath. "Okay," he said, his thumb on the button, but not pressing it yet. "This is something that I hadn't planned on doing just yet, but . . ."

A loud, low-pitched *BEEP!* made us both jump, and I looked over to see a bus chugging up to our driveway. It started to turn in, but then stopped and backed up a few feet with a *beep-beep-beep* sound that seemed unnecessarily loud on our totally quiet street, sending some birds from nearby trees into flight.

"What the heck?" my dad asked, striding down toward the end of the driveway, sounding annoyed. I followed a few paces behind, and as I got closer, felt my steps slow.

There was a giant picture of my dad's face on the bus, taken from his last campaign photo shoot. WALKER FOR CONGRESS, it read in giant red and white letters. Underneath this, but only slightly smaller, was printed, TOWARD THE FUTURE.

"Peter!" my dad yelled, as he walked up to the bus. His face was starting to turn red, and since he'd been fine just a moment before, I had a feeling this was due to the bus and not the heat.

The doors opened with a *squeak* and a sound of air releasing, and a moment later Peter was striding down the steps and smiling at us. "Morning," he said, then winced. "Jeez, it's hot out today. Luckily, the bus has AC."

"Why is this even here?" my dad asked, staring at it. "When did we decide we were going ahead with this?"

"We didn't," Peter said as he pulled out his BlackBerry. "An intern forgot to cancel, and it had already been paid for, so it showed up this morning. Along with the driver, Walt. Hey, Walt," Peter called into the bus. The driver—Walt—who had a short blond crew cut and looked to be in his late fifties, just lifted an eyebrow at Peter before raising the paper in front of his face, hiding it from view. "Anyway, thought we might as well get some use out of it. Ride to this rally in style."

My dad just looked at the bus, a small frown still on his face.

"Great," Peter said as though my dad had agreed, eyes on his phone screen. "I've got to catch up on some e-mails, but let's plan on leaving in ten, okay?" He looked up and frowned at me as his eyes drifted down to the pajamas I was wearing. "Andie, you're, uh, not coming, are you?"

"No," my dad and I said at the same time.

"Gotcha," Peter said, relief clearly etched on his face. "See you later, then." He climbed back onto the bus, fingers already flying over his keypad.

"Bye," I called, even though I had a feeling Peter could no longer hear me. Behind the wheel, Walt lowered his paper and rolled his eyes before raising it again—he'd clearly had more than enough of Peter already.

"Okay," my dad said, holding up the garage door opener, smiling at me again. "Ready to do this?"

We walked back up the driveway, the asphalt warm under my bare feet. I looked back toward the bus for just a second, my dad's huge face giving a confident but trustworthy smile to the street. Despite whatever Peter had said, campaign buses didn't show up by accident—not unless there was a campaign that would require them. "Dad—" I started, right as the garage door opened and I found myself looking at a yellow '65 Mustang.

"Surprise!" my dad said, making a little flourish with his arms, smiling big as he looked from me to the car.

"Is that . . . ?" I asked, taking a step closer to it. "Is it Mom's?" It looked just like it, but I couldn't be sure. "Didn't you say you didn't know where it was?"

"I said that, yes," my dad said, grinning now, and I could see that he was incredibly pleased with himself. "I didn't want to give the surprise away. It's been in a storage facility upstate. Your mother asked me to give it to you when you turned eighteen, but when you started asking about it, I thought maybe now was the moment."

"This is great," I said a beat too late. "Really great," I repeated, trying to bring some enthusiasm into my voice. "Thank you."

"I've made sure that it's ready to be driven," he said, walking toward the car, running his hand along the side of it. "It got fully overhauled, detailed, everything. And I'll have to teach you how to drive stick, but after that, you should be good to go." He looked at me and his smile faltered a little.

"Awesome," I said, making myself smile, knowing I wasn't reacting the way he wanted me to. I felt terrible about it but wasn't sure I would be able to fake it. Because there was a bus with his face on it at the bottom of the driveway, reminding me of everything that was going to happen and how little I could do about it. When was he planning to teach me how to drive a stick shift if he was going to be not only working, but campaigning in the fall's election? I looked at the car, pretty sure that it was going to sit there, undriven, for a very long time.

"Sorry," my dad said, his excited energy ebbing away as he ran his hand over the back of his neck. "Maybe . . . this was probably the wrong day. But when they called and said it was ready, I just wanted you to have it."

"No, it's great," I said, feeling even worse than I had a moment ago. "Really, Dad. Thank you."

"Well," my dad said, after an awkward silence had fallen, "I hope you like it, Andie."

He turned to head inside, but before he'd reached the door,

I blurted out, "You're running again, aren't you." It didn't sound like a question because it wasn't one. All the proof I needed was sitting at the bottom of the driveway.

My dad turned back to me. "I told you, I haven't decided anything."

"You can at least tell me the truth." I said, shaking my head, realizing that I should not be getting mad at him right after he'd given me a present, but knowing that it was happening anyway.

My dad raised his eyebrows. "I am," he said. "I'm still weighing my options."

"It's just . . . this summer, having you around, it's been really . . ."

"Alex!" Peter was standing on the bottom step of the bus, tapping at his watch in a hugely exaggerated manner, like we were involved in a game of long-distance charades. "We have to get going. Walt can't make traffic miracles happen!" Peter stepped back inside the bus, and I looked back at my dad.

"I . . ." My dad looked down at me for a moment. "I won't decide to run without talking to you first. Okay?"

I looked back to the bus, which was contradicting everything he was saying. "Right," I said, nodding and looking away from him, my voice flat. There was no point in arguing if he was just going to leave anyway. "Sure."

Ten minutes later I sat in my mother's Mustang as the bus made a painfully slow three-point (in this case, more like an eighteen-point) turn before heading back down the road. I realized as it departed that TOWARD THE FUTURE was printed on the back of the bus as well, and the very slogan seemed to mock me for ever doubting that this was the choice my dad would make.

I'd gotten into the passenger side out of habit—I'd been years away from driving the last time I was in this car. I shut the door behind me and looked around. I had hoped, in some absurd way, that it would still somehow feel like my mom. That even after five years in storage, her perfume would be lingering or there would be the feeling I always had in this car with my mother—that adventure was somehow just around the corner, that any minute now, exciting things were going to happen.

I sat there for just a moment, looking through the motes of dust in the shafts of sunlight to the empty seat where my mother should have been sitting, the view I'd always had. When that got to be too much, I slid over to the driver's side, pulling the seat forward and placing my hands on the steering wheel for the first time.

I flipped down the visor mirror, expecting the keys to drop down into my lap, because that's where they always seemed to be in the movies. But there was nothing there, and a quick glance around the car didn't show them to me either. I realized as I looked that I actually wasn't sure how the car had gotten here—if it had been driven or towed.

I opened the glove compartment and starting flipping through the papers—mostly what appeared to be sale and insurance documents—and found them toward the back, the car keys on the key chain that I'd gotten her for Mother's Day when I was nine, a bright-purple heart dangling from a chain. I smiled as I held it up now, the silver of the chain catching the light and reflecting it back at me. When I'd bought it from a mall kiosk eight years ago, I had been convinced that there had never been

Morgan Matson

anything so beautiful. Now, though, I could see just how tacky it was—and how wonderful my mother had been, to carry it around for years after that anyway, just because I had given it to her.

I started to put the papers back inside the glove compartment when I saw my name. I started flipping through them more slowly, and there, almost at the end of the stack, I saw it—a plain white square envelope with my name written across the front of it—in my mother's handwriting.

I just stared at it, holding it with both hands, not wanting to even breathe in case this somehow went away or disappeared. I looked at my name on the front of the envelope, in the handwriting I hadn't seen in so long—the looping *A*, the circle over the *i*. I turned the card over, and what I saw there made me let out a short laugh with a sob mixed into it. Across the back flap she'd drawn the Mustang with a horse in sunglasses sitting in the driver's seat, one elbow out the window. *Lots of horsepower!* she'd written below it, and I laughed, even though I could feel tears prickling the corners of my eyes. The drawing wasn't as sharp as the ones she usually did—the lines were a little unsure and wavy, and I knew just by looking at it that this was one of the ones she'd made toward the end, before even picking up a pencil hurt her hands too much, before she lost all the energy she'd once used for things like drawing mustangs in Mustangs.

I took a deep breath, then slid my hand under the flap and pulled out the note, which had been written on her stationery. MOLLY WALKER was printed across the top in raised letters, and I ran my finger over them once before I bit my lip and started to read.

Andie!

Hello, my love. Happy 18th birthday! I so wish that I could be there to celebrate with you.

I have loved this car, and I'm so happy it's yours now. I hope you'll use it for so much more than getting around. This car, like you, is made for extraordinary things.

So have adventures. Go exploring. Drive around at midnight. Feel the wind running through your hair.

Life is so short, my darling. And there's no day like today. Drive safe. Have fun. I love you so much.

(But of course you knew that already.)

—Mom

PS—I know you already are, but take care of your dad for me. He needs help sometimes, even if he's bad at showing it.

I set the paper down in my lap and wiped under my eyes, not trying to get myself to stop crying, just trying to dry my face off a little. I looked down at the note, still a little unable to believe it had happened—that my mom had left something behind for me after all.

I read it through again, still crying, when one line jumped out at me—*no day like today*. And I knew, just like that, what I had to do.

I had to find Clark and tell him how I felt—how I *really* felt—and see if he might want to give it another chance. Even if he said no, at least I would have tried. At least I would have tried to be as honest as I could be. Because right now I was just running away when things got too real.

I carefully put her note back in its envelope, folded over the

Morgan Matson

flap, and placed it back in the glove compartment, closing it and then resting my hand there for a moment. Then I got out of the car and ran full speed into the house.

Fifteen minutes later I glanced at my reflection in my bedroom mirror and decided it was the best I could do under the circumstances. I hadn't wanted to take much time, but even I knew that when you are going to tell someone that you love them and want them back, it's probably best not to do it in the T-shirt you've slept in, especially if you've stolen it from them. I'd thrown on a skirt and a white T-shirt after rejecting almost everything else in my closet, since nothing seemed right for this—even though I had never done this before and had no idea what one actually wore for it. But I could feel my heart pounding as I ran a brush through my hair and slicked on some lip gloss. I needed to do this now, soon, before I lost my nerve, before I actually started to think about what I was going to do.

I stepped into my flip-flops, then took the stairs two at a time. I had a very strong feeling this was a have-in-person conversation, and even though I knew I probably should, I didn't want to call first, didn't want him to be able to tell me not to talk to him anymore. I wanted to see him—to talk with him face-to-face. To tell him how much I missed him.

I launched myself out the front door and hurried to my car. I'd just tossed my bag in the front passenger seat when I saw someone walking up the driveway.

I lifted my hand to cut the glare, then let it fall it when I saw it was Palmer.

I stood by my car, not really sure what to do. My heart was

hammering as I raised a hand in a wave. I half expected that at any moment Palmer would change her mind, but she kept coming toward me until we were only a few feet apart.

"Hi," Palmer said. She gave me a nervous smile, then stuck her hands in the back pockets of her jean shorts. "Sorry for just showing up like this."

"No, it's fine," I said, smiling back at her, hoping she hadn't come over here to tell me that she'd decided we could never be friends again. "You know you can always come by." Palmer nodded and took a breath. But before she could speak, I jumped in. "I really, really messed up," I said. "I'm so sorry."

"I know it was coming from a good place," Palmer said, shaking her head. "But—"

"I know," I said. "I was trying to control everything, because the thought of not having you guys . . ." I let out a shaky breath. "But I shouldn't have interfered like that."

Palmer nodded. "I know you were trying to help, in your own, very not helpful way," she said, and I smiled. "But I overreacted. And I'm sorry, Andie."

We just looked at each other for a moment, and then Palmer reached out to hug me, and I hugged her back, tight, neither of us moving for a few moments. When we broke apart, it felt like I'd just put down a really heavy burden I'd been carrying for too long, like something had finally been set right.

"What's happening with them?" I asked when we stepped apart, hoping somehow that would have worked everything out.

Palmer shook her head, and those hopes were dashed. "Bri's trying," she said, shaking her head. "She's apologized over and over again, but Toby won't listen. I've barely seen her." She looked over at my car and seemed to notice the keys in my hand for the first time. "Wait, are you leaving?"

"No," I said, then hesitated. "Well, kind of. I was going to go talk to Clark. . . ."

"Clark," Palmer said, her eyes widening. "Really? I was sorry to hear about you guys. . . ."

"Well—" I started, taking a deep breath, "Here's the thing. I need to go tell him that I love him."

"Andie!" Palmer looked at me like she wasn't exactly sure who I was.

A *beep* sounded from my bag on the passenger seat, and we both looked over at it, just as another one sounded. "Just a second," I said, leaning in and pulling it out. "It's Topher," I said, looking at the screen, turning it so I could read it in the glare.

Palmer raised a disapproving eyebrow at me. "Topher?"

"No," I said immediately, then realized this wasn't entirely correct. "Well, kind of. A little, but never again." Palmer frowned, and I realized just how much there was to catch her up on. "I'll tell you later."

"What's he want now?" she asked, folding her arms over her chest.

I stared at the texts, trying to make sense of them. "I'm not sure."

TOPHER

Hey, don't let your dad do the campaign thing today
Heard my mom saying something
Think it's a bad idea.

I looked at Palmer, who was reading over my shoulder. "Okay, what is wrong with him?" she asked, shaking her head. "He can't be bothered to give you like a smidge more information?"

"I'll call him," I said, pulling up his contact info, wondering why this was happening *now*. I was supposed to be halfway to Clark's by now, practicing what I was going to say to him, gathering all the courage I could muster. I wasn't supposed to be trying to decode Topher's texts. But I had a not-so-great feeling as I waited for his phone to ring. Topher almost never told me things like this, mentioned things that could impact either of our parents.

"Hey," he said, picking up on the fourth ring.

"Hey," I said, pulling my phone back from my ear to look at the texts once more. "I got your texts."

"I figured," he said. "Hang on." There was a small pause, and then I noticed that things had gotten much quieter on Topher's end—like he'd just stepped inside, or gotten into his car, or something.

"What's he saying?" Palmer whispered, poking my arm.

"Nothing yet," I whispered back to her.

"Sorry," Topher said, his voice much clearer now. "Look, I shouldn't even be doing this. But I heard my mom saying something last night . . . something about how the governor is just using your dad as a prop."

"A prop?" I repeated, feeling myself frown. "What do you mean?"

"I guess people have been saying he's not aggressive enough. So when your dad's onstage, he's basically going to point to him as an example of everything that's wrong with politics."

"To his face?" I asked, feeling sick. I couldn't even think

about what this would do to Peter's plan. If this happened before my dad's announcement, his press conference, the whole narrative Peter was crafting wouldn't work. Which was maybe what the governor was counting on.

"I think so," Topher finally said after a silence. "From what I could hear, at least."

"Okay," I said, nodding, trying to figure out what to do with this information. "I'm going to call my dad." I looked over at Palmer, who mouthed *What?* at me.

"Probably a good idea," Topher said. Silence fell between us for a moment, and I thought back to how we'd left it, how awkward it had been—and then realized that he had texted me anyway.

"Thank you," I said, hoping he would know that I meant it.

"Sure," Topher said, then, "I'll see you, Andie."

"What's going on?" Palmer asked, when I'd hung up. "Is your dad okay?"

"I don't think so." I looked down at my phone once more. "Topher said this thing he's doing today—this rally—might not actually be so good."

"Wait, so he's running again?"

"Apparently," I said as I pulled up my dad's number and called it. It didn't even ring, just went right to voice mail, and I suddenly remembered a campaign tic of my dad's—he turned his phone off every time he was going to be interacting with voters. He always said he didn't want to be tempted to take a call, or look at a text, or do anything that might be read as not giving them his undivided attention. "His phone's off," I said, scrolling through my contacts again. "I'll just call Peter."

But Peter's number went right to a recording that told me the number was no longer in service. I lowered my phone, realizing that Peter must have gotten a new phone during my dad's leave of absence.

"No good?" Palmer asked, as I lowered my phone and bit my lip.

"No," I said, looking at the time. I didn't even know where this event was in New York, but it must have been close-ish. If it was starting in less than two hours, it couldn't have been up in Albany or anything. I tried to do the driving math and realized that there was no way I'd be able to go stop my dad and then get back home to see Clark before he left for his bookstore event. Because it was looking like I'd have to go up there—I wasn't going to let my dad just get attacked like that. And there didn't seem to be any other way of contacting him. I let out a breath and turned to Palmer. "Up for a road trip?"

Palmer grinned at me. "Always."

Twenty minutes later I looked across at Palmer from the passenger seat. She was driving, and had been since we'd stopped by the gatehouse. I'd taken three wrong turns just trying to get us out of Stanwich Woods, which was when Palmer suggested that maybe I should just ride for a while.

It wasn't a bad idea, especially since my thoughts were spinning triple time. We'd done some preliminary research into the governor's schedule, only to find out that he was speaking at three events today. Rather than waste time—and also because it was getting *really* hot out on the driveway—we'd gone inside to see if we could find anything about the location of today's event in my dad's study.

I'd gone to my dad's desk to try and find any information while Palmer had made herself useful mostly by looking at all the paraphernalia on the bookcases. His laptop was on the desk, and even though I was pretty sure that I would need a password, I opened it up just in case I could get into his calendar. To my surprise, it wasn't locked—and there was a window open to a fan site for Clark's books. I smiled at that, then minimized it, only to see a document with my dad's speech for today. I didn't get any further than glancing at his opening remarks before I minimized that, too. I started to pull up his calendar when I realized I was looking at the background image on his screen. I knew it—I knew it better than almost anything—but I'd never seen it like this before.

I found myself sitting down in his leather chair and leaning forward, trying to understand what I was seeing. Because it was *Stars Fell on Alexandra*—but not the painting. It was a photograph.

It looked like it had been taken at early dusk, with long blue shadows everywhere. There was no flash, but you could still see details—you could see my yellow Converse and their broken laces. And you could see that I was looking off to the side, just like I was in the painting—but that I was looking at my father.

He was standing just at the edge of the frame, waving at me, and I was smiling at him like I'd never been so happy to see someone.

Clark had been right after all. I had been looking at something—at some*one*.

I'd been looking at my dad.

My mom had wanted her last work to be the two of us, in frame, together.

"Did you find it?" Palmer asked, making me jump and shaking me out of this reverie. She walked around behind me to see what I was looking at, and I heard her draw in a breath. "Is that . . . ?" she asked, and I nodded. "Wow," she said softly, shaking her head. "We'll have to tell Tobes. She'll flip."

The words seemed to hang in the air for a moment before I cleared my throat and said, "Okay. Goals. Address." It had been the first item in my dad's calendar for today, and we'd grabbed bottles of water for the car and hit the road.

Now I looked down at my phone, holding my hair back in one hand to keep it out of my face. Palmer was a windows-down driver—it was one of the fights she always had with Bri, who liked to keep the Grape Escape air-conditioned and as close to the temperature of a meat locker as possible. Normally I liked a windows-down drive as well, but it was hot enough that it was beginning to feel like a hair dryer was blowing in on us.

"How are we on time?" Palmer asked, glancing over at me.

"We should be there in forty-five," I said, looking down at the map on my phone.

"Will that be enough?"

I nodded. "It should be." I twisted my hair up into a knot, pulling it through on itself. "I know it goes against your belief system, but do you think we could turn the AC on just for a bit?"

Palmer sighed and nodded, then put up both our windows as I cranked the air-conditioning as high as it would go. "Every now and then you have to concede defeat," she said, angling her driver's-side vent so that it was pointing right toward her. "So what about Clark?" Palmer asked, after we'd been driving in silence for the amount of time it took to pass two rest stops.

I looked over at her. I'd already told her about my revelation at the party and given her the bare outline of my mom's note. That one still felt a little too raw for me to go into much detail about it, but I knew I'd tell her everything soon. "What do you mean?"

"I mean what now?" she asked, looking over at me for just a second before focusing back on the highway. I wasn't worried like I would have been if Toby were driving—Palmer was the best driver out of all of us, by far. "What's the plan?"

I opened my mouth, then closed it when I realized I didn't have an answer. For the first time in a long time, I didn't have a plan. And I didn't want one. "I'm going to play it by ear, I think," I said. I just wanted to tell Clark how I felt, without practicing or preparing anything.

Palmer looked at me, a smile spreading over her face. "Hi. I'm sorry, have we met?" she asked. "I'm looking for Andie Walker."

"Ha," I said, smiling back at her. "I'm not going to plan anything out. I'm just going to talk to him tonight and see how it goes. When he's back from his signing."

"Or," Palmer said, looking significantly over at me.

"Or what?"

"Or just go to New Hampshire and tell him at his book thing."

"New Jersey," I corrected. "And I'm not going to do that."

"Why not?" she asked, changing lanes smoothly and speeding up slightly.

"Because," I said, shaking my head, "it's a work thing for him.

And it's in public. I don't want to tell him in front of a ton of people. . . ." My voice trailed off as I remembered the argument Clark and I had had about Karl and Marjorie and the declaration of love in the crowded tavern. I closed my eyes for just a moment, remembering how seriously Clark had seemed to take it, how he'd fought for it. "Oh god," I said hollowly, as I opened my eyes, realizing what I had to do. "I think I have to go to Clark's reading."

Palmer grinned at me. "Okay, so we'll go tell your dad, and then we'll head to . . ."

"New Jersey," I filled in for her. "Do you have a mental block about this state, or something?"

"New Jersey," Palmer said, talking over me like I hadn't said anything.

"You don't have to come."

"You think I'd miss this?" She looked at me incredulously. "Not a chance."

"Thank you."

She nodded, and I watched as she tapped her fingers on the closed driver's-side window, then brought her hands back to ten and two, then moved them again. "What is it?" I asked.

She glanced over at me before looking back at the road. "Bri and Toby," she said, shaking her head. "We have to fix it."

I nodded. From the way she said it, though, I could tell that she had about as much of an idea for how to do this as I did. "Yeah," I agreed. "But how?" The question hung between us in the car for a moment before I reached over and turned on the radio, sensing that both of us needed a break from our thoughts.

When we were ten minutes away from the fairground where the event was being held, something started happening to

Morgan Matson

the car. The engine was making a groaning sound, and though Palmer had started driving more slowly, it didn't seem to be helping. "What is this?" I asked, leaning over to try and see the dash. "Why are you breaking my car?"

"Do you think it knew you got another one?" she asked, "and so it's mad or something?"

"It's probably nothing," I said, hoping that if I said it out loud, it would turn out to be true. "Right?"

Palmer frowned as she looked down at the dash, tapping it once. "This is moving over toward the *H*," she said. "It's the temperature thing. I have a feeling that's not good."

"It's probably just because it's hot," I said, nodding, glad to have an explanation for this that made sense. "It's just really hot out. I'm sure it'll get better once it has a chance to cool down."

"Maybe," Palmer said, still frowning at the gauges, most of which I'd never paid any attention to before now. Right as we turned into the parking area, however, the CHECK ENGINE light came on, which didn't seem like a good sign to either of us. We both got out of the car, and I felt myself wince. Things seemed to be even hotter here than they'd been at home. "Go find your dad," Palmer said, leaning against the car and pulling out her phone. "I'm going to call Fitz and see what he says about the engine. He's the only one in my family who knows anything about cars."

"Great," I said, shouldering my bag and heading toward the area where a stage had been set up. "I'll meet you back here," I called as I started to run toward the stage, then stopped when I realized that this was walk-fast weather, not running weather.

I'd been around enough of these things that I knew my

way around. But there was nobody behind the stage where the sound guys were running mic checks, and the assembled crowd was still aimlessly milling around, people trying to find as much shade as possible or lining up by the food trucks. So it was clear that I wasn't too late—but I also didn't know where I was going to find my father.

I turned in a circle, as though I would see a labeled politician holding area, or something—when I saw two campaign buses parked on the other side of the street and realized that maybe I just had.

"I don't understand," my dad said, frowning, as he stood outside the bus with me. He'd been inside with Peter, enjoying the air-conditioning and reading through his speech, and I was just glad that I'd met Walt earlier this morning, since he had recognized me and opened up the doors, rather than calling security when I started yelling about how I needed to get onto the bus. "Topher said this?"

I nodded, then had to look away from the very strange optical illusion of my dad standing in front of a giant picture of his head. "I don't think you should do this," I said, looking back toward the stage where things now seemed to be happening, the crew guys moving with more purpose as they hustled around the stage, even in this heat.

"And you came all the way here? Just to tell me?"

"Of course," I said, and just for a second, remembered the picture on his computer, the moment my mother had captured. "Wouldn't you have done it for me?" I asked, hoping I knew the answer but needing to hear it anyway. "If I was about to get hurt?"

"Of course," he said without even a moment of hesitation. "You know I would."

"There was a note for me in the car," I said, and my dad looked at me, suddenly going very still. "From Mom. She told me to take care of you." I felt like I'd already spent far too much of this morning crying, but nevertheless, tears were starting to flood my eyes.

My dad smiled, his chin trembling just the smallest bit. "You do, sweetheart," he said, and I started to cry for real as he wrapped his arm around my shoulder and pulled me into a hug. "Of course you do."

"Uh . . . Alex?" We turned around to see Peter coming down the steps of the bus, his frown deepening when he saw me. "Hey, Andie. When did you get here?" He didn't wait for me to reply, just turned to my dad and said, "They're ready for you."

My dad looked at me and then nodded. "All right."

"Wait," I said, stepping into Peter's path, like that would somehow stop this from happening. "You're still going through with it?"

My dad gave me a smile. "It'll be okay," he said, and nodded toward the stage. "Want to come watch?"

I shook my head. I'd come all this way—I'd done this instead of talking to Clark when I still might have been able to—and my dad was going to go ahead and do this. "No," I said, taking a step away. I wasn't sure I could stand to see my dad get humiliated, especially when I'd come so far to try to stop it. "I have to . . . go to New Jersey."

"Oh," my dad said, eyebrows flying up. "Why?"

"Alex," Peter said, gesturing toward the stage, speaking in his *I mean business* voice. "We're on a schedule."

"I'll see you at home," I said, giving my dad a nod. "Um. Good luck." I turned around then and started walking back to the car, wondering why I'd even tried if it had made absolutely no difference.

I got turned around in the parking lot, the heat coming off the baking asphalt messing with my sense of direction as I turned down one wrong row after another. Finally, Palmer dropped a pin at her location, and I was able to track her down. I'd heard the sound system come on during my third wrong turn, though I was too far away to hear anything specific, which I was glad about. I didn't need to hear the governor of New York making a fool of my dad, especially when I hadn't been able to stop it from happening.

"Bad news," Palmer said, hopping off the trunk when she saw me coming.

"Me too," I said, nodding to her. "You go first."

"So Fitz says the car overheated," she says. "He thinks we probably need to tow it, or at the very least, add coolant if we have it—"

"Which we don't."

"Or water to the engine, but only after we've let the car cool down."

I felt my stomach sink. "How long is that going to take?"

Palmer winced. "He said to give it a couple of hours."

"But—"

"I know," she said, shaking her head. "What happened with your dad?"

"Nothing good," I said with a sigh, wondering how it was possible to feel this exhausted when it was just a little after noon.

"He didn't listen to me and just—" I stopped when I heard my phone ringing in my bag. I pulled it out and saw it was my dad calling. "Hello?" I asked, utterly confused, wondering if it was Peter or someone calling from his phone. Because I was pretty sure my dad was still onstage at the moment.

"Hey," my dad said, causing me to look over toward the stage, as though I could see anything there except faint dots.

"What—" I started. "How are you—"

"I'll tell you in a minute," he said. "Where are you?"

"I'm in the parking lot with Palmer," I said. "Oh—Palmer's here. And the car overheated, and I really need to get to New Jersey. . . ." I trailed off, still trying to grasp what was happening. "I still don't understand what's going on."

"So you need a ride," my dad said, and I could practically hear the smile in his voice. "Want to use mine?"

"So this is a campaign bus," Palmer said, from her seat by the row that surrounded a table, where strategy sessions usually took place. She ran her hand over the tabletop and nodded her approval. "I like it."

"Explain it to me again," I said, leaning more into the aisle. My dad was sitting across from me, in the aisle seat as well. He and Walt had picked us up in the TOWARD THE FUTURE bus, and my dad had called AAA to tow my car back to Stanwich. Peter was not on the bus, and I was pretty sure my dad had left him back at the fairgrounds, which Walt seemed particularly happy about.

My dad smiled and shook his head. "I told you, you should have stayed to hear it."

"So . . . you didn't let the governor say anything," I said, now really regretting that I hadn't stayed, if only to see the look on Peter's face when things started going off script. "You just started talking?"

"I said I had an announcement," my dad said. "And one that couldn't wait."

"People are talking about it online," Palmer said, scrolling through her phone, and my dad let out a short laugh.

"I'm not surprised," he said.

"Me either." I was still trying to get my head around it. My dad had given the speech he'd planned to give all along, the one that Peter had no knowledge of—the speech that said he would finish out his term but would not run for another one. That he wanted to spend more time with his family.

"So what now?" I asked.

My dad took a deep breath and gave me a smile. "I'm not sure," he said. "I'm going to finish out my term and then . . . I guess I'll figure it out."

"So I bet Peter's freaking out right about now," I said, not quite able to stop myself from smiling.

My dad nodded. "Probably," he said, then shrugged. "He'll get over it. And if he doesn't, it's not really my issue any longer."

"Congressman?" Walt called from the front of the bus. "I'm going to need an address. Unless you just want me to go back to the pickup spot?"

"Coming," my dad said, ruffling my hair like he used to do when I was little, then making his way to the front of the bus.

I crossed back to join Palmer at the table. She was looking like I felt—a little stunned by everything that was happening.

"Busy day," she said, shaking her head, and I smiled as I sat in the seat across from her.

I nodded. "It has been."

"And we're still going to New Jersey," Palmer said, fixing me with a look that let me know she wasn't going to let me out of this. "We'll just get my car and I'll drive us."

I nodded, pulling out my phone and looking at the time. I'd found the address of the bookstore on Clark's website, and mapped it from Stanwich—it was still another hour to get there. It would be cutting it close, but we could almost make it. I wasn't letting myself think about what would happen once I got there. For the moment it was enough to know that we were going. "Okay," I said, nodding a few more times than I needed to. "Okay."

"So I was thinking about Bri and Toby," Palmer said, and I looked up at her, putting my phone away, glad to have some distraction from what we were heading toward. "I think we need to get them to sit down together and talk this out."

"I agree," I said, "but I don't see that happening, do you?" Palmer sighed and bit her lip. "I mean, even if we get them both to the diner, or wherever, when Toby sees Bri, she's just going to leave."

"Or you," Palmer pointed out. "They're both still pretty mad at you."

"Right," I said. We sat in silence for a moment, the weight of the situation—the hopelessness of it—seeming to press down on me like a physical force.

"We need to get them together," Palmer said slowly, "somewhere they can't leave."

I nodded, thinking that sounded good if we could work it

out. I suddenly remembered *Rio Bravo* and all the secrets and resentments that had come bubbling to the surface when the men were stuck in the jail together. We needed that, but hopefully with less singing. "That would be good," I said, "but . . ." I looked over at Palmer to see that she was looking at the bus with newfound interest. "What?" I asked.

Palmer smiled at me. "Are you thinking what I'm thinking?"

I had not expected, when I'd woken up that morning, that by the afternoon I would be in this situation. In all the vague ways I'd imagined my day going—maybe getting a coffee and picking up some dog-walking shifts—this had not been one of the options. Riding in a bus with my dad's face on it, barreling across New Jersey, en route to tell Clark I was in love with him, while trying to get Toby and Bri to talk to each other, had been nowhere in my list of possibilities. And yet here we were. We weren't in the Mustang, but I had a feeling my mom would have approved.

"Say something," I said to Bri, who sat across the bus table from me, her arms folded, looking hard out at the window like she couldn't hear me.

"I'll say something," Toby snapped, from her seat across the aisle. "This is kidnapping. You can't just force people to be on a bus together."

"Nobody forced you onto the bus," Palmer pointed out from where she was standing in the aisle between Toby and Bri's rows. "You came on voluntarily."

Both of them scoffed in unison, and Palmer and I exchanged a look. When we'd asked my dad if this would be possible—leaving out, for the moment, that Bri and Toby were currently

Morgan Matson

not speaking to each other—we'd made it seem like we all just wanted to ride down to Clark's bookstore event together and that Bri and Toby were excited by the idea of being on a campaign bus.

My dad had bought this and checked with Walt, who just shrugged and said he'd been paid for the whole day, so as long as we didn't go over the mileage, we were okay, and that it didn't make any difference to him where we went. Once we'd gotten the go-ahead, Palmer and I had strategized. When we'd decided on the plan—we'd pick up Bri and Toby as we went through Stanwich en route to New Jersey, and they'd just have to work it out as we all rode down to the bookstore together—we'd realized we had to actually get them both on the bus, together, in order for this to work.

We'd finally decided to go with the nuclear option—Palmer telling both of them that she and Tom had broken up and that she needed to see them at once. Palmer had knocked on every piece of wood on the bus afterward, convinced she was somehow jinxing her relationship by lying about it. But we knew this was the only thing that would get both of them to agree. They'd figured out the ruse pretty quickly, but there's not a whole lot you can do when you're riding on a campaign bus that's flying down the New Jersey Turnpike, with a driver who refuses to stop at the rest stops.

My dad had figured out that Palmer and I had been doing some creative embellishing but had only told me sternly that we'd talk about it when we got home and had gone to the front of the bus to sit with Walt, casting occasional glances into the back of the bus and shaking his head. I got the sense that I'd probably be grounded again in the near future.

But I also had the feeling, like on the night of the scavenger hunt when he got to drive like James Bond, that he was secretly enjoying this.

Bri and Toby were still refusing to talk to each other, and as the miles whipped by outside the window, I found myself getting more and more nervous. What if even getting them trapped in a space together wasn't enough? What if we really weren't going to be able to get past this?

"Guys," Palmer said in her best reasonable voice, "Andie and I really think that if you just talk to each other . . ." Toby just shook her head, and Bri looked down at her hands.

"I mean, we're stuck on a bus together," I pointed out. "We might as well make the best of it."

"We're stuck on this bus *because* of you," Toby snapped. "Don't make it seem like it's just a big coincidence."

"I know," I said, looking between them. "And I'm really sorry, guys. I truly am. I shouldn't have interfered like I did. I just . . . wanted us to be okay."

Toby let out a short, humorless laugh, and Bri stared hard out the window, neither one of them speaking.

Palmer and I exchanged a look, but there didn't seem to be a ton to say after that. Silence fell, while I tried to think of a new approach we could take, something that would shake this up.

"Toby," Bri said ten minutes later, breaking the silence. "Please just talk to me."

Toby folded her arms tighter across her chest, and I saw Palmer take a breath, like she was about to jump in, but I caught

Morgan Matson

her eye and shook my head, hoping that maybe, if we gave her enough space, she'd come around. "What do you want me to say?" Toby finally asked. "I don't have anything to say to you."

"You can't . . . ," Bri said, then stopped and tried again. "I never meant to hurt you, T. You have to know that. It was the last thing I wanted."

"And yet," Toby said, and I could hear the anger in her voice, the way she was biting off the ends of her words, "guess what happened. Gosh, who could have foreseen that totally bizarre occurrence?"

"I'm so sorry," Bri said, and I could see that she was on the verge of tears. "I wish you would just listen to me—"

"So you can say what?" Toby snapped. "That you went ahead and did something you *knew* would break my heart, but you didn't care enough about me to stop? Or even to tell me what was going on so I didn't have to find out like that?"

"Tobe," Palmer said, leaning toward her. "Maybe—"

"Although why am I even surprised?" Toby asked, shaking her head. "Of *course* this is happening to me. Of course not only can I not be with the guy I like, but he falls for my best friend." She looked right at me, and I felt myself drawing back. "You don't believe I'm cursed," she said with a short, unhappy laugh, "but what the *hell* do you call this? I'm the only one of us in this situation. Everyone else is happy and in love with their perfect boyfriends, and I'm alone, just like I always am." Toby's voice broke, and she wrapped her arms around herself and looked out the window, her chin shaking.

"Well, Andie's not," Palmer said, clearly trying to lighten the mood. "That's one of the reasons we're going to New Jersey."

"We're going to *New Jersey*?" Toby asked, closing her eyes for just a moment. "Perfect."

"Tell me what I can do," Bri said, leaning across the table toward her, and I could see she was getting blotchy, the way she did when she was trying to stop herself from really crying. "There has to be something. We can't just keep not talking like this. I miss you so much."

I thought I saw something in Toby's face soften for just a moment, but then it was gone. "Okay," she said, turning to face Bri and folding her arms. "Are you still with Wyatt?"

"Toby," I started, but she was already talking over me.

"Are you still *sleeping* with Wyatt?" she asked, and from the front of the bus, I heard my dad clear his throat and then start asking Walt very loud questions about the bus's gas mileage.

"Look," Bri said, leaning toward Toby. "If you'd just listen—"

"You want to be friends again?" Toby asked. "You want to stop fighting?"

"Yes," Bri said, her eyes searching Toby's face. "I do."

"Fine," Toby said. "If you break up with him, we can be friends again."

Bri drew back. "That's not fair."

Toby let out a short laugh, the kind with absolutely no happiness in it. "What's not *fair* is that you snuck around behind my back and stole the guy I was in love with. That's what's not fair."

"You weren't in love with him!" Bri yelled. "You were in love with the idea of him, just like you always are."

"Excuse me?" Toby asked, her voice rising as well.

I glanced to the front of the bus, worried, but if Walt seemed bothered by the fact that he was driving a busful of teenage girls—two of whom were screaming at each other—it did not seem to be fazing him in the slightest.

"Guys," Palmer said, her voice soothing, "maybe just—"

"A real friend wouldn't ask me to break up with him," Bri said, shaking her head. "I can't believe you're asking me to do that, Toby."

"A real friend wouldn't have done it in the first place," Toby shot back, and I could hear the raw pain underneath all her anger and bravado. "Especially not you. Especially not my *best* friend."

"So let me understand this," Bri said, and I could hear the pain in her voice as well. "You want me to break up with Wyatt for you?"

"What am I supposed to do?" Toby asked, her voice anguished. "Am I supposed to still be your best friend and hear everything about this? Listen to you talk about how in love you are? I'm supposed to be *happy* for you?" Toby's voice broke, and she drew in a raggedy breath. "I can't do that," she said, shaking her head, just once, to either side. "I just can't. And I want to be friends again, Bri, god," She said, starting to speak faster now, the words coming out all in a rush. "I miss you so much, you have no idea. I want to be friends again and I hate that you're doing this to us—"

"*I'm* doing this to us?" Bri asked. "What about you?"

I looked at Palmer, alarmed, and saw her swallowing hard. "Guys," I said, looking between the two of them, "let's not . . ."

"But this isn't about him," Bri said slowly, like she was hearing the truth of the words as she was speaking them. "You just asked me to stop seeing the person I love. Do you realize that?"

"What?" Toby asked, frowning.

"That is just so far from okay," Bri said, shaking her head. "What kind of friend would ask me to do that? And what kind of person would I be if I said yes?"

"What kind of friend leaves me behind like this?" Toby said, her voice cracking. "You were only thinking about yourself!"

Bri just stared at Toby for a moment, then drew in a big, shaky breath. "I don't think you know just how little I've thought about myself," she said. "And now you want me to break up with him. So it's easier for you." Bri shook her head. "That's not good," she whispered, not even bothering to brush away the tears that had started to fall. "I need you to be *happy* for me when I fall in love for the first time, to want good things for me because you're my best friend."

"You knew I wouldn't be *happy* for you," Toby snapped. "Don't try to make me the bad guy here."

"I'm not," Bri said, her voice getting more and more composed. "I'm just . . . This is the first thing I've done without you. Without consulting you. And that's why you're mad."

"No—"

"Maybe this wasn't about Wyatt, not really," Bri said, talking faster, latching on to this and holding tightly. "Maybe we really needed this break. I mean, it was really hard, but it gave me some perspective. And now I think we can move on from it and it'll be better. More balanced. Don't you think?"

I held my breath as I waited for Toby to answer—it seemed like even the bus's machinery was quieter.

"No," she finally said, and I watched Bri's face crumple.

"What do you mean?" she asked, her voice barely above a

whisper, like she wasn't just afraid to hear the answer, she was afraid to ask the question.

"I mean you're right. Maybe we did need a break. Maybe we still need it."

"Toby," Palmer said, casting a worried glance my way, "maybe—"

"Do you know how horrible I've felt over the last two weeks?" Toby asked, turning to look at all of us. "It's been the worst time of my life. And I couldn't even talk to my best friend about it, since it was her fault."

"I felt the same way—" Bri started, but Toby talked over her.

"I realized I don't know who I am if I'm not your friend," she said. "Like I have no idea at all. And that's a problem."

"So that's it?" Bri asked, and I could hear the fear beneath her words. "We're done?"

"Yes," Toby said, her voice cracking. "I can't do this anymore. I'm done."

Bri just stared at Toby for a long moment, then wiped her hand across her face, got up, and walked to the back of the bus, holding on to the empty aisle seats for support.

"We'll be there in five!" Walt yelled toward the back of the bus, and Toby leaned over to the window and looked out.

"I need you to let me off at that Starbucks," Toby said, her voice quiet but decisive, as she pointed out the window.

"Uh, Toby," my dad said, frowning, "I really don't think I can do that. I can't leave you off in the middle of some strange town...."

"I'll call my mom to come pick me up," she said, picking up

her bag and slinging it over her shoulder. "But I can't be here any longer."

Walt looked at my dad, waiting for instruction, and my dad shook his head. "Even so," he said. "I don't think—"

"If she can't come get me, I'll text Andie and you guys can pick me up on your way back to Stanwich," Toby said, a firmness in her voice that was hard to argue with. "But I really need to get off this bus now."

After making Toby promise to check in with us in an hour either way, my dad relented, and Toby got off the bus, crossing in the crosswalk and walking toward the coffee shop. The light changed and Walt drove forward, and in the glass behind Toby, I saw the bus slogan reflected as she slowly pulled open the door, her head down and her shoulders hunched. TOWARD THE FUTURE.

"Girls?" my dad called, a little fearfully, toward the back of the bus.

"Just a second," Palmer and I yelled in unison from where we were sitting on either side of Bri, who had collapsed into the middle of the back row and was crying into a wad of toilet paper she'd taken from the bathroom.

"I can't believe it," Bri said, wiping her arm across her face. "I didn't think—I mean, she just *left*."

"I'm so, so sorry," I said, patting Bri's arm, unable to shake the completely illogical thought that it was Toby who would know how to handle this situation best.

"Toby doesn't even *like* Starbucks," she sobbed.

"It'll be okay," Palmer said, adding quickly, "eventually. I promise."

"Why don't we head back home," I said gently, realizing

that if my world had collapsed around me, the last place I would want to be was stuck on a campaign bus in New Jersey. "We'll get ice cream on the way, how does that sound?"

"Really?" Palmer asked quietly, and I met her eye above Bri's head and nodded. After all, this had mostly been a romantic gesture. Clark was going to be back in Stanwich tonight—I'd just talk to him then.

"No," Bri said, looking up at me, her face stricken. "Andie . . . You have to go talk to Clark."

"I'll talk to him later," I said. "It's not important. So . . ."

"It *is* important," Bri said, looking right at me, her eyes puffy from crying. "That's why we're here, right? And you love him?"

I nodded. "I do."

"Then," Bri said, sitting up straighter and crumpling up the toilet paper in her hand, "you're going to tell him that."

"Are you sure?" I asked.

She nodded. "You know how you're always saying that real life isn't like those movies, and it doesn't actually happen that way?" I nodded, and she gave me a trembly smile. "Go prove yourself wrong."

In all the movies Toby had made us watch, it was always somewhere very romantic. On top of the Empire State Building, on a rain-streaked airport runway, at a New Year's Eve party. This moment did not, in any of the movies I could recall, take place in a bookstore in New Jersey packed with fantasy-novel readers, many of whom were in costume.

And yet there we were, fighting our way through the crowd

that seemed to be taking over most of the downstairs of Clymer Books. A podium was set up at the other end of the store and there was a table next to it with both of Clark's books on it. Chairs were lined up in rows, an aisle between them, but it looked like every single chair was taken, and a large crowd was filling in the rest of the space—it appeared that Clark's event was standing-room only.

It probably didn't help that there were so many of us suddenly trying to crowd in—me, Palmer, Bri, my dad, and Walt. It turned out that Walt was a big fan of the movies and so was happy to tag along with us after he found a lot to park the bus in.

Now, a guy who was dressed in a very detailed Elder costume glared at me as I tried to take a step forward, craning my neck to see if I could spot Clark.

"Andie?" I turned and did a double take when I saw Tom, looking as shocked to see me as I was to see him. "What are you doing here?

"What are *you* doing here?" I asked, just as Palmer spotted her boyfriend and ran over to him.

Tom broke away from kissing Palmer to answer me. "I'm here to support Clark, as a friend and as a reader."

"Thomas," my dad said, holding out his hand, causing Tom to turn bright red.

"Congressman," he said, shaking my dad's hand. "I mean, hi. How are you doing?" He looked behind my dad. "And Bri, too. And . . ." He frowned when he saw Walt. "Do we know him?" he asked in a whisper to Palmer.

Before she could answer, though, a bookstore employee— in an apron, for some reason—walked toward the podium, tapping on the microphone twice. "Hello," she said, smiling at the crowd. "Welcome to Clymer Books." She then launched into an introduction, covering how the signing following the reading would work and that we were required to buy books before having them signed. Then she started to introduce Clark, and as she listed his résumé and accomplishments—so impressive, for someone so young!—I could feel my pulse picking up. Clark was here. He was probably just feet away from me, hiding behind a bookshelf or something. I was here, and so was he, and it really seemed like this was going to happen.

I didn't even hear the end of her introduction, but realized it was over when people started clapping, and then Clark was coming out, adjusting his glasses the way he always did when he was nervous, looking so handsome in his dark-blue button-down that it took my breath away.

"Hi," he said, stepping up behind the microphone and giving the crowd a nervous smile before looking down again. "Thank you all so much for coming. I'm . . . actually going to read from my work in progress, if that's okay."

It was like the crowd all held their breath for a moment before everyone started talking at once. I noticed that Tom had an incredibly pleased look on his face, like he was thrilled he had known about this before the rest of the world.

"Uh—" Clark said, and everyone quieted down pretty quickly, seeming to realize that if they kept talking, they wouldn't get to hear any of the new book. "It's still pretty new. So it might change. Just letting you know so you don't hold me to anything here." There was low, polite laughter, and then Clark cleared his throat, looked down at the paper in front of him, and started to read.

For the next ten minutes the room was silent except for the sound of people's camera phones clicking. You could have heard a pin drop as Clark read from a section of his new, untitled book. I listened, my hands twisted against each other and my heart in my throat, not quite able to believe what I was hearing, but for different reasons than the rest of the crowd in the bookstore.

Because it was about us.

It was about all of us—me, Palmer, Tom, Toby, Bri, even Wyatt—and the summer we'd had together. It was still set in Clark's fantasy world, but it was about a group of friends off on an adventure together. And when Clark finished and there was deafening applause, I felt a piece of responsibility for it. Like maybe this new book wouldn't be happening if it hadn't been for me—if it hadn't been for all of us.

Clark started taking questions then, and it seemed like every hand in the crowd was going up. People wanted to know why he'd taken so long to write the follow-up, where he got his inspiration, and what he thought about the casting of the movies. They wanted to know how to get an agent, when the new book would be out, and who his favorite authors were. The questions kept coming, until the aproned bookstore lady announced that they had time for only one more. Palmer gave me a look and I took a breath. I knew this was the moment. Clark was searching the room through all the hands that were waving frantically, but I didn't wait to be called on. I just stepped forward into the aisle and said, a little too loudly, "Um. I have a question?"

"I'm actually calling on—" Clark started before he saw me. I saw his eyes widen before he composed himself, and I could tell that I'd surprised him. "You had a question?" Clark asked, giving me a small, tentative smile.

"Yes," I said, making myself take another step forward, trying not to think about the fact that my dad and my friends and a middle-aged bus driver—as well as a crowd of hundreds of strangers with smartphones—were there, and that everyone was watching me. "I actually had a question about two of the more minor characters."

"And who might those be?"

"Karl and Marjorie," I said, and I heard the guy on the aisle next to me ask, "Wait, *who?*"

"It's canon," the guy next to him scoffed, and I made myself take another step forward.

I could do this. If whole galaxies could change, so I could I. For just a moment I thought about Palmer calling the play. She asked if the cue was ready but then didn't wait to hear the response before giving the go-ahead. You got a warning, but not time to change your mind or come up with another plan. You just had to act.

"What about them?" Clark asked, and I could sense the restlessness of the bookstore lady next to him, probably wishing he'd just called on someone else.

"Just . . . I was wondering if you were committed to their ending," I said. I heard the guy on the aisle scoff loudly again. "If . . . maybe there was any way it could be different."

"Thanks so much for that question!" the bookstore lady said brightly, clapping her hands together, and my heart sank. Was I really going to be stopped by a random employee in an apron? Without even getting an answer?

"No, it's okay," Clark said, not looking away from me. "I'll answer that." He took a deep breath, and I could see his eyes searching mine, like he was looking for an answer. "I had thought that was the ending," he finally said. "But I might have been wrong."

"I was just thinking," I said, sure that the rest of the crowd could probably hear how hard my heart was beating, since it seemed deafening to me, pounding in my ears, "that maybe Marjorie realized she was in love with Karl. And told him that. And said she was sorry for being scared."

Clark nodded and glanced down at his papers, and suddenly a terrible fear shot through me. What if I was about to get rejected, here, in front of all these people? Was I about to be turned down in an incredibly public way?

"Well," Clark said, after a pause. When he looked up at me, he was smiling, both dimples flashing. "I think that would certainly change things."

I smiled and felt tears spring to my eyes. "Oh," I said, my voice coming out wobbly, and I could feel that I was torn between laughing and crying and on the verge of both. "That's really good to hear."

Clark smiled at me, and from his expression, I could see that he was feeling pretty much the same way.

And then Clark was stepping out from behind his podium and walking toward me, and I was running toward him and into his arms, and Clark was picking me up, and I wrapped my legs around his waist and we kissed, and it was like I was blocking out the commotion all around us, the people yelling and talking and laughing and trying to figure out what was happening, and the bookstore lady clapping her hands and trying to get control of the situation.

"Hi," I murmured when we stopped to breathe and Clark set me down to the ground on legs that felt wobbly.

"Hi," he said, running his hand over my hair and cupping my face in his hands. "I missed you."

"Me too," I whispered. I knew that this couldn't last—that there were people waiting and he had things to do and this couldn't go on forever. But in that moment it was like everything else faded away and there was only me and Clark and the possibility of us—whatever we might become—stretching forward in a hundred different directions, all of them unexpected, each one better than the last, the ending not yet written. And with this thought in mind, and Clark's hands in my hair, I stretched up to kiss him once again.

J ack looked around at them—the five who would be accompanying him on this journey. "Are we met?" he asked, dreading the answer.

These were the comrades-in-arms who would help him avenge his sister's death and find the message he knew for certain Tamsin had left behind in the castle for him? This collection of rogues and misfits?

He looked at them one by one, realizing as he did that most of them weren't even paying attention, despite the fact that he was (technically) now the king. There was Lord Thomas, who was sulking on a nearby stump, still in the player's costume he'd been wearing when the king's guards had pulled him out of the performance. "I had a matinee today," he said petulantly, shaking his head. "I've been rehearsing for *weeks*. My accent's finally perfect. But I suppose you don't care about that?"

Next to him were the ladies Sabrine and Hannah, who were, as usual, laughing together at something the rest of them weren't included in. He knew he needed them—Lady Sabrine was the best tracker he'd ever encountered, able to pick out the spot where a deer paused for a second and changed direction. And Lady Hannah had a way with horses that was unmatched. But that didn't mean he wanted to feel like they were giggling about him behind his back, like they'd been doing since he was a boy of fifteen.

Leaning up against a tree, not paying attention to any of this, and certainly not the looks Lady Hannah was sending him, was Sir Wylen, who was, as usual, strumming the lute he seemed to carry with him everywhere.

"*No*," a voice at his side said, dripping with disgust. He turned and saw Lady Andrea, who had insisted for the past week she was coming along, until he'd finally stopped arguing. "I'm not coming unless you get him to stop playing that thing. I cannot abide it. I'll break it up myself and use it for kindling."

Jack felt himself smile, and prayed he wasn't blushing, or he knew he'd never hear the end of it from Sabrine and Hannah. But he couldn't help it—he'd been in love with her from the moment he'd seen her, when she'd stormed into his court and demanded to know what idiot claimed to be running the kingdom.

Rather than risk her seeing him blush, Jack knelt down to rub the ears of Bernie, the huge dog that seemed to follow her everywhere and which he had a suspicion was actually part wolf. "I'll leave that to you," he said, backing away slightly when the dog bared inch-long fangs at him. "I think you can handle it."

"We're going to have to be careful," Lady Sabrine said, as she stood and pulled Lady Hannah up, ignoring Wylen, who'd reached out his hand to help her. "I've heard rumors that the assassin Margery is unaccounted for. And for a prize such as you, my lord, I doubt she'd have to settle for the lowest bidder."

"Who?" Wylen asked, frowning.

"I have an idea!" Thomas said, standing up as well and clapping his hands together. "What if we leave *later* tonight? Then I can get the evening performance in, and—"

"No," Hannah and Sabrine said in unison.

"It'll be dark soon," Lady Andrea said, sheathing her dagger and taking a step toward the woods, dog at her heels. "We should get started."

Jack took a breath, then let it out as he looked west, toward Haverhall, where they would journey. "Well, then," he said, looking around at the assembled group. "Let's begin."

—C. B. McCallister, "The Coin of the Realm." Hightower & Jax, New York.
Advance reader's copy. Not for review or quotation.

Chapter TWENTY

I took a sip of my latte and looked across the table at Flask's. I'd switched to hot lattes at the end of September, when it officially got too cold for iced drinks, and now that we were getting close to Halloween, the leaves outside the coffee shop window had all turned color and started to cover the ground. "How are you not done yet?" I asked, shaking my head.

Toby glanced up from where she was currently doctoring her caramel pumpkin latte with sugar packets and cinnamon sprinkles, as she had been doing for, I was pretty sure, the last twenty minutes.

"You can't rush these things," she said, dropping in a very precise amount of sugar, giving it a stir, tasting it, then nodding and looking back at me. "Perfect. What were we talking about?"

"I don't know. It was ten years ago, and I've forgotten." I looked automatically to the chair next to Toby—the one that was sitting empty. This was when Bri would have chimed in, defending Toby or making a joke. But silence just fell between us, and we both took a sip of our drinks in unison.

"So," she said, before the pause could grow uncomfortable. "How's it going with the DMV thing?"

"You mean DVM?"

"Sure," Toby said with a wave of her hand. "If you say so."

I smiled. I was pretty sure Toby actually knew what it was called and was just doing this to tease me. But there was a chance that she was actually still getting used to it—the change had taken me by surprise as well. In the last month I had switched my focus from premed to veterinary medicine. Now, whenever my dad and I went through my college options, narrowing down where to apply, we were focusing solely on schools that had good veterinary programs. I wasn't sure if the idea had taken root during the night of Bertie and the chocolate, but by the end of the summer, I'd come to my decision. Maya was thrilled.

Even though I was no longer working full-time, I was still doing weekend walks for Maya and Dave. Folding a dog into my regular routine seemed like good practice for the winter. Because now my dad and I were spending far too much time on pet rescue websites, either when he was here or video chatting when he was in D.C., arguing about what kind we wanted to adopt when he was out of Congress and home in January. One thing that seemed to be clear was that the dog was going to be named Duke. Every time we talked about our potential puppy, that's what my dad called it, and I was trying to accept that I was going to have a dog with John Wayne's nickname.

"It's good," I said, before Toby could ask me if I would be the person who took people's license pictures—I'd heard all these jokes from her before. "How's the track team?"

Toby groaned, but good-naturedly. "It's killing me," she said. "These people are maniacs. And did I tell you that we have practices on Saturdays? Like, in the mornings?"

I smiled as I took a sip of my drink. "You may have mentioned it."

She shook her head and started going off about how weekends were for *rest*, not running, but I had a feeling it was mostly just Toby being Toby. She'd joined the track team right after school started and seemed to eat lunch most days at the track table, laughing with her new group of friends, wearing a ribbon in her hair on the meet days. Palmer and I had gone to one, holding up the signs she had made, but that was before we'd realized just how long they could take. "Anyway," she said with an exaggerated sigh when she'd finished complaining. "We have a meet next Saturday. You know, if you're free."

I pulled out my phone, scrolling through the social media apps that were now mine to do with as I pleased, until I got to my calendar. "I'm in D.C. next weekend," I said, dropping my phone back in my bag. "My dad's giving a speech and he asked me to be there."

I shrugged as I said it, and Toby made a face, but the truth was, I didn't mind at all. Seeing my dad return to work, safe in his lame-duck status, had been beyond fun to watch. He'd returned to the House, kicking butt and taking names, determined to use his last few months in office to the best of his ability, no longer pulling any punches or having to say things he didn't mean. As a result, he'd told me last weekend over pizza, he was getting more done than he ever had before. When his term ended in January, he was already set up with a job at the Stanwich Public Defender's Office. Until then, though, he tried to be home whenever he could, and was shooting down the rumors that he was going to run for governor.

It wasn't like it had come out of nowhere—my dad's speech at Erikson's event, coupled with the media narrative about being cleared of wrongdoing *and* leaving at a political high point to spend time with his family, had made him the star of a few news cycles. It was around then that the sitting governor of Connecticut had called him in for a meeting. He wasn't planning to run for another term, which—coupled with news of their meeting—had sent the rumor mill into overdrive. But my dad was denying them all for the moment. He'd promised me he wouldn't consider doing anything until I was at college, and I was very relieved he wouldn't be uprooting my life to Hartford anytime soon.

"So," Toby said, when the conversation had started to wind down and we'd both finished our lattes. Toby had been folding and refolding her empty sugar packet for the last few minutes, and I knew she was getting up the nerve to ask the question. "How is she?"

Our coffees and lunches usually ended like this, with the reminder that things were not as they had been. When Toby and I met once a week, for the hours we were hanging out, I could almost let myself forget that things had changed, pretend that maybe Bri and Palmer were just running late or something. But we always came back to reality at the end.

"She's good," I said carefully, searching Toby's expression, wondering if maybe this was the moment that she'd say she wanted things to go back to how they were, or ask me to reach out to Bri for her, anything.

But Toby just gave me a half smile and pushed the sugar packet away. "I'm glad."

Toby and Bri didn't speak for several weeks after Toby walked off the bus in New Jersey. And even Bri and Wyatt breaking up when he went back to school didn't change this, even though Palmer and I had hoped it might. Bri, Palmer, and I had tried our best to adjust to our three-person group—four, if you included Tom, who always got offended when he was left out. Things between Bri and Toby had gotten better since school started—they'd chat in the hallways occasionally—but they weren't Bri-and-Toby any longer. "Do you think," I started, then reconsidered my words. "I mean, maybe you two . . ."

Toby raised an eyebrow at me. "You were there on the bus, right? You saw the meltdown?" She shook her head. "I know I went a little crazy."

"Well, I had kidnapped you and forced you onto a campaign bus."

A smile flitted across her face and then disappeared. "I know I shouldn't have said the things I did. But . . ." She shrugged. "I think maybe this hasn't been the worst thing for me and Bri."

I was about to try and argue with this, but Toby continued. "We needed some space," she said, her voice quiet and sure. "I needed to figure out who I was without her." She looked away from me and folded her sugar packet again. "Without all of you guys."

"And?" I asked. Toby and I had talked around this over the last few months, but never this directly. And now that we were addressing it head-on, I couldn't help but notice that she seemed . . . calmer, somehow. More centered, like her energy wasn't flying off in a hundred directions any longer.

"And I'm good," Toby said firmly, looking me right in the eye. "I promise."

"So maybe someday," I said, hearing the hope in my voice, "you guys might be friends again." I knew we'd probably never go back to what we'd had before. But maybe that would be okay.

"Maybe," Toby said, giving me a smile. "I hope so," she added a second later, in a voice so quiet I almost didn't hear her.

We said our good-byes and headed out shortly after that. I got into the Mustang, running my hand over the steering wheel for just a moment before checking the time and realizing I had to get going. There was someone I needed to meet.

I always thought about my mother a little bit more when I was driving her car, and its presence in the senior parking lot had already attracted a lot of attention—mostly from the science teachers, for some reason. But between the car and the portrait of Stabby Bob hanging in the foyer, it was like my mom was around more now. Or maybe it was just that my dad and I were talking about her more. It still wasn't easy, but it no longer felt impossible. We were finding our way through it, together.

I drove away from the coffee shop, glancing at the time, hoping that for once I would be there first—whenever we arranged to meet at our spot, he had an annoying habit of beating me there.

And sure enough, when I pulled up in front of Winthrop, there Clark was, sitting on one of the picnic tables, reading a book, a big white dog waiting at his feet—the dog we walked every Sunday.

I got out of my car and walked toward him, glancing away from Clark and looking at Winthrop for just a moment. I saw the statue differently now. I'd decided that he wasn't pointing to anything or anyone. Now all I could see was that he was reaching out his hand to someone. For me that explained the expression on his face that I'd never quite been able to understand before.

He was hopeful and nervous and scared and a little bit proud of himself for doing it—extending his hand to someone, not knowing if they'd take it. This was, I had realized, one of the scariest things of all, requiring much more courage than sailing across an ocean and landing on an unknown shore.

At least that's what I saw. Clark and Tom's new theory was that he was a time traveler who'd somehow been transported to the past and was just trying to hail a cab.

We all still hung out by Winthrop a little—but we hadn't done another scavenger hunt since Toby left the group. This was much to the dismay of a very cute college freshman who really wanted another chance to prove his quest skills.

Having a boyfriend in college, I'd learned, wasn't that different from having a boyfriend at school with you—you didn't have any teachers in common, but you could still do homework and complain about classes together. Clark was living in the dorms, finishing revisions on the book while he took classes. He was going to be taking a lighter course load in the spring, when his publisher planned a huge book tour.

Fan interest was already reaching a fever pitch, people clamoring to join a lottery to read the early copies. I'd already read most of it, and so had my dad and Tom, though we'd all been sworn to secrecy.

For the first few weeks after we'd gotten back together, I'd been worried that things might fall apart again, not sure that I was up to being in a real relationship, one with actual stakes and feelings and something to lose. But things were going really great, and I was trying to take it one day at a time, trying not to think about schedules or book tours or what would happen when I went to college. We would figure all that out later. But for now there was just Clark. Just the boy I loved.

"Hey," he said, setting down his book and standing up when he saw me, as Bertie lunged toward me, tail wagging wildly.

"Hey," I said, walking over to Clark, but Bertie got in the way, and I leaned down and scratched his ears, and under his chin, sending his back leg thumping. "Hi to you, too," I said, stepping around Bertie and giving Clark a kiss. We lingered that way for a moment, and then he kissed my forehead and squeezed my hand.

"How was Toby?"

"She was good," I said, smiling at him. "Ready?"

He slung his arm around my shoulders and I wrapped mine around his waist, tucking my fingers through his belt loops, and we started to walk, the dog leading the way, sniffing every available rock. "I was born ready."

"Please don't say that," I said, shaking my head, and Clark laughed. "That sounds like something Tom would say."

"Well, in that case, I'm going to say it all the time," Clark said. He smiled down at me. "Where were we?"

"They were trying to cross the frozen lake," I said immediately. "And Marjorie was telling everyone about frostbite prevention."

"Oh, was she?" Clark asked, but I could hear the laughter in his voice. "Okay. So they're about to cross the lake . . ." He paused, and I waited, knowing that any minute now he'd suggest a possibility, and we'd go from there.

Morgan Matson

And as it slowly started to get darker, we walked together, the leaves crunching under our feet, both of us tossing out ideas, trading off, adding a detail here and a moment there, as the world we were building unfolded and the story, without any end that I could see, continued on.